William Clive was born in
Munich Crisis of 1938, age
in order to join the King's
a rifleman. Following activ
discharged, his records no
soldier. I am sorry to lose him.'
entered the Royal Navy, in which he remained for fourteen years. As William Clive, he has already written one novel about the Indian Mutiny, *Dando on Delhi Ridge* (part of the highly successful *Dando* cycle of novels). As Ronald Bassett, he has published historical novels such as *The Carthaginian* and *Witchfinder General*. Married with two children, William Clive lives in Surrey.

By the same author

written as William Clive

DANDO ON DELHI RIDGE
DANDO AND THE SUMMER PALACE
THE TUNE THAT THEY PLAY
DANDO AND THE MAD EMPEROR

written as Ronald Bassett

THE CARTHAGINIAN
THE POMPEIANS
WITCHFINDER GENERAL
AMOROUS TROOPER
REBECCA'S BRAT
KILL THE STUART

William Clive

Blood of an Englishman

MAYFLOWER
GRANADA PUBLISHING
London Toronto Sydney New York

Published by Granada Publishing Limited
in Mayflower Books 1977

ISBN 0 583 12621 9

First published in Great Britain by
Macmillan London Ltd 1975

Granada Publishing Limited
Frogmore, St Albans, Herts AL2 2NF
and
3 Upper James Street, London W1R 4BP
1221 Avenue of the Americas, New York, NY 10020, USA
117 York Street, Sydney, NSW 2000, Australia
100 Skyway Avenue, Toronto, Ontario, Canada M9W 3A6
Trio City, Coventry Street, Johannesburg 2001, South Africa
CML Centre, Queen & Wyndham, Auckland 1, New Zealand

Made and printed in Great Britain by
Hazell Watson & Viney Ltd
Aylesbury, Bucks
Set in Monotype Plantin

The map of Cawnpore on pages 8 and 9 is taken from Michael Edwards, *Battles of the Indian Mutiny* (Batsford, 1963).

AUTHOR'S FOREWORD

The Massacre of Cawnpore, during the Indian Mutiny of 1857, has been claimed by many historians to have initiated the drastic change in Anglo-Indian relationships that poisoned the next ninety years of British rule.

The term 'Indian Mutiny' is a misnomer, but it has stuck. Only the northern provinces of India were involved; most of India remained peacefully loyal. Even in the affected areas, millions of natives wished to play no part in the revolt, and many thousands risked their lives in actively supporting British counter-measures or in alleviating the suffering of the revolt's victims.

It is true, however, that the senseless horror of Cawnpore aroused in the British an animal fury and provoked reprisals no less despicable than those of the original massacre. One example of anti-Indian feeling was that of the English corporal in 1857, newly disembarked in Bombay, who explained why he had just killed two inoffensive bullock-drivers: 'I seed two Moors talking in a cart. Presently I heard one of 'em say "Cawnpore". I knowed what that meant, so I fetched Tom Walker, and he heard 'em say "Cawnpore". And he knowed what that meant. So we polished them both off.' Later, during Havelock's march to relieve Lucknow, a soldier was given two days CB for 'hanging a native without permission'. Thus cheap had Indian life become to the avenging British. Afterwards, British confidence in the Indian never became fully restored and the two cultures achieved only a veneer of compatibility. The memory of Cawnpore, if only subconscious, was indelible.

And the Mutiny itself was a disaster for India. When, in 1858, the relatively benevolent administration of the East India Company was replaced by all the formality, complexity and remoteness of Crown rule, self-determination for India, albeit inevitable, became vastly more difficult to achieve. It took almost a century, two world wars and a great deal of interim bitterness to accomplish, when it might, without the Mutiny, have developed much more peacefully and certainly earlier.

It was because of Cawnpore.

GUIDE TO INDIAN ARMY TERMS

Sepoy	Private (from Persian 'Sipahi')
Lance-Naik	Lance-Corporal
Naik	Corporal
Havildar	Sergeant
Jemadar	Lieutenant
Subedar	Captain
Sowar	Trooper (from Persian 'Sawar')
Duffadar	Sergeant (cavalry)
Rissaldar	Cavalry troop commander

There were a number of extensions of these titles, such as Subedar-Major and Rissaldar-Major, both being senior native officers.

The Regiment – or 'Ridgement' – was also a *pultan*, derived from the English 'platoon', which in turn is a corruption of the French 'peloton'. The very first Bengal regiment was the *Lal Pultan*, or the Red Regiment, from the colour of its tunics, and later the commander's name would be incorporated, such as *Gilspy-ki-Pultan*, or Gillespie's Regiment. The *Lal Koorti Ka Haspital*, of course, was the Redcoat Hospital.

Rissalah referred to both a troop and a regiment of cavalry, while *sillidar* described those regiments in which recruits provided their own mounts and equipment. Artillery was the *topkhana*.

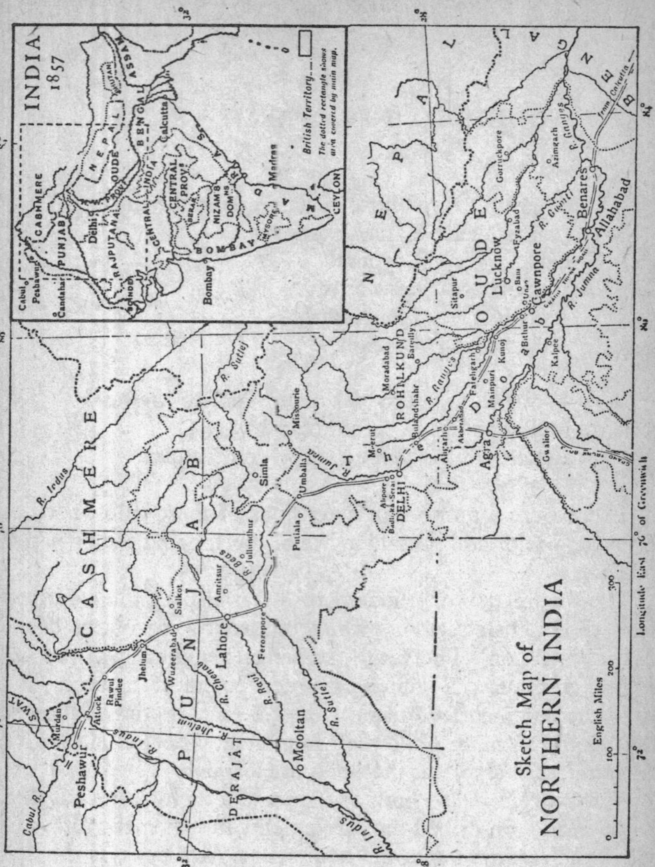

Taken from Michael Edwardes, *Battles of the Indian Mutiny*, published by Batsford.

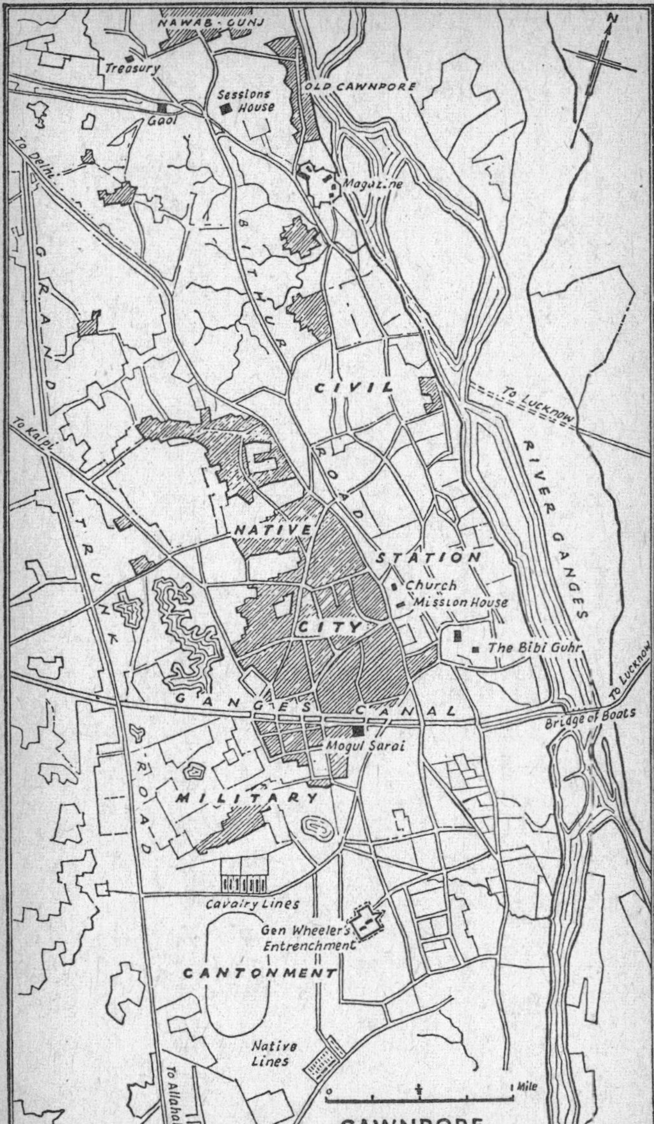

NAWAB-GUNJ
Treasury
Sessions House
Gaol
OLD CAWNPORE
Magazine
To Delhi
BITHUR ROAD
GRAND TRUNK ROAD
CIVIL STATION
To Lucknow
RIVER GANGES
To Kalpi
NATIVE CITY
Church
Mission House
The Bibi Guhr
GANGES CANAL
To Lucknow
Bridge of Boats
Mogul Sarai
MILITARY
Cavalry Lines
Gen Wheeler's Entrenchment
CANTONMENT
Native Lines
To Allahabad
0
½
1 Mile
N

CAWNPORE

Part One

Fee, Fi, Fo, Fum,
  I smell the blood of an Englishman;
Be he alive or be he dead,
  I'll grind his bones to make my bread.

Jack and the Beanstalk

I

Cawnpore, meaning the 'City of Kahn', stood on a flat, treeless and dusty plain on the southward bank of the Ganges – a terrain which, in the hot season, was bereft of a single blade of grass. Vegetation clung to the river bank, tangled reeds and bamboo, a grove of mango trees, sugar cane and wild banana.

Architecturally, Cawnpore offered nothing like the shrines and palaces of Benares or the marble beauty of Agra. On the river's bank was a causeway of limestone *kunkur* – the Suttee Chowra Ghat – where native boats moored and women washed clothes, chattering under a hot sun, flanked by a small Hindu temple that resembled a dilapidated summerhouse. A few cattle stood in the shallows with their red-rimmed eyes brimming with crawling flies, scrawny chickens scratched hopelessly and skeletal dogs sniffed at garbage. For a newcomer, after weeks of weary poling up-river, the first impression of Cawnpore would not be improved by longer acquaintance – glaring heat, dust, neglect, and the unrelieved tedium of a typical Indian military station. The cantonments began about a mile from the river.

The most imposing structure in Cawnpore was the white tower of the church, Christchurch, rising above tired trees. The cantonments covered an area of almost six miles – white-painted bungalows of varying size and condition, each in its compound and a few with watered lawns and jealously pampered shrubs, all alike with a row of red clay jars in which water cooled for the Sahib's morning bath. There was a Roman Catholic Chapel of Ease and a mission house of the Society for the Propagation of the Gospel, a small theatre, a freemasonry lodge, a library and newsroom. Mr Duncan's Hotel boasted a billiards room, a breakfast club where bored Sahibs could take *chota hazri*, and a net-enclosed racquets court. A stretch of the dun-coloured plain was marked out as a racecourse, and there were the Public Gardens surrounding an iron bandstand, deserted during the day except for a sweeper listlessly sprinkling water to lay the dust.

The European population of Cawnpore numbered more than a thousand – civil servants of the Post Office, the Public Works, the Opium Department, a few surveyors of the East Indian Railway, merchants and shopkeepers, and a mixed three hundred British officers and men of the East India Company's Bengal Army. Of the total, some 280 were women, either wives or adult daughters, with a similar number of infants, most of whom at the age of four or five would be shipped to a boarding school in England.

Major-General Sir Hugh Wheeler, KCB, Honourable East India Company, commanding the Cawnpore station, was sixty-eight. He had entered the Company's service at the age of sixteen, fifty-two years before – ten years before Waterloo. Even so, he was more active than his counterpart in Meerut, Major-General William Hewitt, also of fifty years' service, who was too fat and infirm to ride a horse and, outdoors, never descended from his carriage.

Wheeler had been in India for almost his entire adult life, and his record, if not distinguished, was beyond criticism. He spoke Hindustani like a native, had always commanded Indian troops and, furthermore, had even married an Indian and had a grown-up son and two daughters. Queen's officers of less experience might disdainfully refer to Wheeler as a 'sepoy', or an 'old yaller', but he knew his India.

He knew India, perhaps, too well. A man who could scarcely remember the green fields of England, who had seen the beards of his havildars and subedars grow white with his own, knew the names of their sons and grandsons and accepted their respectful 'Huzoor, General Sahib' with a paternal nod, who preferred Indian food to preserved delicacies from the Europe Shop or a ripe native mango to the American apples tasting of the straw in which they had been packed for six months, such a man could become sanguine towards the criticisms or suspicions of his younger subordinates, levelled at the natives. There had been a lot of loose talk about unrest among the Bengal Army's sepoys, but it would come to nothing. Hindus, Moslems and Sikhs, decided Wheeler, would never conspire together or act in concord.

True, military unrest in Cawnpore could be inconvenient. The town was an important link in the chain of stations across the northern brow of India – Allahabad, Fatepur, Cawnpore, Agra, Meerut – and distances were vast. From Cawnpore, Calcutta was 633 miles and Bombay 839. The feeling of remoteness was not alleviated by the fact that, northward, just across the Ganges, lay the recently annexed kingdom of Oudh.

The situation with regard to Oudh was complex and delicate. For a number of years the Honourable East India Company, with an eye constantly on the possibility of expansion, had applied the 'Doctrine of Lapse'. This forbade the princes of independent states to pass on their titles to an adopted male heir in the absence of a natural one, and under this convenient piece of legislation, between 1848 and 1854, the Company had scooped up the provinces of Satara, Sambalpur, Nagpur and Jhansi.

The annexation of the kingdom of Oudh, however, could not be justified by even this legal chicanery. Oudh, stretching from Nepal to Central India, was the last great Moslem state remaining independent, and it provided two-thirds of the recruits for the Bengal Army. Oudh was also green, fertile and productive, and taxation would bring a further million pounds a year into John Company's coffers.

There was another reason, doubtless genuine but hardly the Company's concern. Oudh, it was claimed, was corrupt and vice-ridden, a misgoverned, perfume-reeking orchid house rooted in poverty, crime and flagrant immorality.

In this direction the Company could righteously adopt a critical attitude. Throughout the British-ruled territories a continuous and bitter campaign had been fought against long-established crime. The Thugs – the professional murderers who for generations had garrotted and robbed 30,000 natives a year in the name of the goddess Kali – had been eliminated by 1840. Suttee – widow-burning – had been forbidden since 1829 and was becoming progressively rare. The hard battle against child-marriage, with ten-year-old girls bearing children, was being determinedly fought, as was that against the deliberate crippling of infants to produce charity-earning beggars. Dacoits and budmashes, whom the natives detested as much as the Sahibs, were being hunted down and hanged.

Crime in India owed much to the caste system which, for thousands of years, had stultified all national and economic progress. Originally there had been three castes, or classes, established to discourage intermarriage between Aryan and Dravidian stock – the priestly Brahmin, the soldiers and military leaders of the Kshatriya, and the farmers and small traders of the Vaisyas. Over many centuries the definitive borders of these castes had become blurred, but never for a fourth estate, the Sudras, the Untouchables, the lowest of humanity.

To the Brahmin, all others were subordinate and every trivial event in a Hindu's life demanded payment – when a baby was born, when an infant was free from 'birth pollution', when his hair was first cut, when he was first fed on solids. And so it went on, through childhood, youth, manhood, marriage and death. The taxation imposed by the East India Company was severe, but the Hindu paid five times as much to the Brahmins.

For the millions of untouchable Sudras there was nothing but crippling poverty and unrelieved degradation. The occupations permitted to them were confined to sweeping and scavenging, water-carrying or the removal of night-soil. An Untouchable could not walk near a Brahmin; even his shadow was polluting. He could not draw water from the communal well, nor resort to a *devadasi*, a prostitute, nor possess the Hindu scriptures. And it was from among the Sudras, the outcasts without hope, that came most of the dacoits and budmashes, pilferers, bullies, pickpockets and abductors, who battened on the Indian peasantry, stole from godowns and army storehouses, snatched girls for brothels and murdered for a few rupees.

Independent Oudh, itself a hotbed of vice and intrigue, was a sanctuary for criminals fleeing from the British who, in turn, were obsessed with law and order. If the British were a nation of shopkeepers, they were extremely militant ones, with no patience for an anachronism like Oudh, an ugly fly in the lucrative Indian ointment. The King of Oudh, Wajid Ali, had been warned several times to put his house in order, but Wajid Ali, more interested in his scores of concubines and red-lipped boys than in the eccentric opinions of the British, thumbed his nose and did nothing. It was unfortunate. In 1856 nobody in the world, least of all a shabby Indian prince, thumbed a nose at the British. Oudh was annexed.

2

Amelia Horne was eighteen years old and an Anglo-Indian, a half-caste. Her father had been English and her mother had Indian blood. In India, in 1857, this accident of birth did not suffer quite the disadvantages it would at a later time. True, there were occasional murmurings of 'karanie' and 'baboo', or 'a touch of the tar-brush' but, by and large, the Anglo-Indian – particularly if of an established family – was accepted, with a degree of condescension. Mind, it wasn't *quite* the same as being a 'When-I' – the name given to those with roots in Dorking or Cheltenham who opened every conversation with 'When I lived in Cheltenham—' In any other society – in Cheltenham – Amelia would have been considered of pure English stock. There were many English girls with blacker hair and darker skins, and only the bluish tinge at the base of her fingernails betrayed her mixed parentage. On Ladies' Night or at the amateur theatricals she wore white gloves.

And many a subaltern, new from England, gazed wistfully in her direction until brought to earth by a nudge from an older colleague. Amelia was beautiful, and nobody could dispute it, but she was, after all, a 'karanie'.

'It's fine, old boy, for a little of the you-know-what, eh? But marriage—?' There was a confiding sniff. 'They're all the same, old lad. At twenty-five they go to seed, and at thirty-five they're a ball of lard, spitting betel and smelling like a stable—'

It was viciously untrue, but every Englishman in India for a hundred years considered he had a master's right to the 'khansamah's daughter' – which meant any attractive native female – but marriage to one was something quite different.

For the English exiles, Cawnpore represented a boring existence, or at least they all claimed so. It was fashionable to complain. Few would concede that they struggled desperately to maintain a pseudo-genteel standard considerably higher than they had been accustomed to in Dorking or Cheltenham. The women exchanged martyr-like criticisms of the inadequacy of Indian servants, of the humiliation of an outside water-closet that their less fastidious husbands referred to as a 'thunder-box'. In the Europe Shop one could purchase tinned Cambridge sausages, hams, salmon, Cheddar cheese, Portuguese sardines, ox-tongues, wines and spirits. All these things were painfully expensive, but one had to make a show. It was important that an English atmosphere be maintained, and efforts to achieve this were carried to extreme lengths. Despite the devouring heat, women conceded little in their dress – whalebone corsets, damask, three or four petticoats, perhaps a straw boater with a veil. Beneath, their thighs and breasts streamed with sweat as they fluttered inadequate fans. There were skin balms and unctions which, however, seemed to do nothing but attract flies. Houses or bungalows were furnished with heavy armchairs and couches, thick carpets and curtains, the walls hidden by pictures and the stuffed heads of animals, and every horizontal surface by vases and knick-knacks, oil lamps with glass chimneys, antimacassars and potted plants. A *punkah*, a long rectangle of carpet or canvas, was hauled slowly back and forth over the sahibs' heads by a punkah-coolie.

The white wife's day began at early morning when she consulted with her *khansamah* and *khitmatgar* with regard to the day's menus. Breakfast was gargantuan, and might include porridge, devilled turkey, grilled kidneys, Irish stew, eggs fried, boiled or poached, fresh fish or kedgeree, pigeon pie, with tea, beer and cold claret. In Bombay or Calcutta there would be ice from America, but not yet in Cawnpore.

Occasionally, the English wife might visit the Europe Shop, always by gharri, but more usually she sent a messenger, a *chaprasi*, with a chit. A lady of any quality would write 2,000 chits per annum, to order preserves or dress materials, windsor soap and camphor balls, to extend an invitation to afternoon tea or a social evening. Amelia knew very little about England; she thought Cawnpore was wonderfully exciting, with its amateur theatricals, garden parties, the band in the Public Gardens on Sundays and Wednesdays, and the handsome officers in their summer uniforms. If Cawnpore really compared so unfavourably with England, then England must be a heavenly place, where the Queen and lords and ladies lived on Europe Shop tinned goods all the time, and always had ice as in Calcutta and Bombay.

Her stepfather was John Hampden Cook, the Cawnpore agent of the North-West Dâk Company. The *Dâk* system was one peculiar to India where railways were almost non-existent, providing stage travel by *dâk gharry*, a vehicle not unlike a bathing machine pulled by ponies, and *dâk* bungalows. These latter, at stage intervals on trunk roads, had four to six bedrooms reasonably furnished and clean, allowing accommodation and simple meals for travellers, but no bedding. All travellers were expected to carry their own, and the regulation maximum period of stay, at a fixed rate, was forty-eight hours. Responsible for travellers and mail over 350 miles of roads between Cawnpore, Allahabad and Lucknow, John Cook was therefore a person of no small social standing.

At eighteen, Amelia should be thinking about marriage; in another two or three years she would be considered 'on the shelf' – but not an impecunious army man, John Cook ruled. A John Company civilian was a better catch, known as a 'three-hundred-a-year-dead-or-alive-man', because civilians joined the Company at £300 per annum and were required to subscribe to a fund which, in the event of their deaths, guaranteed their widows a pension of a similar sum. But Amelia had not decided about marriage. There were so many exciting things to do before embracing the semi-purdah of Victorian matrimony, an infant per year of which every second would die before five of the cholera, or smallpox, typhoid or pneumonia.

She adored the amateur theatricals, sitting among the tremulous fans of the languid but secretly sweating mem-Sahibs and their equally sweating husbands who mopped at lobster-red necks with bandanas. She loved the naughty riposte of the half-tipsy subalterns of the 2nd Cavalry and the 32nd Queen's, in the audience, in response to the actors' comments.

When the distinguished stage duke said to his butler: 'James – bring me a whisky and soda,' his colleagues from the darkness would chorus, *'Humara waste bhi!'* – meaning 'For me also!' A pink-and-white heroine, resenting her kidnapping, enquired, 'Do we live in the Middle Ages?' and the happy subalterns would yell, 'No! Much worse! We live in Cawnpore!' Flustered, the heroine would confess to her suitor, 'My dear – I was blind last night.' It was not to be missed. The young men, fresh from a polo finals celebration, roared, 'And so were we!'

There was a Thursday hunt, English fashion, with an MFH, and the hounds a mixed bag of breeds and pedigrees. The young officers rode ponies with gaily dyed tails and manes, and the quarry was a jackal – although the undisciplined pack was always likely to get the scent of a native's bitch in a field of sugar cane and abandon the chase unashamedly. In the house compound, children in sailor suits also rode small ponies, or miniature dog-carts, led by careful servants, or read from picture books or played 'Happy Families' under the shade tree watched by an *ayah*. Their mothers watched them, too, for the diarrhoea that could mean death from cholera within hours, the headache and lassitude that spelled typhoid, or the nausea of dysentery. The European churchyard of Christchurch was filled with small white crosses over tiny graves.

By daytime it was obligatory for an English gentleman to ride horse-back, but at dusk, when there were social functions, he might use a gharri or carriage, driven by a red-sashed *syce*. And there were numerous functions, although not all were suitable for the attendance of a young lady of eighteen – particularly those that drew bachelors to the native quarter, like Captain Mowbray Thompson of the 53rd Native Infantry, with his dashing red hair, or Lieutenant Hamilton Forbes, whose quizzical, dark eyes always made Amelia lower her gaze.

The difficulty, Amelia decided secretly, was that she was too old for children's pastimes but apparently not yet considered an adult. She was aware of a number of things, including a growing interest in handsome young men who, thrillingly, also seemed interested in her.

Occasionally, very occasionally, she visited the bazaar, the *Sudder*, in the native quarter – or at least those accessible parts deemed sufficiently decent for a young lady to see – and always escorted. The native quarter was a different world from that of the Sahibs. Amelia was familiar with Indians; they had been an integral part of her life since infancy. There had always been an *ayah* for the children, a *khitmatgar* to serve at table, a *syce* for the horses, a *chowkidar* to guard the house, a *mali* for the garden, a *mehtar* for sweeping, a *chaprasi* to carry messages. They had been long-serving and loyal servants of the family and, Amelia might have conceded, it was possible to feel fondness, of a kind, for Indian domestics. Without them, it was impossible to imagine the European community surviving for a single week.

But the native quarter was a different world, a mazy warren of narrow, ramshackle streets, bisected by even narrower, twisting alleys, gloomy, damply hot and with windows shuttered against every probing shaft of sunlight. In the *Sudder* there was a pervading, indefinable stench that clung to her clothes for days, and the broken paving underfoot was littered with rotting refuse, drenched with the blood-like betel juice spat indiscriminately. There were mounds of melons and mangoes, pomegranates and grapes, sacks of flour, rice and lentils, hung mutton and goat-meat swarming with flies, live chickens and baskets of river fish. There were tailors and copper-smiths, jewellers and leatherworkers, shouting. She had seen holy men, *sadhus*, shrivelled skeletons of men, smothered with ashes and cow-dung, and children with grotesquely twisted limbs crawling to offer a begging bowl. And there were women.

Amelia's thoughts seldom dwelt long upon Indian women. They were so totally different to English women as to be incomprehensible. There were, she conceded, Indian men of good background and education – like Nana Sahib – who seemed almost English in everything except colour, who could talk about Berkshire, and Lord Canning, or Purdey guns, and knew more about the Company's profits and dividends than Amelia ever would.

But Indian women, like the Sudder Bazaar, were of a different species. She had never achieved the merest glimmer of compatibility with the household Indian women, or the very few she had met socially. The lower-caste women, who washed clothes, cut grass, or broke stones for the roads, were animal-like, their filthy *chudders* not concealing their breasts empty and flaccid from years of infant-suckling, chattering as they pounded their linen or swung their sickles, but falling to obsequious silence when a mem-Sahib passed.

But there were others in the Sudder Bazaar – brazen-eyed, shapely ones at dark doorways with jewelled nostrils and carmined lips, who met her quick glance and thrust it downwards, taunting. And Harry Delafosse hurried her on, talking quickly, irrelevantly. 'These blacks' – it was lately fashionable to talk about 'the blacks' – 'they're suckled on loot, fed on theft, swaddled on plunder, and weaned on robbery—' He had read Mr Heatley's editorial in the *Delhi Gazette*.

On Sundays Amelia accompanied the family to church, to give righteous thanks to God for all good things and to listen to the sermon of the Reverend Edward Moncreiff while the ayah and syce waited outside. It was a wholly European occasion; the few Indian converts in Cawnpore, dubbed 'curry and rice Christians' because of their reputed insincerity, were the responsibility of the American missionary, the Reverend Haycock, who did not always see eye to eye with his more traditional ecclesiastic colleague. In the main, both Hindu and Muslim regarded Christianity with indifference; Christ was probably a good man, but he was a Sahib, and so would be unlikely to have any greater regard for an Indian's welfare than any other Sahib. Neither Hindus nor Muslims made any attempt to convert Christians.

There were four Indian regiments stationed in Cawnpore, the 1st, 53rd and 56th Native Infantry and the 2nd Cavalry, totalling about 3,000 men of the East India Company's Bengal Army, with white officers. British troops consisted of 200 infantry and 60 artillerymen, many of whom were invalids in the *Lal Koorti Ka Haspital* – which was no more than two small and dirty thatch-roofed warehouses for storing sick soldiers until they either died or recovered. The nearest sizeable concentration of Queen's troops was at Meerut, 250 miles distant, where there were six companies of the 60th Rifles, the 6th Dragoons, and two batteries of the white Bengal Artillery, while in Lucknow, 50 miles away, was the understrength 32nd Regiment of Foot.

There were periodical Ladies' Nights in the officers' messes, resplendent with regimental silver and with tables groaning under the weight of roast turkey, lobster, venison pie, curries and lamb cutlets, smoked salmon and trout, jugged hare, Stiltons and Gruyère, pickles and chutneys, jellies and trifles, a magnificent bowl of wine-and-champagne stirrup-cup for the ladies and, for the men, whisky-sodas, gimlets, port and brandy. Soft-footed and turbaned orderlies responded to the 'Jeldee, kubbadar! Yota whisky-soda, ek dum!' with submissive alacrity. The ladies' white and powdered shoulders gleamed under the light of dozens of candelabra, their owners nodding and smiling languidly, but praying for that bedroom moment when they could tear off their punishing corsets to lie naked, with sweat cooling, momentarily, under their mosquito nets, praying again that a drunken husband would not, this night, demand conjugal privileges.

But Ladies' Nights were rare experiences for an eighteen-years Amelia. Her stepfather, John Cook, entertained at home, and his usual guests were John Roach, the Postmaster, with whom he shared certain responsibilities, and Thomas Berrill, an engineer engaged in establishing the route of a proposed steam railway line which might or might not pass through Cawnpore, or might not happen at all. John Cook was very interested in the possibility of a steam railway line, which could render his dâk-gharri network obsolete overnight or, at best, relegate it to less frequented and less profitable roads.

Amelia seldom found the men's conversation illuminating. They talked about Company tolls and taxes, of Leadenhall Street, bills of lading and freight costs, the high incidence of pilfering and the quality of animal fodder. Amelia would have preferred to chatter to someone of her own age about the latest dress patterns and Lancashire prints from Calcutta, or Lieutenant Ashe's beautiful moustaches, or the daring bonnet that Mrs Hillersdon, the Collector's wife, had worn to church last Sunday, but her stepfather, she knew, would ask her to play the German rosewood pianoforte he had brought from Lucknow specially for her. The gentlemen, in their black broadcloth frock-coats and white duck trousers, would stand gazing gravely at the floating punkah as her slim, golden fingers stroked the keys. She was an accomplished pianist, whether reading music or improvising, and John Cook liked to show her off. Although not her father, he was fond of her and their relationship was excellent. Her Dresden china petiteness and her deep brown eyes were capable of winning the compliance of most men, and when John Cook assured his guests that a teen-age daughter was an expensive luxury, to be married off to the highest bidder as soon as possible, nobody, least of all Amelia, took him seriously.

With few exceptions, the British officers of the native regiments shared a unifying, common experience. They had earlier, at some time, been gentlemen cadets of the Honourable East India Company's military college, Addiscombe House, near Croydon – Thompson, and Ashe of the Artillery, Vibart and Bolton of the 2nd Cavalry, Whiting of the Engineers, Delafosse, Moor, Kempland, Reynolds, Turner – and for most of them the memory of Addiscombe remained the most vivid they retained of England. On 'stag' evenings in the mess, with the port circulating, there would inevitably arrive the moment of nostalgia, when they recalled the green lawns and white gates of Addiscombe, the tall walnut and chestnut trees, the football goals and the turret clock. Ashe would tell, yet again, of the time he had felled the flagstaff with a shell from the practice mortar, and they remembered the leg of mutton five times weekly, boiled beef once, and roast beef on Sundays. There had been a stodgy suet pudding, unpopular, but which had to be eaten before the orderly officer allowed cheese to be taken, so they had fixed their puddings to the underside of the table with their forks, reported to the orderly officer, and achieved their cheese. They had worn bell-shaped shakoes with tuft plumes, blue swallow-tail coats with red facings, and on Sundays marched to St James's Church behind the band, along the Lower Addiscombe Road.

Inevitably, someone would recall the college drill sergeants – 'Squasher' Murray, Malster, Foyce, Reid and Cook, and another would quote the inscription over Addiscombe's stately entrance: *Non faciam vitio culpave minorem*, meaning 'I will not lower myself by vice or fault'. It was the signal for the old College song, and the Indian mess servants would stare, blank-faced and uncomprehending.

With his coat faced with red and the shoulder-knots
bright,
His 'bezzars' too large and trousers too tight,
His dress cap and belt quite twenty years old,
Here's our Addiscombe lad with heart true as gold!

Oh, we are the lads for the Army,
Our lass and our grog is our boast;
But, ladies, don't let me alarm you,
Here's our Addiscombe lads for a toast!

There were several John Company regiments of wholly British rank and file – the Bengal Artillery, the Bombay Fusiliers, the Madras Light Infantry, and others of the Bengal, Bombay and Madras commands. These, recruited at their depot at Warley, England, were drawn from the ultimate dregs of society – deserters from the regular Army, ruined gentlemen, ticket-of-leave men. If a man passed the doctor's inspection, no questions were asked of him, and once in India he resigned himself to being one of the 'God's forgotten', uncaring and inhumanly vicious in fighting, blaspheming and incorrigible, drunkenly devoted to arrack and bazaar rum. The combination of climate, hard campaigning, disease and alcohol ensured that few of John Company's Europeans would achieve old age, and the handful that did regain England were fit for little. Even so, their lists of battle honours were as long as any Queen's regiment, their motto, 'Eat, drink – and especially drink – for tomorrow we die.'

In addition to artillery, there were nine such regiments of infantry in the Company's service, but scattered throughout India. The bulk of white troops were Queen's soldiers, some 40,000, hired from the Crown – like the 32nd Foot at Lucknow, nearest to Cawnpore. There were almost a quarter-million native soldiers.

'Orderly! Yota whisky-soda, ek dum!'

Lieutenant Henry Delafosse, of the 53rd Bengal Infantry, spoke from the depths of a nine-months-old copy of *The Times*. 'I say, Mowbray – listen to this. "The comfort of a fixed water closet for one pound. Places in gardens converted into comfortable water closets by the Patented Hermetically Sealed Pan, with its self-acting valve, entirely preventing the return of cold air or effluvia. Any carpenter can fix it in two hours. Price one pound."' He looked up. 'We ought to send for one of those. Our thunderbox is an absolute *sink*.' He calculated. 'Just think of it. We could have it by Christmas.'

Captain Mowbray Thompson was reading the *Calcutta Weekly Review*. 'They've just started using the punkahs in Calcutta,' he noted, 'and Outram's business in Persia is finished.' He raised his eyes musingly. 'It's a pity we missed that. I wonder what the prize money'll be like?' A newcomer had entered, and Thompson lowered his paper. 'Ah, enter the third thief. Whisky-soda, Sinjin?'

The newcomer was Lieutenant St George Ashe, Bengal Artillery, sweating in his formal uniform of a horse-tailed, brass helmet with its badge of three guns and a shot, blue tunic with high red collar, doeskin breeches and jack-boots. He lifted off his helmet and unfastened his collar, then accepted the drink with a grateful nod.

'They've been sentenced,' he said. 'Ten years' hard labour on the roads.'

Thompson and Delafosse knew what he meant.

There had been native troops in the service of John Company for more than a hundred years, both Hindu and Moslem. Although even more poorly paid than white troops, the sepoys enjoyed certain privileges. They could not be flogged, could not be issued with beef or pork, and should not be sent overseas – although this latter restriction had been subject to abuse. Sepoys had served in Java, China, Aden, Persia and Afghanistan, and had suffered damage to their caste status as a result.

There were other annoyances. Punjabi sepoys had been ordered to trim their beards to a consistent shape, while gaoled defaulters all had beards cut off, with often Hindus and Moslems lodged and fed together, which was distasteful to both. In Himalayan regions, where the sepoys suffered considerably from the cold, well-meaning officers issued their men with *posteens* – sheepskin coats with the fleece inwards – and all Hindus disliked touching dead animal skins.

Taken singly, these irritations and many others were minor; the British considered the complaints irrational and obstructive, while British rankers could claim that they had a deal more to complain about, and probably did. In total, however, they were generating a growing mountain of smouldering resentment, to which fuel was added by a number of outrageous rumours until the puzzled sepoy could not separate fact from fiction.

The thousands of English widows resulting from the Crimean War, it was claimed, were being transported to India, where sepoys would be forced to marry them and produce children, who would be Christian. The bones of all killed soldiers, white or brown, were being ground to powder, which in turn was being mixed with the flour issued to the Army; thus defiled, the sepoys would have no choice but to become Christians. Native hillmen were being captured, killed, and their bodies boiled down for fat.

These and many similarly wild stories were ridiculed by the older soldiers, the white-bearded jemadars, but true isolated incidents did not help. Typically, Surgeon Wells of the 48th Native Infantry, in Lucknow, suffering from morning flatulence, had injudiciously drunk with his lips to a medicine bottle. In minutes his native apothecary had spread the news that the

Doctor Sahib had defiled all medicines, and henceforth none must be taken. It was useless for the regimental commander to muster his men, smash the offending bottle before them and publicly rebuke his surgeon. Within forty-eight hours the Surgeon's bungalow was set on fire, and he and his family barely escaped with their lives. It was too late. The sepoys of the Bengal Presidency had reached the stage of looking for affront in every opportune incident.

There were still further troops in India – the private armies maintained by the rulers of the remaining independent states. These troops varied widely in quality, from the superb cavalry, camel corps and infantry of the Nizam of Hyderabad to the rag-bag, undisciplined contingents of numerous minor princes, often years in arrears of pay and dependent upon legalized freebooting for their sustenance. When independent, the kingdom of Oudh had maintained such an army of 60,000. On annexation, John Company had taken 15,000 of the best of these into service, but the remainder had been discharged, some with pensions but many with no provision whatsoever, angrily simmering and looking for any opportunity to injure the Sahibs in Lucknow and Cawnpore.

The sepoys of John Company were armed with the Tower musket, a heavy, robust weapon which, with the exception of a few specialized corps, had also until recently served the British Army. With regard to dress, although the British in India were experimenting with brown-dyed cotton or linen, known officially as 'drab' but more usually as 'khaki rang' or merely 'khaki', no such concession was extended to native infantry. There were variations between regiment and regiment, but a typical uniform would include a black, bell-shaped but peakless shako, scarlet tunic with appropriate facings, dark trousers, white cross-belts, pouches, a haversack and a brass *lotah*. Boots, however, were unpopular, and lighter, native footwear, and even bare feet, were common.

In early 1857 the Army's new weapon was introduced into India. It was the percussion Enfield-Pritchitt rifle, weighing less than nine pounds, long-ranged, accurate, and considerably superior to the musket. First to be issued with the new gun were the Queen's 60th Rifles, stationed at Meerut, near Delhi – but, predictably, there was already a campaign of resistance to the Enfield or, more accurately, its cartridges, among the sepoys.

To facilitate loading, cartridges were greased, and regulation grease was a mixture of linseed oil and beeswax, both innocuous. The musketry manual required cartridges to be torn open by the teeth before loading, and rumour had it that the British had deliberately impregnated the new cartridge with pork and cow fat in order to defile both Hindus and Moslems. There was possibly a grain of truth in the claim about the composition of the grease; contractors notoriously flouted specifications in search of higher profit margins. Even so, the Governor-General, Lord Canning, issued immediate orders that all cartridges already in magazines should be issued only to the 60th Rifles, who had no qualms about beef or pork, that grease-dry cartridges could be issued to sepoys, and finally that the cartridges could be torn open by hand instead of by mouth. The orders made no difference. Determined to be provoked, regiments were refusing to handle not only the new Enfield cartridges but also the smooth-bore ammunition that they had happily handled for decades.

It is very probable that a soft-pedalling administration could have cooled this new situation, but equally probable that the inevitable would thus be only delayed. Compromise was not a notable component of John Company's administration, while the growing number of malcontents in the Bengal Army were on a collision course that they could not abandon without losing face. The fuse was laid. It needed only a match.

The match was applied in Meerut in mid-April. Ninety troopers of the 3rd Bengal Cavalry refused their ammunition. A no-nonsense commanding officer, Colonel Carmichael Smyth, repeated the order to every man in turn but, of the ninety troopers, eighty-five refused yet again.

From that moment nothing was reversible. The Colonel had no choice but to report mutiny to Divisional Headquarters, where an obese General Hewitt could have no alternative but to order a Court of Enquiry. Whatever the misgivings of the Court's officers, all Indian, their decision could be none other but a recommendation for court-martial, forwarded to the Commander-in-Chief, General the Honourable George Anson.

Anson was a disciplinarian and made no secret of his contempt for the recent wave of 'cartridge phobia'. He already considered that the Governor-General's concessions represented a display of weakness that the natives would exploit, but even he might have wished to avoid the new situation. His duty, however, was clear-cut and immutable. He ordered a court-martial, though he never knew the outcome. Eight weeks later he would be dead, of cholera, at a moment when British fortunes were at their lowest ebb, and all India seemed lost.

St George Ashe had ridden from Lucknow, the provincial capital, which had telegraphic contact with Agra, Allahabad and Delhi as well as Cawnpore.

'Ten years,' he repeated. 'They're held in Meerut's Thug Gaol.'

Henry Delafosse whistled softly. 'Pretty damn stiff. Couldn't they have just stripped 'em and drummed them out, deprived of pension? What does that bloody fat fool Hewitt think he's about?'

'It's not Hewitt,' Mowbray Thompson said. 'I'll lay a pony he's cursing Smyth, and the cartridges, and every other damn thing that's upset his sweaty little world of pampered obesity. The officers of the court were all Indian – and there's the rub.' He paused, reaching for his whisky. 'These sepoy officers come in two sizes. They're either falling backwards to demonstrate their loyalty to John Company and the Buna Rhani, or they're Brahmin troublemakers whipping up causes of mutiny *against* British administration. That's why a few half-wit peasants in uniform, after being coerced into refusing an order, got ten years' penal servitude.'

'Flogging,' suggested Delafosse, only three years out of Addiscombe, 'it's a mistake to forbid flogging. There's nothing like an occasional bloody back to encourage discipline. If Queen's soldiers can be flogged, why can't damn sepoys?'

Mowbray Thompson shook his head. 'No, lad. Flogging never did anything except turn a man into an animal. Take the 60th Rifles at Meerut – probably the top Queen's regiment in India. I'll wager they haven't seen a flogging in years. They'll have their bad hats – drunks and brawlers, mostly – but a few days chained to a log, on bread and water – that's probably the worst punishment in the 60th these days.' He contemplated his empty glass. 'The British Army is changing, lad. D'you know that three out of every five Queen's rankers can read and write?'

'And that's why Queen's officers are so damn cock-snooty?' asked Ashe.

'In Bengal,' Thompson nodded, 'and with reason. Goddammit, let's face it. The Bengal Army's the shabbiest of the three. The Madras – and 'specially the Bombay – don't have our problems. In Bengal we have too many blasted Brahmins and too many damn family recruitings.'

That was it in a nutshell. The native Army of the Bengal Presidency differed in several aspects from those of Madras and Bombay. First, it was considerably larger than the two others combined, consisting of 74 regiments of infantry and 10 of cavalry. Second, promotion was rigidly by seniority while elsewhere it was by merit. A sepoy enlisting at the age of 16 could not hope to become a naik, or corporal, before 36, a havildar, sergeant, before 45, or a jemadar, native captain, before 60, and it was usually considered that the native soldier was utterly useless by the age of fifty.

Brahmins dominated the Bengal Army. A veteran Indian officer, if of lower caste, must abase himself before the newest Brahmin recruit, a situation which did nothing for discipline. Equally serious was the nepotism with which all Indian society was riddled – the law courts, police, military, down to the domestic servants of every household. Every sepoy promoted to *naik*, every company *subedar*, each encouraged the recruitment of his own village associates while at the same time making life uncomfortable for the stranger. In consequence there existed a sympathy and freemasonry throughout the Bengal ranks, a unanimity which had its merits, but could be dangerously two-edged.

A Bengal infantry regiment averaged 1,000 sepoys, 120 NCOs, and 20 native officers. Oddly, with the exception of gun lascars in the Artillery, almost no recruits for the Bengal Army were taken from the area of Bengal proper. Bengalis were considered poor military material. Christian Indians were recruited only as drummers and fifers.

Earning seven rupees per month, the sepoy was, in native terms, a wealthy man with access to John Company accommodation and transport, blankets, provisions, employment and, of course, further advancement. From Behtah, Fatehpur and Hamirpur his country cousins came to share his hut and his good fortune, and a column of sepoys on the march was accompanied by a long caravan of small carts, wives and in-laws, local hangers-on, goats and pot-bellied infants.

But when Mowbray Thompson used the word 'mutiny' he really meant insubordination, the symptoms of the ill-discipline of the Bengal Army which caused it to be criticized by its counterparts in Bombay and Madras, as well as Queen's officers. Thompson was as incapable of visualizing an open, armed rebellion as was the Divisional Commander, General Wheeler – or the hundreds of other officers who were firmly convinced that Queen's officers should mind their own bloody business. 'It's a pity,' wrote an officer of the 65th Native Infantry, 'that Europeans abusing a corps can't be strung up!'

3

The Cawnpore native city accommodated a population of 60,000 within an area smaller than that which housed a thousand Europeans. The hot season was approaching, but, by Indian standards, it was still comparatively cool. The only street of note was the wide *Chandni Chauk*, the street of silversmiths, which enjoyed a province-wide reputation for cheapness and excellence, as did leatherwear – saddlery, boots and shoes, bottle-covers, helmets and cheroot cases. A subaltern could harness his horse and trap for three pounds, or his pony for half that. A serviceable if inelegant and hard-mouthed horse could be purchased for a hundred rupees, the equivalent of ten pounds.

Most of native Cawnpore, however, was a labyrinth of narrow streets, with the bazaars jostling with shouting traders, gutter-urchins, prostitutes at doors and windows, crawling beggars, squatting shopkeepers, peasant smallholders with their market wares – mangoes, guavas, shaddocks and limes, peaches and melons. There were piled sacks of rice, flour and lentils, bolts of cloth, sweetmeats, baskets of *pulla*, the muddy-tasting river fish, attracting the flies, and hung Patna mutton and goat periodically splashed with dirty water. Here and there were the shops of immigrant Chinese, an occasional strolling Sahib, civil or military, or a hump-shouldered cow, inviolable, being enticed away from a vegetable stall with a handful of grain.

Many sepoys frequented the native city, but it was difficult to distinguish one as such. Off duty, the sepoy lost no time in removing his uniform and reverting to a peasant *dhoti*, in which he looked the same as thousands of other peasants who swarmed Cawnpore. But Miss Georgina Williams, daughter of Colonel Williams of the 56th Native Infantry, had been quite convinced that it was one of her father's men who had jostled her in the bazaar. She had momentarily feared for her purse, but the man had spoken over his shoulder. 'You will not come here many times more, mem-Sahib. *Sub lal hoga hi*. Everything is to become red.'

It was quite incomprehensible, as she confided to her sister, Fanny. She did not wish to mention the incident to the Colonel, or even Captain Thompson, because of the fuss they might make, but she had felt quite shaken. Cawnpore had not completely lost its ill repute of earlier years, when it stood on the fringe of British-ruled territory, the stage-point busy with criminals travelling in both directions, and stabbed or strangled corpses could be found in every alley. Had the man in the bazaar been uttering a threat or a warning?

Mrs Bridget Widdowson, the wife of a private of the 32nd Foot, was of rather sterner stuff. When a native jeered that there was something thicker than water, and more red than a British uniform, she had told him to shut his filthy clack, then laid him sprawling with a blow of her huge fist. Nobody took liberties with Mrs Bridget Widdowson, as Private Widdowson could ruefully confirm.

But there was something in the air, something vaguely conspiratorial, fed by fragmentary rumours that seemed to have no meaning even to the natives who passed them. There was talk of the Devil's Wind, and *Fouj ki Bheera* – the will of the Army – but no sepoy could have explained what either phrase meant, unless there was some connection with the *chupatties*, the thin cakes of unleavened bread passed from village to village throughout the Ganges valley with laconic instructions to pass them further. For what reason? Nobody seemed to know. British rule in India, ran the legend, would terminate in its hundredth year, and 1857 was the hundredth. But how?

Then, during late March, in Barrackpore, Calcutta, a drug-crazed sepoy named Mungul Pande, of the 34th NI, had shot down his adjutant and sergeant-major. He had been hanged on 8 April, on the Brigade Parade Ground at five past five a.m., and a chill apprehension shivered through northern India. Later the same month a party of discharged Brahmins of the 19th NI passed through Cawnpore from the west. To the wide-eyed sepoys of the 53rd and 56th they told strange tales of polluted cartridges, of hempen nooses, swords glittering under the Ganges moonlight, and the spurting blood of English officers.

The British have always displayed an odd penchant for waltzing all night, or playing bridge, bowls or cricket when disaster was approaching at frightening speed. In a few weeks, 24 May, it would be the Queen's birthday, an occasion on which the monotony of the cantonments would be relieved by a whole series of events. There would be a grand parade of all the regiments, Amelia Horne knew, attended by General Wheeler and perhaps the Rajah of Bithur, with musketry volleys fired at the sky. There would be theatricals, and the subalterns of the 2nd Cavalry might repeat their hilarious impersonation of a ladies' quartet, complete with moustaches. Thinking of moustaches, Amelia hoped that Sir Henry Lawrence, the Chief Commissioner in Lucknow, would send a detachment of the Bengal Artillery to add colour to Cawnpore's celebrations. It was not that she was particularly interested in the polished brass field-guns, but Lieutenant St George Ashe, of the Lucknow garrison, would probably accompany them, and Lieutenant Ashe was very handsome.

Church-going that Sunday would be the ladies' event of the year, and Amelia had a dress-length of gorgeous muslin from Dear's of Manchester that *nobody* in Cawnpore had ever dreamed of. The Reverend Moncreiff at Christchurch and Father Joseph Rooney in the Roman Catholic Chapel would drone religious platitudes at congregations anxious to be released while lace and starched linen remained unspoiled by perspiration. In the mission house the curry-and-rice Christians would sing tunelessly, led by an enthusiastic Reverend Haycock while his aged mother played a harmonium.

Amelia, however, would not be wearing her pretty muslin on the Queen's birthday, although Lieutenant St George Ashe would bring his two battery guns to Cawnpore.

It was fashionable for a bachelor to maintain his quarters in a state of tumbled disorder, and Mowbray Thompson's bungalow was just that. A large, battered table in the sitting-room was strewn with drinking glasses, bottles of soda water, whisky and brandy, playing cards, a box of cheroots, a Hindustani dictionary, several tattered English periodicals, an inkstand and a revolver. The corners of the room were obscured by jumbles of pig-spears, carriage whips, a sword, shotguns and an Afghan *jezzail*, the walls by pinned, fly-specked company orders, muster lists, and a curled, fading photograph of Addiscombe's class of 1853-4. A dusty *punkah*, suspended from an equally dusty ceiling, was slowly oscillated by a long string that passed through a hole in the wall to the nodding punkah-coolie on the verandah, while beyond the wide-flung window Thompson's elderly Kabul pony was tethered in the shade of a clump of mango trees.

Mowbray Thompson, in off-duty silk shirt and linen drawers, reclined uneasily on an old couch with broken springs. 'Damn prickly heat again,' he winced. 'That's the price of having hot southern blood, y'know.'

'Try lemon juice,' suggested Henry Delafosse. 'Rubbing on, I mean, not drinking.' In addition to Delafosse there sat or stood Frank Whiting of the Bengal Engineers, Surgeon Nathanial Collyer, and Athill Turner and Fred Burney of the Native Infantry. Nobody smiled.

Delafosse was very angry. 'It's bloody Hewitt again! Why is it that everyone in the Bengal Army with any authority is so blasted old? We've got brigadiers of seventy, colonels of sixty, and even captains of fifty!' He choked. 'Goddam, if we had to *choose* a place for a sepoy revolt, we'd have *said* Meerut, where there's two thousand British troops – infantry, horse and artillery. Why weren't the blacks torn to shreds with canister and then finished off with those marvellous Enfields that the 60th Rifles are so bloody proud of?'

'I've tried lemon juice,' Thompson said, 'and it made me smell like a mem-Sahib's *mithra-pani*.' He paused, frowning. 'Anyway, we've only got half a story through Agra. It could be just another shave, put up by the Brahmins.'

'Some of the clerks said they heard gunfire last night,' Whiting offered.

Mowbray Thompson laughed. 'Damn bunkum, Frank. Meerut's 250 miles away. As I say, we haven't got the full story. All we know is that the 3rd Bengal Cavalry and the 11th and 20th Native Infantry have cut up some of their officers in Meerut and marched on Delhi—'

'Where there's three more sepoy regiments,' Delafosse insisted, 'and not much more than a corporal's guard of Europeans to hold them. I just don't bloody understand how Hewitt could have let it happen.'

'Something went wrong,' Thompson conceded. 'Perhaps Hewitt is a senile old dodderer, but he's also a John Company man. It'd be damn difficult for any of us to order Queen's soldiers to open fire on our own men – men that've served under us for years. Dammit, Harry, I'm not sure I could do it.' He lit a cheroot carefully and watched the trickle of smoke rise. 'It'll come to nothing. It can't. Without officers they'll be a rag-bag, a mob. It'll be all over as soon as the rains start. They'll be crawling back, shouting, *"Jai Company Bahadur ki!"* Have you ever known Hindus and Moslems to agree about anything? They disagree *because* they're Hindus and Moslems. That's our strength – divide and rule.'

Henry Delafosse was not convinced. 'The 3rd Cavalry are Moslem, and the 11th and 20th are Hindu,' he pointed out. 'They agreed at Meerut, anyway.'

'And the gunfire.' Frank Whiting was not to be denied. 'It didn't have to come from Meerut. It could have been nearer – Kannauj or Fatehpur—' He hesitated, then, 'John Cook, the *dâk* agent, says that the *dâks* from the west haven't arrived.' He shrugged lamely. 'Anyway, it's a bloody queer business.'

Mowbray Thompson was very patient. '*Dâk gharries* lose wheels and break axles. *Dâk* ponies have been known to drop dead, and *dâk* drivers suddenly decide it's a religious festival and go home. Then there are rock-falls, collapsed bridges and sunken ferries, and finally there are bloody passengers who simply change their minds. You don't need a blasted sepoy revolt to delay a *dâk gharry*, b'God.' He chewed gently on his cheroot. 'Cook? Isn't he the fellow with the soldier's-dream daughter?' He chuckled, then winced again. 'All right, Frank, you can tell her that if her father's *gharry* hasn't arrived by tomorrow morning we'll send out a troop of the 2nd as far as Sherajepur. In fact' – he nodded – 'we'll send two troops. With everyone having nightmares about blood, lust, and revolution, a show of strength mightn't be a bad thing.'

'If it happens, Mowbray,' Delafosse enquired, 'what do we do? I mean, just suppose—'

'It won't – not at Cawnpore, anyway. There's one thing we do know. If our blacks aren't quite as dandy as the Coldstream Guards, they're certainly not mutineers, either. This Meerut business'll fall to pieces as soon as they realize there's no paymaster and no commissariat, and every bloody sepoy wanting to be a major-general; you'll see.'

'That,' said Delafosse, 'is what Colonel Finnis of the 11th probably said just before they blew his brains out in Meerut.'

Thompson snorted. 'If – and it's a festerin' big "if" – we

have trouble with our blacks, there are 200 European troops here, and there's the 32nd Queen's, and artillery, in Lucknow. And we'd have Nana Sahib on our side.'

Bithur, with its palace and several temples, was five miles north of Cawnpore although, because of a wide, dog-leg bend in the Ganges, still on its southerly side. Mythology had it that Brahmâ, the Hindu deity, had walked in Bithur, that the pin of his slipper had become detached and imbedded itself in the riverside *ghat* – a legend that attracted a considerable number of pilgrims to the town.

In 1851 Bajee Rao, Peshwar of Poonah, last of a long line of Mahratta princes, died in Bithur. He had earlier been deprived of his vast estates by the East India Company and settled in dissolute retirement on a pension of £80,000 per year. Bajee Rao, however, was without a natural son – an oddly common predicament of many of the degenerate Indian dynasties, and one readily exploited by the Company.

The Peshwar's adopted heir was a man named Sereek Dhondhu Punth. His origins were vague. Some spiteful commentators have made him the son of a Poonah corn-merchant, others a peasant from Venn, near Bombay, or the son of a poor Konkani Brahmin. Notwithstanding, Sereek Dhondhu Punth became the Maharajah of Bithur, better known as Nana Sahib – the 'grandson'.

For several years Nana Sahib petitioned the East India Company in Calcutta for a continuation of the annual pension for himself, but without success. The Nana could retain the Bithur palace and properties to the value of a quarter-million pounds, said the Company, but the pension died with the old Mahratta. Nana Sahib was not satisfied with Calcutta's decision. He decided to send an emissary to the Company's headquarters in Leadenhall Street, London.

His chosen agent was a Moslem opportunist named Azimullah Khan, whose background is less obscure than his master's. Azimullah had once been a *khitmatgar* – a table-servant – for an Anglo-Indian family, acquiring a good command of English and a little French. He later became a pupil, and subsequently a teacher, in the government native school in Cawnpore, attracted the attention of Nana Sahib, and was appointed minister to the Maharajah.

Azimullah Khan travelled to London in 1854. Handsomely equipped, witty and courteous, he was quickly lionized by Mayfair and became the sought-after guest of dozens of society drawing-rooms. The Governors of the Honourable East India Company, however, were less impressed by the plausible ex-*khitmatgar*, and Nana Sahib's suit was again rejected.

Returning to India by the part-overland route, Azimullah passed through Scutari and Constantinople at a time when British military ineptitude had never been more appallingly demonstrated, and when he regained Bithur he was able to offer some small consolation for the failure of his mission. The British, he assured Nana Sahib, were far from invincible. They were paper tigers, and their rule of India was based on a mere illusion of power which was completely unsupported. The Indians had been hoaxed for a hundred years, and a little simple arithmetic suggested that, without John Company's sepoys to do their fighting for them, the British could be swept out of India with ease.

Nana Sahib listened with interest, but for the moment the information was of no more than academic value. He was certainly in no position to initiate any insurrection against the British Raj. Still, he would remember.

Now, in 1857, Nana Sahib was 36, of middle height but fleshy build from lack of exercise, with a sallow, clean-shaven face and a clandestine appetite for hashish, French brandy, and the concubines whose erotic adulation he had enjoyed since childhood. To the British in Cawnpore, however, he represented the best kind of Indian – an Anglophile of the most amicable and acceptable kind.

The Palace of Bithur, although not of outstanding architectural merit, was situated in parkland stocked with peacocks, antelopes, apes and falcons in addition to an excellent stable and kennels which accommodated horses, dogs, elephants and camels. The palace reception-rooms, thickly carpeted and glittering with mirrors and chandeliers, were exquisitely furnished. There were harness-rooms and gun-rooms to widen the envious eyes of any subaltern for whom five years' pay would not have purchased just one of the many magnificent sporting guns from Purdey and Manton, wardrobes overflowing with shawls and jewellery that had visiting Cawnpore ladies sighing wistfully. And there were rooms in the palace that would have shocked and appalled those same ladies had they been allowed beyond their locked doors.

Nana Sahib entertained his European neighbours lavishly and often, mixing freely with his guests and enquiring courteously of this lady's health or that gentleman's hunting accident, congratulating an officer on his promotion or welcoming another back from Simla. A guest's merest whim was unfailingly met – the loan of a carriage, horses for pig-sticking, elephants for a tiger-shoot. Nana Sahib, everyone agreed, was a gentleman, a 'stout fellow' – even if he was only an Indian. His lips smiled continuously, but somehow his eyes never did.

'We can always count on Nana Sahib,' Mowbray Thompson said. 'I'd say he'd be damn flattered if we asked him. He has about four hundred troops, infantry and cavalry, and a few guns. They're a ragged lot, but good enough for guarding the Treasury and the mess-houses.' He shrugged. 'But it'll never come to that.'

4

The field officers' durbar, on the verandah of General Wheeler's house, was attended by the Station Commander, Brigadier Alex Jack, Colonel Ewart of the 1st Native Infantry, Colonel Williams of the 56th, Major Hillersdon of the 53rd, Colonel Larkins of the Bengal Artillery, Major Vibart of the 2nd Cavalry, and Captain John Moore, 32nd Foot, the senior Queen's officer in Cawnpore. Wheeler thumbed through a sheaf of despatches, occasionally raising seamed eyes towards the distant Ganges, glinting in the morning sunshine, already hot, and thronged with small vessels. A narrow bridge of boats rose and fell gently under the constant passage of carts and animals between Cawnpore and the Oudh bank.

'The electrical telegraph wires from Delhi have been cut since 11 May.' The General did not entirely approve of the electrical telegraph. It brought home unpleasant events much too quickly, not allowing a man to think carefully. In his younger days a galloper might require two weeks to carry a despatch 266 miles from Delhi to Cawnpore. Now the stench of disaster could travel that same distance in minutes.

'The situation, gentlemen, is beginning to clarify a little. At least six regiments have mutinied – the 3rd Cavalry and the 11th and 20th Infantry from Meerut, who have brought out the 38th, 54th and 74th in Delhi. The city is in mutineers' hands, and several hundred Europeans have been murdered. There are no lists yet, but some have escaped. As you know, a Mrs Fraser reached Cawnpore yesterday, after a ten days' journey by *dâk gharry*.' He peered at the papers before him, knowing his eyes inadequate, but he could never tolerate the thought of spectacles. 'The King of Delhi, old Bahadur Shah, has been proclaimed Emperor.'

There was a murmer of disbelief from the surrounding officers, none of them, except for Moore, with less than thirty years' service in India. The news was utterly nonsensical. 'Dammit,' Ewart grinned, 'I spent a week with Ripley of the 54th only last month, and his lady—'

'Colonel Ripley and his lady' – Wheeler sucked his teeth – 'are both dead, shot by their own sepoys.'

Nobody said anything for several seconds, then, 'Bahadur Shah, sir?' It was Moore, the Queen's officer. 'He's more than eighty, isn't he?' Immediately, he wished he had not spoken; the white-haired officer at the end of the table was almost seventy.

Wheeler resumed. 'The Commander-in-Chief, General Anson, is already moving towards Delhi, from Simla, with a mixed force of 3,000. He had also been required by the Governor-General to reinforce Cawnpore with infantry and cavalry, but I have sent a message to Calcutta confirming that all is quiet here. I have no desire to weaken the Commander-in-Chief's force. I presume' – he glanced at the men around him – 'that there is no sign of dissension among your people?'

Ewart was mildly uncertain. 'There was a fire in my lines last night, but it seemed accidental, and the men extinguished it quickly enough.' He paused. 'There are a lot of rumours, but – no – there's no sign of anything worse.'

The other officers agreed, with Moore remaining silent. Not a sepoy officer, he was in no position to gauge the temper of native troops and, in any case, he was only a captain. He supposed, dammit, that these John Company men knew what they were about.

'It is important,' General Wheeler ruled, 'that all European officers behave normally, and give absolutely no indication that there is any alarm over the Delhi situation, or that there is any doubt about the loyalty of the Cawnpore regiments. All parades and duties will continue as if nothing has happened. Your officers' calm behaviour will also reassure the European civilians.'

The durbar, Captain Moore realized as he walked away, had been so brief and superficial as to be almost useless. There had been no discussion of measures to be taken in anticipation of a local mutiny simply because none of the elderly John Company officers would concede that a local mutiny was possible; they were deliberately pushing their heads into the warm sand of regimental pride. Other regiments *might* mutiny. Theirs would not.

He halted, his eyes half closed against the sun's glare as he gazed eastwards toward the river. He did not belong in Cawnpore and knew little of its characteristics. The sweat was already soaking his shirt, and he could smell hot dust and cattle dung, hear the faint, incomprehensible shouts of distant boatmen at the *ghat*. Southward from the river were the cantonments – bungalows and compounds, the church, and Duncan's Hòtel. Beyond, he could see the race-course, the old hospital, and a line of eight partially-built barrack-houses on which all work seemed to have stopped. There was a pervading sense of tiredness and stagnation, of today being exactly the same as yesterday, as tomorrow, or last week. Cawnpore presented a depressingly unmilitary appearance.

'I know what you're thinking.' A voice spoke from close behind him. 'There's not much on which to base a defence position – and you're damn right.'

Turning, Moore found himself in the company of a tall young man in the scarlet shell-jacket and white, curtained forage-cap of John Company's native infantry. The young man smiled. 'Delafosse, 53rd. You're Captain Moore of the 32nd Queen's from Lucknow? We were introduced in the mess, but you'll probably not remember.'

John Moore did not, but he nodded. He had met forty or fifty officers during the past few days, and he had a poor memory for names. He was a solitary Queen's officer of modest rank in a John Company world, and a polite wariness existed between the soldiers of the two services. A John Company officer, particularly one of mature years, considered the East India Company the only authority in India and Queen's regiments merely time-servers who might be in India this year, Hong Kong the next, and Jamaica, Portsmouth or Capetown the year after. In response, the Queen's officer regarded the other as a mercenary in the service of a vast commercial organization, pretending to be real soldiers and, after all, commanding only native troops. Both, to a degree were right, and equally prejudiced.

'It's a problem,' Moore agreed. 'Not that there's likely to be any need, of course – but there just might.'

'There's nothing here that couldn't be knocked to pieces by a six-pounder in minutes,' Delafosse said, 'but there is at Nawabgunge, on the other side of the town. It's the magazine – built like a fortress, big enough to accommodate all Cawnpore's Europeans, and with enough artillery and ammunition for a major campaign. It's got a good well, and its rear is protected by the Ganges – just a *brahmakund* where the Hindus bathe. Then the Treasury and public offices are nearby, so specie and records could be easily transferred, and the gaol gates would be covered by our guns. Properly provisioned, the magazine could be held for a year.'

Moore was surprised, and his face showed it. Delafosse laughed. 'We're not *all* military antiques in John Company's army, y'know. Some of us can actually think.'

It was Moore's turn to laugh, and the gap between them was closed. Moore dabbed at his neck with a bandana. 'What's good for prickly heat?'

'Lemon juice.' Henry Delafosse offered the other a cheroot. 'You've just come from the General's durbar.'

'That's right, lad. There's been bloody mayhem in Delhi, with six regiments known to have mutinied, and probably more by now. All *dâk* travel has been suspended; the roads are crawling with dacoits – a lot of 'em in uniform. Four of your regiments in Lahore have been disarmed at gunpoint, by Queen's soldiers.' He paused. 'Between us and Delhi there's only the 60th Rifles, the 6th Dragoons raw from England, and a few penny packets of infantry and artillery that aren't worth a gnat's spit.' He sucked at his cheroot, eyes narrowed. 'What's the mood of your sepoys?'

'Not openly defiant, but they're gloating over the Meerut and Delhi affair. You can see it in their faces – a sort of smug malice that you want to wipe off with your fist, but daren't. And there are new rumours with every damn camel train or troupe of dancers that passes through Cawnpore. The latest is that the Queen has given the Governor-General permission to kill three hundred thousand holy men, Hindu and Moslem – all part of the plot to convert India to Christianity.' Delafosse was thoughtful, 'They seem to be *waiting* for something.'

Amelia Horne was finding it difficult to suppress her excitement. The Queen's birthday was only a few days away, and her new dress was finished. She and her mother, Emma Cook, had sat with their sewing-baskets until midnight, with the moths fluttering at the oil-lamps, and she had stood nervously as her mother pulled out the last pins and tacking, and then she had pirouetted before the mirror in a whirl of gossamer muslin.

On Sunday, of course, she must be demure and self-possessed, holding her prayer book in a gloved hand and pretending to be unaware of the surreptitious glances of Lieutenant Henry

Delafosse, or Captain Thompson, or Lieutenant St George Ashe from Lucknow. She hoped it would not be too hot. It was always difficult to appear dainty, cool and fragrant when corsets and petticoats were becoming sodden with perspiration, and feet scalded in pinching shoes.

John Cook was in a bad humour and worried. *Dâk* transport on the Grand Trunk Road, from the north-west, had ceased, and he had heard that *dâk* bungalows in the Khyabad Division had been broken into and ransacked. European travellers en route westward could get no further than Cawnpore. Nearer home, the growing sulkiness of the sepoys had spread to domestic servants. The *bhistie* failed to fill the bath, the *khansamah* cooked carelessly, a *chaprassi* needed an hour to walk two hundred yards with a chit, and other servants simply failed to arrive for work. Native shops in Cawnpore were being closed and shuttered, their owners pleading sickness, and a number of Europeans had already packed bags and departed by steamer for Calcutta.

The palace at Bithur swam with the aroma of the thickly growing mustard flower that carpeted the banks of the Ganges, mingling with the less subtle scents of palace women with their eyes smudged with lamp-black and lips wet-crimson with the juice of betel nut. They twisted on slim brown ankles with bangles chinking, fingers drumming softly on tiny *madals*.

Gharib Parwar, urged Azimullah, this is the moment we have spoken of many times. In Delhi the old king has raised the banner of Shah Jehan, and the rule of John Company is finished. But the King of Delhi is old, and will soon die. Then there will be many princes claiming the title of Badahur Shah, Ruler of the Universe. At the moment they are uncertain, for they do not know – as we know – that the British have no more soldiers than those in India, that all the others have been killed at Sevastopol. Have I not seen the mountains of their corpses in Scutari? And see, the Indian sepoys only wait for a leader. Who better than the Prince of all the Mahrattas? First Wheeler Sahib in Cawnpore, and then Lawrence Sahib in Lucknow. It will be easy. But it must be now, Gharib Parwar.

Nana Sahib was very tempted, and he had cause. Had not John Company refused him his rightful pension, and further humiliated him by declining to even recognize his title of Maharajah of Bithur? For many months he had not visited Cawnpore because the garrison was not permitted to fire a salute in his honour. The Sahibs accepted his hospitality as if it were their right, but they winked at each other behind his back and he knew they referred to him as a nigger. It would be satisfying to see them humbled, to see those pink-faced subalterns and haughty ladies grovelling and broken.

But he wasn't sure yet. Not yet.

Azimullah Khan was right, of course, about the East India Company's weakness in India. Delhi was already in rebel hands, and its recapture, in the face of further disaffection that was spreading like a grass-fire, would require the undivided attention of all the puny British forces in the north-west. It was more likely that Delhi would never be recaptured. And he, Nana Sahib – if he destroyed the British in Cawnpore and Lucknow – the only relieving force, equally puny, must come from Calcutta, 633 miles away. A half-built railway might carry that force as far as Ranigunge, leaving a march of more than 500 miles through country in which population, climate and terrain were viciously hostile. There would be ample time to consolidate before the remnants of a relieving force reached Cawnpore – if it ever did.

And Azimullah was right in claiming that the leader who raised his banner and shouted his cause now would recruit the boldest rebels, and be in a strong position when the time came to dispute rulership.

But was Azimullah really right about the collapse of British military power? He, Nana, had seen a map of the world, of which vast areas were coloured red. How could such a tiny splinter of red marked 'Great Britain' be overlord to a whole quarter of the earth's surface

Cawnpore's sepoy lines comprised long rows of huts built of mud brick and bamboo, thatched with straw, the narrow lanes between rutted and stony. Each sepoy had his own hut, in which he also quartered his women and numerous dependent relatives, and each regiment had its own small bazaar, thronged with vendors of corn and rice, tobacco, cotton fabrics, with prostitutes, fakirs, barbers, moneylenders, and reeking street kitchens. There was a new and ominous excitement in the lines, among the anxious native officers and the off-duty sepoys who, reduced to their *dhotis*, squatted on their heels in small groups, gossiping, eating, or engrossed in the ritual of lengthy ablutions. Until now the news of mutiny and massacre had related to places hundreds of miles away, but now, it was told, the towns of Etawah and Aligarh, much nearer, had been plundered, and the insurgents were marching towards Cawnpore. It had already been reported to General Wheeler that the son of a trooper of the 2nd Cavalry had been boasting to his juvenile fellows that he knew all the secret details of a bloody uprising of his father's regiment.

Wheeler had dismissed it all as bazaar trivia, but almost immediately there was a further report of a Mussulman sepoy of the 56th, one Khan Mohamed, who was assuring his comrades that, on 5 June, the regiment was to be assembled, ostensibly to draw pay, and would then be blown to pieces by a huge bomb which even now was being prepared by the Sahib officers in the billiards room of Mr Duncan's hotel.

Not satisfied, the sepoy took his story to the cavalry lines, with the added embellishment that several squadrons of British cavalry were to receive the horses and sabres of the Indian troopers following their destruction. The lines rocked with anger and vociferous defiance, and arrests were made. Charles Hillersdon, the Collector, complained that the sepoy guards at the Treasury were accosting people leaving with money and stamp-papers, and were talking mutiny. What did the Station Commander intend to do about it? Was he waiting for everyone to be murdered in the streets, as in Meerut and Delhi? What was the delay in making safe the European district, and sending for Queen's soldiers from Lucknow?

The General's breakfast durbar was joined by Mr Hillersdon and Sir George Parker, the cantonments' magistrate. Both officials were clearly uneasy – Hillersdon with regard to more than £100,000 in specie in the Treasury vaults and Parker for the increasing level of local lawlessness. The police were in control still, but only just. Information from the surrounding country indicated that the whole of Bengal was on the brink of mutiny, and thousands of native merchants and shopkeepers were closing their businesses and departing eastward. It needed only one more provocative rumour, one more loud-mouthed sepoy, and the situation would be beyond retrieval.

Events were moving too quickly for Wheeler; he still could not believe that the sepoys he had commanded for half a century would ever turn their weapons against him. The very thought was anathema. His old regiment, the 48th Native Infantry, was in Lucknow, and they, he knew with certainty, were staunch. All these ridiculous rumours were grossly exaggerated.

'I do not believe the situation is as black as some people suppose,' he decided. 'We must remain calm. Any hasty action on our part will only provoke further suspicion, perhaps retaliation, among the natives. If we have patience, and show that we are completely unconcerned, all this nonsense will die a natural death.' He paused, considering. 'I am quite sure that Calcutta will have the matter under consideration. Meanwhile, Sir Henry Lawrence has the 48th Native and the 32nd Queen's in Lucknow, and the 3rd Bengal European Fusiliers are in Agra. We are in communication with both by electrical telegraph.'

Colonel Ewart cleared his throat. 'Sir, if the situation does get worse, both Lucknow and Agra will be as badly placed as ourselves. Agra even worse; they're between us and Delhi. If Calcutta began organizing a relief force *today*, it could hardly be with us in less than a month.'

Mr Hillersdon nodded. 'With respect, General, the European civilians, particularly the women, would be grateful to see some arrangements made for their protection in the event of a worsening state of affairs. The European residences are scattered, and would be helpless. There should be a prepared sanctuary, some fortified place—'

Captain John Moore, junior of the dozen men surrounding

the table, held his peace. Ewart and Hillersdon, at least, were talking sense and, in any case, this distinguished company would be unlikely to welcome a suggestion from, and would probably resent, a mere Queen's captain. Colonel Ewart resumed. 'The Magazine, sir,' he suggested. 'It's the obvious place. If there *is* a mutiny – Heaven forbid – then Cawnpore and Lucknow will both be involved. In that event, Sir Henry Lawrence *must* fall back on Cawnpore to pool his resources with ours. To have two understrength garrisons defending themselves less than fifty miles apart would be military idiocy – and in Lucknow Sir Henry has nothing like the Cawnpore magazine.'

That's it, Moore triumphed mentally. The Magazine. Since his meeting with Henry Delafosse he had walked around the huge building. Delafosse was absolutely right. Adequately provisioned, a tiny force of determined men could hold the Magazine against the entire Bengal Army – with or without Sir Henry Lawrence from Lucknow.

The General straightened, then walked a few short paces to the verandah's edge. The scene had not changed since last week, or last year. The white paint of the Baptist Chapel was still peeling, and the weather-vane over the old Assembly Rooms was still crooked. It was barely nine in the morning, but already the early freshness was almost lost, and a warm, dry breeze carried the noise of river activity. Clumsy native boats with high sterns and thatched canopies looked like floating cottages. The pontoon toll-bridge spanned three-quarters of the Ganges to a mid-stream eyot before continuing to the Oudh side and the road that ran north-eastward to Lucknow. There were plans for a steam railway, Wheeler knew, to run clear across the breadth of India, following the route of the Grand Trunk Road, from Calcutta to Peshawar, and travellers would journey in an hour as far as they did during a whole day by *dâk gharry*. The General sighed. There were so many new things to comprehend – electrical telegraphs, steam railways, and now there was talk of breech-loading artillery. Campaigning in India would never again be the prolonged, leisurely business it always had been.

He turned. 'Not the Magazine. It would be a hostile act which the sepoys could easily misunderstand – almost an insult. Besides, the Magazine is at Nawabgunge, on the wrong side of Cawnpore. If there were an insurrection, and if we were defending the Magazine, a relief force would have to fight its way through the town to reach us. No.' He shook his head. 'We shall entrench and provision the *Lal Koorti Ka Haspital*, the old Dragoon Hospital.'

There was a long moment of shocked silence, then Brigadier Jack choked. 'The Dragoon Hospital, sir? There are only two flimsy brick buildings, with one of them thatched, and both exposed on all sides. How could we accommodate and victual a thousand Europeans, half of them women – and more if we get refugees from the out-stations – in a miserable place like the Dragoon Hospital?' He sucked in his breath. 'The position is not defensible.'

Colonel Larkins of the Artillery followed quickly, keeping his voice respectful only with difficulty. 'In the Magazine, sir, there are 200,000 pounds of powder and similar stocks of cartridges and percussion caps. And there are thirty-six boat-loads of shot tied in the river alongside. Dammit, sir – if there *is* trouble, and we abandon all that—'

'And the Treasury, General,' Hillersdon insisted. 'How do you hold that secure if you're several miles away in the Dragoon Hospital?'

'The necessity will not arise, Mr Hillersdon.' The white-haired little General placed his hands behind his back. 'We are passing through a period of native unrest. It will pass, and it will pass more quickly if we keep our heads and behave like Englishmen. The Dragoon Hospital will be entrenched behind a *sangar* and victualled for twenty-five days. To quieten the fears of the civil I shall send an electrical telegraph to Lucknow, asking for a detachment of Queen's soldiers. So far as the Treasury is concerned' – he played his trump card – 'the Maharajah of Bithur, Nana Sahib, has already offered a force of fifteen hundred men to meet the threat of any mutiny in the Cawnpore garrison.'

5

Amelia did not remember her own father, and there existed no pictorial record of him. He had been Captain Frederick Horne, RN, and he had died of yellow fever in the Gulf of Oman during an anti-slavery patrol in 1840, when Amelia was a year old. 'A fine, large man,' Emma Cook had told her daughter, a little wistfully, 'with thick black hair you'd scarcely push a comb through.' John Cook, the *dâk* agent, was not a fine, large man, and his hair was sandy and thin, but he had provided well for Emma and her small daughter since he had brought them from Bombay to Lucknow, and then to Cawnpore.

Further children had arrived at regular two-yearly intervals by a process that Amelia only vaguely and uncomfortably understood. It was a subject not discussed between mother and daughter, and Amelia's interpretation of it had been achieved by a process of observation and deduction that sometimes perturbed her. It was breathlessly indelicate, but there was no logical alternative.

There were a number of puzzling gaps in her knowledge. She had never seen a European gentleman exposed, but she had seen her smaller brothers, and occasional natives. What she had seen had been interesting but hardly impressive. Once, when nursing her infant half-brother, Herbert, he had pushed his face against her, and she had quickly opened her bodice and given her proud young breast to his hungry mouth. His lusty sucking had provoked a sudden, hot emotion that she had never before experienced. She had been frightened, and she pushed him away, buttoning her dress, her throat choked, and ashamed. There were things she still did not know of. If an infant could do this, what could a man do? What was her step-father doing when, through her thin bedroom partition, she listened to her mother's desperate sobbing? And why, next morning, was her mother so apparently composed?

It was the same with newly-married brides, of her own age, who departed, innocent virgins, for Simla or Ambala, and returned, ten weeks later, smugly confident with a new, exclusive knowledge that, like Emma Cook, they never divulged.

Now, in May 1857, her mother's waistline was again embarrassingly swollen, but everyone pretended not to notice – nor the visits of Dr Boyes.

The Reverend Alban F. Haycock was a beanpole, ungainly New Englander who had brought the Gospel from Connecticut, USA, to the heathen millions of British India. He had also brought his mother, an obese old lady in unrelieved black who played the harmonium during prayer meetings of the Society for the Propagation of the Gospel, but whom nobody could recall ever having heard speak.

The Reverend Edward Moncreiff of Christchurch and Father Joseph Rooney of the Roman Catholic Chapel – and most of their congregations – considered Haycock to be something of an eccentric. Anyone who came from the United States, where slavery was widespread, to teach Christianity to the subjects of the British, who had outlawed and fought slavery for years, must indeed be an eccentric.

Haycock never penetrated beyond the outer fringe of Cawnpore's European society. He was never deliberately snubbed and, indeed, his presence was tolerated at many functions because the British considered that any suggestion of a 'poor white' was damaging to their status in the eyes of the natives. Haycock, however, either through ignorance or perversity, did little to improve his own image. He dressed oddly, with a green veil stitched to the brim of his hat, indulged in neither tobacco nor alcohol and, since he owned no means of conveyance, usually walked. His mother seldom emerged from seclusion except for the hymn-singing meetings of the curry-and-rice Christians.

The American preacher's interest in Amelia seemed to have begun immediately upon the arrival of the Cook family from Lucknow. In this he was far from alone; few Cawnpore bachelors could resist speculation on the subject of the charming young lady's future. Exile in Cawnpore had become marginally less disagreeable. Macassar oil was applied to whiskers, cleanly starched shirts became more evident, and the Reverend Moncreiff was flattered by the unusual number of spruce young subalterns, behind the Cook pew, who listened with apparent absorption to his sermon on the perils of sloth.

Haycock, however, ignored the subtleties of British protocol. Before even leaving his card – if he possessed a card to leave – he presented himself at the Cook bungalow and introduced himself.

John and Emma Cook were surprised, but polite. Mr Haycock was a clergyman, of sorts, and it was difficult to be discourteous to a visiting clergyman. Mr Haycock's visits, unfortunately, were frequent and painfully prolonged, until even good-natured John Cook frowned with annoyance when the *chowkidar* announced yet another visit of Haycock Sahib. His chosen cronies, John Roach and Tom Berrill, were equally ill at ease with the newcomer, who had no sensible conversation, no interest in *dâk gharries*, railway routes, freight costs or road tolls, who declined a whisky-soda, and merely sat on the edge of his chair smiling blandly at Amelia whenever she appeared, his eyes following her every move.

Amelia was mildly perturbed, but only mildly. The Reverend Haycock was all of forty years old. He was thin, gawkish, with watery eyes, and smelled of camphor. She was totally unable to think of him as a suitor, even if he found favour with her stepfather, which was unlikely. If John Cook decried the prospects of army officers like Henry Delafosse and St George Ashe he would hardly encourage the attendance of a gospel-reader with no income beyond a stipend from some obscure mission society in Hartford, Connecticut. Amelia was therefore puzzled but not alarmed, when the Reverend Haycock invited her to a meeting of the Society for the Propagation of the Gospel, and to meet his mother. 'I will send a carriage for you, Miss Amelia,' he promised, towering over her.

Amelia had been unable to quickly think of an excuse for declining, although when too late she thought of dozens. The carriage was a hired *gharri*, and she wished she had taken Gulab, the house-*ayah*, with her.

In the humid mission house a dozen natives wailed 'How sweet the Name of Jesus sounds' to the accompaniment of Mrs Haycock's harmonium. The preacher's rendering of the parable of the prodigal son did nothing to remove the apathy from the congregation's faces, but the distribution of flour and *ghee* was more enthusiastically received. The natives bowed over their hands, reaffirming their intention to return tomorrow, and then departed hurriedly. The Reverend Haycock wiped his floury hands on a bandana and beamed at Amelia.

In the adjacent Haycock residence, which reeked of camphor, Mrs Haycock examined Amelia from the depths of a basket armchair into which she had laboriously lowered herself. Her crinkled face was putty-coloured and she wheezed asthmatically. Amelia seated herself tentatively, wondering how soon she could politely make her departure. There was no *punkah*, her underclothing was beginning to soak, and the room was suffocating.

'Alban has told me everything about you, Miss Horne,' the old lady panted. 'Everything.' Amelia wondered what the missionary knew that he might tell. He stood awkwardly at her shoulder.

'Do you know, Miss Horne,' Mrs Haycock revealed her yellow teeth in a smile that was more like a snarl, 'that Alban has made more converts in one year than the Reverend Moncreiff and Father Rooney have in ten?' The missionary coughed modestly and smiled at his large feet.

'The Haycocks are New York stock,' Mrs Haycock laboured on. She snarled benignly at her son. Alban's second name is Fayette.'

'Alban Fayette Haycock,' the missionary affirmed.

'I think,' Amelia suggested, 'it must be almost time for *chota hazri*—' She stirred, but the Reverend Haycock's hand was on her shoulder, gentle but firm.

'Fayette is in New York State, Miss Amelia,' he explained. 'The birthplace of the Church of Jesus Christ of Latter-Day Saints.'

Mrs Haycock snarled at her. 'Alban and I are both Saints, to whom the Risen Christ has made known the fullness of the

Gospel.' She drew a noisy breath. 'You know, of course, of our patriarch, Mr Brigham Young?'

Amelia nodded, then shook her head. For the first time in her life she was a little frightened. The Reverend Haycock laughed jerkily, and she tried to shrug off his hand, but failed. She felt a little faint.

'Your folks are good church-going people?' Mrs Haycock enquired. 'It wouldn't do otherwise.'

Otherwise than what? Amelia dabbed her face with an inadequate handkerchief. 'We attend Christchurch,' she said.

'Episcopalian,' the old lady sniffed. 'Well, it might be worse. Alban tells me you play the pianoforte, my dear. You'll find the harmonium is a little different. When we were in Manila we didn't have anything – just a tuning fork and the voices the good Lord gave us.' She paused. 'You'll be Alban's first. I don't hold with more than one until a man's got snow in his hair and sense in his head. Good seed don't spoil with keeping.'

Amelia was quite confused. The Reverend Haycock cleared his throat. 'I have not, of course, interviewed Mr Cook.' His hand on Amelia's shoulder was wetly hot.

'The Reverend Cockey will come from Benares to bless the union,' Mrs Haycock went on. 'John Cockey was one of the first Elders, Miss Horne. In 1846 he drove four hundred head of cattle from the Missouri clear to the Rocky Mountains, so two hundred miles for a marriage won't be a hardship.'

'No hardship at all,' the Reverend Haycock agreed.

'In Hartford, Connecticut,' Mrs Haycock bared her teeth, 'I'm referred to as Mother Haycock, but English folk don't seem to care for it. It's not usual for Brethren to marry outsiders, Miss Horne, but I don't see harm in it, if the choosing's wise.' She halted to measure Amelia with her eyes. 'You've not an easy child-bearing body, Miss Horne. Narrow hips usually mean bringing forth in sorrow, my dear. And Alban will need children; happy is the man that hath his quiver full of them.'

Amelia was shocked and bewildered. Minutes later, free of the bungalow's choking atmosphere, she gulped clean air as she clambered thankfully into the *gharry* 'Mr Haycock – I don't quite understand—'

'It was necessary for Mrs Haycock to see you first, Miss Amelia,' the missionary explained, 'and I am delighted to think she was most impressed. There was no point, you see, in speaking to your father unless Mrs Haycock approved. It might have been embarrassing to have agreed matters with Mr Cook, only to have my mother decide that you were unsuitable.' He put on his hat with the green veil. 'I always believe in behaving like a gentleman, Miss Amelia.'

'I am a church-going man,' said John Cook. 'I do not beat my wife, I drink liquor in moderation, and I never use strong language.' He rammed buckshot into his old twin-barrelled flintlock. 'And I have never fired this gun except at crows and thieving monkeys. But' – his usually mild eyes were narrowed in anger – 'if the Reverend Alban Fayette Haycock comes within one rod, pole or perch of this *bloody* bungalow I'll send him back to Hartford, Connecticut, with an *arseful* of hot, smoking lead!'

6

The mutiny was spreading outwards from Delhi, across northern India. By 16 May all telegraphic communication had been cut between Meerut, Karnal, Muzaffarnagar, Saharanpur, Ambala and Patiala. All news from an area the size of the southern counties of England had suddenly ceased, and eastward and southward the European refugees streamed, seeking sanctuary, behind them the flames of their houses and the murdering mobs that had once been disciplined regiments. Women, children, many in nightclothes, trudged afoot or rode gharries, bullock tongas or tired ponies, many moving only by darkness, hiding during the day, begging handfuls of food from villagers who, in turn, were unpredictable. Many of the poorest gave generously, others demanded and forcibly took money, valuables and clothing. A village headman might guide a party of Europeans to safety or he might betray them to the nearest gang of sepoy mutineers. Hundreds of refugees never reached safety. Their stripped, bloodied corpses lay in fields and monsoon ditches, blackening and swelling in the sun.

Still further north, in Peshawar, Mooltan, Amritsar and Ferozepore, sepoy regiments were being disarmed under the bayonets of their British counterparts – a course of action which provoked angry protests from military pundits in safer locations. As late as 22 May, twelve days after the horror of Meerut and Delhi, a letter appeared in the newspaper *Englishman*, written by Colonel Simpson commanding the 6th Native Infantry in Allahabad. He ridiculed the suspicions directed towards his sepoys, who 'evinced the utmost loyalty. So far from being mistrusted, they are our main protection.'

Only a few days later Colonel Simpson was grateful to settle for a bullet in his arm when most of his officers had been butchered by the loyal sepoys of the 6th.

On the night of 20-21 May, Sir Henry Lawrence, Chief Commissioner for the territory of Oudh, and resident at Lucknow, received a telegraphed despatch from General Wheeler in Cawnpore. The message asked briefly, but in urgent terms, for military aid in anticipation of disaffection among the Cawnpore native regiments.

Lawrence was in a quandary. His own situation was scarcely different from Wheeler's. Outside Lucknow, all civil authority had broken down, and nobody could travel the roads without an armed escort. Further, almost all his cavalry were irregulars of suspect loyalty. Incendiarism was rife, and attempts had been made to fire the thatch of several bungalows by the oddly primitive method of shooting arrows wrapped with burning rags. The lines of two regiments, the 13th and 48th, had been gutted, and placards calling upon all true Hindus and Moslems to join in exterminating the Sahib overlords were posted by night in several places. True, Lawrence had the Queen's 32nd Foot, but he would need them all, and more, if the native regiments actively mutinied.

Even so, Cawnpore was an important station, the gateway

between Oudh and Central India, and the defences of both Cawnpore and Lucknow, only 49 miles apart, were complementary. Further, the two European communities were well acquainted, while the wives and children of the 1st Company of the 32nd Queen's were quartered in Cawnpore. Lawrence must do what he could. Before first light, 50 bemused men of the 32nd were crammed into *dâk gharries* and despatched into the darkness of the Cawnpore road. With them rode an escort of two squadrons of Oudh Irregular Horse under British officers, and Captain Fletcher Hayes, military secretary to the Commissioner, ordered to establish with General Wheeler a co-ordinated plan of action.

Few of the sleepy soldiers in the jolting vehicles could have predicted that this might be their last journey. In Cawnpore, at least, John Cook of the North-West Dâk Company would experience a brief satisfaction at the return of his long-absent *gharries*.

Captain Mowbray Thompson of the 53rd Native Infantry was tall, red-haired, twenty-five years old and an eligible bachelor. Speculative young ladies and their mothers, however, seldom enjoyed opportunities for drawing his attention towards the possibility of matrimony. Mowbray Thompson expertly avoided drawing-rooms and teacups; he preferred hunting and duck-shooting, pig-sticking, whisky, and the *Ridgement*.

Now he was gazing apprehensively at the old Dragoon Hospital. The two hospital buildings, on a flat plain, were of brick, each with a wooden verandah on three sides. One had a roof of *pukka*, or concrete, the larger was thatched. Inside, the rafters were uncovered and the walls unplastered, festooned with cobwebs and scuttling with tiny geckos. A few broken, string *charpoys* stood among scattered debris. The *Lal Koorti Ka Haspital* had been intended as a depository for sick, common soldiers of no account, with a maximum capacity of one hundred men per building, and even for that purpose had been abandoned as obsolete. Outside, detached, were a small cookhouse, two dilapidated native huts, and a well encircled by a low brick wall. As a sanctuary for a thousand people, half of them women – or, equally important, as a potential defensive position – the location was ludicrously inadequate

General Wheeler had ordered the site to be surrounded by a rectangular *sangar*, a mud wall, with embrasures for field guns. For days the thousands of baskets of Ganges mud, brought by camels and on the backs of coolies, had been spilled onto the dusty *maidan*, and now the wall was finished – roughly two hundred yards square, but only four feet high, three feet thick at the base, and tapering to a mere twelve inches.

If the two buildings could be demolished by a few rounds of six-pound shot, the top of the *sangar*, lower than a man's chest, was not proof against a rifle bullet. The artillery embrasures were simply gaps. Gun crews would be completely unprotected.

Small knots of off-duty sepoys watched the wall being built, talking amusedly among themselves and grinning, falling silent and glancing away when an officer passed within earshot. Nana Sahib's contingent – 300 men, cavalry and infantry, and two guns – stood guard over the Treasury, and Azimullah Khan had ridden over to gaze at the Dragoon Hospital. 'What do you call this?' he asked. 'Your Fort of Despair?' He laughed as he cantered his horse away.

A week earlier Mowbray Thompson had ridiculed any suggestion of a sepoy mutiny in Cawnpore. Now he knew differently. *There was going to be a mutiny*. He could see it in his men's faces, in their every gesture, their defiant swagger, their surly responses. The only questions were *when*, and *how*. Tomorrow? By day or night? The sepoys had given no cause for disciplinary action yet; a mutiny couldn't be suppressed until it had begun, or at least until there was positive evidence of it. Even then, there simply were not enough white troops in Cawnpore to disarm the native regiments. They would have to rely on the wretched Dragoon Hospital and Nana Sahib. And victuals for twenty-five days? From where, in God's name, would relief come in twenty-five days?

Nana Sahib, of course, was solidly reliable. But his troops? They were a ragged-arse bunch, paid three rupees a month with a new uniform once a year. Using them to guard the Treasury was like expecting a pack of starved jackals to protect a sheep-pen. At the first sign of trouble the vision of hundreds of thousands of silver rupees behind the Treasury doors might well be too much for their questionable loyalty.

There had been a suggestion that all women and children should take refuge in the Palace of Bithur instead of the Hospital, but none was anxious to be separated from menfolk and, for the same reason, relatively few had taken the last river steamboat for Allahabad. In any case, it would be improper to leave Cawnpore while General Wheeler's wife and daughters remained.

Seven guns of various calibre had been positioned within the entrenchment, and the watching sepoys hawked and spat, muttering. Stocks of rice, lentils, flour, butter, salt, tea and sugar, brought in by native carts, seemed pitifully meagre for the support of a thousand people, and doubtful officers contributed canned meats, beer and spirits from their mess stores. There was a pervading feeling of inadequacy, an unspoken persuasion that none of this was worth while.

During the last few days Nana Sahib had visited Cawnpore several times, but had avoided contact with Europeans. On the native side of the town was a yellow-painted building which had once housed a religious order, but was now a hostelry for Indian merchants and businessmen. It was still known as the *Savada Kothi*, a convenient place for the Maharajah, accompanied by Azimullah Khan, to receive a deputation from the sepoy regiments. They came furtively, Subedar Teka Singh and Trooper Shumshoden Khan of the 2nd Cavalry, Jemadar Dulgunjun Singh of the 53rd Native Infantry and Subedar Gunga Deen of the 56th. From Bithur, also, was Mudud Ali, once of Nana Sahib's military service, now a horse dealer, and Jwala Pershad, a hanger-on from the Palace.

'What can the soldiers of John Company want with the Maharajah of Bithur?' His tone was disdainful, cold, but he was harassed by a thousand doubts. He knew why they were here. The room was hot, with a vague, stale odour of tobacco, hashish, and unwashed bodies. Beyond the open window he could see the grey-white plaster façade of a Hindu temple, like a shabby, discoloured wedding cake. This was the inevitable moment he had exulted in, and yet dreaded, for months. 'Have you no officers, no magistrates, of your own? Why do you plague me with your petty business?' Azimullah Khan, he knew, had been the go-between, had engineered this meeting, had probably boasted great things on his behalf.

Subedar Teka Singh placed the palms of his hands together respectfully. 'Excellence, your soldiers have come to Cawnpore to take charge of the Magazine and Treasury of the English, yet we all, Hindus and Moslems, have united for our religions, and the whole Bengal Army has become one in purpose.' He paused. 'When the time comes to choose, Excellence, what will you say?'

Nana Sahib fixed his gaze on the temple beyond the open window. He could guess what was happening, at this moment, on the other side of those plaster walls. A score of worshippers knelt before Kali, with shadows fluttering grotesquely as two great flares guttered over their heads and made the loathsome figure of the goddess contort. Loose-haired and black, her only garment was a girdle of human hands and a necklace of skulls. One of her own four hands held a sword, another the severed head of a giant, and her bloody tongue protruded from the corner of her mouth as her bulging eyes rolled. Her feet were on the body of Siva, her husband.

A white-robed priest knelt, in his arms a white kid surrendered to him by one of the worshippers. The priest raised the animal to his mouth, then pressed his teeth into its throat. The kid bleated, struggling, but the arms held it tightly, the teeth biting deeper. Blood gushed over the face of the priest and saturated his white garments. Then the animal, kicking away its last few seconds of life, was placed before Kali.

Nana Sahib turned away. Was he not, also, of the Mahratta? What rewards could the English offer, that he should support them? If John Company had denied his income, dismissed his title of Maharajah, and inferred that he was no more than a commoner and a speculating opportunist, how could he now be expected to provide the troops and guns, that they sneered at, to protect them?

He nodded, then spoke slowly. 'I, also, am at the disposal of the Army.'

The hands of Subedar Teka Singh came together again, and Azimullah Khan smiled.

But Trooper Shumshoden Khan had gone straight to the *Anunga Runga*, the Stage of Love, in the bazaar, where there was a public woman, a *devadasi*, named Azezun. She was the favourite of the 2nd Cavalry and much sought after – young, shapely-limbed, more intelligent than the drunken patrons who grappled with her, whispered impossible promises, and brought *gup*, or gossip, from the *Ridgement*.

And Shumshoden, intoxicated by his meeting with the Maharajah, had whispered more than everyday gossip. In a few more days he would no longer be a mere trooper of the 2nd Cavalry; he would be a colonel, or perhaps even a general, like Wheeler Sahib, at the right hand of the new King of the Mahrattas. He would fill the house of Azezun with gold mohurs, from cellar to roof, and she would be his first woman.

Azezun had heard many such boasts and seldom allowed them credence. She only smiled and nodded, stroked and mouthed her patron to a condition of animal lusting, then offered her body in any of twenty-five different positions for his culminating pleasure. This time, however, there was an oddly authentic ring about the trooper's claims. Azezun had no love for the English; they frowned upon her centuries-old profession, and English officials could not be bribed, or otherwise cajoled – at least, not by a public woman. By the same token, they hunted down and imprisoned the native pimps and bullies who enslaved and exploited prostitutes. All things considered, the English were a lesser evil and, in any case, it was always wise to have a foot in both camps. Azezun told her fears to another client, an Indian lawyer named Nanukchund. He, in turn, had no doubt that his interests were better served by English law and order than by native anarchy. He took the story to General Wheeler.

'You mean we might have to *live* in the old Dragoon Hospital?'

Mrs Emma Cook shuddered. It was inconceivable. 'But what will happen if—?' She smoothed her skirts. 'Will Dr Boyes be there?'

'It may never happen, my dear,' her husband assured her. 'Even if it does, it'll only be for a few days. It's my opinion that the whole thing will have blown over before the end of the month.'

Four-year-old Florence squealed with excitement. 'We're going to *live* in the Hospital? Really *sleep* there, Mamma? With the soldiers?' The prospect was intoxicating. 'I don't mind if it's for years and years.'

John Cook grunted. If there was much more of this nonsense there could be a complete suspension of *dâk* travel in northern India; the threat of the steam railway was bad enough. Things had come to a pretty pass when a few insubordinate blacks could jeopardize the future of the North-West Dâk Company. He had a mind to write to the *Calcutta Weekly Chronicle* about it.

Amelia had equally serious problems. What clothes should she pack? Would she need nightdresses? Would ladies *really* be sharing rooms with men? She would take her fringed silk shawl, just in case, and the bonnet with the chaplet of rosebuds, and the grey court shoes because they showed off her ankles so nicely, and the blouse with the lace cravat, and white gloves for evenings—

7

Calcutta had not forgotten the threatened towns of Bengal. Government House was desperately scraping together European troops from every possible source – Madras, Bombay, Burma, and even ships on passage to China – but there were daunting problems of distance and transport. On 25 May a telegraphed despatch from the Governor-General, Lord Canning, outlined the military predicament.

'It is impossible to place a wing of Europeans at Cawnpore in less than twenty-five days. The Government *dâk*, and the *dâk* companies, are fully engaged in carrying a company of the 84th to Benares, at the rate of eighteen men a *dâk*. A wing of the Madras Fusiliers arrived yesterday, and starts today by bullock train, part by steamer. The entire regiment of the Fusiliers, about 1,000 strong, cannot be collected at Benares in less than nineteen or twenty days. One hundred and fifty men who go by steamer will scarcely be there so soon. I expect that from this time forward troops will be pushed upwards at the rate of 100 men a day from Calcutta; each batch taking ten days to reach Benares. From Benares they will be distributed as most required. The regiments from Pegu, Bombay, and Ceylon will be sent up this way. Every bullock and horse that is to be had, except just enough to carry the post, is retained; and no troops will be sent by steamer which can be sent more quickly by other means. This is the best I can do for you.'

The best he could do. One hundred men a day to put down a mutiny in a native army totalling 232,000.

And events were gathering momentum. General Wheeler in Cawnpore, still reluctant to admit the possibility of a local revolt, had nevertheless consented to all women and children moving into the entrenchment of the old Dragoon Hospital. Officers, he insisted, must remain with their regiments to prevent alarming the sepoys. The weather was becoming progressively hotter, with the dust of the plain stirred by the slightest breeze, the sky cloudless and golden. The Queen's birthday, Sunday 24th, which coincided with the Moslem festival of the Eed, had come and gone without the celebrations for which Amelia Horne had sewed and planned so long. There was confusion in the Hospital and its enclosure. Ladies who had hitherto performed few tasks more arduous than pouring tea or passing the caraway cake stared askance at their new quarters, crowded, filthy, and blatantly communal, with long queues at the well and the make-shift kitchen. In such circumstances, was one really expected to disrobe, or wash, or let down hair, or – horror of horrors – use the reeking thunder-box, hidden by only a hung blanket and frequented by a hundred others?

Captain Moore and two sergeants of the 32nd Regiment's contingent were training civilians in the use of the new Enfield rifle – railway engineers, writers, postal and commissariat officials and merchants. Ammunition, at least, was plentiful; three field magazines held 2,000 pounds of powder and adequate ball cartridge and round-shot. The regimental officers slept in tents close to the sepoy lines, reporting daily that, so far, all was quiet, and Wheeler, despite his years an excellent horseman, rode regularly and alone around the station, taking salutes. All, so far, was quiet.

Spirits began to rise. Had the old General been right all the time? Each evening a regimental band rendered light airs from the bandstand, 800 yards from the Hospital. Ladies began to think wistfully of their comfortable bungalows, and young officers of the possibility of a duck-shoot. Amelia yearned for a bath, to wash her hair, to change into clean, lavender-scented underwear, while her stepfather fretted at the revenues being lost by the North-West Dâk Company. Telegraphic despatches told of similarly returning confidence in Lucknow, Agra and Allahabad. Was this whole stupid business beginning to blow over?

On 26 May there was even better news. Two companies of the Queen's 84th Regiment – 150 men – had left Allahabad to reinforce the Cawnpore garrison, and would arrive during the first few days of June. The difference such a force would make in the event of a major insurrection might be negligible, but the effect on morale was immense. Cawnpore had not been forgotten.

Then two events occurred to dampen the spirits of the Europeans. Nana Sahib's troops guarding the Treasury had become insubordinate and completely unmanageable. General Wheeler ordered them to be dismissed from their posts and replaced by the fifty men of the 32nd Queen's loaned by Lucknow. Then, more ominously, the naked corpses of a white man and woman, unidentifiable, floated into the canal from the Ganges. They had been in the water for several days, floating from the westward, lacerated by the probing sticks of small boys who had never seen the genitals of a Sahib and mem-Sahib.

Lieutenant Tom Fayrer rode his Cape gelding at the head of a detachment of Oudh Irregular Horse along the Grand Trunk Road towards Etah. He was young, confident, and life was good. At this moment, he mused, hundreds of regimental officers were suffering the daily boredom of cantonments' duties, frustrated by endless red tape and protocol, sweating over commissariat returns and muster lists in stifling barrack offices. He, Fayrer, was master of all he surveyed, at least for the present. Behind and ahead of him was the long, clip-clopping column of irregular cavalry – raffish, bearded men in turbans and frock-like *alkhalaks*, carrying native sabres and pistols, each with a bag of flour on his crupper. True, they lacked the immaculate bearing of the Sikh Lancers, but he would not have changed. 'Fayrer Sahib,' they had assured him, 'have we not eaten of your salt? Are we not yours until death?'

Ahead of him, also, were Lieutenants Carey and Barbor, and Captain Fletcher Hayes, military secretary to the Chief Commissioner. Some days before, the column had ridden from Lucknow as escort for the fifty men of the 32nd Regiment hurried to Cawnpore. Having safely delivered their charges, Hayes had telegraphed Lucknow for permission to reconnoitre, and demonstrate a military presence, along the Grand Trunk Road to the westward, from where reports of increasing lawlessness had been received.

Permission given, the column had snaked leisurely towards Mainpuri, and then Etah. There was no sign of dacoits or civil unrest. Every village headman emerged to 'huzoor' and bless the Company's munificence, and small boys chased after the horses. Young Fayrer had slept under the cool stars with his saddle for a pillow, awakened stiff and damp to breakfast on eggs, *chupatties* and bad coffee, and he enjoyed every moment. This was the real business of Empire, he knew – the maintenance of peace and the administration of justice, a task for which the Englishman was the Lord's chosen. It was a pity there were not more men like his senior, Captain Hayes, who believed that a show of strength and a bold confrontation was the only answer to threatened insurrection. Weren't they proving it now? If the Grand Trunk Road had been a hotbed of unrest, it had become amazingly peaceful at the approach of the irregular cavalry.

It was nearly noon, with the sun uncomfortably hot, but the head of the column was jingling into native houses among stony, crudely-ploughed fields. They would halt here, water their horses, then decide whether to camp or push further up the road.

There was no warning of treachery. Fayrer dismounted at the well, from the depths of which two troopers were hauling a filled bucket. He leaned over the low surrounding wall, peering into the cool gloom below as the bucket climbed towards him, and was in the act of reaching forward to steady it when, from behind, a third trooper lifted his sabre and struck the young officer a scything blow on the back of the neck. Fayrer jerked, his head half severed. His shako fell into the well and he knelt, vomiting blood, and then crumpled without a sound.

It happened so quickly and unexpectedly that Hayes, Carey and Barbor, all still mounted and further along the column, had observed nothing. From yards away a native officer hissed a warning, and then they could see. Fayrer was a sprawled, grotesque, blood-drenched thing, and dozens of sabres were rasping from scabbards. 'Christ!' Hayes choked. 'Ride for your bloody lives!'

They wrenched their horses around, but Hayes's horse was tired, and responded slowly. Before he could kick the animal into motion he was surrounded and cut from his saddle. Lieutenant Barbor got clear, spurring in the direction of Aligarh, but in minutes he found his road barred by his own advance vedettes. He tugged his sword free, lowered his head, and rowelled his mount to a thundering gallop, hoping to burst through, but the barrier of men and horses was too solid. Animals fell, screaming and kicking. Barbor slashed, saw two troopers reel away with hands clutched to bloodied faces, and then he stood for seconds as a dozen sabres butchered him.

Only Carey, an officer of the 17th Native Infantry, on leave, who had accompanied the column only because he wanted to rejoin his own regiment to the north-west, achieved safety. The cavalrymen pursued him doggedly for several miles, but he was better mounted and gradually outdistanced them. Eventually they reined, their horses blown, and Carey, shaken but relieved, pressed on to Mainpuri

In Kerowlee, a rissaldar of the 1st Oudh Cavalry announced that all Hindus and Moslems were now joined, and all would march to Delhi, where Bahadur Shah had raised the banner of a new India.

By the last week of May the evidence of an impending mutiny had become so overwhelming that even General Wheeler was forced to accept it. Twice on the 25th he had telegraphed Lucknow, warning that a rising was imminent. However, already two squadrons of Oudh Irregular Horse, with Captain Fletcher Hayes, were making a reconnaissance sweep to the westward and, so far, Hayes's reports of a peaceful countryside contradicted the despatches of Wheeler and magistrates on the border. Chief Commissioner Lawrence decided to send out a second force of cavalry and infantry, with a half battery of field artillery, along the 49-mile road towards Cawnpore, and then probably southward.

The mixed bag of native militia mustered on the *maidan* behind the *Kaisar Bagh*, the old King's Palace, at dawn on the 26th, then moved raggedly to the Cawnpore road – one squadron of irregular horse, five companies of Oudh Irregular Infantry, and the half battery, under Lieutenant St George Ashe, comprising two 9-pounder field guns and a 24-pounder howitzer. The officers were in good spirits. Lucknow was not the pleasantest of localities in which to be confined, and they had all been envious of Captain Hayes's foray along the Grand Trunk Road. Now they too could do something more positive than watching the dirty Gomati River from the Mound. Ashe in particular had no objection to a visit to Cawnpore. There was excellent male company, all Addiscombe men, in the messes of the 53rd and 56th, and there were the ladies – Charlotte Newman, provokingly bosomed, Bella Blair whose demure eyes never left his tightly tailored breech-front, and Amelia Horne, a peach-skinned little Venus whose fan had fluttered signals towards him that could have only one interpretation. With all three, mused handsome Lieutenant Ashe, the only problem was opportunity.

The reconnaissance force, however, was to achieve little. It crossed the Sai River and then the Ganges, but here the infantry refused to leave their native Oudh. All but forty of them were sent back towards Lucknow. The cavalry and infantry turned up the Grand Trunk Road, and had progressed only one day's march when the news of the fate of Fletcher Hayes's party met them from Mainpuri. The situation, it seemed, had deteriorated drastically, and a few miles further the road swarmed with mutineers, both horse and foot.

For the six accompanying English officers, any further operation in the field with a wholly Indian column was out of the question. The cavalry and remaining infantry turned back to Lucknow, but Lieutenant Ashe, not unwillingly, found himself ordered by General Wheeler to bring his half battery to reinforce Cawnpore's Dragoon Hospital.

When the three guns rumbled into the entrenchment, Ashe stared about him, aghast. The General had just ordered all officers to cease sleeping in the sepoy lines and to move into the Hospital compound. The dusty enclosure teemed with women slightly dishevelled and children scampering everywhere, thinking the whole business a wonderful adventure. There were seven guns of varied calibre crewed by a mixture of Bengal Artillerymen and apprehensive civilians, invalid infantrymen of the Queen's 32nd on unsteady feet but trying to appear military and, at a distance around the perimeter of the surrounding *maidan*, the gathering throngs of sepoys, in their hundreds, watching and jeering. Was this supposed to be a defensive position? Against what, b'God?

Somewhere in this crawling antheap were Mowbray Thompson and Henry Delafosse, Whiting, Turner and Burney. And, dammit, the ladies. What would happen in five or six weeks, when the rains came? This pitiful mud wall would be washed away in twenty minutes.

And there was a further shock for Lieutenant Ashe. His native gun crews were ordered at gunpoint to climb down from their caissons. No natives, Wheeler had ordered, would enter the entrenchment. Ashe turned away to avoid the incredulity in his men's eyes. They walked slowly, heads bowed, to join the sepoys on the edge of the *maidan*.

Moodily, Ashe picked his way around the wall. To the northward an outer earthwork redan faced in the direction of the Ganges, commanded by Major Vibart and Captain Jenkins, both of the 2nd Cavalry. Ashe's own battery had been placed to the northeast, assisting him Lieutenant Ashburner and 2nd Lieutenant Sotheby of the Bengal Artillery. Three 9-pounders formed a south-east battery under Lieutenants Eckford, Burney and Henry Delafosse, while three more covered the westward, commanded by Lieutenants Dempster and Martin, supplemented by a little, rifled 3-pounder piece under Major Prout of the 56th. None of the guns was masked. The mud walls between the batteries were manned by the infantry of the Main Guard, both professional and civilian, with each defender having at least three loaded muskets at hand and the trained men with seven or eight.

Ashe had his role outlined to him by a fair-haired Queen's officer who seemed to have more authority than any of the several John Company colonels and majors – or, indeed, subsequently more than General Wheeler.

'While the position is not under close siege,' ordered Captain John Moore, 'you will hold your two light battery guns ready to be limbered up at any time to accompany a sortie party, for which thirty men will be detailed. We must show the blacks that we can still take offensive action if we need to. No action was ever won by sitting behind a damn wall and letting the enemy decide when and where to fight.'

'Who, exactly,' Ashe asked Henry Delafosse, 'is this bloody chap Moore? Haven't we any blasted field officers of our own?'

Delafosse grimaced ruefully. 'Plenty, but they're just not up to it, old boy, although at least they have the sense to concede it. The General's dazed by the whole damn business; he can't seem to recognize priorities, and he can't make a decision without changing it an hour later. Brigadier Jack's trying to fight off a bout of malaria, and the rest – well – they're just nice old gentlemen who never thought they'd have to lead fighting troops in the twilight of their years. That's why' – he shrugged – 'it's a bloody mercy we've got Moore, you'll see.'

The last mail had already left Cawnpore by steam pinnace, downriver towards Allahabad, when, on 2 June, two dusty companies of the Queen's 84th Regiment swung off the Grand Trunk Road from Fatehpur, tramped along the canal bank, and halted on the race-course. The sight of 150 sweat-streaked scarlet tunics, brick-red faces and curtained shakoes brought hundreds of excited men and women to the wall. Two companies represented a meagre reinforcement when 3,000 sepoys, well supported by artillery, threatened the Hospital, but at least these were trained soldiers and not men dragged from sick pallets, or clerks and tradesmen who clenched their eyes when they fired a musket.

There was hand-shaking and back-slapping. Now let the bloody blacks talk drivel about mutiny, and cutting Sahibs' throats, eh? Bottles of warm Moselle were produced and treasured tins of ham and sardines broached. The worst was over, wasn't it? If the sepoys didn't shout *'Jai Company ki!'* now, then they'd eat dirt in three or four weeks when the real relief column arrived from Calcutta, b'God.

On the few square feet of verandah occupied by the Cook family, Amelia Horne was teaching her younger sister, Florence, how to knit. She had seen Lieutenant St George Ashe, but shrank from meeting him. How could she when she had slept in her clothes for a week, when her hair was tangled, and she was beginning to smell her own unpleasantness? The new dress that she and her mother had sewed for the Queen's birthday was probably gone; she knew that, in the family's absence, their bungalow had been ransacked. It didn't matter. This nightmare was about to end. There were dresses and materials to be bought in Cawnpore – not exclusive patterns from Dear's of Manchester, of course, but adequate. Most of all she thought of a bath with fragrant soap, her waist-length, black hair washed and silkily combed, lavender water, and powder for her shoulders. Only then would she have the confidence to meet Lieutenant St George Ashe.

And Captain John Moore was suddenly ignored, even snubbed. Only hours before he had walked the entrenchment like a Titan among pygmies, tirelessly detailing, explaining fields of fire and cross-fire, inspecting field guns, encouraging the nervous civilians and calculating ration issues. Now, however, the elderly Company field officers resumed their authority – Colonels Ewart, Williams, Wiggins, Hillersdon, and portly Sir George Parker. General Sir Hugh Wheeler emerged from the Hospital with his lady, accepting congratulations on his stoic refusal to be unnerved by the hysteria of lesser men. Even Henry Delafosse was half ashamed of his championing of Captain John Moore.

For the remainder of the day feelings of relief and expectation remained high. Native vendors reappeared with melons and peaches, and several of the more daring ladies and gentlemen strolled as far as the bandstand, or watched the sun set and the sky turn to orange, to purple, then jewel-scattered blackness. It was the next morning that the sound of tramping feet and shouted orders brought the curious again to the wall, and they did not believe what they saw. General Wheeler had ordered the entire company of the 32nd Regiment, and all men of the 84th's reinforcement except 60 men, to march to Lucknow, to supplement the garrison of the Chief Commissioner, Sir Henry Lawrence. Despite yesterday's welcome arrival of two companies of infantry, there were now only ten more soldiers defending the Hospital than there were before.

And Wheeler's telegraphed despatch to the Secretary to the Government of India, reporting his action, was the last to reach the outside world. Cawnpore's lines had been cut.

But news was coming in – chilling news. At Sitapur, 50 miles north of Lucknow and only 80 from Cawnpore, twenty-four Europeans had been hunted down and killed by the local sepoys. The victims had included six women and six children, the Commissioner, Mr Christian, and his wife, Mr and Mrs Thornhill, and the Clerk, Mr Craneburgh. They were names that many in Cawnpore knew, and the elation of yesterday drained. Sitapur today could mean Lucknow tomorrow and Cawnpore on the next. Why, in God's name, had General

Wheeler sent away two whole companies of trained soldiers to Lucknow – when Lucknow already had a European regiment? Did the old fool think he was being chivalrous, when the lives of more than a thousand people were at stake?

Moore strode the vast, crowded compound of the Dragoon Hospital with his face twisted by a scowl, and men moved hurriedly out of his path, sucking their teeth and looking away. It was bloody odd, he fumed mentally, that all those Company field officers, who yesterday looked so martial and confident when the 84th's companies marched in, were suddenly not seeking attention. General Wheeler was in command, they replied to questions, and he was an officer of long experience. General Wheeler, however, despite his long experience, seemed to have no notion of preparing a siege defence.

Well, something had to be prepared, confound and blast it, and there wasn't much time. Moore began to calculate his resources. First, there were approximately 65 John Company officers, 60 men of the Queen's 84th, 59 artillerymen, 15 of the 1st Madras Fusiliers, and 70 invalids of the 32nd. That totalled 270 soldiers, to whom could be added 200 civilians capable of making some contribution. It was bloody thin, but it could be worse. It wasn't lack of numbers that worried Moore, but the complete lack of protection against artillery fire. Wheeler's piddling little mud wall achieved nothing but a few feet of shade from the sun. Christ's blood, Moore seethed, why weren't they all behind the masonry of the Magazine?

Secondary problems were food supplies, sanitation, and medical services. Even if relief did arrive in twenty-five days, which was debatable, Moore was convinced that the commissariat had underestimated the needs of a thousand people for that period, and he was equally certain that supply contractors had given short measure anyway. The *gomashtas* were adept at unloading the same sack of flour several times. Sanitary shortcomings could kill more people than enemy bullets, and already the primitive thunder-boxes were over-spilling and reeking. Finally, there would be sick and wounded. There were eight doctors, civil and military, but were there medical supplies for a four-weeks' siege? Where, among these teeming refugees, would the surgeons operate on the wounded? Where would the wounded lie? Where would the dead be buried? General Wheeler seemed oblivious even to the questions. He had withdrawn into a state of dignified amnesia which none of his field officers seemed willing to disturb.

In the 2nd Cavalry lines the Indian troopers were sharpening their sabres. 'Glory for all, and Heaven for those who bleed!' urged Subedar Teka Singh and Trooper Shumshoden Khan. Women and infants had been sent from the regimental lines into the native quarter of the city, and there had been a further meeting between the ringleaders and Nana Sahib, on a boat in mid-river. All was ready. It needed but a word.

On the Hospital verandah, four-year-old Florence had grown tired of knitting and now, with a loop of wool, experimented with a twisting cat's cradle. As with most of the other children, the novelty of living and sleeping within the Hospital entrenchment had palled. 'When can we go home, Amy?' What had happened to Dot the pony, and Sacha the spaniel, left in the care of indifferent servants? Florence itched under her clothes; she was tired of mutton and peas, bored with her confined, insect-infested quarters. 'Shall we go home soon, Amy? And why is Mamma always being sick?' Mrs Emma Cook was pregnant, and her periodical nausea, which might have been experienced in the privacy of her own bedroom, had now to be exercised in the full view of everyone. Amelia combed Florence's hair and then her own, repeatedly, terrified at the thought of lice. Yesterday, when the native fruit vendors had come to the wall for the last time, she had purchased some mangoes with her remaining money. When she had cut them apart, however, the yellow flesh of every fruit had been crawling with maggots, and Florence had cried.

Colonel Ewart, commanding the 1st Native Infantry, penned a letter to a friend – which might or might not ever leave Cawnpore. 'I do not wish to write gloomily, but there is no use in disguising the fact that we are in the utmost danger; and, as I have said, if the troops do mutiny, my life will almost certainly be sacrificed. I hope in God that my wife and child will be saved.' Beyond the line of half-built barrack-houses, three to four hundred yards away, he could see the twinkle of the sepoys' cooking fires, the climbing ribbons of smoke. At least, he knew, he might describe himself as elderly; for a soldier he was simply damn old.

He should have taken his retirement years ago, but how did a Colonel and his family live on £300 a year after the artificially high standards of the English in India? It meant a small house in Godalming or Norwich, a cook-general, two housemaids, and the painful choice between a coachman/ostler and an indoors manservant. Could he have afforded the subscription of a London club, or a moderately good cellar? And would his wife's wardrobe have survived the constant scrutiny of local ladies with bank-manager husbands?

He should have taken his retirement, but every year he had postponed it. Just one more year, one more year. Now, it could be too late. He was too old for fighting.

There were a number of Europeans who did not mix easily with the majority. They were the common soldiers of the Queen's 32nd and 84th, and the handful of John Company's Madras Fusiliers. All were experienced troops – the 32nd having been in India for eleven years, although cholera, dysentery, smallpox and typhoid had taken a heavy toll of the battalions' muster-rolls since 1846. For active service the men were relieved of their red shell-jackets, thick trousers and Albert shakoes; these were now substituted by duck trousers, a smock frock, and a forage cap with a flapped cover, the latter of white for the Queen's soldiers and blue for those of the Fusiliers. Until a few days earlier only the Fusiliers had carried the new Enfield rifle, but now all had been issued from Cawnpore's magazine. A waistbelt carried a bayonet and ammunition pouch.

These were the men of the Main Guard, posted fifteen paces apart behind the flimsy cover of the mud wall. They had little in common with the officers and civilians who outnumbered them, and who, in turn, seldom considered the existence of slum-reared rankers, tough, blasphemous, paid 1s. 8d. per week after stoppages. Many John Company officers regarded their own sepoys more highly.

They remained apart, these men, standing their duty, sleeping where they stood and when they could, relieved only briefly to draw rations and fill their canteens. Common soldiers on foreign service were permitted to be accompanied by wives – referred to, disdainfully, as 'other ranks' women' – at the rate of six wives to a company, chosen by lot, with no quarters provided other than the barrack-room. The handful of army wives in Cawnpore, however, were those of rankers of the 32nd Regiment, stationed in distant Lucknow. The men of the recently-arrived 84th had left theirs in Allahabad, where they must fend for themselves.

One in three of the common men was Irish, one in four was illiterate, capable of only laboriously signing his name. Of those names, despite their owners' heroism, very few would be considered worthy of record, and the three or four condescending references to private soldiers that would survive Cawnpore would confine themselves to surnames – just Private Donavan, or Private Murphy, or Sergeant Brownlow – empty, limbo references that typified the Victorian attitude towards the lower orders. Only gentlemen made history.

Captain John Moore, at least, had been joined by three more Queen's officers. They were Lieutenant Wainright and Ensign Hill, both of the 32nd, and Lieutenant Saunders of the 84th. It was young Hill's first posting, and he had so much to write about – when the next mail left.

The Moslem festival of the Eed had passed without serious incident – at least, no more serious than that of an alcoholic Englishman, still occupying his bungalow and surrounded by bottles, who emerged to fire a gun at a nocturnal noise. His erratic shot narrowly missed some Moslem troopers, who complained to the cantonments' magistrate. Sir George Parker declared the matter to have been an accident, and the Moslems seethed. There would, they promised, be a lot more guns being fired by accident before the week had passed.

8

At midnight on 6 June, Subedar Teka Singh, on picquet duty with his troop, decided that the time had come.

Behind the *sangar* of the old Dragoon Hospital the chilled, drowsy sentries roused themselves as three distant pistol shots, in rapid succession, broke the night silence. Minutes later, as the Main Guard scrambled from their blankets, the sky over the far cantonments was aglow with flame.

The 2nd Cavalry lines swarmed with excited, jostling troopers, their bravado fed by a few shouting ringleaders and sustained by the anonymity of darkness. Some ran to fire the bungalow of the English riding-master, following this with the heaped bales of horse fodder behind the stables. Tons of dry hay exploded into white-hot fire, vomiting sparks skyward.

Other men ran for the guardhouse, where there was a money-chest and the regimental colours. Here they were checked, but only briefly. The duty subedar-major, white-bearded Bhowani Singh, stood his ground with sabre drawn. He was sworn to his duty, he shouted, and he would not betray it for a mob of mutinous sowars. 'Old fool!' they taunted. 'What duty do you owe the Sahibs, who have made you a servile dog for forty years?' They crept nearer, and then pounced, cutting him to the floor. Bhowani Singh lay in his own blood as they tore open the money chest.

Not all were intent on mutiny. Older soldiers slipped away in the darkness and confusion, reaching the Dragoon Hospital, but it was too late for any action to be taken against the 2nd Dragoons. The troopers, it seemed, were all mounted and congregating on the Grand Trunk Road, each with a spare horse, swearing that they were marching to join Bahadur Shah in Delhi, who had unfurled the green flag of the Prophet. The long, untidy column jingled through the darkness of the circuit road, the troopers chattering, low-voiced. There was safety in numbers. Old Bhowani Singh, the subedar-major, was dead, and the Sahibs hanged men for killing – but could they hang a whole regiment? But, in any case, so far the Sahibs had done nothing.

The native infantrymen of the 1st, 53rd and 56th had not yet moved from their lines. Many were still sleeping, or emerging from their huts, rubbing swollen eyes to peer at the flickering glare over the cavalry stables, but a party of mounted cavalrymen reined among the thronging sepoys of the 1st. A bugle sounded, then, 'Our Subedar-Major sends his compliments to the Subedar-Major of the first. Why is there delay, when the cavalry are drawn up and waiting on the road?'

None of the sepoys knew that their subedar-major lay sprawled on the floor of the guardhouse, few knew the reason for the noisy commotion that had aroused them from their charpoys. They scattered to their huts to struggle into tunics and cross-belts, fill knapsacks and load their muskets. Native officers, equally uninformed, mustered their companies on the drill-ground. The ranks dressed by their right, the jemadars shouting orders in the gloom as if this were any routine parade.

Colonel Ewart and his Adjutant, Athill Turner, both hastily dressed and unarmed, strode onto the drill-ground from the direction of the guardhouse. There was a sudden, uneasy silence.

'My children.' Ewart spoke in Hindustani, and his voice was strained. 'My children – why is this wickedness? This is not your usual conduct. Have you not given your oath to the Ridgement – that which is numbered First of the whole Bengal Army? How can you do this wicked thing and hold up your heads among your people? How will you face General Wheeler, who has been your father?'

A reply came from an invisible subedar. 'Colonel Sahib, you are a good man, and we do not wish to kill you.' There was another shouted command and the flank company turned into file, followed by the second and then the third. Hundreds of muskets rose to shoulders as the battalion wheeled onto the road that led to Nawabgunge, where the cavalry waited. The two Englishmen stood in silence until the tramp of departing feet had become almost inaudible.

'Mutiny,' Ewart said quietly. 'I've been telling myself for weeks that it just wasn't possible, Turner.' He shivered in his greatcoat. This, then, was the end of forty-five years of soldiering for John Company. A bloody mutiny. There'd be a court of enquiry, then the courts-martial, and hundreds of his men in leg-irons, breaking stones on the roads for years. The Regiment would not live down the disgrace of it. And he, Ewart, would be the object of condescending pity in every mess and club in India and England. It might have been better, he decided, if his sepoys had shot him down – but they had marched off as if he had never existed.

'At least they're not in a violent mood, sir,' Athill Turner offered. 'Likely they think they'll be sitting with their damn feet up in the United Service Club in Calcutta next week, smoking cheroots and calling for chota pegs.'

The Colonel shook his head. 'They'll make for Delhi, I shouldn't wonder, to join Bahadur Shah.' He straightened. 'Subedar-Major Bhowani Singh is in the guardhouse, and he's still alive. We must get him to a surgeon in the Old Dragoon Hospital. Think on it, Turner – only one loyal soldier in a whole blasted regiment.' He shook his head, puzzled. 'What have we done wrong?'

They were both mistaken. The 1st Native Infantry would march to neither Calcutta nor Delhi – only as far as Nawabgunge, on the other side of Cawnpore. Then they would return to the Old Dragoon Hospital. And the Magazine and Treasury were at Nawabgunge. The tired Treasury guard of Queen's soldiers had been relieved by a company of the 53rd.

The Adjutants of the 53rd and 56th Regiments reached their lines within minutes, mustered the native officers, and ordered both battalions to stand to arms. It was a course of action earlier agreed – that if mutiny threatened, the men would probably be more easily restrained under disciplined drill conditions than if left to their own devices. The glow over the cavalry stables was dying, and the sky to the eastward was streaking with dawn yellow.

The two regiments paraded in column, with colour parties,

bands, drums and pioneers. Subedars stamped forward to report their companies, and the ranks shouldered, fixed and unfixed bayonets, advanced, retired, changed front to left, to right, halted and deployed, until the sun was well above the horizon.

'What do you think, Mowbray?' Delafosse asked quietly. 'Are they safe?' The sepoys had marched and counter-marched for two hours without hesitation or any sign of ill humour.

Mowbray Thompson hummed softly. 'God knows, old son. But we can't keep 'em here all bloody day.' The men must be dismissed soon to cook breakfast, for ablutions – and, once dismissed, anything might happen.

At 8 a.m. Colonel Williams, commanding the 56th, decided upon a calculated risk. Sooner or later the men's loyalty must be tested, and it may as well be now. He ordered his regiment to scour the deserted lines of the 2nd Cavalry, to secure horses and arms abandoned by the mutineers. By half companies the sepoys spread among the empty huts, the scattered debris and skeletons of stables. There was little to retrieve, but a naik and four sepoys of the 1st Regiment emerged from the elephant sheds, having barricaded themselves and refused to surrender the elephants to the mutinous cavalrymen. Colonel Williams promoted the naik to havildar.

Dismissal, now, could not reasonably be further delayed. Williams ordered the 56th to be dispersed, and Major Hillersdon followed suit with the 53rd. The men went off to their lines, to shed their uniforms and crouch on their heels around their clay stoves. If the 2nd Cavalry and the 1st Infantry had marched clear of Cawnpore, it was just possible that the 53rd and 56th would remain uncontaminated.

The morning sun climbed higher and grew hotter. Behind the entrenchment one man in two of the Main Guard and the gun-crews was sent away to the field kitchen, or to queue at the well. Awnings and sunshades were being raised against the sky's glare, and in a corner of the hospital building lay Subedar-Major Bhowani Singh, next to an Englishwoman, a Mrs Wade, who tossed and sweated in a feverish coma.

It was quiet, except for the interminable humming of flies. Northward across the dusty *maidan*, just beginning to shimmer in the sun's heat, they could see the curving race-course with its white-painted markers and, beyond, the church with its cross-scattered cemetery, the reading room, the riding school and the racquets enclosure. All seemed deserted except for scurrying flocks of bunting among the vegetable gardens. North-eastward, four hundred yards distant, was the 56th Regiment officers' mess-house, and in the opposite direction, by the same distance, the long echelon of partly-built barrack houses that Captain Moore had been regarding with growing uneasiness. The nearest of them would provide excellent cover for an attacking force, and a simpleton could see that the Europeans should occupy them in advance – but with whom? Even if there were troops to spare, it would be a no-return, suicidal position.

There was no telegraphic communication now with the outside world, even with Lucknow. All messages would have to leave or enter Cawnpore by runner. That might be possible if the 53rd and 56th remained firm, but difficult and dangerous otherwise. There had been no reliable news of events in Oudh and Bengal for several days.

They had heard about Etawah and Aligarh, of the massacre at Sitapur, and Lieutenant Ashe had brought news of the mutiny of Captain Hayes's irregulars at Kerowlee, but they did not know that the red tide of revolt had already engulfed Azimgarh, Bareilly, Fategarh, Benares and, on this very morning, was devouring Allahabad, so that Cawnpore was now a tiny island surrounded by bloody rebellion.

Something would have to be done, Captain Moore decided, about those damn shells of barrack-houses – but, God alive, he couldn't think what. He walked the *sangar* perimeter and ordered all artillery pieces to be run in and loaded, discovering to his disgust that there was no round-shot for the 3-pounder rifled gun.

As the dismissed sepoys squatted in small groups, smoking and gossiping, a trooper of the 2nd Cavalry, from the Treasury at Nawabgunge, trotted into the lines and dismounted. Why were the sepoys sitting at their doors in their *dhotis* when a holy war against the British had begun? For many years the Indian had been enslaved and robbed, and his women dishonoured by white men who were no better than sweepers of filth. What were they waiting for now? Their comrades who guarded the Treasury had said that they would allow no division of silver until their own regiments came to claim their share. There were lakhs and lakhs of silver, all that the Sahibs had taken from the sepoys. And there were many mem-Sahibs here for the sepoys to dishonour – as their own wives and daughters had been dishonoured by the English. Blessed be the Hindus, the Mohammedans and Sikhs! If the sepoys of the 53rd and 56th were unwilling to avenge their outraged daughters, they should drown themselves in the water-tank of the Deputy-Commissioner's bungalow.

It was fighting talk, and the men of the 56th, by threes and fours, dragged on their tunics and equipment and began to drift away towards Nawabgunge. If there were thousands of rupees to be had, why should they not share? In thirty minutes the huts of the 56th had emptied except for a handful of men still unconvinced. One of these was an officer named Khoda Bux, who raced to the Dragoon Hospital to find Colonel Williams. He was an Indian who had once enjoyed the rare experience of a visit to London, as a servant, and had seen sufficient evidence of British power and sophistication to be immune to the predictions of bazaar rabble-rousers. Making his report. Khoda Bux added contemptuously, 'If those fools of sepoys had ever been to Battses' Hotel, Vere Street, Oxford Street, they would not be so bold, Colonel Sahib!'

General Wheeler made one of his rare appearances to gaze towards the native lines. 'Lieutenant Ashe, are your guns shotted?'

St George Ashe saluted, surprised. 'Yes, sir.'

'And the sepoy lines are in range?'

'Yes, sir.'

The General nodded. 'Then open fire.'

Ashe glanced quickly at the distant sepoy lines, then at his two 9-pounders, and finally back at Wheeler. 'Sir?'

Major Hillersdon stepped forward. 'Sir, the mutineers have

gone. The only sepoys left in the lines are those of the 53rd – *my* sepoys! I've got a dozen native officers here who'll swear their men will stand firm. Dammit, sir – we've allowed three regiments to march off with their arms, and we haven't fired a shot. Now we're going to fire on the only regiment that's remained loyal?'

'I appreciate your concern, Major.' The little General placed his hands behind his back. 'We all think our own are lambs, when others have only goats. It's time they were all taught a sharp lesson.' He turned back to Ashe. 'Lieutenant, lay your guns, if you please.'

Ashe crouched over the sights of his two guns as artillerymen pushed on handspikes. He rose. 'Laid and ready, sir.'

Wheeler nodded again. 'Then carry on, Lieutenant.'

Ashe swallowed, then, 'Numbers one and two – prove your fusees! Ready! Fire!'

The two guns crashed almost simultaneously, rearing back on their trails and enveloping the crews in black smoke. The artillerymen were instantly spongeing, reloading, and ramming. Seventy yards away, Moore, Thompson and Delafosse whirled, aghast. 'Bloody Christ!' Thompson screeched, 'Ashe's festerin' battery's firing on the 53rd. *Our* 53rd! What the hell's he thinking about? What the—'

His voice was drowned by a second thunderclap as the guns fired again. Men, women and children were flocking excitedly towards Ashe's battery to watch the distant, mushrooming falls of shot, and the sweating gunners as they spilled around the 9-pounders.

'Sponge! Reload! And ram! Ready! Fire!'

'Festerin' Lazarus, Moore—?' Mowbray Thompson flung his hands in the air. 'Why? Why?'

Moore flinched. Why did these damn Company men always look at him when things went wrong? He was only a bloody Queens' Captain, wasn't he? 'It's not Ashe,' he said. 'It's General Wheeler.' Why didn't the old fool stop interfering in a situation he didn't understand? Still, dammit, the 53rd were unlikely to have remained in their lines for more than an hour or two. Wheeler had only precipitated the inevitable.

Thompson's face was in his hands. He choked and vomited. Delafosse looked away.

The hurtling round-shot tore through the wattle and bamboo huts as if they were only paper, smashed down cooking stoves and hurled fire-embers and boiling *ghee* over scrambling, half-clad sepoys who, seconds earlier, had been unconcernedly eating their day's first meal of fish and rice. There was thatch smouldering, acridly smoking. Bewildered men clawed up clothing and haversacks and scrabbled desperately along the narrow, rutted alleys, away from this incomprehensible insult. Why was this happening? Where was Hillersdon Sahib, and Captain Thompson, and Delafosse Sahib? Weren't they in the *Lal Koorti Ka Haspital*, from where the guns were firing? Why?

In minutes, the 53rd's lines were deserted. The sepoys streamed towards Nawabgunge. 'That,' said Henry Delafosse, 'is bloody *that*!'

For the time being there was no lack of information from native informers on the mutineers' movements, in exchange for a few rupees from Mr Hillersdon, the Collector, but it was plain that much of it was being invented. Still, there was no doubt that the mutineers had moved no further than Nawabgunge, where they had released all prisoners from the gaol, broken into the Treasury and distributed silver and other loot, then scattered the thousands of documents in the public offices. It seemed likely that soon the sepoys, having pillaged all they could in Cawnpore, would now move north-westward along the Grand Trunk Road towards Delhi – or at least away from the eastward, where the forces of retribution were mustering. With few exceptions the sepoys wished to be quit of Cawnpore but they lacked a commander with authority. Nana Sahib, waiting at the *Savada Kothi*, descended to the street to meet a deputation from Nawabgunge – those of the original conspiracy joined by a throng of other native officers and sepoys. Subedar Teka Singh was the spokesman, and he bowed, his hands placed together.

'The time has come, Excellence, that we have spoken of. What will you say? Will you lead us to Delhi? A kingdom awaits you if you join with us.' He paused, glancing up. 'But only death if you support our enemies.'

Nana's voice was more disdainful than he felt. 'Have I not said before? What have I in common with the British? I am altogether yours.' He condescended to place his hands on the lowered head of each member of the deputation, assuring them of his fidelity to the cause of all Hindus and Moslems. He was committed now.

Meanwhile, at Nawabgunge, the storm of vandalism and plunder was continuing. The magistrates' office and the court-house were fired, and with them all civil and criminal records. All European residences on the western fringe of Cawnpore were ransacked, then burned to the ground, and a dozen shouting, flag-waving mutineers, clinging to the back of an elephant, cut the cables of the bridge of boats that spanned the Ganges. The long line of linked boats swung gently into mid-river, broke up, then drifted downstream. The sepoys cheered.

There were, surprisingly, still Europeans who had declined General Wheeler's orders to take shelter in the entrenchments of the Dragoon Hospital – in Cawnpore's suburbs and the nearby villages of Shirajpore and Chobipore – clinging to their conviction that nothing serious would result from all this nonsense and, in any case, evacuating property was only asking for it to be looted. Fortunately, the mutineers were, so far, too concerned with loading scores of bullock tongas with their booty and women, ready for the trek to Delhi, to be very concerned about killing Europeans. Only one, a supervisor of highways, was pursued along the road he had recently been building, and shot dead.

By late afternoon the long, straggling caravan of laden bullock carts had reached as far as Kalianpore, the first easy stage on the Grand Trunk Road towards Delhi. In the Dragoon Hospital entrenchments the Europeans did not celebrate; they had been disappointed before. They held their breaths and waited. One more day, perhaps two, and the four regiments of mutinous sepoys would be at a safe distance. Let them all go, and good riddance. At the moment all British forces seemed to be converging on Delhi – 2,900 men from Ambala and Meerut under General Sir Henry Barnard, who had assumed command on the death of General Anson from cholera. Within days Barnard, too, would be dead, from cholera. Of these things Cawnpore was ignorant, but if Delhi justified priority attention, then let Delhi have the mutinous sepoys. Cawnpore was content to be left alone.

But neither Nana Sahib nor Azimullah Khan wanted to exchange Cawnpore for Delhi. In the Cawnpore district Nana was Maharaja, lord of all, but at the court of the old Mogul, Bahadur Shah, he would be only one of the many minor princes competing for preference, and he had achieved nothing yet to establish himself as the valiant leader of a rebellion. The four mutinous regiments were needed in Cawnpore to form the nucleus of an army that both the British and Bahadur Shah would take notice of. Alone, Nana Sahib could not even challenge Wheeler's garrison, far less campaign against the British Raj. No, the sepoys must be brought back.

Nana ordered elephants and took the road in pursuit of the sepoy column. With him rode Azimullah and his own younger brothers, Bala and Baba Bhut. It was dusk when they reached Kalianpore, and the sepoys' untidy bivouac, of tents, carts and smoking fires, was sprawled along the road and the adjacent fields. The mutineers' ringleaders were loud in their appreciation of Nana Sahib's arrival. He had come, as he had promised, to march with them to Delhi, to join the growing army of Bahadur Shah – Mohammed Surajoo-Deen Bahadur, King of Delhi and Ruler of the Universe.

They were less enthusiastic when he explained his real purpose, but Azimullah, supporting his master, was a persuasive talker. It would be tactically unwise, he argued, to leave General Wheeler's force in their rear when it could be destroyed so easily. Besides, the sepoys from Cawnpore had hardly mutinied; they had merely deserted. They would be better received in Delhi if they had killed a thousand Europeans in Cawnpore. And there was much loot to be had in the Cawnpore district, besides a magazine, filled with guns and ammunition, that remained untouched. Finally, Nana Sahib would give every sepoy a gold ankle bangle when the Cawnpore entrenchment had been taken – and how could three thousand trained sepoys fail to quickly overrun such a miserable fortification? It was Nana Sahib, not old Bahadur Shah, who was the rising star of Hindostan, and all these men now listening would be promoted to colonels of regiments, and generals of brigades, immediately they embraced the cause of Nana Sahib. Could they be sure of the same from old Bahadur Shah in Delhi?

They were uncertain. Delhi was the resurgent, rallying point of all native India, the bastion to which all mutinous regiments were flocking. Cawnpore was a shabby substitute. But Azimullah was right. In Delhi, havildars would remain havildars, and sepoys would still be sepoys. But in Cawnpore? It was tempting. And, it was true, Wheeler Sahib's flimsy position would surely delay the sepoys' march to Delhi by only a few hours. The Europeans would have taken all their jewellery, coin and valuables into the *Lal Koorti Ka Haspital*, packed in those black tin trunks with the steamship labels. It could be even more lucrative than the Treasury. And promotion to Colonel. Would the Colonel Sahib's uniform fit? And the Colonel's mem-Sahib – that pallid, haughty lady with the fish-like, contemptuous eyes, to whom sepoys were sub-human, vermin creatures to be tolerated, but never, never spoken to. It would be exquisitely satisfying to see her stripped and beaten with *lathis*, to see her debased and pleading before her throat was cut and her corpse flung into the filth of a monsoon ditch. That would be most satisfying.

9

In the locality of the Dragoon Hospital all had been quiet, and again the bolder residents were venturing out of the entrenchment. Sir George Parker, the magistrate, led a party of his friends to his bungalow for a civilized breakfast, and four Company clerks strolled to the native shops on the canal bank in search for coffee. The brown ribbon of the Allahabad road, the distant, charred skeletons of the cavalry stables, the curving race-course and the long echelon of half-built barrack houses, all seemed deserted of life. At first light, to Major Hillersdon's satisfaction, the grenadier company of the 53rd Regiment had approached from the direction of the Treasury where, their native officers reported, they had remained when the other sepoys had marched for Kalianpore. They had no wish to mutiny; they came to honour their oath in defence of the *Lal Koorti Ka Haspital*. They had brought their weapons, and their cartridge pouches were full. What would the Sahibs have them do?

When Hillersdon returned from a brief interview with General Wheeler his face was grey. The need for reinforcement, he explained, was diminishing with every hour, and the sepoys' services were not now needed within the entrenchment. In any case, food supplies were insufficient to allow any increase in the garrison's number. Like Ashe's native artillerymen, they stared at him, not comprehending. Hillersdon emptied his pockets of money, and wrote for each man a certificate of fidelity. They could, he said, station themselves in a small sepoy infirmary, six hundred yards to the eastward of the Dragoon Hospital. He would not forget them; he would remember every name as he remembered those of his nearest family.

The grenadier company, 150 men, trooped away, eastward, toward the isolated infirmary building – a position they would defend on behalf of the Sahibs for nine bitter days before the last of their muskets fell silent.

Mowbray Thompson lowered his bi-ocular glasses thoughtfully, raised them again to his eyes, and then drew a deep breath. 'Don't look now, Moore,' he said quietly, 'but I have an uncomfortable feeling that our prodigal sons have returned. And there's a bloody lot of 'em.'

Moore fumbled for his own glasses and swore. Simultaneously the sentry on the roof of one of the hospital buildings shouted an alarm. The distant trees around Christchurch, the gardens, riding school, the southerly Allahabad road, every copse and clutter of buildings, all teemed with tiny scarlet-coated figures. Moore could see bullock-drawn guns being unlimbered, with ammunition carts behind. From the direction of the small sepoy infirmary, six hundred yards distant but obscured from sight, came the sudden chutter of musketry fire.

The regular soldiers of the Main Guard, without orders, were already at their allotted places at the mud *sangar*, and they were looking towards Captain Moore, not at the hospital building from which General Wheeler had not yet emerged. Ewart, Williams, Vibart and Hillersdon, all senior, were glancing at each other enquiringly.

Henry Delafosse began singing softly. 'Alice, where art thou—?'

Moore grunted impatiently, then, 'Officers to your commands, if you please! Prove all gun charges, and fill all water-buckets. Clear away carriages. Mr Ashe, we'll have your guns limbered and ready to accompany a reconnaissance party in fifteen minutes. All horses are to be brought to the redan. Civilians under arms, stand to your positions, please. Major Prout, sir – the three-pounder will have to be loaded with case shot. Sergeant Grady – take a detail to bring out all metal baggage trunks to reinforce the battery positions. And I mean *all* baggage trunks. Battery and Main Guard officers, report your detachments when mustered and ready, please. Women, children and infirm will remain behind walls for the present. Extinguish all fires—'

There were sufficient horses, mostly officers' Cape or Australian ponies, to mount twenty men. The little column, with Ashe's two 9-pounders behind their galloper carriages, jingled out of the entrenchment followed by hundreds of eyes. 'It's information we want, Mr Ashe, not bloody heroics,' Moore ordered. 'Don't get involved. Look for gun positions. It's artillery fire that's going to give us most trouble; our Enfields out-range their muskets. And keep your detachment together.'

The last order was difficult to satisfy. The ponies were undrilled and most carried strange riders. Ashe led them in a wide sweep towards the Ganges canal. All its bridges, he noted, were posted with sepoys. He turned away. Heavy mortars were in battery between the racquets court and the reading room, a heavy battery in the churchyard, and another behind the riding school. The lines of the 1st Native Infantry, recently deserted, now teemed with men. On his flank he could see the silver-grey of mounted cavalry and hear distant, shouted commands. Ashe had seen enough, and it was time to return to the Hospital before encirclement threatened.

'About wheel!' He threw a hand high, rotating it. 'Trot! Trot out!'

The two teams of gun-horses, abreast, turned the guns and carriages in their own lengths, with the artillerymen clinging to their narrow seats to prevent being thrown off. The following twenty riders, unprepared for the manoeuvre, were less adept. The ponies tugged and jostled, and the column was in confusion with hooves churning dust. To hell with drill, Ashe decided. They were hardly more than five hundred yards from the safety of the Hospital entrenchment but, if the native cavalrymen had their wits about them, there was ample time to be cut off and surrounded. Ashe pointed, shouting. 'Ride for it—!'

The dust rose in a dense, choking fog. All semblance of order had gone. The gun wheels were bouncing and there seemed to be galloping ponies everywhere, but the *sangar* of the Hospital was ahead, and they could see Dempster's battery and its gun-crews with rammers and spongers. Moments later, Ashe's detachment poured into the entrenchment, the riders sweating and laughing. Ashe grinned at Moore.

Moore was not amused. 'Who was the man you lost?'

Ashe, dismounting, gazed at Moore in surprise. 'Lost?'

'We were watching you when you wheeled. One of your riders broke away with his pony out of control, then he was thrown and his mount bolted. The native cavalry cut him down.'

'Sir, I'm sorry – I didn't know—'

Moore nodded. 'I suggest you muster your detachment, Mr Ashe, so that we know who is our first casualty.'

There was nausea in Ashe's throat, and his men had stopped laughing. It needed only seconds. 'Ashburner's missing, sir,'

Ashe said quietly. 'Lieutenant Ashburner, Bengal Artillery. He was the rear-marking officer. Goddam—!' He choked. 'I was commanding. When we withdrew, I ought to have taken the rear.'

'No, Mr Ashe. Officers commanding, whether they're lieutenants or lieutenant-generals, do not place their persons in jeopardy. But you should have kept your detachment more firmly in hand, and remembered that polo ponies aren't drilled troop horses. However' – he sniffed – 'there probably wasn't much you could have done about Ashburner, and he won't be the last. The Maharajah of Bithur has informed us by formal letter that he intends to attack this position. Kindly make your report, Mr Ashe.'

Sir George Parker and his breakfast guests escaped from his bungalow with bullets spitting about their ears, and scrambled through gardens and bamboo scrub to reach the Hospital breathlessly shaken but unharmed. The four clerks who had crossed the canal were less fortunate. They were shot dead as they ran from the native shop in which they had been drinking coffee.

A few minutes after Lieutenant Ashe's detachment had regained the entrenchment a railway engineer named Murphy reeled in, shot through a lung and vomiting blood. There was little that the surgeons could do for him, and he died within the hour. A single, dusty coffin had been found in one of the hospital buildings, and this Murphy shared with Mrs Wade, who had succumbed to fever. They were the only Europeans to be buried within the perimeter of the mud *sangar*. The old subedar-major, Bhowani Singh, still clung to life.

No other Europeans achieved the doubtful sanctuary of the Dragoon Hospital. Those who remained at large were being hunted down by baying packs of armed sepoys, pursued from house to house, dragged from hiding-places in outhouses, ditches and culverts, shot or bayoneted. Informers who had recently taken British money now tracked down the Sahibs still in hiding. One elderly man, with his wife, sixteen-year-old son and infant daughter were taken from a tool-hut by the post-house. Another similar family were found under a canal bridge, disguised in native clothes and with faces stained. Alone, or in groups, belligerent men, tearful women and shocked children were hauled from their pitiful refuges and butchered immediately.

Nana Sahib, carried by elephant, had led his new army from Kalianpore to Cawnpore, consisting of three infantry regiments, one of cavalry, and a detachment of Oudh Artillery in addition to the troops of the Maharajah's own household. It was an impressive force, but Nana's authority was thinly stretched. There were too many men, recruited from the Oudh principality, who had mutinied only for an opportunity to loot with impunity. Almost all sepoys were heavily in debt to the bazaar money-lenders. Here was a glorious chance to kill the money-lenders, burn their receipts and, as a lucrative bonus, take their hoarded silver. Azezun, the public woman, the favourite of the 2nd Cavalry, was lifted to the saddle of a troop horse and led before the column, more loudly attended than the Maharajah of Bithur himself.

At 10 a.m. precisely the rebel battery in the cemetery of Christchurch opened fire. There was a distant, mushroom-puff of black smoke, and the 9-pound ball soared skywards, deceptively slowly, then plunged. It smashed through the lip of the mud wall beside Lieutenant Eckford's battery, bounced from the ground, and then sheared through both walls of the *pukka*-roofed hospital building.

It was debatable which was more uncomfortable, the exposed balconies poorly shaded from the day's blazing sun and chillingly cold at night, or the crowded, oven-like interiors, rank with the smell of dust and unwashed bodies. Noon temperatures were rising to 115 degrees in the shade. Several trenches had been dug during the first few days of inactivity, but these were only eighteen inches deep, and offered little protection against either sun or enemy shot. Women and children huddled in their family groups, drenched with sweat and filthy, flinching as the sepoys' battery-fire shuddered the brickwork, splintered timber, or gouged clods of earth skyward. It had suddenly become hazardous to move in the open, and men did so crouching, running.

John Cook, the *dâk* agent, and the gentlemen who had once listened respectfully to Amelia's pianoforte exercises, had been issued with rifles and ammunition, and held themselves ready to man the wall at any time. Amelia's mother, Emma Cook, had reached her seventh month of pregnancy and sat damply pale and listless. In addition to Amelia, there were five smaller Cook children – two boys and three girls aged from ten months to ten years – and all were now Amelia's responsibility. For as long as she could remember, in Lucknow and Cawnpore, there had always been an impassive, competant *ayah* to cope with the children while the Sahib and mem-Sahib were more importantly engaged. Now Amelia choked back her own revulsion as, with a single bucket of water, she must clean up her mother's vomit, keep herself and the five children clean and, with what remained, wash dirty clothing.

Days before, a friend of her mother's, Mr Frederick Briant, with his wife and children, had arrived in Cawnpore from Fatepur. Emma Cook had urged them to seek safety eastward, and they had boarded the last steamboat to leave for Allahabad. If only, Amelia prayed, they had all gone. By now they would be in Allahabad, perhaps even Benares.

More probably, however, they would not. Amelia was unaware that the escape route to Allahabad had been cut, and Lucknow and Cawnpore now sheltered the only European communities of any size for hundreds of miles in every direction.

The first death from the mutineers' artillery fire was that of Gunner M'Guire, of Lieutenant Dempster's westward battery. The black speck of the round-shot seemed to approach so slowly, and M'Guire watched it, fascinated and unmoving, until it smashed him to the ground. His corpse was covered with a blanket and left behind the embrasure until nightfall.

By the Maharajah's hand, Subedar Teka Singh of the 2nd Cavalry had been appointed Commander of Horse, with the rank of General. Jemadar Dulgunjun was promoted to Colonel of the 53rd and Subedar Gunga Deen raised to Colonel of the

56th. Others were majors and captains, dressed in ill-fitting regimentals looted from officers' bungalows. Azezun, on her troop horse, was festooned with medals and stolen jewels. Whatever her misgivings, she had little choice. The mutineers were masters in Cawnpore, and the Europeans in the Dragoon Hospital would never admit a public woman.

With European residences ransacked, the spoilers were turning their attention to the property of wealthier Indians, native Christians and Eurasians. The house of Bhudri Nath, one of the commissariat contractors who had provisioned the Hospital, was stripped of all furnishings and valuables. Forty thousand rupees, belonging to a Hindu merchant, were taken from a cart in the Post Office compound, and in the *Chandni Chauk*, the Street of Silver, shop doors were being beaten down. In the Moslem quarter the residence of Nunhe Nawab, the most influential Moslem dignitary in Cawnpore, was stormed by Brahmin sepoys, who blew open the gates, smashed priceless glassware and porcelain, and looted the plate-chest and wardrobe.

Elsewhere, however, discipline was beginning to prevail. General Teka Singh had taken a force to the Magazine to unload the thirty-six ammunition boats tied in the river. Serviceable guns in the Magazine were being hauled by government bullock towards the Dragoon Hospital, those in poor condition taken to be refurbished on the lathes of the armoury by native artificers.

Within thirty-six hours it was unlikely that any Europeans, other than those in the Dragoon Hospital entrenchment, remained at large in the vicinity of Cawnpore, but occasional refugees from the mutinies westward stumbled into the town's outskirts, sometimes having survived miraculously for weeks. On Monday, 8 June, a young woman with a small child, both exhausted and emaciated, were seized by cavalry on the Grand Trunk Road and dragged triumphantly before Nana Sahib. The woman's condition was such that she could no longer speak; she merely croaked from lips broken and blackened by the sun, and so remained unidentified. The child was unconscious from heat exhaustion.

Nana regarded them both with a degree of uneasiness. He had not yet become involved in the killing of Europeans, but neither did he desire the inconvenience of maintaining prisoners – particularly white female prisoners. In general, religious taboos forbade both Hindus and Moslems to have sexual relationships with women of a different creed. So far as a white woman was concerned, the more religious sepoys would more likely prefer to humiliate her by stripping her naked and compelling her to acts unspeakably shameful to a mem-Sahib; there might be others, however, who wished to go further, to determine how a white woman compared with a brothel *devadasi*. A captive white woman, Nana Sahib decided, could become a source of contention.

'Every Englishwoman,' he said, 'is only the mother of English children, and any English child is a sucking tyrant. The wolves, and their mates and whelps, have been herded into their den. We must smoke them out, and make an end of that vicious breed.' He paused. 'Kill them both.'

Ten days later, along the same road from Fatehgarh, appeared a dusty, slow-moving *gharry* pulled by a horse lame with fatigue. In it rode a woman of mature years, a teen-age girl, and three smaller children. The woman's husband, she explained to the troopers of the 2nd, had been killed on the road further westward, but the killers, with a rare show of chivalry, had allowed the woman and children to go free. The troopers of the 2nd had no similar feelings of compassion; they ordered all five to climb down.

Brought before Nana Sahib, whose appearance suggested someone of better quality and education than the soldiers, the older woman brightened. Would the gentleman protect them, and perhaps conduct them to safety? And could he please give the children water?

Nana Sahib now knew exactly what to do with white women. He shook his head, drew a finger across his throat, and turned away. One of the children was plucking at the woman's skirt. 'Mamma – there's a bungalow, see? Can't we get water from the bungalow?'

The woman's tired eyes were on the Maharajah's retreating

back. She had seen his gesture, and she knew. She had brought her children from the butchery at Fatehgarh only to find death at the side of a dusty road in Cawnpore. She hoped, dear God, that they would kill the children first and quickly, so that they would not have to watch the mutilation of their mother. 'Please,' she asked, 'could you take us into the shade?'

But they would make not even that small concession. They tied the captives together on the road, wrist to wrist, then shot each through the face with their pistols.

10

Calcutta and Government House were 633 miles away. The Honourable East India Company had been negligent in the planning of railway communitication, and by mid-1857 a rail track under construction, following approximately the route of the Grand Trunk Road, reached only as far as Ranigunge, 120 miles from Calcutta. Beyond that point travel was still by *dâk gharry*, bullock tonga, river boat, horse, elephant, or foot. If any place had been specifically designed to favour a military rebellion, it was north-west India. Stretching fifteen hundred miles to Lahore, then on to Peshawar on the Afghan border, the Grand Trunk Road was laid with limestone *kunkur* that allowed reasonable if dusty travel in the dry season but could be a glutinous quagmire during the rains. Off the Trunk Road there were seldom better than primitive tracks through parched plains and thick jungle.

In Calcutta the Governor-General, Lord Charles Canning, had achieved several near-miracles in mustering three European regiments for the desperately necessary punitive campaigns to relieve Benares, Allahabad, Cawnpore and Lucknow. These were the 1st Madras (European) Fusiliers, the Queen's 64th Foot, and the 78th Highlanders. All were tough, climate-hardened soldiers who knew their business, with an arrogant contempt for native troops that gave them a psychological advantage in all encounters. In anger they could be sadistically brutal, and the sepoys regarded them with apprehension. What Canning lacked was an army commander of the same calibre. And there wasn't much time.

Henry Havelock was 62 – six years younger than Sir Hugh Wheeler. He was a short, ramrod man, with grey hair and trimmed side-whiskers beginning to whiten. The lowered eyebrows over stern but not unkind eyes, a strong nose and unsmiling lips all contributed to a face which might have been that of a Covenanter, or perhaps a Cromwellian captain; it was an uncompromising but honest face, to dampen frivolity in subordinates but engender their respect.

At twenty, in 1815, Havelock had followed two older brothers into the Army, but Napoleon's final defeat and exile promised, or rather threatened, a long and unprofitable peace for a professional soldier, and in 1823 Havelock transferred to India.

Promotion was still painfully slow. He was a King's, later Queen's, soldier, and most plum appointments went to officers of the Honourable East India Company. Additionally, Havelock was not a sociable type. He was religious, his reading material Clausewitz, Jomini, Tempelhof, and the Bible. In cantonments he organized a chapel, a temperance society, and a coffee-house to counterbalance the beer-and-grog canteen. The men of his company, pointedly encouraged to attend divine service, were sneered at as 'Havelock's Saints'. It was 1838 before he achieved his captaincy, and a further sixteen years before promotion to Colonel, but during that period he campaigned in Burma, Afghanistan, Gwalior, and in the bloody Sikh War. Early 1857 found him involved in the brief Persian campaign which terminated on 5 April. Five weeks later, on 10 May, the Sepoy Revolt exploded in Meerut.

Havelock regained Bombay on 29 May, anxious to reach Calcutta on the far side of the subcontinent, but a journey across country was now unthinkable. He snatched a passage on the steamship *Erin*.

The steamship was wrecked on the coast of Ceylon, in heavy

surf. The lascar crew panicked, but Havelock quietened the Europeans, characteristically denying access to the spirit room, and there was no loss of life. He wrote later: 'The folly of men threw us on shore; the mercy of God found us a soft place near Caltura.'

He reached Calcutta, where the arrival of an officer of his experience was a gift from heaven. He was immediately given his first independent field command – the patchwork force intended for the relief of Cawnpore and Lucknow. It was an assignment with shuddering problems, but he threw himself into it without question. At 62 he was still only a Colonel, and he would not sign himself Major-General for a further six months, just eight days before his death.

Even before Havelock's arrival, the relief force had begun to move out of Calcutta. The situation westward was deteriorating so rapidly that days, even hours, had become important and a commander, when appointed, could easily overtake the column. The mutiny was drawing closer and closer to Calcutta, in whose streets disbanded or deserted sepoys were blatantly selling their regimentals. Quite apart from distant Lucknow and Cawnpore, nearer Benares was simmering with unrest, while Allahabad, similarly unsettled and with its fort and arsenal strategically placed at the junction of the Jumna and Ganges, had no British garrison. Either city could fall to mutinous regiments at any moment.

The advance detachment of the relief force constituted four companies of the 1st Madras Fusiliers commanded by Brevet Lieutenant-Colonel James Neill. The Fusiliers had been loaned by the Madras Presidency and had reached Calcutta by sea, blissfully unaware that they were expected to do any fighting. So ignorant were they of the gravity of the situation that Neill had left behind seven of his most experienced officers who had been appointed members of a court-martial.

In Calcutta, Neill was quickly disillusioned and, equally quickly, he took action. He put one company into barges to be towed up-river by steamers, then ferried four across the Hooghly to Howrah railway station. They would at least cover the 120 miles to Ranigunge as rapidly as possible.

At the time scheduled for the train's departure, much of Neill's baggage remained unloaded, but the station superintendent, more concerned with his time-table than with the future of India, ordered the engine-crew to proceed. Neill requested a few minutes' grace, but the superintendent refused. The train, he said, would start at the scheduled time, and anyone or anything not aboard could take another train tomorrow. Within seconds the superintendent, driver and fireman were shrinking before the bayonets of several unsympathetic Fusiliers. Neill loaded his baggage, entrained his men, and the cramped wagons jolted out of Howrah only ten minutes behind time.

Neill, an Ayrshireman, was forty-seven years old and had been a soldier for thirty. During the recent Crimean War he had been seconded to the Turkish service, in which the rules of warfare were somewhat different from those observed by the British. He possessed much of the character of the men he now commanded – familiarly known as the Lambs – and during the months to follow his ruthlessness would earn him reprimands, even under circumstances when barbarity had become commonplace.

On the four companies' arrival at the rail-head of Ranigunge, Neill commandeered every *dâk gharry* in the locality, but these were insufficient for his entire force, so that many had to follow by painfully slow bullock tongas. Neill, with only 25 men, reached Benares on 3 June.

Benares, the holiest city of Hinduism, was a hair's-breadth away from insurrection. Two regiments of native infantry and one of cavalry were balanced by only a small detachment of the Queen's 10th Foot and a single battery of artillery. European women and children had already taken refuge in the Mint.

Even for the impatient Neill, the force at his disposal was too small to take any initiative against three regiments of potential mutineers. During previous weeks, however, the British in India had learned one very painful lesson – that they must move first, that the native troops must be disarmed. Neill waited one more day, for 200 of his slower-travelling Fusiliers to reach Benares, and then ordered a parade of all troops in garrison for 5 p.m.

On the open *maidan* the four guns of the Bengal Artillery, loaded with grape, were flanked by 200 Fusiliers and the few men of the 10th Foot. Facing them, separated by fifty yards and in close order, were the 37th Native Infantry, a regiment of Sikhs, and the dismounted troopers of the 13th Irregular Cavalry.

'Fall out all officers. Markers forward. Pile arms by companies!'

There was a moment of hesitation, but the markers of the 13th and the Sikh Infantry stamped forward and turned inward. Muskets and carbines clattered to piles, the men slouching back to their ranks and standing sullenly. Only a few of the 37th, however, had moved.

The order was repeated. 'Markers forward! Pile arms by companies!' Behind the field guns an officer spoke urgently. 'Prove your fusees!' The artillerymen in their horse-tailed helmets began to adroitly whirl their short lengths of slow-match until the ignited ends glowed. Dozens of curious native bystanders on the fringe of the *maidan* began to edge away, and officers' hands strayed to pistol holsters.

The sepoys, too, had paraded with muskets loaded, but for a few more moments the black muzzles of the field guns held them in check. Then all uncertainly ended. There was a flash, a whip-crack report, and a musket-ball whirred within feet of Colonel Neill. Instantly there was a second, a third, and within seconds scores of sepoys were firing widly, with the cavalrymen and Sikhs stumbling and jostling to get clear.

The reply from the British was immediate and devastating. Fuses came to vents, the field guns erupted, and a blizzard of grapeshot scythed the sepoys down in swathes. Fusiliers and Queen's infantrymen presented, cocked, volleyed, then fixed bayonets and surged forward. It was enough. The sepoys' ranks had disintegrated into chaos, the men flinging down their muskets and struggling through the lines of equally shocked and helpless Sikhs and troopers. Blaspheming British stabbed and clubbed, treading over the fallen and tearing down the few knots of native soldiers who dared to stand. In less than three minutes there remained nobody to kill. Several hundred dead sepoys lay among a debris of weapons and equipment; the rest had fled, and mutiny had been quelled in Benares.

II

Cawnpore's old Dragoon Hospital was now completely surrounded, and communication with the outside world by all normal means had been severed. There remained a few natives, several of them pensioned sepoys, who stole in and out of the entrenchment under cover of darkness and maintained a tenuous liaison with Sir Henry Lawrence in Lucknow. The British, however, could never be sure that despatches would reach their destinations. Messengers often simply disappeared; they may have absconded or, worse, delivered their messages to the mutineers. It soon became customary to write significant words or phrases in French.

It also became clear that Sir Henry Lawrence, similarly surrounded at Lucknow, did not intend to fall back on Cawnpore; and the Cawnpore garrison abandoned all thought of breaking out and fighting a way through to Allahabad or Benares. Two hundred determined soldiers supported by a similar number of armed civilians might conceivably succeed, but the hundreds of women and children, and the growing number of sick, put the possibility beyond consideration.

For the moment, Nana Sahib seemed content to confine his activities to a leisurely but incessant bombardment. He had immense ammunition resources, he had plenty of time, and the Hospital was a ludicrously exposed and fragile target. The British guns replied as best they could, probing for the enemy batteries, but the mutineers protected their guns well, and they had the freedom of movement; they could fire a dozen rounds, then move fifty yards. The British needed mortars, and they had none. From the westward race-track, near the reading room, the mutineers were pushing forward a sap, protecting a 24-pounder mortar, and there was nothing the British could do about it. There were two more heavy mortars firing from the racquets court and three heavy artillery pieces from the 56th Regiment's officers' mess.

Moore's first concern, however, involved the line of partly built barrack buildings, the nearer of which dominated the Hospital entrenchment. There were eight of them, each 200 feet in length, staggered in echelon to achieve the maximum benefit from northerly breezes, and of red brick that had not received the coat of plaster that reduced all Anglo-Indian buildings to a monotonous uniformity. The walls of Number 1 were seven feet high, those of 2 and 3 about forty, Number 4 boasted a temporary roof, and the remainder had reached seven or eight feet. None had floors, and the interiors and surroundings were littered with bricks, bamboo scaffolding and builders' rubble.

As cover for the sepoys, who could move progressively and unhindered along the line of buildings, they represented a vicious threat. 'We should have demolished them weeks ago,' Moore said, but he knew the objections there would have been to the deliberate destruction of John Company property. 'We can't occupy them all, dammit, but if we can get men into one of them, we might stop the rot spreading along the line. It'll have to be Number 4. And God help them, because there's not much support we can give from here if things go badly.'

With more guns being hauled from the Magazine, the enemy artillery fire was intensifying, and during the first day the men crouching at the *sangar* could hear the shrieks of women and children as hurtling round-shot rocked the hospital walls, splintering brickwork or shearing through roof-thatch. After that first day, however, the shrieking ceased. Surgeon Donald Macaulay of the Bengal Artillery and Surgeon Collyer of the 53rd crawled with splints and swabs, seeking the injured who moaned in the gloom with throats parched and stung with brick-dust.

At dawn, when a sepoy half company moved forward to occupy Barrack Number 4, they found themselves walking into a blast of rapid rifle-fire that cut down a dozen of them and sent the remainder scrambling for cover.

The unexpected rebuttal had come from a party of sixteen civil engineers of the East Indian Railway, whose years of surveying experience and distance calculating made them peculiarly expert marksmen. Each had eight or ten loaded muskets or rifles at hand, and most carried a double-barrelled sporting gun with a lead slug loaded in one barrel and a rammed charge of shot in the other for close quarters. A volley of Eley's No. 4 in the face at six feet was calculated to stop anything on two legs. After three bitter days and nights of repelling every attack mounted by the frustrated sepoys, the railwaymen were joined by Captain Jenkins of the 2nd Cavalry. No mutineers ever set foot in Barrack Number 4 and lived to boast of it.

General Wheeler was still nominally in command, but he seldom left the company of his wife and two daughters. Punctiliously, every morning and evening, Captain Moore reported to the General – the casualties, the ammunition stocks, the food supplies and the water situation, and the General nodded, agreeing. Very good, Mr Moore. Proceed, if you please. And it was Moore, growing daily more strained, who seemed to be everywhere, cajoling, encouraging, bullying, tenderly comforting to an injured child and brutally contemptuous towards a fit man who shrank from his place at the *sangar*.

If only, if only, Amelia wished, she had the help of Jemdani, the children's *ayah*, or even Gulab, the *khansamah's* daughter. The care of five small children and her mother in the frightening conditions of the Hospital occupied every moment of her day. Mrs Cook's sickness was undoubtedly worsening. She vomited repeatedly, complained of dizziness, and cramps in her legs, and was experiencing seizures lasting several minutes during which her body went rigid and her face and limbs twitched uncontrollably. It was eclampsia, Dr Newenham explained. Under different circumstances, and if Mrs Cook's pregnancy was a little further advanced, he would bring on the delivery, which was the only remedy he knew, but here it was unthinkable. He could only offer a sedative, and Amelia used precious water to soak cloths with which to cool her mother's sweating face. Additionally, her younger stepbrother, three-year-old Herbert, had diarrhoea. She prayed that it was not the dreaded sign of cholera. But only feet away Dr Newenham's wife had a headache and her nose was bleeding. She would be dead before little Herbert.

Amelia's understanding of military matters was small. In happier days she had seen lancers and shining artillery guns jingling behind confident young officers in scarlet and gold, the horses with leopard-skins, sheep-skins and throat-plumes, and the band playing 'Bonnie Dundee'. It had never occurred to her that a 24-pound round-shot from one of those pretty guns could scythe through thirteen feet of rammed earth or sandbags, or that a .75-calibre musket ball could make a hole in a man's skull as big as a fist.

By the third day of the siege every door and window in the hospital buildings had been smashed in, the screens and piled furniture wrecked. Women and children were being killed or maimed hourly, by round-shot, canister or bullets, by falling masonry or splinters. Occasionally a heavy shot would smash through both walls as the dust-caked occupants clung to the ground; one mortar shell plummeted, hissing through the roof to kill seven women.

In the open, heat exhaustion and sunstroke were taking an increasing toll of the men at the *sangar* and in the redan. Colonel Williams of the 56th was carried in, unconscious and with face purpling with apoplexy, to die in hours at Amelia's feet. His widow choked in a mask of blood, a shell splinter having struck her in the face and carried off her nose, while a daughter lay comatose in fever.

Drawing water from the single well in the entrenchment had become a perilous task. The sepoys, who could see it clearly, had the range to an inch, and the constant riddling of grape-shot had torn down the surrounding brickwork and the timber superstructure. The bucket had to be drawn up, hand over hand, from the water seventy feet below. Even at night the unavoidable rattle of the bucket was the signal for a blizzard of shot from guns ready laid and waiting. John McKillop, a civil servant, confessed that he was no fighting man but he would make himself useful in some capacity. He did, on his knees at the well-head, hauling, panting, sprawling for his life again and again, for four days, until struck by a spinning enemy missile that spilled his bowels over his knees.

There would be no more water for washing, John Moore ordered, only for drinking. Still, many of the more wealthy were willing to pay handsomely for a half-bucket of dust-filmed water, and soldiers of the Main Guard would crawl to the well under cover of darkness for ten shillings – until quickly money lost all significance, when they continued to crawl, unpaid, for the wounded and sick.

Foiled by Jenkins and the railwaymen in Barrack Number 4, the sepoys edged around it to occupy Number 1. Moore cursed. It was a possibility he had dreaded; he could ill afford men to meet it, but he had little choice; he had to occupy Barrack Number 2. The force detailed for the unenviable assignment consisted of Lieutenant Glanville of the 2nd Bengal Fusiliers, Ensign Henderson of the 56th, five men of the Madras Fusiliers, eight of the Queen's 84th, and two railway plate-layers – a total of seventeen.

Within forty-eight hours Glanville was seriously wounded and carried to the railwaymen's position, which had been joined by Surgeon Macaulay. All the Fusiliers were dead, with four men of the 84th.

'We've got to hold Number 2, sir,' Moore explained to General Wheeler. 'It's the key outpost to the whole position, and the blacks know it. Fortunately they can't bring artillery to bear, but they're sending in hundreds of men, and it's going to cost us a lot of lives that we can't afford. We've already lost Glanville and nine good men.'

The General nodded. 'Quite so, Mr Moore.' He tried to visualize which of the barrack buildings was Number 2. 'But it won't be for long. The relief force from Calcutta should arrive any day, and I shall send a despatch to Lawrence at Lucknow, asking for two hundred men. You must see that the men in the outposts receive extra grog and rations. And whom do you intend to replace Glanville?' Moore did not wish to protest that there was no knowledge of a relief having even left Calcutta, that Lucknow was as closely invested as Cawnpore with losses probably as severe, that there was no grog, and rations were already reduced to horse-meat, lentils, rice, with a few luxuries for the wounded. 'I'll be sending Captain Mowbray Thompson, sir.'

The General nodded again, frowning, trying to put a face to the name. 'Ah, yes – Thompson. An excellent choice, Mr Moore. Please proceed.'

Moore sent for Mowbray Thompson.

'I know what you're going to say, Moore,' Thompson grinned. Like many red-haired people he suffered painfully from sunburn, even after several years in India. His face and neck were blistering badly, his lips cracking and beginning to fester, and his inner thighs were raw. He walked gingerly. 'If I only had prickly heat I could use lemon juice. Not that we have any lemon juice.' He grinned again. 'D'you know what's happening in London today, Moore? The Oxford and Cambridge boat-race! I've always wished I'd gone up to Oxford, but my old fellow was a John Company man, y'know – Bengal Artillery – and it had to be Addiscombe. But think of it, Moore. I might have been on the tideway between Putney and Mortlake today, with half the riff-raff of London shouting their damn heads off.' He paused wistfully. 'We'd burn the boat, then off in cabs to the West End – buckets and *buckets* of iced champagne, Moore—'

Moore gazed beyond the guns of Dempster's battery, beyond the dust-whirls of the *maidan* and the Allahabad road, and further to the distant, dim-blue smudges that told of high *jkow*, and bamboo thickets, banyan and kikr trees. Champagne, b'God! He'd settle for water for the rest of his life. A river of cold crystal, like the Maigue in Limerick, or the gushing Test above Chilbolton, under green willows and cool blue skies. Water – a trivial thing that nobody gave a thought to until they were in a place like this, where children sucked at pieces of old water-bags, and fetidness was everwhere.

'We'll replace your losses as far as we can,' Moore told

Thompson, 'but you'll need to send two men daily for rations and ammunition. It's my guess that the night hours will be your most troublsome; in daylight the blacks will have to run the gauntlet of fire from the Hospital as well as your own. And watch for the sudden quiet period. It can mean they're preparing to mount an assault.' He held out his hand. 'Good luck, Thompson. When it's all over I'll buy you a damn cartload of lemons, and you can borrow Nana Sahib and Azimullah Khan to squeeze 'em.'

Day followed hideous day. The entire surrounding terrain, as far as the eye could see, was an ant-hill teeming with mutineers. Every few minutes a distant, tiny burst of smoke gave warning of a hurtling shell, and the men in the entrenchment would watch for the approaching shot which might plough deep into the earth, or bounce high, skidding and flailing.

The British guns were replying, but the exposed officers and men of the Bengal Artillery were being shot down or were collapsing under the pounding heat of the sun, to be replaced by telegraph clerks and bandsmen whose determination was no substitute for their lack of expertise. Sunstroke killed Major Prout at the breech of his little 3-pounder, Captain Kempland lay insensible in the shade of the *sangar*, while his second officer Lieutenant Eckford, was killed instantly by a falling shot while snatching a few minutes' sleep on a verandah. At the western battery Lieutenant Dempster was shot dead, and Martin carried into the surgeons with a perforated lung. By the end of the first week all fifty-nine artillerymen were dead or wounded. They had earned their pay of 1s. 8d.

Several guns had been damaged. One lost its entire muzzle, others blew their vents, and the sole 24-pounder, brought by St George Ashe from Lucknow, was smashed from its carriage. Then came the most disheartening blow so far. All artillery shot remaining in the field magazines was for 6-pounder guns, and the serviceable pieces defending the old Dragoon Hospital were all 9-pounders.

Across the Ganges, in the village of Chobipur on the road

northward, had been posted a detachment from Lucknow consisting of a squadron of 7th Oudh Horse and two companies of sepoys commanded by Captain Staples of the 48th NI, four subalterns and a European sergeant-major. They had been there for several days, and by Tuesday 7 June the officers were aware of the situation in Cawnpore; their own position was hazardous.

At 2 p.m., after a lunch of curried mutton and tea tasting of wood-smoke, the Captain's tent was stifling as the six men discussed their predicament. To advance on Cawnpore was out of the question, to fall back on Lucknow seemed advisable, but how would the men behave? They, too, would have heard of the insurrection only sixteen miles away. In the cavalry lines the troopers would be grooming their horses under the eyes of their native officers, and in a few minutes a bugle would sound 'Water and Feed'. The sergeant-major was explaining that in the sepoys' bivouac he had smelled crushed geraniums, the sure betrayal of hashish-smoking.

Beyond the tent wall the distant bugle sounded. The sergeant-major paused in mid-sentence, then frowned. 'That's not—' He rose to his feet. 'That's not "Water an' Feed", sir. It's "Assembly"!'

The six men tumbled from the tent, their eyes blinded by the sun. Captain Staples shouted. 'Rissaldar-Major—?'

There were musket shots and shouts, and they knew. Their horses, however, were saddled and tethered only yards away, and they ran, praying that knotted halter-ropes could be quickly unravelled, that the animals would not decide to be perverse. Captain Staples was shot with one foot in a stirrup, and fell. Two of the subalterns went for the river and kicked their horses over the bank, crouching low as their animals swam like hunted stags, but neither reached the far side. The sergeant-major and another subaltern turned away through Chobipur, but here were met by a mob of armed villagers and driven back among the pistols and sabres of the cavalrymen.

Lieutenant Bolton of the 7th Oudh Horse, with a bullet-hole through his cheek, thrashed his gelding southward and reached the Ganges, only to find the boat-bridge destroyed. Under his threatening pistol a native boatman ferried him across, two miles above Cawnpore, and Bolton reached the town's outskirts at nightfall. Incredibly, and unaware of the precise location of the old Dragoon Hospital, he led his exhausted horse unobserved through the scattered sepoy positions and reached the open *maidan*. Here he remained for the remainder of the night, listening to the chutter of gunfire all around him but still uncertain where the British entrenchment lay. At dawn he could see. He mounted and urged his horse to a final gallop. Only yards from the mud *sangar* the sentries opened fire at the thundering apparition in the half light. A ball tore out the throat of Bolton's mount, but the game creature cleared the wall with its rider, to expire in a froth of blood minutes later. Bolton had exchanged death in Chobipur for a death in Cawnpore.

The following day the mutineers from Chobipur marched triuphantly into Cawnpore, bringing with them the severed heads of three of their late officers, which were displayed to shouts of '*Kali ma ki jai!*' On their route they had also seized Joseph Carter, the toll-keeper on the Oudh side of the Ganges, and his young wife who had reached the last days of pregnancy. Carter was shot, and his wife would have shared the same fate were it not for an unexpected intercession from the Palace of Bithur. The several widows of Bajee Rao, Nana Sahib's predecessor, pleaded for her life.

Nana Sahib was annoyed. His involvement in the mutiny had reached a stage from which there could be no possible withdrawal. He had staked everything and, when ultimate victory was achieved, Indian history would hail him as a saviour, a Shah Jehan, another Tamerlane. He wanted no hostile survivors with stories to tell of atrocity and child-murder to tarnish his glory. The mouths of all European witnesses must be silenced.

The ladies of Bithur insisted. The old Peshwar had never made war on women and unborn infants, and the line of the Mahratta should not be disgraced by his adopted son. If Nana Sahib killed Mrs Carter, then they, the Peshwar's widows, would publicly commit suicide.

The threat startled Nana Sahib. The Bithur women did not lack influential friends, and the scandal of their suicides could be damaging.

It was annoying. '*Hut, hut!*' He tossed a disgusted hand. 'You may take her to Bithur, but she must be kept in *purdah*, and there will be a guard on your quarters.' Besides, he could deal with Mrs Carter later.

It was impossible to dispose of the dead in the daytime. The corpses were piled at one end of a verandah, where they lay, teeming with black flies, until night, when the burial detail dragged them over the *sangar* to a dry well, into which they were thrown. The verandah was beyond Amelia's nearest window, and as the sun grew hotter the stench of putrescence was overpowering. She tried not to look at the corpses because she shrank from identifying them – and yet there was a morbid fascination difficult to resist. There were so many people of the Cawnpore community that she had known – young officers who had made her blush with tingling excitement, ladies she had admired or sometimes resented, dignitaries of the Company whom she had never met but whose names filled her with awe. Now she saw them in their final indignity, dead, dishevelled and bloating, with mouths agape and clothing torn and awry to expose pubic hair, long-hidden breasts and pale buttocks. The daily tumble of dead was repugnant, but it was hypnotically fascinating, and in the darkness she lay listening as, yards away, the men of the burial detail hauled corpses by their feet, bumping down the wooden steps.

She was ashamed, but the picture-image refused to be pushed away. This must be Sir George Parker, the pompous cantonments' magistrate, dead from sunstroke, with his bat-wings of white hair, cultivated to hide his baldness, drooping over his ears. And now—here was Miss Yeates, that cream-and-gold goddess who queened over every Ladies' Night, now with her tresses dirtily tangled and her eye-pits clogged with flies. And young Lieutenant Martin, who had arrived in Cawnpore only two days before the outbreak and who, the ladies had giggled, rubbed a flour, salt and water mixture into his upper lip every night to encourage the growth of a reluctant moustache. He had drowned in his own blood after being shot through a lung.

There were worse things in daytime. Peering through her broken window-frame, Amelia had seen a young man mount the verandah, swaying with fatigue and his face flushed. Was it someone she knew, someone with whom she might exchange a few words of conversation? She rose to her knees, but she never did know. An enemy round-shot struck the ground ten yards from the verandah, reared, then smashed the young man's head from his shoulders. Amelia screamed. The man's torso jerked, deluging blood and with hands raised as if in supplication, outstretched, before spinning to the boards.

12

Colonel Neill, in Benares, was fretting to be on the march for Allahabad, the next major stage on the Grand Trunk Road westward, but there were matters demanding his attention. In Benares captured sepoys were being hanged on a gallows that could accomodate four at a time, and it did, repeatedly. The route beyond this point would now become progressively more hostile, and Neill's 200 Fusiliers were hardly adequate for the purpose of maintaining a hold on Benares; the surrounding country was still rebel-held. It would be foolhardy to push on until both he and the city were reinforced.

Still, Neill was desperately anxious about the fort at Allahabad. In mutineers' hands it would be a daunting obstacle to any lightly-equipped relief force. Neill made another gamble. On 6 June he despatched fifty of his Lambs, under a subaltern, towards Allahabad, with orders to simply secure the fort. The next day, plagued by the worry that the detachment was too small for its task, he rushed off another fifty-seven.

The leading fifty, under Lieutenant Arnold, reached Jhusi, on Allahabad's opposing bank, on the 7th. They were utterly exhausted by forced marching in pounding heat, many in a state of collapse, and they were bitterly frustrated to find that the bridge of boats over the Ganges was in the hands of mutinied sepoys of the 6th Native Infantry.

Arnold and his little band had arrived just too late, but perhaps it was just as well, for they might otherwise never have survived. Twenty-four hours earlier the sepoy regiment, the 6th, had butchered fourteen European officers, fired the cantonments and thrown open the gaols. Colonel Simpson, who had recently written to the *Englishman* ridiculing all suggestions of disloyalty among his men, galloped to the fort with a bullet-smashed arm.

The fort's duty officer was middle-aged Captain Brasyer, an ex-sergeant commissioned from the ranks. His garrison consisted of a regiment of Sikh irregulars and a company of sepoy infantry – the latter waiting to open the main gate on the expected arrival of their mutinous comrades. The Sikhs, too, were in a ferment of disaffection.

Brasyer, however, was no man for nonsense from a crowd of damn blacks. Under his lashing tongue the Sikhs mustered and disarmed the sepoy guard at the gate. Then, when the Sikhs also began murmuring mutiny, Brasyer stood at the open door of the magazine with a burning torch inches from a laid fuse, swearing by Baba Nanak, Ram Das, and every other festerin' *guru* of the Sikhs that if they did not obey his orders he would blow the entire regiment to the Sikh equivalent of kingdom come. The Sikhs believed him, and for the moment the fort of Allahabad was reprieved.

Meanwhile, Lieutenant Arnold and his fifty fatigued Fusiliers had managed to cross the Ganges, but expected to find that the fort had fallen, in which case they would have difficulty in extricating themselves. They were unaware that another fifty-seven men, under Lieutenant Beaumont, followed them on the road, a day behind. Beaumont had been attacked and had lost all his baggage, but he had not stopped marching. On 7 June Arnold's party reeled into the fort, and Beaumont arrived on the 8th.

In Benares, Colonel Neill was teaching that city a lesson in savage reprisal that would not be forgotten. For generations thereafter, father would tell son, and son would tell grandson how Neill's Lambs brought the Sahibs' vengeance to Benares, how the long file of shrinking sepoys climbed to the rope, and when the rope was too slow they were shot, and to save reloading they were bayoneted. It was useless for a man to plead that he had not been a mutineer; all sepoys were mutineers. All Indians were suspect – Hindu, Moslem, Sikh, Buddhist, Jain. It made no difference. Never again, Neill swore, would these animals dare raise a finger against the British Raj.

With further small detachments of Madras Fusiliers trickling in from Calcutta, the Colonel left Benares late on the 9th, accompanied by forty men and several *gharries* to convey his baggage. The seventy miles took him a day and two night marches. His horses failed, so he put natives between the shafts. At Gopiganj he found his road blocked by sepoys who did not know Neill. He swept them aside with cold steel. Five men died from sunstroke on the march, and two more in crossing the Ganges a mile below the bridge. On the final mile between river and fort, Neill himself collapsed, but his men kept him conscious by continually emptying their water-bottles over him.

Entering the fort on the 11th, Neill waited only until the following day before attacking the mutineers holding the bridge. It was an operation he had to direct from the fort's batteries, prostrate, and sustaining himself with repeated draughts of champagne and water. The bridge was cleared and repaired in time for the arrival of a hundred more Fusiliers from Benares. Immediately, the incredible Neill launched his entire force into Allahabad and the suburbs of Jhusi and Kydganj. Within four days of his arrival Allahabad was secure, the streets quiet, the magistrates' court re-opened, and the gallows erected. Neill's casualties were two killed and five wounded.

Neill now knew that both Cawnpore and Lucknow were under siege, and that Cawnpore in particular was in danger of being overwhelmed. The possibility incensed him. Beyond Allahabad there had been a further forty miles of railway track under construction, as far as Lohanga, but the mutineers had torn up the rails, burned rolling stock, and disabled engines by artillery fire. 1,500 draught bullocks had disappeared, and carts, stores and tents destroyed. Neill was handicapped not only by his lack of numbers but also the brutal heat of the Indian summer. Cawnpore was still 125 miles away, a march of at least ten days during which the sun would decimate his force. Colonel Havelock was somewhere in his rear with the 64th Foot and the 78th Highlanders, but Wheeler's situation at Cawnpore would not wait and, anyway, Neill and his Lambs were snarling to get at Nana Sahib. On 14, 16 and 18 June further small parties of Fusiliers tramped into Allahabad, and Neill sent a despatch to the Governor-General in Calcutta.

'As soon as a sufficient number of Europeans arrive I shall push on as large a body of Fusiliers to Cawnpore as I can, but almost fear it will be impossible until a shower or two of rain falls. The heat here is fearful; all are suffering from its effects. No European soldier could survive beyond a day or two a forced march, badly provided with carriages, and consequently tents and provisions, on the Cawnpore road, which has for some time been in the hands of the insurgents. When cooler weather sets in, after a little rain, I will make the attempt, and I doubt not, if it is to be done, with success. I will also endeavour to send up men by steamer when the river rises. However, of this feel assured, I will push on troops to Cawnpore with the utmost despatch.'

Then, on 22 June, around a bend of the Ganges from Benares, threshed the paddle-boat *Mirzapore*, her tall funnel vomiting black smoke and her horn barking like an excited terrier. On board were 240 Madras Fusiliers, fresh, armed with new Enfield rifles, and looking for a fight.

Neill now had more than 400 European infantry, two 9-pounder field guns, 300 Sikhs and 120 irregular cavalry. He also was looking for a fight, and he was determined to march to Cawnpore, heat or no heat, within four days.

13

Throughout the night hours Mowbray Thompson and his sixteen men crouched at the loop-holes of Barrack Number 2, powder-blackened and aching with fatigue. Except for Barrack Number 4, still grimly held by the European railwaymen, all other adjacent buildings were crawling with sepoys, and all night they could be heard, like scampering rats behind a wainscoting, chattering and shouting taunts. From every door, window and drain there came a continuous musketry fire which the defenders tried to ignore, watching for the enemy's careless moment when, emboldened by hashish or bravado, he emerged into the open, singly or in swarming droves.

Thompson had constructed a crow's-nest platform, twenty feet above the ground, from which a man could overlook the surrounding approaches and give warning of an impending assault upon either of the British-held buildings. An eager occupant was Lieutenant Stirling of the 2nd Cavalry, a superb marksman with his breech-loading Terry carbine. It required only a distant glitter of brass, a momentary glimpse of a red tunic, for Stirling to aim, fire, and grunt with satisfaction as another mutineer spun and fell.

By day a few hours of sleep were possible, so far as the intense heat permitted. The men would curl themselves among the sharp-edged bricks and rubble and be asleep in seconds, their grimy faces cradled in their arms and their shirts rotting from the sweat that soaked them continuously. A shout from the look-out would waken them, stupid with weariness, to crawl again to their positions and grope for their guns.

All ammunition and rations had to be brought daily from the Dragoon Hospital entrenchment, two hundred yards away across the naked *maidan*, and the mutineers watched and waited for the occasion. Two men of the picquet undertook the hazardous duty, running, crouching, as the garrisons of both British-held barracks and the Main Guard in the entrenchment gave covering fire. The return journey, hampered by a heavy box of cartridges and a bucket of pea-mash or boiled rice, was no less dangerous. As a reward, the two men of the 'cook detail' were exempt from the next night duty – if they had survived.

Captain Moore insisted, and Mowbray Thompson agreed, that the mutineers in the other barrack-houses should not be permitted to congregate, to build up their numbers and confidence towards the mounting of a major attack that might sweep away the two British outposts. At least once a day the men of both picquets, totalling about thirty, would combine forces in a counter-assault with bayonets to clear the vicinity, stabbing and clubbing among the rubble and splintered timber. The sepoys seldom stood. They scattered, but many were too slow. They were dragged from drains and culverts or shot from scaffolding, and when they ran from cover into the open *maidan* there was Dempster's battery waiting for them, its guns rammed with canister made from musket-balls packed in women's stockings.

Occasionally the daily sortie hauled in prisoners, cringing Hindus who swore that the mutiny was not the fault of the sepoys, but of the *Rakshasas*, the malevolent devils, who could assume any shape they wished.

Prisoners were an embarrassment to both barrack-house picquets; there were neither guards nor rations to accommodate them. For the first few days they were transferred to the Dragoon Hospital entrenchment. Eleven of them, roped wrist to wrist, sat on the ground under the unsympathetic eyes of Mrs Bridget Widdowson, the massive wife of a private of the Queen's 32nd. She held a naked cavalry sabre in her hand, and the prisoners sat very still. Nobody took liberties with Mrs Widdowson, as Private Widdowson had rued for years.

Later, when the belligerent lady had been withdrawn, the prisoners, under male surveillance, all contrived to escape. It was a pity, because they took with them the knowledge of the Europeans' destitute circumstances. The British could not hold out much longer, they told Nana Sahib, and they were fools who did not shoot captives. The *Lal Koorti Ka Haspital* would be taken by the first general assault.

Henry Delafosse was becoming increasingly irritated by the activity of a rebel gun position beyond Barrack Number 1, within his own field of fire, but to achieve accuracy with a worn 9-pounder loaded with 6-pounder shot was impossible. There was only one remedy, he decided. It was to turn his gun into a monster blunderbuss.

He loaded a double charge of powder into the barrel, followed this with three 6-pounder shot and then rammed home a stockingful of grape. A delicate shell pink, he noted, and wondered from whose leg it had come. The loading was a hazardous business. With temperatures rising to almost 140°, guns became so hot that they were capable of firing spontaneously. Delafosse waved everyone away, laid his sights with meticulous care, put his slow-match to the vent and then flung himself to the ground.

There was a deafening roar as the old gun erupted flame and screeching round-shot, leaping backwards. Delafosse had his arms over his head, but the barrel had not burst. The rebel gun beyond the Barrack Number 1 was never heard from again.

The children no longer asked when they were going home, or enquired of Sacha the spaniel. They crouched, blank-eyed with shock, occasionally sobbing with the unfamiliar ache of real hunger. The last meal of substance had been horse-meat soup, made from the last of Lieutenant Ashe's battery horses. Thereafter, for women, children and wounded the daily ration was a handful of dried peas and one of flour, and for able-bodied men without regard for rank a half pint of gram, or chickpea, intended as animal fodder.

The wounded now had to be laid among the crowded families in the hospital buildings; there was no space elsewhere. The heat and stench increased hourly, and ladies who only weeks before would hardly have acknowledged the existence of a common soldier now found themselves sharing the same floor-space with bloodied, filth-encrusted men who blasphemed as the surgeons probed and splinted, then lay silent in a stupor of pain. The ladies tore their dresses and petticoats into strips to provide bandages, and gave their stockings to the batteries for grapeshot casings. Privacy for even the most personal activities was impossible. Breasts had to be exposed to feed babies, and other undertakings of an intolerably embarrassing nature performed under a spread blanket. Several women bore stillborn infants.

Amelia, who for several days had hoarded tiny amounts of rice and lentils with which to make a mess of *kitcheree* for the five children, fed the hard-won luxury between the lips of a wounded artilleryman – a man she had never seen before, his face grime-coated and with creases swimming with blackened sweat. He croaked his gratitude, but the eyes were glazed and staring by the next dawn, and the burial detail dragged him to the verandah.

Mrs Emma Cook, in a coma, muttered incoherently of her own mother, whom she wanted to see, and called repeatedly for a carriage to take her. An Indian *ayah*, walking in the open, was struck by a round-shot that took off both her legs and sprawled her blood-drenched remains over the broken wall at the well-head. The water ration that night was streaked with crimson, but Amelia choked it down, clenching her eyes.

The men at the *sangar* were becoming wearily accustomed to seeing mirages in the heat-shimmering, distant plain, of luxuriant green forests and vast stretches of silver water, but the Brahmin bull was no mirage. It was solidly tangible, hump-shouldered and tan-coloured. A wanderer from Cawnpore, it stood on the *maidan*, three hundred yards from the Dragoon Hospital, grazing lazily and arrogantly confident of its sanctity. The animal was secure from the muskets of the sepoys from whose lines it had strayed, but positively not from the Europeans' Enfield rifles, the bullets of which could penetrate four inches of pine at one thousand yards. The beautiful Brahmin jerked, amazed at the sacrilege, fell to its knees, then rolled over, defecating.

To shoot the animal was one thing, to bring it into the entrenchment something different. The men of the Main Guard gazed speculatively across at the distant, pale brown hummock on the darker brown of the *maidan* – a half-ton of beef that, with nightfall, would provide a feast for jackals and pariah dogs, but long before then would be putrefying in the sun.

'B'Jasus, there's a lot ev mate, axing ter be took,' an Irishman mused.

'An' ox-tail in gravy,' someone else said, 'Jes' think o' stewed ox-tail in bleedin' gravy.' They thought of it.

Captain John Moore had his bi-oculars to his eyes, calculating. He turned doubtfully. 'No. It's tempting, but too damn dangerous. Anyone going out there will be shot to bloody rags.'

He was ringed by unkempt, crestfallen faces. Private Sullivan of the 84th touched his cap. 'Beggin' ye pardon, Captain sorr – we might as well be shot as be starrved. With a baste like that' – he pointed – 'we cud make enough holy broth ter feed the wimmin an' children fer wayks an' wayks.'

Moore considered. 'I think your estimate of the potential of one Brahmin bull is highly optimistic, Sullivan.' But he grinned and nodded. 'All right. I'll take six volunteers, and we'll need rope. Mr Ashe' – he glanced about him – 'I'd be grateful if your guns would spread a little alarm and despondency among the blacks' position around the reading room.'

'I seem to remember, sir,' St George Ashe protested, 'that officers commanding do not place their persons in jeopardy.'

'Quite so, Mr Ashe,' Moore nodded again, gravely, 'but even officers commanding are entitled to a little recreation. Besides, I doubt whether any officer is more highly qualified. I was once a champion ice-skater.' Ashe stared, baffled.

Both cow and bull were sacred to the Hindu. To offer insult to either could have angry consequences; European officials who had occasionally attempted to drive off animals who obstructed and fouled streets, ate from market stalls and grazed indiscriminately, had been faced with mob riots. To deliberately kill a Brahmin bull with a view to eating it was an act of inexpiable wickedness.

As Moore and his detail went over the *sangar*, a fusillade of musket shots came from the enraged sepoys around the reading room, and a dozen men even advanced from cover, but Ashe's guns sent them scuttling back. Moore's equally frantic men flung themselves to earth around the prostrate bull, roped its hind legs and horns, and then turned for home, heads down and hauling like madmen. From behind the *sangar* the filthy scarecrows of the Main Guard were cheering, and Ashe's men sent another blizzard of shots screaming towards the reading room. Moore, his men, and the dragging, tumbling Brahmin bull spilled over the wall. Three men were bleeding.

'Jasus an' Joseph,' panted Private Sullivan, 'that wuz better than Phaynix Park on St Patrick's noight!'

The Dragoon Hospital was now completely ringed by batteries – in the cemetery of Christchurch, the racquets court, the Roman Catholic Chapel of Ease, the riding school and the 56th Regiment's officers' messhouse – totalling three mortars, two 24-pounders, three 18-pounders, two 12-pounders, two 9-pounders and one 6-pounder.

Nana Sahib's first reinforcements were several hundred ragged survivors of Colonel Neill's action in Benares, mostly Sikh irregulars, who had struggled 190 miles to Cawnpore on horseback, in bullock *tongas*, or on foot, goaded by the knowledge that somewhere in their rear were the savage Lambs of the 1st Madras Fusiliers. Nana Sahib's sepoys had yet to make the acquaintance of Neill's Lambs, and were consequently loudly contemptuous of the Sikhs' account of the Benares affair. The Sahibs had no soldiers such as the Sikhs described. The Sahibs had very few soldiers; they had almost all been killed at Sevastopol; but of course these miserable Sikhs were not real fighting men like those of the regiments of John Company – they were just nervous Punjabi peasants, and they would each have to pay a rupee to be ferried across the Ganges to Cawnpore.

There was the beginning of frustration among the mutineers in Cawnpore, generated by the lack of quick success against the *Lal Koorti Ka Haspital* and not alleviated by the inherent resentment between religious sects which was never far below the surface. During the first few days of revolt, Hindu sepoys had looted Moslem premises and insulted Moslem dignitaries; now the Sikhs from Benares had been belittled. Two general assaults on the Dragoon Hospital had been made – the first by the 2nd Cavalry and Oudh Horse, the second by sepoy infantry and bazaar riff-raff. Neither assault was enthusiastic, and both were turned away by the vicious fire of field pieces, rifles and sporting guns from the mud *sangar*, accompanied by the blaspheming jeers of the Main Guard. Hindus and Moslems blamed each other; both blamed Nana Sahib. Had he not promised that the *Lal Koorti Ka Haspital* would fall in hours? Why was the *maidan* scattered with Indian dead? Should they not all abandon profitless Cawnpore and march for Delhi?

A further embarrassment for Nana Sahib was to follow. John Moore carefully selected fifty men from the most aggressive of his regulars – Irishmen, slum-reared Scots and English – and in the dark of night led the unholy company towards the Roman Catholic Chapel and then the racquets court in an orgy of killing. A score of native gunners were bayoneted as they slept, five heavy guns were spiked and upturned, and one battery emplacement blown up by powder-charges before the mutineers could muster sufficient men to retaliate. Moore's men shot their way out, carrying four wounded and leaving one dead, to regain the Hospital with their blood-lust exultantly satisfied. The Captain, breathing hard, lowered himself to the ground in the darkness, his back against the *sangar* and licking congealing blood from torn knuckles. St George Ashe offered him a canteen. 'I must learn this ice skating, sir. It seems a damn necessary attribute if I am to get one of those Victoria Crosses we've heard about.'

Moore gulped at the dirty water gratefully, then nodded, smiling. 'Ice skating, Mr Ashe. I'd be delighted to show you the basic principles – given the ice.' He rose to his knees to peer into the blackness of the *maidan*. 'I wonder if it was worth it, Mr Ashe? One dead and four wounded – and tomorrow the blacks can replace those guns from the Magazine six times over. Who did we lose? Private Peel?' He spat. 'I've broken him twice from sergeant, for drunkenness – but in a fight, they don't make 'em any better. You can put it on record that I gave him back his stripes yesterday. He's left a widow and three children in Lucknow.'

Amelia would never forget the long suspense of that night. Sleep was impossible with the knowledge that Captain Moore and fifty of the garrison's fittest men had disappeared over the *sangar* into the darkness. John Cook and Tom Berrill, the railway engineer, knelt at the broken window, talking in low, worried voices, and she lay in the dust with Florence and Herbert clutched to her. Feet away her mother muttered, a woman sobbed quietly, and the wounded moaned. Old Subedar-Major Bhowani Singh, who had defended the guardhouse, lay on his back, staring at the invisible rafters above him. He would have given much to have accompanied the Captain Sahib, just this last time, to take his bayonet to the pigs who had defiled the colours of the 1st Regiment of Bengal Infantry. He had served for forty-five years – since Colonel Ewart was a pink-cheeked boy of an Ensign, and himself a bare-foot peasant boy from the Rajmahal Hills. He had not known his left foot from his right, and a disdainful havildar had stuck a straw between his toes. The young Ensign Ewart had laughed, and called him Sepoy Bhowani Strawfoot, but there had been no scorn in his laughter, only the merriment of a boy-Sahib, with the long, boundless road of life ahead of him, and their eyes had met. They had become men together, their hair had whitened, but their eyes still met and they both still remembered Sepoy Bhowani Strawfoot on the hot drill-ground at Aligargh. Had not the Colonel and Captain Turner carried him from the guardhouse, when his eyes were filled with blood? He had tried to explain about the colours and the money-chest, but the Colonel-Sahib had only laughed. 'It is of no importance, old Bhowani Strawfoot. What matters a rag on a pole, old friend, and a few rupees that will be spent in the brothels before Tattoo? There are more important things.' And the Colonel-Sahib had lifted the Subedar-Major gently.

He gazed into darkness. He would give everything, his four medals, his pension, his remaining hours of life, to have accompanied the Captain Sahib tonight, but the sabre cuts across his head had paralysed him from the waist downward, and he had lost an eye. Still, a man needed only one eye to sight a musket; he had his hands, and he had the comforting hardness of the loaded musket against his chest. The first pig of a sepoy that came through the door of the *Lal Koorti Ka Haspital* would never know that he had been shot dead by Subedar-Major Bhowani Singh.

The following day, however, the mutineers' guncrews, stung by the night's losses, opened fire with redoubled ferocity, and men and women clawed at the earth, praying, as shot after shot smashed into the entrenchment. A single, stray bullet that struck and killed a soldier also passed through both arms of his wife, at his side, and wounded one of the twin infants she carried. Amelia had already torn the frills and sleeves from her dress, relinquished shawl, stockings and petticoat, and now she shredded her undershift to bind Mrs White's broken arms. The woman lay on her back helplessly, but with her bodice opened and a child at each breast. She did not weep.

Injuries were being suffered more rapidly than they could be attended to by the surgeons who crawled among the debris. Surgeon Newenham of the 1st, and the civilian Dr Garbett were both dead, and medical supplies were almost exhausted. The Reverend Moncreiff and Father Rooney knelt over the dying or distributed rations to the living, until the Roman Catholic priest collapsed in apoplexy. Moncreiff, now alone, ministered to all, regardless of faith, and the hard-bitten Irishmen of the Main Guard knelt before him as readily as they had for their own chaplain.

For some, the daily horrors of the siege were becoming too much for sanity. They sat or crouched with eyes wide and vacant, speechless or, like Emma Cook, stammering nonsensically. One woman, dragging her two children, flung herself from the hospital building and ran for the *sangar*, shouting that she could tolerate no more and that she would beg the lives of her little ones from Nana Sahib, or release them by death. A soldier grappled with her, and she was hauled back to shelter, shrieking and kicking.

Amelia had seen little of the Reverend Haycock. He and his mother were not among those who shared the hospital building with the Cook family, and nobody crossed the bullet-torn entrenchment to neighbouring buildings except for a very good reason. In any case, Amelia was far too involved with her own charges, her mother and the crowded wounded around her. She had assisted in two childbirths and had stifled her nausea as surgeons amputated among filth and swarming flies. She had almost forgotten the Reverend Haycock and the Society for the Propagation of the Gospel.

Unlike his fellow churchmen, Haycock did not apply himself to any spiritual duties. It was not that he lacked either courage or inclination but rather that few Europeans believed in the validity of his office. Nobody heeded his exhortations to join together in prayer or hymns, or believed that a loud chanting of the 23rd Psalm would provide immunity against bullets or round-shot. The presence of Haycock, even more than before, was tolerated but not welcomed. Declining to man a defensive position at the *sangar* when even women and older children packed grapeshot and carried ammunition to the soldiers, he had little to offer except biblical platitudes, a poor exchange for the rations and water he consumed. Worse, there was a suspicion that Haycock and his mother had a private stock of provisions in their baggage – tinned ham, sardines and sausage – that they ate in the dark of night, but it was only a suspicion.

It was the custom of many civilians to venture to the verandahs during the last cool hours of dusk, to gulp clean air and stretch cramped muscles. The luxury was a dangerous one, but twenty hours in the stifling, dust-choked fetidness of the hospital buildings were sufficient to outweigh the possibility of a musket shot finding a haphazard target. Such a shot, however, killed old Mrs Haycock.

For her son, the gaunt missionary, the loss was crushing. For twenty-four hours he sat in silence, staring at the cracked brickwork of the hospital wall, declining food and drink and making no response to the Reverend Moncreiff's conciliatory hand on his shoulder. Then, at noon, Haycock roused himself. Slowly he drew off his shoes, shirt and trousers, and stood white and scrawnily naked. Women looked away, not yet having lost all delicate feeling, and children scuttled to their mothers. Haycock ignored them all. He walked to the verandah, then into the pounding heat of the open entrenchment. He lifted his thin arms.

'Deliver me from mine enemies, O my God! Defend me from them that rise up against me! Deliver me from the workers of iniquity, and save me from bloody men! For, lo, they lie in wait for my soul; the mighty are gathered against me!'

At the *sangar* the Reverend Moncreiff was kneeling over Lieutenant Godfrey Wheeler, son of the General, who had just been wounded. Seeing the naked missionary, Moncreiff scrambled to his feet, but the filth-encrusted hand of a soldier restrained him. 'Reverend, sorr, shure he's not worrth risking yeself for. The man's *ghazi*, like them holy men that swear they're immortal, till ye stretch their necks wid rope. Ye watch now, Reverend. He'll not walk fifty yarrds.'

Haycock did not walk fifty yards. He staggered and his voice faltered. Then he fell to his knees, choking, and finally crumpled – an untidy, pallid heap in the hot dust, mouth wide and eyes bulging.

Godfrey Wheeler, of the 1st Native Infantry, was carried into the hospital building, where the Wheeler family enjoyed the privilege of a small, partitioned space. He was laid on an old sofa to await a surgeon, and was being fanned by his sister when a round-shot screamed through the open door and left him a headless trunk, spattering walls and floor with crimson.

14

Nana Sahib issued his proclamations, printed on the press of a local schoolmaster, from his headquarters in the *Savada Kothi*. He had a number of growing problems, the first of which was the establishment of a disciplined organization among the increasing military forces in and around Cawnpore. The thoughts of most of the mutineers were turned towards Delhi, where the old King had raised the banner of revolt against the British Raj. The fragile old man's involvement was perhaps not whole-hearted, but he was the last of the Mogul dynasty, the most illustrious figure-head that the mutineers' leaders could find, and Delhi was the capital city of Hindustan, a bastion, and the obvious rallying-point for rebellion.

The lure of Delhi was strong. A publication from the old King offered thirty rupees per month for cavalrymen and ten rupees – later raised to twelve – for sepoy infantry. Nearly 100,000 men, it was claimed, were already mustered, the colours of thirteen British regiments captured, and fourteen districts had been liberated. There were hundreds of guns and masses of treasure already accumulated. Not a single Christian in India was to be left alive.

Nana Sahib, in Cawnpore, had little to offer in competition with the Peacock Throne in Delhi, even if Bahadur Shah was a doddering octogenarian more interested in new aphrodisiacs to enhance an appetite for small girls than in being reinstated Mogul Emperor of all India. All regiments, the Nana decreed, would have a colonel, a major and an adjutant, each company a *munshi*, or clerk, to prepare pay-lists and muster-rolls showing wounded and absentees. Pay would be similar to that offered by Delhi. There would be pensions for those who grew old in the service as well as for the dependants of men killed. It was difficult to predict where finance for such obligations, even in the short term, might be derived. In previous times all money had come from the Finance Department of the Honourable East India Company, and nobody needed to question it. Now, Nana Sahib did not have sufficient funds to cover his army's first month's pay – but, of course, it had not yet served a month.

There were other complications, of varying annoyance. The *Lal Koorti Ka Haspital*, with its ridiculously flimsy defences, had been under siege for almost two weeks, but it still defied him – or rather it defied the half-hearted efforts of the sepoys, who seemed to have no stomach for real fighting. They preferred to lounge in the shops and brothels by the Canal, consuming sherbets and sweetmeats, or riding horses and carriages taken from the Sahibs' stables. The artillery was being manned by army pensioners attracted by the prospect of twelve rupees a month.

A court of law was established in the billiards room of Duncan's Hotel, presided over by Nana Sahib's younger brother, Baba Bhut, supported by Azimullah Khan and Jwala Pershad. A thief was sentenced to have a hand severed, a Moslem butcher to mutilation for having killed a cow, but the tribunal was soon exercising its authority beyond matters of common law and order. Commissariat contractors were imprisoned for shortcomings, including one who insisted that it was impossible to provide five hundred tunics for one rupee each. A public offices writer, Williams, was found still in hiding, and executed, and the head of young Mr Duncan, son of the hotel's owner, was brought to his father's house for a reward of ten rupees.

Time, so recently on the side of Nana Sahib, was beginning to run out. There would soon be thousands of cavalrymen, sepoys and hangers-on demanding their promised pay, but there was something else. Incredibly, a British relief force was reported to have reached Allahabad, 125 miles away, commanded by a man named Neill. The confident calculations of Azimullah Khan, who had sworn that the British were running for their ships in Calcutta and Bombay, had been utterly false. There were even stories of warships entering the Hooghly river, including the line-of-battle ship *Sanspareil*, with four decks of guns. Fortunately the Ganges was too low for anything other than small native boats, and it was still beyond belief that an overland relief force could reach Cawnpore soon enough, or in sufficient strength, to cause Nana Sahib embarrassment, but he could not be sure. His plans had not allowed for a prolonged resistance by Wheeler Sahib's pitiful little mud-walled entrenchment. It was sickeningly frustrating.

Perhaps most worrying was the fact that Nana Sahib's position as exclusive leader was beginning to be challenged. The Meer Nawab, a distinguished Oudh Moslem, had arrived from the east with two thousand infantry of the Nadiri and Akhtari regiments and a full battery of artillery. The new arrivals were a mixed blessing; Nana did not want a rival.

The Oudh troops swaggered in droves to the *maidan* to laugh and spit in the direction of the *Lal Koorti Ka Haspital*. They did not hide their contempt for the generalship of Nana

Sahib or the fighting ability of his army. 'Is this the mighty fortress that defies the *Lal Pultan*, the red regiments, of *Jan Kompanie*? Are these not the brave sepoys who abused us because we are not real soldiers, only Oudh locals? See, with no Sahibs to lead them, they are only sheep that bleat, pretending to be tigers, but running in terror when a dog barks.' Tomorrow, they promised – when they had rested and eaten – the Oudh regiments would storm the *Lal Koorti Ka Haspital*. Tomorrow it would be finished, and then they would see who should be Rajah in Cawnpore.

Next morning, 18 June, two thousand Oudh infantry exploded into the *maidan* and swarmed towards the Dragoon Hospital. The whistles of the Main Guard shrieked, and infantrymen, gunners, clerks, railwaymen and shopkeepers snatched up guns and ran for their posts, but many failed to reach the wall before the leading mutineers spilled over it into the entrenchment. For several moments it seemed that the *sangar* had been taken. Behind the leading mutineers surged a sea of gesticulating, shouting Indians, eager to kill.

The redan, commanded by Major Vibart, was overrun, his little force of Queen's soldiers firing, stabbing and slashing as they were swept back. A gun of Dempster's battery was overturned and one of the two field magazines was surrounded. The men of Ashe's battery, however, with hand-spikes and torn fingers, were clawing around one of their 9-pounders, double-loaded with grapeshot. Ashe, crying with rage, flung himself over the trail, and the gun roared.

Grapeshot and canister were seldom employed at ranges of more then 300 yards, but at distances of less the effect on a massed enemy was brutally devastating. Taken in enfilade, the jostling Oudh infantry were torn down in their scores by a shrieking hurricane of packed musket-balls, each penetrating two, and sometimes three men. Suddenly there was an empty avenue between the *sangar* and the horde of following mutineers. The swarming assault, only seconds earlier seeming irresistible, stumbled to a shocked halt, and the mutineers already over the *sangar* were cut off. They died quickly as the savage professionals of the 32nd and 84th demanded payment

– a 'Cawnpore pudding'; a bayonet thrust into the abdomen and ripped upward, then a brown face stamped into the ground by a steel-shod boot.

Ashe's cursing gun-crew were reloading like madmen, spongeing, ramming, and Ashe was crouched over the vent, his face powder-blackened, but Meer Nawab's men from Oudh had taken enough. When the 9-pounder belched again, it clawed only at the retreating, scattering backs of a terrified mob. On the *maidan*'s edge the sepoys jeered. '*Jeldee, kubbadar!* Make way for the brave ones! Ah, what a story they will have to tell to their sons and grandsons! What men! What warriors! Who now are running like sheep when a dog barks?'

Nana Sahib was not displeased at the discomfiture of the Meer Nawab's regiments, but the *Lal Koorti Ka Haspital* still defied him. If the British could not be overcome by force, then perhaps they could by stealth.

In the Main Guard's shelter, Lieutenant Armstrong, Adjutant of the 53rd, was experiencing the nausea and diarrhoea that could mean the approach of cholera, or it could be merely the result of foul food. During the last few days, rations had included dog-meat, and a broth boiled from the head of an old troop-horse shot by Mowbray Thompson's men in Barrack Number 2. Thompson had just crawled in from his outpost, and with Lieutenant Prole was crouched under the ragged canvas-and-bamboo canopy when a musket ball struck Prole in the groin, and he fell with an obscenity.

Mowbray Thompson raised him, pulled an arm over his shoulder, and began the hazardous forty yards across the entrenchment to the nearest hospital building, where a surgeon might be found. He had taken only a dozen stumbling paces when a second ball tore into his right shoulder, and both fell together in a tangled heap. Several soldiers scrambled to drag the officers to cover, and Lieutenant Gilbert Bax, leaning over the prostrate Thompson with a few wry words of condolence, was silenced by a bullet in the back.

Amelia gently squeezed a soaked rag against the lips of a wounded man, and then realized that the red-rimmed eyes and blistered, unshaven face were those of Captain Mowbray Thompson. Instinctively, she lifted a hand to her hair, ashamed of what he might be seeing, but his scab-crusted lips broke upwards into a grin. 'Miss Horne? By hokey, it's wonderful to see you. We haven't met since Sir George Parker's garden party – remember?'

Amelia blushed under her dirt. She remembered. A native magician had placed her garnet brooch under a cup and turned it into an egg, then broke the egg to release a live chick. And she remembered Mowbray Thompson in his immaculate mess scarlet, his fine red side-whiskers smoothed with pomade and his white-gloved hand on her waist as they waltzed to the music of the 53rd Infantry's band. And there had been Henry Delafosse, and Freddie Burney who lisped, and Captain Athill Turner who had no eyes except for the glorious Miss Yeates—

'Captain Thompson,' she smiled. 'I trust you are well?' It was a stupid question to ask of a man with a .75-calibre ball in his shoulder. She swallowed. 'I'm sorry – I mean—'

'I'm alive, at least,' he nodded. In fact, he felt damn ill, with a desperate need to retch. He did, and she reached for her precious water bottle, but he shook his head. 'No, Miss Horne – thanks. Never touch the stuff, y'know, except for shaving. If you have a whisky-soda, now, or a champagne fizz—?' He tried to grin again, but vomit filled his throat, and she took his hot face against her until he had finished, and lay back exhausted. 'Miss Horne – I am sorry—' He paused, breathing deeply but amused still. 'Can we both stop being sorry and talk about something else? That wet rag tastes delicious, Miss Horne. What is it?'

'I tore it off my—' Amelia stopped, then laughed for the first time for several weeks. 'The question is indelicate, Captain Thompson.' She rolled an old camel blanket to place under his head, then smeared his broken lips with the last scraping from her jar of Muller's Cold Cream of Roses. 'This,' said Mowbray Thompson, 'is worth being shot for. When this business is over, Miss Horne, I shall buy the Europe Shop's entire stock of cold cream – rose, lavender, honey and flowers – and have it delivered to you in several bullock *tongas*. Never again will you stand in need of cold cream, Miss Horne. You have my word as an officer and a gentleman.'

'This "business", Captain Thompson—' Amelia hesitated. 'When will it end? When will the relief force get here?'

It was Thompson's turn to hesitate. He had disciplined himself to think no further than today. Speculation only bred hopes, and dashed hopes could tear morale to shreds quicker than anything else. People were capable of enduring incredible hardship and deprivation for long periods without complaint, but the disappearance of a treasured anticipation would make them whimpering animals in seconds. Still: 'There *is* something,' he said slowly. 'A native came into the lines yesterday – a *bhistie* – from the Oudh side. He said that two companies of European troops, probably the 84th's, had marched from Lucknow with several guns, and had reached the river. They intended crossing today.'

'Today!' Amelia's eyes widened. 'You mean we shall be relieved *today*?' The prospect was so exhilarating that she barely stifled a scream of delight.

Thompson raised his good arm to put a finger to his lips. 'No, Miss Horne. We don't know yet. In any case, two companies couldn't relieve our situation, although they'd be a welcome reinforcement. And it's provisions and ammunition we need as badly as more men. The *bhistie* went out again with a message, then came back at dawn today. He said that the European force had been delayed by an unexpected flood, but they were building rafts, and expected to reach us within forty-eight hours.' He paused thoughtfully. 'Now the native has gone out again.'

The lack of enthusiasm in Thompson's tone was a warning. 'You really don't believe it,' Amelia said, and the excitement within her drained.

Mowbray Thompson shrugged and winced. 'Whoever heard of a flood in the dry season? The Ganges hasn't been lower for months, Miss Horne. Besides, if one native knows about our infantry and guns crossing the river, so does Nana Sahib and a lot of others, but there's no sign of movement to meet any threat, nor any gunfire from that direction, and by now we'd expect a few more natives to be currying favour by bringing in information. The word of one miserable *bhistie* isn't enough.'

'So it's not true.' Amelia's voice was flat. 'But why did the man say so?'

'It's my guess that he was sent by Nana Sahib, Miss Horne. I'd say the Nana is getting a little worried. It's possible he *knows* of a relief force approaching from Allahabad, and he needs to finish with us before it arrives. He calculates that, if we were convinced of a European force only a mile away, fighting to reach us, we might abandon the entrenchment in an attempt to join with it. Then we'd be caught nicely in the open.' He shook his head. 'Captain Moore has persuaded General Wheeler to sit tight, and we don't move an inch until we see red coatees, kilts, or rifle green right there on the *maidan*.'

The *bhistie* did not return for the second time, and there were no European troops on the opposite bank of the Ganges. Nana Sahib's ruse was hardly likely to have succeeded but, if nothing else, his agent could provide a detailed description of the entrenchment's impoverished condition.

As Captain Moore had dreaded, the mutineers' mortars began to fire incendiary carcasses. A single burning missile lodged itself in the tinder-dry thatch of the hospital building, which in seconds was aflame. Inside, among dense smoke and falling, incandescent brands of roofing straw, there was terror-crazed confusion as women and men snatched up children or dragged the helpless wounded to a door or window, only to find that all enemy field guns and hundreds of muskets were pouring a concentrated fire on the blazing target. With neither pumps nor water, the flames were completely uncontrollable. Rafters collapsed, bringing down masonry. Amelia's smaller sister, Florence, screeched as a wall leaned, bulged, and then fell. Amelia clawed at her, but Florence's trapped leg was fractured. A woman crawled with a foot severed, men with amputated stumps of arms or legs cried as they were flung from the verandah. Old Subedar-Major Bhowani Singh died in the smoke, his white beard burning and his musket still clutched to his chest.

Few of the men at the *sangar* could leave their posts. Hundreds of jubilant sepoys were congregating on the edge of the *maidan*, and Ashe's battery was already hurling grapeshot to discourage any attempt at a general assault. John Cook's family, with many others, huddled to the ground as, yards away, the hospital building burned to a charred ruin. In addition to Florence's injury, both Amelia and her mother bled from head wounds, and now there was no protection against the sun. It was four days before the crumpled shell of the hospital cooled sufficiently for it to be re-entered. Everything within had been utterly destroyed, including medical instruments, medicines and dressings, and men of the 32nd raked among the ashes with their bayonets, searching for the blackened discs of their Punjab campaign medals.

There was little, now, that the surgeons could do for the wounded and sick. Bullets could not be extracted or amputations performed. There were no narcotics or quinine. Burns and mutilations quickly became putrescent, blackening and foul-smelling, crawling with flies. Men demented with pain tossed and swore, craving for water that was not available, and it seemed impossible that misery could be more intense. Dear God, Amelia prayed, was it right that human beings should have to endure so much? Was there to be no end to this nightmare?

And for some the nightmare had become beyond toleration. If they could only escape from the entrenchment dressed as natives, if they could only get past the mutineers' picquets and avoid using the Grand Trunk Road, it might be possible to reach the safety of Allahabad. It was worth trying. Anything was better than remaining in the Dragoon Hospital.

Several families joined forces in requesting permission of General Wheeler to leave, but Moore was angrily opposed. 'They can never succeed, sir. Even Blenman failed.' Blenman, a Eurasian, had attempted to penetrate the enemy outposts disguised as a *khansamah*, a native cook, and had passed seven cavalry picquets before being halted by the eighth. 'Blenman, is naturally dark-skinned and he speaks colloquial Hindi, but he failed. These people, with no language worth mentioning, think they can disguise themselves as natives and pass through 125 miles of hostile country? They'll never manage it, sir. They'll not get a mile.'

Wheeler lifted his tired eyes to Moore. This time he would make a decision, good or bad. He must regain touch. He must participate. 'I am sure you are right, Mr Moore, but they must surely be aware of the hazards. If they are determined to do this thing, then I do not see that we have the right to forbid them. They are civilians. They are entitled to our protection, but are also entitled to refuse it.' It sounded logical.

Moore controlled his impatience. 'I submit, sir, that under the circumstances they are subject to military law, and what they want is little better than desertion. But that's not the point. Do they really believe, in their condition, that they can walk 125 miles? Or do they think there'll be *dâk gharries* or horses for hire, and travellers' bungalows every night? And when they're caught – as they will be – they can only expect to pay with their lives.'

The General nodded. Moore, of course, was right. He wished the younger man had supported the civilians' request to leave, so that he, Wheeler, could take the more sensible view and refuse. 'If they wish to gamble with their own lives, Mr Moore, that is their own affair. And if we refuse, there is little to stop them leaving the entrenchment after dark. We must give them rations and water, and assist their departure as best we can.'

The three civilians and their wives left the entrenchment as the afternoon was cooling. The women were dressed as Indian *ayahs*, with their heads covered by cotton *chudders*, the men shabbily clothed as *bhisties*, carrying water-skins. They hurried, stooped, across the *maidan*, feigning a frightened escape as several soldiers at the *sangar* fired blank shots in their wake. Moore followed them with his bi-oculars. He could see curious sepoys strolling forward, closing around the group of fugitives and gesticulating. Seconds passed, then a commotion as a concealing drape was wrenched from a woman's head and a water-skin flung to the ground. Muskets were levelled, and the six, surrounded, were herded out of sight in the direction of the *Savada Kothi*.

15

By the end of the third week the last flicker of hope had almost died. In the pitiless, pounding heat of day the men lay behind the mud wall, their faces obscenely raw and scab-covered, clothing sweat-rotted and stinking. They rarely stirred, their bloodshot, slitted eyes on the hazed *maidan* where jackals and pariah dogs roamed, snarling at each other, and vultures floated to earth and sat ghoulishly. Eastward, beyond the brown plain, beyond the hidden river, a mirage shimmered above the horizon, of green forests, hills, and glassy water, but the men had seen such things often. They listened still for the sound of artillery fire more distant than that of the mutineers' batteries, or the faint rattle of ordered musketry, the whine of bagpipes or the faint teeter of a cavalry bugle. But they had listened for three weeks, and there had been nothing.

More than half of the surviving fighting men were wounded, including Colonel Ewart of the 1st Native Infantry and Major Hillersdon of the 53rd. The Major's brother, the Collector, was dead after being disembowelled by a round-shot, but Mowbray Thompson, with his shoulder strapped, was back in Barrack Number 2. Major Lindsay of the 56th had been blinded by shell splinters, but was now dead, as was Heberden, the senior railway engineer, after a shot had passed through both hips. Henry Delafosse had hands and arms cinder-black and shredding after tearing to pieces a burning gun-caisson that might have blown to pieces half the Main Guard, while John Moore, although miraculously unharmed, was an emaciated parody of a man, sometimes incapable of coherent speech, but still in command and making it very plain that he was.

The ruined hospital buildings and the trenches screened by tattered canvas were flooded with a nauseating stench, of human excreta and putrefaction. There was little movement, little sound except the hum of flies and the occasional weak wail of an infant. Women and men slumped dejectedly with haggard faces expressionless. Hair once silkily brushed and curled daily by a house *ayah* now hung tangled and matted, hands and nails were begrimed. Men were unkempt and unshaven; all had skins leprously blotched and peeling, and wounds were wrapped in filthy rags.

It was 9 a.m., and among the rubble of Barrack Number 2 Sergeant Grady pulled himself to his knees. 'It's bleedin' quiet all of a sudden, ain't it? Why's the blacks stopped soddin' shooting?' He shaded his eyes with a hand, and then turned urgently. 'Captain Thompson, sir! There's someone approaching from the blacks' lines – a woman!'

Mowbray Thompson scrambled to the barricade. 'Hold your fire!' It was, as Grady said, a woman, and she was European. Without shoes or stockings, she carried a small child, and she sobbed as she stumbled towards the curious soldiers behind the barrack loopholes. Several men reached out for her, lifted her to safety, and she sank to the ground hysterically weeping.

Thompson knelt, uncorking a water-bottle as Grady took the child. 'Gawd strewth,' said the Sergeant, 'it's Mrs Jacobi – Henry Jacobi's lady. You know, sir – the watchmaker in the *Chandni Chauk*. We all thought they was dead.'

The woman lifted her face. 'I have a letter from the Rajah of Bithur for General Wheeler, and I must go back with an answer. I must go back. My children are in the *Savada Kothi*—'

Three weeks before, when most Europeans in Cawnpore had taken refuge in the Dragoon Hospital, the watchmaker Henry Jacobi and his family had chosen to seek safety in Lucknow, fifty miles distant. They had crossed the Ganges just before the bridge of boats had been destroyed, but the following day, in Oudh territory, they were taken by mutineers and dragged back to Duncan's Hotel in Cawnpore. On arrival, Mr Jacobi, who had been carried on a *charpoy*, was found to be dead from heat apoplexy. His distraught wife had reviled the Nana in terms shockingly unbefitting a mem-Sahib, and she must have been very near death at that moment, but for reasons known only to Nana Sahib she and her children were herded to the

Savada Kothi and then, for the moment, apparently forgotten.

When Mrs Jacobi reached the *Savada Kothi* hostelry she found that another family had already been detained there. These were Mr Edward Greenway, an Englishman of considerable property and wealth, with his wife, sister, and several children. The Greenways, suggested Azimullah Khan, were too valuable to be immediately killed, and Nana Sahib agreed. He had fixed their ransom at forty thousand pounds, and was debating how a bill of exchange, authorized by Edward Greenway, could be presented to a Calcutta bank for payment.

By the third week in June the Nana's situation was bordering on the critical. His Moslem rival, the Meer Nawab, who paid his followers, was growing in popularity and influence, holding court in the racquets enclosure, attended upon by an increasing number of troopers of the 2nd Cavalry who, in turn, were joined by the public woman, Azezun. Nana Sahib's own sepoys were complaining. They wanted their pay and they wanted to march for Delhi; meanwhile they would not face the guns of the *Lal Koorti Ka Haspital* again. General Teka Singh was under arrest in his tent, charged with accumulating a private store of looted treasure.

There was further news, too, from the eastward. The stories that the Sikhs had told, that the sepoys had derided, were not exaggerated. Colonel Neill had taken Allahabad and its fort, and with only 140 men had routed the 6th Native Infantry. Neill had sworn to stuff Nana Sahib with cow fat and then roast him alive over a slow fire, and the Nana wished to allow no opportunity for the threat to be realized. He had to finish with the *Lal Koorti Ka Haspital* within the next forty-eight hours, or abandon it.

The daily fare of chupatties and water, although meagre, was probably better than that in the besieged Dragoon Hospital, but Mrs Jacobi had lost all her clothes except those she wore, and her earrings had been wrenched from the lobes of her ears.

On the evening of Tuesday, 23 June, Azimullah Khan and the sycophantic Jwala Pershad, from Bithur – now a brigadier-general – were admitted to Mrs Jacobi's room. For a few moments she thought they had come to kill her. She had been chosen, Azimullah said, to convey a message to Wheeler Sahib, and if she valued the lives of her children she would agree. Mrs Jacobi agreed. Next day she was interviewed by Nana Sahib himself.

The Nana had lost a little weight during the previous few weeks, but he could still be described as a fleshy man. Thick eyebrows, a small, delicately-groomed moustache, and a pale, pock-marked skin contributed to a face that lacked noteworthy features and might have been that of any prosperous corn-merchant or money-lender. His brief instructions to Mrs Jacobi were interpreted by Azimullah Khan, and she refrained from mentioning that she spoke and understood Hindi.

Tomorrow, she was told, she would carry the Nana's letter to Sir Hugh Wheeler, but her two older children would remain in the *Savada Kothi*. She would return with Wheeler Sahib's answer. If she did not, her children would be killed before the sun set.

The two men conversed in Hindi, ignoring her presence. There was talk of Colonel Neill and Allahabad, and references to the time required for a European relief force to march 125 miles. The killing, said Nana Sahib, must be done quickly, and none must be allowed to escape. It would be done at the *Suttee Chowra Ghat*, as they climbed into the boats.

'In England, Highness,' said Azimullah Khan, never missing an opportunity to air his knowledge, 'the *ayahs* tell the children stories of demons and giants, and there is one giant – a *Kumbhakarma* – who says, "Fee, fi, fo, fum, I smell the blood of an Englishman! Be he alive, or be he dead, I'll grind his bones to make my bread!"' Nana Sahib laughed.

When Mrs Jacobi brought the letter to the *Lal Koorti Ka Haspital* she was aware of the capture of Allahabad, of Neill's intended advance, and she knew that the letter was the prelude to an act of barbaric treachery. But Mrs Jacobi mentioned none of these things. She held her peace. Her children were in the *Savada Kothi*, and she must go back. . . .

The letter, written by Azimullah Khan, was addressed 'To the subjects of Her Most Gracious Majesty Queen Victoria'. Its text was brief. 'All those who are in no way connected with the acts of Lord Dalhousie and are willing to lay down their arms, shall receive a safe passage to Allahabad.'

A council of war, comprising General Wheeler, Captain Moore, and Captain Frank Whiting of the Bengal Engineers discussed the note's implications. To Wheeler the thought of surrendering to his own sepoys was anathema, particularly after the losses suffered by the Europeans in the entrenchment, including his own son. Had these lives been lost for nothing? His choice of a defensive position had been bad, as every day of the past three weeks had proved, but he would prefer to remain in it, to justify it, if there remained the faintest hope of survival. He was an old man, with a life expectancy to be measured in months rather than years. Was it worth marring his not discreditable military career with the indelible blot of a surrender?

'Mr Moore,' the General requested, 'I should like your report on our situation, if you please, with a view to our continued defence.'

'Yes, sir,' Moore nodded. Malnutrition, lack of sleep, and the hourly punishment of the siege had almost broken him. Almost, but not quite. For three weeks he had walked almost alone. A few had supported him whole-heartedly, but there had been some, the resentful senior officers, who had been content to stand back and watch.

'We have ample stocks of powder,' he reported, 'but no nine-pound shot. Six-pound shot is running short, but adequate for a further week, and even better stocks of small-arms ball. That's the best of it.' He paused. 'Food supplies are reduced to two pints of cattle grain for each person – three days' rations at most. There are no medical stores. I estimate we have imposed one thousand casualties on the mutineers. We have buried two hundred and fifty of our own people.' It was a statement of fact.

Wheeler turned his head. 'You agree, Mr Whiting?'

'Yes, sir. We know that we can expect no help from Lucknow. Sir Henry Lawrence is closely contained and must look to his own defence.' He hesitated. 'Any further resistance on our part will be justified only if a relief force is *at this moment* within three or four days' march of Cawnpore – and that means fifty miles. If any troops were that close, sir, we would surely have received some intelligence.'

'If that is the situation, gentlemen,' Wheeler countered, 'then why is Nana Sahib offering terms? He has sufficient knowledge of our circumstances to predict that our resistance will be ended by starvation within a few days. He has only to wait. Can it be that he *does* know of an approaching relief force?'

Moore reluctantly disagreed. 'There are several possible reasons for the Nana's offer, sir. He may be having troubles of his own – dissension among the sepoys and irregulars, commissariat difficulties, demands for pay, desertions. If the sepoys have mutinied once, they're capable of doing so again. Unfortunately we cannot wait to find out. And another thing, sir. The rains are almost upon us.'

The General frowned. 'Possibly. Ten days – fourteen?'

'They could start earlier, sir. If they do, the mud *sangar* will be washed away and the trenches flooded in minutes. The hospital buildings, in their shaken state, wouldn't last much longer. It will be impossible to keep our powder stocks dry, and with the wounded and sick—' He halted, eyes narrow. 'Sir, we couldn't face the rains in the Dragoon Hospital.'

There was a long pause. Beyond the verandah it was strangely quiet; the sepoys' batteries had not fired since dawn, and Cawnpore, from a distance, seemed deserted and dead. The heat was oven-like and energy-draining, scorching the lungs with every in-drawn breath, the sun blinding to eyes raised skyward. There was not the slightest breeze to stir the dusty trees surrounding the church.

General Wheeler roused himself. 'Can we trust Nana Sahib?'

'No.' Both Moore and Whiting spoke simultaneously, but Moore continued. 'No, sir. And if we had any choice – the *slightest* choice – I'd recommend it. If this were a wholly military situation I'd throw everything into a break-out, carrying our wounded. Some of us might get through. But with four or five hundred women, children, and infirm – and no provisions, transport or medicines—' He choked. 'Godammit, sir – there's *no* bloody choice!' Moore drew a deep breath, then probed at blistered lips with his tongue. 'There's something in our favour, sir. Our numbers. There's eight – nine hundred of us. We're not just some indigo-planter's family, or a few regimental officers. We're *eight hundred people*, sir, and this is 1857, not the Dark Ages. What can Nana Sahib do to us? His note offers a safe passage to Allahabad, but if he does play us false he can only put us in leg-chains, work us on the roads, humiliate us, or perhaps march us to Delhi to give the blacks a Roman holiday – but he can't kill *all* of us, can he?'

Mrs Jacobi had been questioned lengthily on the situation in the sepoys' lines and the reasons behind Nana Sahib's offer, but she had little information to give, pleading that she had been confined in the *Savada Kothi* and knew nothing of events outside. She exhibited an increasing anxiety to return to her children in Cawnpore, and in the late afternoon she was allowed to go, carrying an answer to Nana Sahib's letter. Major-General Sir Hugh Wheeler, in company with his senior officers, was studying the purport of the Nana Sahib's communication of 24 June. The Nana Sahib or his representatives were requested to meet the representatives of General Wheeler at a mean point on the *maidan* at 9.30 a.m. on the morrow, to discuss the possibility of an evacuation under arms of the Dragoon Hospital.

The news that the three weeks' siege might be ended had spread through the entrenchment within minutes, but initial elation was dampened by doubt. There were many officers and ladies who had earlier enjoyed Nana Sahib's hospitality and apparent friendship, who had loudly agreed that he was a 'good type' even if he was only Indian – who were subsequently incensed at being hoodwinked, and equally loudly claimed that they had, of course, always suspected something sinister about the Rajah, and they had anecdotes to prove it. Natives could never really be judged by European standards; they came, after all, from a different branch of the human species.

'Can he really be trusted, Mr Delafosse?' Amelia asked. With dozens of others she had come to the wall to watch for the appearance of Nana Sahib's deputation. The sepoys' guns were still silent, and many people were emerging cautiously to walk in the open. At the well stood a long queue with buckets, kettles and bottles.

Henry Delafosse's voice rang with a jovial confidence that he did not feel. 'In twelve or fourteen days you'll be in Allahabad, Miss Horne. Just think of it – I'm going to spend the whole of the first day lying in a bath, just eating and drinking. Then I'm going to sleep for a week. Then, for another week, I'm going to apply myself to doing *nothing* – more seriously than anyone's done before, except for eating and drinking, of course. I shall grow obese. Do you know Allahabad, Miss Horne? No? It's a smaller version of Calcutta, y'know, and a lot greener than Cawnpore. They have ice, now, with the railway. Just think, Miss Horne. Strawberry water-ice, smoked salmon, grouse with buttered parsnips, lamb chops so tender that they positively melt in the mouth, with mint sauce, but no peas. I swear I'll never eat another pea for the rest of my life. And Stilton with port—' Goddam, he wasn't sure about Nana Sahib. He wasn't sure at all.

'There they are!' There was an excited murmur, and officers' bi-oculars were raised, directed towards the sepoy positions beyond the barrack-houses. 'Azimullah Khan and Jwala Pershad,' Henry Delafosse said, 'with an escort.' Two hundred yards from the entrenchment the group of mutineers halted. A hundred fingers crooked around triggers, and the sights of Lieutenant Stirling's carbine were precisely aligned on the centre of Azimullah's chest, but nobody fired.

From the entrenchment marched Moore, Whiting, and John Roach, the Postmaster. As they approached, Azimullah Khan smiled, inclining his face over his hands. 'Ah, Captain Moore! I am indeed glad that you are safe. And Captain Whiting, of course, and Mr Roach also? God has been merciful. General Wheeler, I trust, is in good health? We have thought sadly for him.'

'That,' Moore snapped, 'we can imagine.'

Azimullah shrugged apologetically. 'Ah, my dear Captain Moore – please, you must not allow bitterness to spoil our meeting. Did not Shakespeare say, "To mourn a mischief that is past and gone, is the next way to draw new mischief on"? It has been a cruel experience for the distinguished General but, see, we are here to promise that no further harm shall threaten that old white head, to offer your people a truce and a safe passage in exchange for the evacuation of the *Lal Koorti Ka Haspital* and the surrender of your artillery.'

Moore's face was expressionless. 'The Nana Sahib's proposal has been considered, and will be accepted under certain conditions. I have those conditions written here, and they are required to be agreed and signed by the Nana Sahib.' He drew a folded paper from a pocket of his creased tunic. Azimullah Khan nodded, smiling again, and Moore read aloud.

'The entire garrison will be permitted a free exit from the Dragoon Hospital, each man under arms and with sixty rounds of ammunition. Carriages are to be provided for the conveyance of wounded, women and children. An adequate number of boats, with crews, shall be ready at the *Suttee Chowra Ghat*, and the boats shall be provisioned with sufficient flour for a twelve-days' passage to Allahabad. Our people will be allowed to board and proceed down-river without interference, and to ensure this will be accompanied by hostages of rank.'

There was a moment of silence, and then Azimullah Khan answered. 'Those appear to be perfectly reasonable conditions, Captain Moore, and I am sure the Maharajah will agree.' From his side, Jwala Pershad added, 'And we will give your people sheep and goats also.' Behind the two principals the throng of others murmured approval, nodding amicably and clapping their hands quietly.

Moore was puzzled. With Whiting and Roach he shared General Wheeler's authority to negotiate and finalize the terms of evacuation. He had expected an hour of bitter wrangling under the hot sun of the *maidan*, and he had damn little collateral with which to bolster his demands. Moore had never known either Hindu or Moslem to acquiesce so easily. He glanced enquiringly at Whiting and Roach, not wishing to betray the slightest uncertainty in his gaze, but they, similarly taken aback, could only hold their faces rigid, eyes stony.

'Then it is agreed, gentlemen,' Azimullah Khan beamed.

'Your terms I shall present to the Maharajah within the hour, and you have my word that I shall do everything possible to persuade him to accept and sign them. The welfare of your people, Captain Moore, is uppermost in my heart. Your ladies and gentlemen may walk freely; they will not be fired upon. Perhaps you will watch for our messenger, who will bring our answer to you this afternoon.' He bowed over his hands. 'Peace on earth, goodwill to all men.'

Regaining the entrenchment, Moore, Whiting and Roach were surrounded by anxious associates. 'What's going to happen, Frank?' Delafosse asked. 'Is it a go?'

Whiting, doubtful, rubbed an unshaven chin. 'I'll be hanged if I know, Harry. John Moore read out our conditions, Azimullah took 'em without blinking, and that was all. It was just too bloody easy.'

It was just too bloody easy, as Moore conveyed to General Wheeler. John Moore had a feeling in his lower belly that had nothing to do with lack of food and bad water. He had been in India for a shorter period than almost all of his John Company colleagues, and had not yet achieved an understanding of these festerin' Orientals.

'There's something about it that smells,' he said, 'but I'll be damned if I can see what can go wrong, assuming Nana Sahib ratifies the terms. If he does, then we'll insist that a couple of officers go to the *Suttee Chowra Ghat* to check on the boats and provisions. The boats *must* be thatched; our sick and wounded will never survive 120 miles otherwise. A lot of 'em won't anyway, blast it.' He sucked in his breath. 'If the Nana has a trick up his sleeve, he can't just kill eight hundred Europeans in cold blood, can he? No.' He shook his head. 'No. It's inconceivable.'

At 2 p.m. the entrenchment was approached by a mounted trooper of the 2nd Cavalry. The message from Nana Sahib was brief. General Wheeler's terms were accepted, but the *Lal Koorti Ka Haspital* must be evacuated, and its guns surrendered, before dusk.

'That's damn impossible, and he knows it!' Whiting exploded. 'How in Hell's name can we prepare all our people, with our sick and wounded, for a twelve-days' journey, convey them a mile to the river, and get them into the boats – which we haven't seen – before dusk?'

Moore agreed. 'It's not on. And you're right, Frank – the Nana knows it. What's he up to, I wonder?' The 200 yards of Wheeler's entrenchment stretched dustily around him. Despite the truce, there was now almost no movement. Hundreds of emaciated, heat-tortured people crouched in scraps of shade, waiting, with only their aching eyes watching for some sign from him that their days of bitter siege were really over. A dozen would die today, he knew, and twenty tomorrow—

He had so little time with which to gamble, so few resources with which to defy Nana Sahib's demand, but to comply would mean a mile of corpses between the Dragoon Hospital and the *Suttee Chowra Ghat* – and Nana Sahib could claim that he had not been responsible. 'It can't be done,' John Moore repeated. 'We will surrender our guns at dusk, but we will evacuate the entrenchment at dawn tomorrow – other conditions prevailing. In the meantime our officers will inspect the boats and provisions. And that is final.' By God, he hoped he was right. He prayed he was right.

An hour later the native cavalryman returned, to be met by Frank Whiting and Mowbray Thompson. The trooper was truculent, neither saluting nor bothering to dismount. The Maharajah, he retorted, would concede nothing. The Sahibs must evacuate the *Lal Koorti Ka Haspital* by dusk today. If they did not, the batteries would re-open fire and continue until every ramshackle building was levelled to the ground. Nobody would be left alive. His Highness knew exactly how impoverished the Europeans' circumstances were. They had nothing left with which to bargain. They would abandon their pitiful defences before dusk, or they would die in them.

Frank Whiting did not take kindly to being sneered at by a native *sowar* from the height of his saddle. He lost his temper. 'You can go back,' he snarled, 'and tell his fat Highness, Sereek Dhondha Punth – or whatever his name was when he hawked betel-leaf in Poona – that if he wants the *Lal Koorti Ka Haspital* he can come and take it. If he knows our circumstances, then he'll also know that we still have enough powder to blow to pieces every damn thing on this side of the Ganges, and that's just what'll happen, tell him, when the first rot-gutting sepoy sets foot inside this entrenchment!'

The cavalryman was startled. He spat, then turned his horse.

Mowbray Thompson was thoughtful. 'Do you think that was wise, Frank?'

'No, I don't. It was a bloody fool thing to say, but it's too damn late now.' He heaved a breath. 'Still, you never know. If the Nana's bluffing, it might just do the trick. I hope so, b'God.'

When Nana Sahib's emissary made his third appearance he was less surly. The Maharajah, who had every desire to be reasonable, conceded the Europeans' conditions in full, and would give his signature to them. The boats, of which twenty-four had been promised by local contractors, could be boarded tomorrow morning. Ample supplies would be loaded, and he suggested that the Europeans should breakfast and dine on board, then start for Allahabad in the cool of the evening. He regretted that there would be insufficient accommodation for native servants. Elephants and an escort would convey a party of officers to the *Suttee Chowra Ghat* to inspect arrangements.

It was really true. It was finished, Amelia thought. The Cook family had all survived so far, and it needed only another two weeks for them to be finally safe. Emma Cook had emerged from her fever weak and wan, and on the brink of childbirth, but lucid and uncomplaining. She could stand and walk shakily – and little Florence had a broken leg – but there would be transport to the river tomorrow.

And then cool sheets scented with lavender, pomade, tooth powder, perfumed soap, cologne, curling cream, and Captain Mowbray Thompson, and Lieutenants Delafosse and St George Ashe—

All remaining rations were shared, the bottoms of casks scraped of rock-hard residues of rice and lentils, the seams of sacks combed for dustings of yellowing flour, and the kettles were steaming with the last paltry meal to be eaten in the entrenchment. A soldier produced a battered flute, another pummelled an overturned tub, and children skipped a jig to unrecognizable music. Everywhere people were scratching in the earth to retrieve modest treasures earlier buried – lockets, brooches, watches, rings, letters and money. Others, less confident, were burying their valuables more deeply, carefully memorizing the spot for an expected later return – for there *would be a return,* they vowed, supported by British infantry, horse and artillery, and there would be a gallows where the Dragoon Hospital now stood, hanging fifty sepoys every hour, seven hundred a day, with the corpses left on the *maidan* to be picked clean by scavengers. And there would be an even more satisfying spectacle – men being blown from the muzzles of guns, scattering crimson slubber for hundreds of yards. That would be worth waiting for, even if it was slower than hanging. Then, for a generation, every Cawnpore native would crawl on hands and knees when a European approached. In all, it was a prospect to be savoured. By God, there would be a return.

When the afternoon had cooled, Captain Athill Turner and Lieutenants Delafosse and Goad, accompanied by an escort of native cavalrymen, rode the mile to the *Suttee Chowra Ghat.* The troopers were conciliatory, almost apologetic. They regretted the deaths of their Sahib officers, Captain Jenkins and Lieutenant Harrison, who had been good men to the Ridgement. Everything had been a mistake, the result of misunderstandings, but now it was all finished. Tomorrow the Sahibs could leave for Allahabad in safety. They swore it.

At the steps of the *ghat* the boats were moored. sterns to shore. They were dilapidated native river barges, fustily reeking from years of varied cargoes, of grain, rice, fish, mutton, but adequate for a last journey down-river, and their owners had little hope of seeing them again. They swarmed with conscripted coolies, plaiting thatched shelters, hammering repairs, or loading sacks of dry provisions. Throngs of sepoys lounged on the bank, sitting on their haunches or strolling, smoking, gossiping, and eyeing the three white officers from the corners of their eyes, then looking away and whispering. But everything seemed in order, as Nana Sahib had promised. There was nothing to dispute. The three men walked away, glad of an opportunity to stretch their legs after three weeks of confinement.

'Well, chaps,' Henry Delafosse said, 'that's it.' He pulled his watch from a shirt stiffened by weeks of dried sweat. 'This time tomorrow we'll be damn near home and dry.'

Athill Turner was silent, gazing across the river, where village smoke from cow-dung fires hazed the far side. The river was low, moving slowly and floating with debris, the yellow, dried banks pock-marked by the hoof-prints of cattle. A few naked, golden-skinned infants splashed in the shallows, and their shouts came faintly on the heavy, still air of evening. A dog barked, and then another.

'Harry, you were never any good at bloody Hindi,' Athill Turner answered slowly. 'Did you hear what those sepoys were saying? No?' He paused. 'Of course, they might have been referring to the sheep and goats, but—' There was a far-away look in his eyes. 'It was "*kuttle*". And do you know what "*kuttle*" means, Harry? It means massacre!'

16

The dawn sun had barely streaked the eastern sky when people began to congregate hopefully in the vicinity of Lieutenant Ashe's battery. It was unusually chill, and a thin white mist clung to the surrounding *maidan*. Men, shirtless and with legs torn from breeches, women reduced to an almost indecent lack of clothes, shivered in the half light. There was water, but no food. The wounded and sick were being brought, with difficulty, from the hospital buildings, and a dozen people were grouped silently around the dry well that provided a tomb for two hundred and fifty corpses – men, women and infants. Sepoys and curious townspeople strolled outside the entrenchment, followed by the challenging eyes of the Main Guard.

Within an hour of first light the promised conveyances for

the sick and wounded were arriving at the north-western corner of the entrenchment – sixteen elephants, some seventy litters and a few bullock tongas, accompanied by still more sepoys and town natives curious to see how the Sahibs looked after three weeks of siege. No help was offered in handling the disabled, nor would the *mahouts* order their animals to kneel. Emma Cook, helped by Amelia, was one of dozens with no choice but the embarrassment and exhaustion of pulling themselves to an elephant's back by its tail, as the natives sniggered at the bared, struggling legs of dishevelled mem-Sahibs. The maimed, dragged and lifted by others who should themselves be in hospital cots, suffered excruciatingly. The natives jeered, and as the first detachment moved off towards the *Suttee Chowra Ghat*, the bolder loot-seekers began to snatch at valuables and trinkets, and women shrieked. One sepoy made the mistake of demanding Frank Whiting's rifle, then found its muzzle under his chin. 'You can have its contents, my little brown friend, but not the gun,' Whiting suggested, and the sepoy melted into the throng.

John Moore and thirty of his fittest men, with rifles loaded and bayonets fixed, trudged in the lead of the long, straggling column of Europeans. They were haggard, emaciated men, incredibly filthy and with skins blotched by sun sores. Several staggered as they marched, but their grim faces were sufficient to persuade the gloating natives to edge backwards. Nana Sahib had sent his own elephant for General Wheeler; the old officer declined the privilege, preferring a litter.

With people afoot, carts, litters and animals moving at different speeds, there was considerable confusion, with women losing sight of husbands and children sobbing for lost parents, but Moore halted on the *ghat*, waited to see the first of his people begin to board the nearest boats, then turned his men to march back to the entrenchment. With every minute he was growing more apprehensive. The swelling crowds were becoming more vociferously belligerent, and all the sepoys were armed. He could see no piled provisions in any of the boats, as Athill Turner had reported, but he had noticed the muzzles of a gun battery, covering the *ghat*, protruding from a careless curtain of chopped bamboo. He had the same gnawing gripe in his belly that he'd had yesterday. He snarled his men on, but they needed no urging. Christ, there was something wrong. The *maidan* teemed with natives – and his thirty flagging men could never hold off a horde of thousands.

The boats, all about thirty feet long by twelve, were moored with their sterns aground on the long, stone steps of the *ghat* – the Hindus' bathing place. The river was low, but they lay in several feet of water; there were no planks for boarding, and it was necessary for the Europeans to wade several yards to the boats' sides, struggling with children, wounded and sick as the crewmen watched from the decks. The hidden steps underfoot brought many crashing full length, to stumble upright again as the sepoys and town coolies roared with laughter. The flimsy apparel of the women clung to them wetly like translucent skins, so that bosoms, bellies and thighs were exposed almost as if naked. Charlotte Newman's magnificent breasts, that so many young officers had speculated upon, were revealed to all eyes as she scrabbled desperately, and Bella Blair's sodden shift rose to her waist as she was tugged bodily over a side. The crowds of watching natives hooted, and a few stones were being thrown.

Amelia, carrying Florence, had lost sight of her mother in the jostling confusion, but a search was impossible. Somehow she scrambled into a boat, grazing her knees painfully, but relieved to see that already under the stern awning were her stepfather, two sisters and two brothers, John Kirkpatrick, a Company clerk, and an Indian *ayah* who had evidently evaded the proscription on native servants. Amelia and Florence crouched on the foredeck, breathless, with two soldiers. John Cook shouted above the noisy discord. 'She's all right, Amy! She's in the next boat!' And, thank God, she could see her mother now, across thirty yards of water that threshed with a chaos of refugees. How soon could they leave this wretched *ghat*? Dear Lord – how soon?

John Moore and his men were shouting on the long caravan of bullock carts and litters that had now been segmented into a dozen shuffling groups interspersed by mobs of natives.

Thompson, Whiting, Turner, Delafosse, Ashe, Burney and Bolton were bringing up the rear, shepherding the slower moving. Behind them a horde of looters swarmed into the deserted entrenchment, to find only a few broken artillery pieces and eleven corpses laid on blankets.

In the mêlée, however, the European rearguard had failed to notice the wounded Colonel Ewart, in a litter carried by four coolies, and Mrs Ewart, compelled to walk, who had been late to depart for the river. The two were accompanied by a throng of the Colonel's own troopers of the 2nd Cavalry, who edged their horses uncomfortably close to the stumbling lady, laughing, until her prostrate husband slashed at them with his cane. The European rearguard, ahead, was gradually retreating from view and, when it had disappeared entirely, the troopers ordered the litter to be put down. They pressed around the helpless officer.

'Ah, Colonel Sahib! Is this not a fine parade? Why is the Colonel not on his fine horse with his sword and gold lace? Where is the mem-Sahib's silk shawl, and her little fan with the pearls? See, we are mustered, Colonel Sahib. Will you not shout your orders at us, and have us walking and trotting, and trotting out? Shall there be the Colonel's inspection today, with the Ridgement standing in the sun while the Sahibs sit in the shade, smoking cheroots and drinking whisky-sodas? *Huzoor*, Colonel Sahib!'

They drew their sabres and chopped at him savagely, until his head and face were crimson pulp, his hands severed, and the ground for yards drenched with blood that blackened in seconds.

Mrs Ewart, who for so many years had been the distinguished First Lady of the Regiment, saluted respectfully by all ranks, whose slightest frown could silence a loudly-talking subaltern or reduce a young wife to stuttering confusion, had stood unmoving and rigid. A Colonel's Lady did not sob or scream. They turned to her, panting from the exertion of the killing. 'We do not harm women, mem-Sahib. Give us your jewels, and you may go in safety.' She gave the nearest a small bundle tied in a kerchief, scarcely larger than a man's fist. 'I have no jewels, only a few toiletries.' The trooper snatched the bundle and tore it open impatiently. Mrs Ewart had spoken the truth. It contained only a small fragment of soap, a tiny square of damp linen, a comb and a few hairpins.

The trooper threw them down, angry at his comrades' laughter, then raised his sabre with both hands. 'I would not wish it otherwise,' Mrs Ewart said, unflinching.

It was almost 9 a.m., with the early mist dispersed and the sun warming, before Moore, Major Vibart, and the dozen officers of the rearguard were satisfied that they could do no more, that further delay would become increasingly hazardous, and began themselves to climb aboard the last boat which, by virtue of its position at the *ghat*, would logically be the first to be slipped. It was unfortunate; Moore and his fellows would have preferred to remain the last to leave, but there could be no thought of changing the cumbersome arrangements now . . .

None of them knew that the sunken road along which they had recently marched, which led down to the *ghat*, was now occupied by several companies of armed sepoys under command, that batteries hidden above the *ghat*, down-river, and on the opposite bank, were being uncovered, and both cavalry and infantry were crowded behind the nearby Hindu temple, messhouses and residencies. From the steps of the temple, a hundred yards distant, watched a group of senior mutineers – Azimullah Khan, Jwala Pershad, and the two younger brothers of Nana Sahib. They did not care to come nearer to the *ghat*. With them waited a bugler of the 56th Native Infantry, speculatively moistening his lips with the tip of his tongue.

A mile away, Nana Sahib slowly paced the carpeted floor of his marquee, listening. He was nervous. It was nine o'clock, and soon it would begin, he knew. Everything had been meticulously planned, and could not fail. When the distant noise of summer thunder ceased, a galloper would bring him a report from the *ghat*, that all was finished. He did not wish to see it done.

And on the steps of the temple Azimullah Khan nodded. 'They are taken out of their fortress – and see, they go gladly, without knowing what is before them. Now let them repent of their misdeeds, and ask pardon of God.' He turned to the waiting bugler. 'Now,' he said.

'In Heaven's name, Moore,' Major Vibart gritted, 'let's be going.' Precious minutes had passed as they waited for possible stragglers to board. 'Let's get this blasted place behind us—'

'There's General Wheeler and his ladies,' Moore frowned. Godammit, why did the old man insist on being the last European to leave Cawnpore? 'We'll have to lead off, then pole across towards the Oudh bank. That'll take us out of range of musketry fire. These damn boat-coolies don't seem very enthusiastic, but we can pole ourselves.'

General Wheeler's litter was carried several paces into the shallows and then halted. Ahead of him the English schoolmistress was ushering twenty-two small girls, English and Eurasian, through the mud-churned water towards the dozens of arms outstretched from the boats' decks. Wheeler leaned from his seat. 'Please be so kind as to take me a little nearer.' A trooper spoke from his saddle. 'No, General Sahib. Get out here.' He grinned.

Wheeler hesitated, then swung his legs from the litter. As he emerged, with head lowered, the trooper's sabre scythed savagely, and the General lurched forward into the water, face downwards. The wading schoolgirls screamed, flailing hysterically away from the floating corpse.

And from the steps of the temple, which resembled a dilapidated summerhouse, there came the urgent and sinister notes of a bugle.

The General's death was hidden from Amelia's boat, and the schoolgirls' screams were lost among the babel of shouts and cries that surrounded her, but she heard the bugle. Momentarily it meant nothing, but suddenly there was a fusillade of shots and the crump-crump of heavy guns that was so sickeningly familiar. Bewildered, Amelia began to climb to her feet, but one of the soldiers pulled her to the deck. 'Keep yer 'ead down, Missie. Gawdalmighty, them blacks 'ave welshed on us!' He groped for his rifle.

The nearest houses and their surrounding gardens twinkled with gun-flashes through a haze of smoke, and the boat-coolies were jumping into the river and clambering for the steps of the *ghat*. 'The bastards!' the soldier spat. 'Beggin' yer pardon, Miss.' He fired at one of the bobbing heads, then mouthed another obscenity as a musket ball smashed into his ribs and jack-knifed him to his knees.

On the crowded and exposed deck of every boat people were dying helplessly – targets almost impossible to miss by the hundreds of hidden sepoys. Bullets stippled the river's surface like rain, and the noise of shots and shouts was deafening. Amelia lay over a sobbing Florence, clawing at the woodwork, praying that there was some mistake, some stupid misunderstanding—

'All men over the side!' Moore was roaring through cupped hands. 'Push off the boats and pole for the Oudh bank! Get the boats away!' Scores of men leapt for the water, to strain their shoulders against the heavy timber hulls, their feet thrusting desperately, but the boats' sterns were firmly aground as if embedded in rock. Man after man was being cut down, slumping, choking, into the river's mud. Amelia was numbly aware of thick, stifling smoke in her nostrils, the crackle of flames and a new crescendo of screams from the neighbouring vessels. Boat-coolies had ignited the tinder-dry thatch before bolting for shore. The maimed and sick were trapped in the cramped stern shelters, while dozens of the more able had no choice but to abandon the doubtful protection of the boat-decks for the waist-deep, bullet-whipped river.

There was a new sound, terrifying. '*Allah, il Allah, din din din! Maro! Maro!*'

From behind the temple deluged an untidy mêlée of mounted troopers of the 2nd Cavalry, kicking their horses over the rutted, scrub-strewn ground. Dogs and chickens scattered as two hundred screeching horsemen urged their mounts down the stratified bank above the *ghat* and plunged into the shallows among the seething chaos around the burning boats.

Moore, Thompson, Delafosse, and dozens of others were faced with an impossible choice – to turn to face the new, overwhelming threat of the approaching, sword-slashing cavalrymen or continue to strain to heave off the boats which so obviously had been deliberately run hard aground.

Of the twenty-four boats, half were ablaze – several from stem to stern, so that anyone remaining aboard must have perished. A choking blanket of thick, acrid smoke shrouded the entire length of the *ghat*, and through it the troopers rode, hacking indiscriminately at the exhausted Europeans, adult and infant, who crawled against the boats' sides or flailed desperately to reach the shore. Behind the horsemen followed swarming sepoys, bayoneting and clubbing. Amelia, with Florence's hands tearing at her, had lost sight of her father and the other little ones. Her mother's nearby boat was in flames, and she could see women with hair burning like torches and mouths cavernous with screeching as they flung themselves into the river, towards the waiting sabres. She saw Mr Kirkpatrick, waist deep in the water only yards from her, his arms raised over his head as two cavalrymen rose in their saddles above him, and she saw his arms hewed from his trunk. He disappeared, but Amelia would see him again, floating helplessly in the blood-tinted river an hour later, still alive.

Florence was crying hysterically. 'Amy! Don't leave me! Amy! Amy!' Both the soldiers who had boarded with her had fallen. One had dragged himself towards the stern, but exulting sepoys were clambering over the sides, and he was finished quickly. A snarling man tore Florence from Amelia's grasp and threw her to the planks. The child screamed as a heavily sandalled foot stamped on her factured leg. Amelia was gripped by her hair, her head tugged viciously backwards, and her necklace of modest garnets was wrenched from her throat. The next moment a blow from a gun-butt sprawled her, dazed, terrified and whimpering. She felt the blood wet and warm on her face.

Amelia did not know how long she remained on her knees and elbows, with her stinging head lowered. It could have been seconds or minutes. She only knew that she could not move, could not reach Florence, and that at any moment death would come to her. Vaguely, very vaguely, she was aware of a mounted cavalryman alongside the boat, with the filthy water up to his saddle. He was shouting something at her and beckoning, half hidden by the smoke and swirling sparks. Amelia was very close to fainting, and she wanted to vomit. She closed her eyes. When she opened them again the trooper was still there, still mouthing unintelligibly at her and with his carbine levelled threateningly. Amelia did not care. It would be now.

The man's face twisted with anger. He kicked his horse nearer, then directed his shouts at a sepoy on the boat's deck. Moments later she felt herself being lifted roughly to her feet, but her legs would not support her. An arm encircled her waist, raising her high, a clawing hand tore her bodice from neck to waist, and there was spiteful laughter in her ears. She was being bared for men to look at, she knew, but she did not care, nor even when cruel fingers scrabbled at her most private body. There was nauseating bile in her mouth, and she did not care.

The mounted man, alongside, exploded into savage abuse, and his carbine rose again. The hands that had insulted her – whose owner she could not see – lifted her again, bodily, and flung her. She struck the water and the trooper's horse reared. Darkness closed over her, but her wrist was clutched and she was wrenched upright, unashamedly vomiting with her face pressed against the horse's wet, heaving flank. From a great distance she could still hear Florence. 'Amy! Don't leave me! Amy – *please* don't leave me!'

By the frenzied efforts of the surviving Europeans, four of the boats were pushed free from the *ghat* and launched into deeper water. Even although the current was only sluggish, steering was almost impossible; there were no oars or punt-poles, and each vessel carried more dead than living. One was struck by a round-shot within seconds and gradually became waterlogged. Two others drifted slowly across the Ganges where, on the Oudh bank, impatient sepoy contingents waited to finish what their Cawnpore fellows had begun.

Only one boat got clear. Not surprisingly this was the boat manned and defended by Moore's party, reinforced by Mowbray Thompson, Whiting, Henry Delafosse, and others of the rearguard. The men's Enfields and the officers' Adams' pistols had kept the blood-crazed mutineers at a respectful distance, and as the laden vessel lurched from the *ghat* and wallowed towards mid-stream, Moore shouted at the men around him. 'Jump for it!'

A dozen did, hauling themselves over the stern, but an equal number were left. Their only hope for life, now, was to swim. Mowbray Thompson took his father's Ghuznee medal and a miniature of his mother from his shirt and flung them into the water, then turned and plunged after the departing boat, followed by the frustrated howls and wild shots of hundreds of mutineers. There were a few others with him – a ragged soldier of the Queen's 84th and two young subalterns of the 56th, brothers, named Henderson. Nobody else escaped from the *ghat*, and Thompson had no time to look back. Those that remained were either unable to swim, or were shot dead as they tried to.

The water was muddily thick, almost glutinous, and all four men were exhausted. The younger Henderson, who had been in India so briefly that Thompson was unaware of his first name, began to weaken and flounder, and then, choking, disappeared under floating filth. His brother, John Henderson, turned frantically, but scything grapeshot tore off his right hand. Gripped by panic, the boy threshed madly, pain-racked, but Thompson and Private Murphy took his arms over their shoulders and dragged him on, themselves near to collapse. Frank Whiting leaned from the deck of the boat. 'We thought you'd never get here, Mowbray. What bloody kept you?'

Thompson lay prostrate on the planks, sucking in breath and with his eyes closed against the sun. 'Frank, my dear boy. Fair stands the wind for Allahabad?' He lifted his blackened, sore-pocked face. 'There's no more to come, old horseman. No more. There was a red sky this morning.' He lay back, drained. His lungs threatened to explode with pain. 'We're all that's left.'

'And half of us,' Frank Whiting nodded, glancing around, 'are dead.'

17

At Allahabad, Lieutenant-Colonel Neill, who had planned to strike out for Cawnpore four days after the arrival of the steam-boat *Mirzapore* on 22 June, had been thwarted. Cholera raged among the Madras Fusiliers, and eighty men had died in three days. Neill could cope with mutinous sepoys, but not with cholera. A secondary problem was drunkenness among the Fusiliers, a consequence of their comparative idleness and a plentiful supply of looted spirits. Neill flogged a man, threatened the same for every man in his force, then collected and destroyed all the liquor that could be found in Allahabad's abandoned warehouses.

By 30 June, however, Neill would tolerate no further delay. Piecing together scraps of intelligence from the direction of Cawnpore, it was evident that General Wheeler's resistance could not be sustained for more than a further few days, and Neill's desire to come to grips with Nana Sahib had become a savage obsession. He mustered his entire force of effectives – 200 Madras Fusiliers, 200 of the Queen's 84th Foot, two guns manned by invalids from the fort, and 120 irregular cavalry who would have to be carefully watched.

Now, at last, he was ready – but on that very morning there was another arrival, of uncertain significance. It was Colonel Henry Havelock.

The two men, Havelock and Neill, could hardly have been more different in character. Havelock was religious, highly principled, and painstaking in everything he did, while Neill was a fire-ball, impulsively energetic, with little regard for the more gentlemanly aspects of campaigning. He wanted the enemy dead, by any means but preferably the quickest, and the Turks had shown him the most economical policy with regard to prisoners. Neill's military philosophy would often cause Havelock to shudder, Havelock's to provoke Neill to cursing frustration, but for the moment they had to work in harness.

And Havelock's first decision was a disappointment for Neill. The small force mustered outside the fort would proceed, not led by Neill but under Brevet-Major Renaud of the Madras Fusiliers, as an advanced, flying column, to be followed by Havelock and Neill as soon as the bulk of reinforcements reached Allahabad from Calcutta. These would include the 78th Highlanders, the 64th Foot, more of the Madras Fusiliers and 84th, and both Queen's and Company artillery. Renaud's command swung onto the hot Grand Trunk Road, gun-caissons jingling, on the first stage of a 120-mile march towards Cawnpore, followed by Neill's disgruntled gaze.

Three days later the gate of Allahabad's fort was swung open to admit an officer flogging a jaded horse. He carried a despatch from Renaud, forty miles away, of the Cawnpore massacre. General Wheeler's garrison had surrendered, and Nana Sahib had butchered every European man, woman and child in Cawnpore.

The effect on the troops now pouring into Allahabad was cataclysmic. Insensate, hard-mouthed soldiers who could walk away contemptuously from fifty lashes over a gun-wheel, be clubbed to insensibility by a provost patrol and still spit defiance, now openly wept with bitter rage, snarled vengeance by every blasphemous deity born of barrack-room vocabulary, shouted to the sky that the heathen animals of Cawnpore would pay for their crime as none had paid before. From that moment no native would walk secure, no thatched hovel be safe from the torch, no reprisal be too barbaric. Never before had the common British soldier been so incensed with vicious hatred for his enemy.

Part Two

O lang, lang may the ladies stand,
  Wi' their gold kems in their hair,
Waiting for their ain dear lords,
  For they'll see them na mair.

Sir Patrick Spens

18

He was Mohammed Ismail Khan, a *sowar*, or trooper, of the 2nd Cavalry, a *sillidar* regiment. He was twenty-eight years old, of medium height and build, with a sallow face badly pocked and a black beard forked and curled outwards in the manner of the Sikhs. But he was a Moslem, and he slept with his head to the westward, towards Mecca, for the mind of Islam was the Ka'aba, the holy shrine of Allah.

In earlier days the men who came to serve in John Company's cavalry brought their own horse, saddlery and weapons. Later, in order to maintain standards of quality and uniformity, it became more convenient for a recruit to deposit a sum of money with the Regiment against the provision of a horse and equipment or, if unable to do so, to be subsidized from the regimental *chanda*, a loan fund, and to repay the loan by instalments from his pay.

Mohammed Ismail Khan had come as a boy from the village of Payagpur, which the Sahibs recorded as simply the Bahraich No. 8 District, whatever that meant. He had taken pride in the fact that his family was remotely related to one of the several mothers-in-law of the King of Oudh, but the Sahibs had not been impressed. They had not appointed him a Rissaldar-Major, or even a Rissaldar, only a *sowar* recruit, to be shouted at by a Sahib-subaltern, *pei-makhe halak*, a milk-faced boy with fewer months in India than fingers on one hand.

There were many such frustrations. The Sahibs were obsessed with cleanliness. What harm did horses suffer from a little mud? But every day they must be groomed – five minutes for their backs, ten for their bellies, five for faces, and five for dirty docks. A whistle would blow and the Colonel Sahib would appear followed by his entourage – the Captain Sahib, the Adjutant Sahib, the Rissaldar-Major, the *Woordie* Major, the Drill Major, and that *zenana*-fed brat of a subaltern. The

Colonel Sahib probed with his cane at a staring coat, a tail to be pulled, teeth to be filed. Mohammed Ismail Khan had been fined fifteen rupees for allowing his own horse to be rope-galled.

He had not been a natural horseman, and his first few weeks in the jumping lanes had been difficult. Jenkins Sahib had been a lieutenant then, and had called him a mutton-fisted oaf for cutting a horse's mouth, ordering extra drills when the other recruits swaggered the bazaar in their new regimentals and jingling spurs. He had been placed in an 'awkward squad', and his pride had been stung by the possibility of being dismissed from the Ridgement – 'sent away' – as unsuitable. This would have been a disgrace, and he could never have faced the *maliks* of his village. Mohammed Ismail Khan had compelled himself to gallop without stirrups, to jump with arms folded, and he had broken a collar-bone and several ribs, but the Ridgement had retained him.

True, he might by now have expected promotion to Lance-*Naik*, but he had always refused to learn to read and write. He could quote long passages from the Holy Koran. What need was there for pot-hooks? What did learning do except breed worms in the brain? Books had not saved the Sahibs. Captain Jenkins was dead, killed in the *Lal Koorti Ka Haspital*, and with him Chaplain-Captain Seppings and Lieutenants Sterling and Quin, of the Ridgement. There may have been more. As Mohammed Ismail Khan had watched the long column of ragged Europeans straggling towards the *Suttee Chowra Ghat* he had observed only Major Vibart and Lieutenant Harrison, and a wounded Lieutenant Daniell being carried in a litter. What had reading and writing done for them?

He had observed something else – a honey-skinned young woman riding in a bullock-cart, with a small child clutched to her. She was slight, slender and beautiful, and like most of the European women was reduced to a single garment which, to Moslem eyes, conceded an indecent and provocative exposure of bust, calves and ankles. Mohammed Ismail Khan walked his horse just to the rear of the *tonga*, looking at her. There were more white women with large breasts and plump thighs, but this one, the dainty golden one, was the queen of them all.

This was no pallid, sweat-damp mem-sahib with cold-fish eyes and hairy armpits, bathing every day because she smelled so much. This was a little goddess that any man would want to walk behind him, veiled and shapeless in a *chudder*, but he knowing what was hidden. He sidled his horse nearer, tolerating the dry-flung dust of the carts, but Trooper Shumshoden Khan, who was now a Colonel, was shouting for them to muster behind the Fishermen's Temple, above the *ghat*. There was to be a *jehad* against the *shaitan* British, against Company *Bahadur*, and they must wait for the bugle.

It was hot and confined behind the temple. The crowded horses, plagued by flies, excreted and pawed ill-humouredly. They were obscured from the boats at the *ghat*, but they could still see the passing draggle of carts and litters, the stumbling Europeans and an occasional plodding elephant. Mohammed Ismail Khan recognized a few of the people. Dr Boyes had treated him for a contusion following a horse-kick, and there was the Reverend Moncreiff with his Bible in one hand while the other supported a limping, rag-swathed soldier. And there were sepoys, hundreds of them, mingling with the Europeans, chattering and laughing. They were Hindus, and he detested the Hindus, their religious depravities, their veneration for the organs of generation, the male *linga* and the female *yoni*, their caste obsessions, their repulsive *sadhus* smeared with dung and ashes, their supercilious Brahmins. But if it was the will of God the Highest that Moslem should join with Hindu against the British, then so be it.

None of the mounted troopers behind the temple was fully prepared for what happened next. Nobody had explained, and they could only guess. The bugle sounded, and a gun battery roared. The next moment the ill-ordered cavalry were spurring over the broken, pot-holed ground that fringed the *ghat*, tugging their swords free and shouting. Musket-fire spat from every direction. Boat-thatch was burning, spewing black smoke, and women and infants shrieked. Mohammed Ismail Khan slashed at a European, saw him sprawl, saw a comrade lift a small girl from the water by her long hair and then scythe head from trunk with a single sweep of his sabre. He hauled his horse about, suddenly drunk with blood-lust, lunged twice at a woman who screeched hysterically for pity before his third blow split her skull.

Then, through the smoke and chaos, he saw the golden one. She knelt on the deck of the nearest boat, unmoving. There was blood on her face and a sepoy stood over her. Mohammed Ismail Khan shouted at her, and she turned her head to stare at him, uncomprehending. He shouted again. 'Jump to me, little one! Jump—' But his voice was lost in a sea of noise, and she lowered her face again. He sheathed his sword and dragged his carbine from its bucket. 'You, there!' He addressed the sepoy. 'Pass down the woman that kneels!'

The sepoy had no love for arrogant Moslem cavalrymen, but the carbine was pointed at his chest. He hauled the woman upright, roughly, resentfully. So the Moslem pig wanted a mem-Sahib to rut with, did he? Were white women different, then? Were their breasts nippled with rubies, their secret parts smelling of jasmine? Let us then see! The sepoy shredded the little mem-sahib's dress from her neck, enjoying the fury in the trooper's face. Then, lifting her from behind with an encircling arm, he raised her petticoat with his free hand. She moaned without struggling, but the trooper, below, was savagely incensed. Mohammed Ismail Khan had acted on impulse; he could not think what he might do with the little golden one when he had got her, but the sight of her insult at the filthy hands of a Hindu sepoy brought the bile of hate to his throat. 'Throw her down, eater of cow-dung, uncircumcised *utni* – or I shoot!'

The Hindu was tempted to return abuse for abuse, but there was something in the Moslem's eyes that bridled his tongue. Instead, he lowered the young woman and threw her towards the cavalryman. 'Take her!' he snorted, shrugging. Then, to himself: 'And may you have scabs in four weeks!'

For an age Nana Sahib had paced nervously, listening to the rattle of gunfire from the distant *ghat*. He had taken the final leap, irrevocably; nothing, now, could turn back the clock. Whatever his prospects of reconciliation or compromise with the Europeans might have been yesterday, from today he would be the inexpiable Butcher of Cawnpore. He was secure only if the British were totally expelled from India. If they were not, he could expect to be remorselessly hunted down like a rabid dog until the day of his death. He had received messages of encouragement from the mutineers in Delhi, but little else. Now, he had heard, the walls of Delhi were under attack by a force of British and loyal Ghurkas and Sikhs. Azimullah Khan had assured him that the Shah of Persia would send many soldiers, and the Khedive of Egypt would destroy any British reinforcements on passage to India, but Nana Sahib had not heard that either promise had been fulfilled, or was even remotely likely. More ominously, intelligence from Allahabad that very morning told of the arrival of further white troops, bringing Neill Sahib's force up to 400 Europeans and 300 Sikhs – and there were even more on the road from Calcutta. It was true that Neill still had the worst part of his march ahead of him, but so far, it appeared, he had flung all opposition contemptuously aside, and Nana Sahib's confidence in the ability of the sepoy mutineers to stand against Europeans under anything like equal terms had been sadly undermined. The tactical appreciation of native jemadars and subedars, now posing as generals, seldom extended beyond visual range; strategy was a closed book. It had taken blatant treachery to overcome even the puny obstacle of the *Lal Koorti Ka Haspital.*

Had he aimed too high? Had he allowed himself to be duped by the plausible Azimullah Khan?

His deepening morbidity was interrupted by the chutter of hooves as a *sowar* galloper reined outside the marquee and swung from his saddle, breathing hard. 'Excellence, all has happened as you ordered. The Sahibs' corpses cover the *ghat* and the river runs red. Only one boat has got off, but it cannot get far; our guns and picquets are on both sides of the river for many miles. In a few more minutes, Excellence, the *Feringhees* will all be dead, and the turtles will have their feasting.'

'There are some, then, still alive?'

'A few, Excellency, but they will be finished quickly.'

Nana Sahib was biting his knuckles. 'It may not be wise to kill them all,' he murmured, as if to himself. 'Not all. Hostages have a value. Perhaps we should not have killed any.'

The trooper shrugged, puzzled. 'Even God cannot change what is past, Excellence. But how can we be rid of the *Badshah* in Calcutta if we do not kill the *Feringhees*?'

Nana Sahib gazed eastward. He could not see the *Suttee Chowra Ghat*, but he could see sunlight glinting on the surface of the river and the Ganges Canal, dusty trees, thorn scrub, and the road that had led to the destroyed boat-bridge, which only weeks ago had flocked with people, a mixing mass of colour, of bullock carts and dark blue elephants, white-robed women priests in saffron, wedding processions with drums and flutes, the gilded glitter of a nawab's palanquin. Now the road was empty, for it led nowhere except to the river bank and an abandoned, ransacked toll-house.

It was strange, the Nana mused, that apart from the criminal fraternity very few of the Indian civil population had displayed much enthusiasm for the Bengal Army's mutiny against the British Raj. Hundreds of Cawnpore merchants had closed their businesses and moved elsewhere, usually to British-held territory. It was not the British who should be expelled, they pleaded. The Sahibs were arrogant, pompous and domineering, but they were also incorruptible. Nobody offered a bribe to a Sahib. It was the thousands of *Indian* clerks, minor officials and lawyers who demanded *batta* from every petitioner or subordinate, who extended favours or twisted justice for those who paid and ignored those who could not. The Sahibs were dictatorial and insolent, but they placed law and order above all other things. What law would there be when the Sahibs had gone?

'There are matters of which you know nothing,' Nana Sahib said. He frowned. 'Ride back to the *Suttee Chowra Ghat*, quickly. Tell them that, of the English that remain alive, the men are to be killed, but women and children are to be spared. They are to be brought into Cawnpore, to the *Savada Kothi*, and we shall decide later what shall be done with them.'

The trooper hesitated, but then brightened. 'Defender of

the Poor,' he nodded, 'perhaps we can have them stamped on by elephants?'

When the surviving men had been killed in the shallows, the women and children were herded ashore, driven from under the charred, steaming woodwork of the boats or dragged, sobbing, from deeper water. All were sodden, filthy with mud, most with clothing torn and bloody, barefoot and exhausted almost to collapse. One hundred and twenty-five, including infants and a few boys of ten or twelve years, huddled together on the trampled sand, uncaring as sepoys snatched at ear-rings and brooches. Yards away the water's edge floated with corpses – mutilated, obscene shapes with here and there an outflung arm or a twisted, lacerated face turned to the sky. A few native *bhisties* braved the sepoys' insults to offer the women mouthfuls of water from their goatskin *massaks*.

Presently, when some order had been established, the women were ordered to their feet and prodded towards the sunken road. Dull-eyed, numb with shock, they retraced their steps of two hours earlier, past the mud *sangar* of the Dragoon Hospital, now thronged with curious scavenging natives, past Christchurch and the Chapel of Ease, to the fringe of the native quarter of Cawnpore and the yellow-painted *Savada Kothi*.

Behind them, however, the horror of the *Suttee Chowra Ghat* was not yet finished. On the evening of the 29th, from the Oudh bank of the river, were ferried the luckless refugees who had been recaptured when their craft had run aground some distance downstream. Sixty men, twenty-five women and four children scrambled ashore to the ghat they had prayed never to see again, eyeing in silence the blackened skeletons of boats and the floating debris of clothing rags, hats, shoes and scattered papers that lapped against the steps.

The grinning sepoys pushed among them, ordering the women to stand clear and the men to sit on the ground. There was a long, chattering rattle as two companies of the Nadiri Regiment cocked their muskets. Chaplain-Captain Seppings, with a broken arm, pulled a prayer book from a pocket and began to read aloud, the women, grouped together, began to sob. A man shouted: 'If you're going to kill us, for God's sake get it over with!'

A woman broke from the group and ran. It was Dr Boyes' wife. She flung herself to her knees beside her husband and clasped him fiercely. 'I'll not leave him! If he has to die, then I'll die with him!' She pressed her cheek against his shoulder, her eyes choked with tears. 'How could I stay without my old love?' Within moments a dozen other wives had copied her, breaking through the surrounding sepoys and unashamedly sprawling with their arms tightly around their men. 'If you kill them, then kill us too!' Doctor Boyes, his wrists tethered, shook his head desperately. Tears furrowed his dirty face. 'No, my dear, no. Please. You must leave me, and look at the sky. My dearest lady—' The sepoys were laughing, dragging the women away by legs or hair, clubbing with their gun-butts. Captain Seppings closed his prayer book, but his lips still moved. There was a prolonged, deafening crash, smoke in the throat, women shrieking. Men contorted, jerking, kicking and cursing in the dirty sand. Only a few were dead; most of them coughed and writhed with vomiting mouths agape, straining at their cords and with faces ludicrously slimed with the dung and filth of the *ghat*. Their watching women cried, clawing at their faces, and the sepoys roared with laughter again. See, now, the haughty Sahibs grovelling and squealing like speared pigs! See, there is Seppings Sahib, the *bahut bhari baba*, with his jaw smashed, mouthing like a monkey to his Lord God. And the fat Doctor Sahib, who tells us to boil our water. See, he now drinks from the Ganges, flailing his arms—

They watched, savouring. There was no need to waste further powder and ball. They fixed their bayonets.

Amelia saw none of her family again, nor knew how they died. There were shots, shouts and screams in her ears as the mounted trooper hauled her unceremoniously up the *ghat* and to the climbing ground beyond. The noise became gradually distant. Her wrist was tightly gripped, tugging her upright as she stumbled, and her wet, blood-caked hair hung stickily over her face. She had lost both shoes, but her feet, it seemed, did not belong to her; they moved, but she did not know how. Nothing was real. This was a horrifying nightmare from which, presently, she would awaken. She would shiver from the night chill because she had kicked her bed-covers away, and she would see the stars in a black velvet sky through her open window. Then she would snuggle deliciously into her pillow, knowing that there was a *chowkidar* on his string *charpoy* on the verandah, Sacha the spaniel snoring gently outside her door, the children sleeping pinkly innocent, and her step-father puffing through his thin, sandy whiskers, and dear Mamma—

But the nightmare persisted. Her face was battered against the hot, steaming, heaving flank of the horse, her feet burned and her vice-gripped wrist flared with pain.

'Miss Horne! Miss Horne!' She could hear her name called, and she compelled herself to turn her head. Some yards away another Indian trooper was leading a horse, to the saddle of which clung a young white woman dressed in a soaked, green chintz gown. Amelia recognized Ulrica Wheeler, the youngest daughter of the General, but only momentarily. Her captor tugged her on.

Their trek seemed endless, across rubble and neglected gardens, patches of coarse *dhub* grass, past the officers' mess-house of the 56th and the hoof-pitted dust of the race-course. Twice they halted when groups of sepoys shouted at them, and the trooper answered. She heard the words '*maulvi sahib*' and '*kutcheri*', but her curiosity was submerged in misery, and she did not care. Soon, she noted, they had entered the native lines of the 2nd Cavalry.

She had never before been in a native cantonment. It was one of those places completely beyond the experience of any white lady, like the house in the bazaar where painted *devadasis* writhed and postured in front of men. Here it was hot, reeking of cattle ordure, curry and frying *ghee*, humming with flies. Everywhere men sat on their heels, talking, smoking hashish, or playing *andhabazi*, spitting betel juice. A few rose to their feet as the trooper dismounted, but before they could gather she was pushed through the door of a hut, into musty gloom, and the door rattled shut behind her.

There were shafts of sunlight penetrating chinks in the door and a flimsy, louvered casement. From beyond came a confusion of voices, the reedy fluting of a *serenai* and the clucking of fowls. The hut held little; a string bed, a small charcoal stove and a hookah, a few cooking utensils and, hanging from nails, various items of uniform clothing.

Amelia drew a shuddering breath, attempting to impose some pattern on the mental chaos which was causing her teeth to chatter and her head to ache. What was going to happen? She tried to recall the cavalry trooper's appearance and demeanour. If he had wished to kill her, surely he could have done so at the *Suttee Chowra Ghat*, but he had carried her off. His manner had been uncouth, but hardly malevolent. He had worn white pyjamas, tight at the ankles, an *alkhalak* – the long coat of the Indian cavalry – and a white turban. His eyes, she remembered, had been black and hard in a pock-scarred face. Amelia shivered. It was not a pleasant face, and this was no nightmare. It was bitterly real. If only she were not alone. If only she had her mother, or even little Florence, with whom to share her terror. Would she see Ulrica Wheeler again? *What was going to happen?*

It was two hours before she began to learn. The rusty hinges of the door suddenly screamed, and Amelia's eyes were blinded by the sun as the trooper led her again into the open, and then strode along rutted alleyways among a maze of thatched huts so that she could hardly keep pace. A retinue of natives followed, chattering and jeering that she was a *kaffir soor*, a pig, and should be butchered like one. She cringed, and the trooper's grip on her wrist tightened viciously, hauling her on, stumbling.

In an open space tangled with weeds stood a large tent, marked with the imprint of the East India Company and surrounded by an increasing throng of native idlers. Their eyes were on her, and there were more spiteful jibes. This, Amelia shuddered, was to be the place of her killing.

Inside, the tent was a sudden haven of quietness and shadow. Released, she halted uncertainly. Under her lacerated feet was a heavy, turkey-red carpet which had perhaps once lain in the magistrates' office. There were a few scattered chairs and, facing her from behind a table, two robed men as motionless as stone, their eyes lowered.

In that moment Amelia remembered. The trooper was a Moslem, and he had mentioned a *maulvi*. Moslems did not have priests, but they followed the direction of *maulvis*, teachers of religion, who exercised considerable authority. Were these men *maulvis*?

'There is no God but Allah,' the trooper said respectfully, 'and Mohammed is His Prophet.'

One of the *maulvis* raised his eyes, but did not glance at Amelia. 'Mohammed Ismail Khan. Is this the woman? You are aware that one of the True Faith may take a Christian or a Jew to wife, for they are "peoples of the Book".' He placed the palm of a hand on the Holy Koran before him. 'But first she must submit to God and His Divine Will. Is she so willing?'

Mohammed Ismail Khan inclined his head. 'In the name of God, the Merciful, the Compassionate.'

On the table beside the Koran, Amelia noted, there lay a naked sword. The *maulvi* transferred his gaze to her. 'You may sit,' he said, and as she glanced around for a chair, added, 'on the floor.' Amelia lowered herself to the carpet. Behind her moved another man, his drawn sword inches from her throat.

The *maulvi* deliberated, then broke into droning Pushtu. Amelia kept very still with her eyes closed, allowing the voice to roll over her, incomprehensible and almost soothing in its monotony. Perhaps she was not going to be killed. The tent was not as cool as she had first supposed, and she felt the prickle of sweat on her neck and chest. The carpet under her knees was soft and warm. Her senses began to float, and she surrendered herself to an overwhelming drowsiness. She would be compliant, and perhaps they would not kill her.

But the voice was speaking to her in English, and she dragged her attention back to the moving lips of the *maulvi*. '... Forbidden to you are carrion, blood, the flesh of swine, what has been hallowed to other than God, the beast strangled, the beast beaten down, the beast fallen to death, the beast gored, and that devoured by beasts of prey ...'

The man's lips, Amelia noted vaguely, were pink-lined, with a globule of saliva at each corner. A pomegranate was placed before him, and he spoke over it as he halved it with a small knife, offering one portion to her and raising the other to his own mouth. Amelia bit into seeds and skin which were bitterly sour, and swallowed with difficulty, wanting to choke but daring not.

'O Prophet, when believing women come to thee, swearing fealty to thee upon the terms that they will not associate with God anything, and will not steal, neither commit adultery, nor slay their children, nor bring a calumny they forge between their hands and feet . . .'

He drank from a glass of sherbet, then offered it to her. 'Praise belongs to God, the Lord of all Being, the All-merciful, the All-compassionate, the Master of the Day of Doom . . .'

It seemed that the droning voice would never end, and Mohammed Ismail Khan was making responses in Pushtu, but then a woman, with veiled head bowed, beckoned, and Amelia rose to follow. Again the hot sun-glare blinded her as they emerged from the tent, but this time only for seconds. Behind a wall of grass matting was a large iron hip-bath bearing the legend 'Spears & Jackson – Sheffield' and filled with water. 'Please to undress, mem-Sahib,' the woman said.

The companionship of another woman, even a strange one, was something to be clung to, but this was no stranger. Amelia paused in her unlacing. 'Aren't you—?'

The woman pulled her *chudder* over her face. 'Yes, but they do not know, mem-Sahib.' She was, Amelia had recognized, the native wife of a bandmaster of the 56th, and a Christian convert who had attended the services of the Reverend Haycock of the Society for the Propagation of the Gospel. 'If they knew—' She avoided Amelia's frightened eyes. 'You must be bathed, mem-Sahib, and then returned to the *maulvi*.'

Amelia lowered herself into the bath. It was exquisitely cool to her hot and sweaty body, and she uttered an involuntary gasp of thankfulness. The woman gave her a tablet of cheap soap, violently scented. 'We must not delay, mem-Sahib.'

'Please, what is to happen to me?' Amelia pleaded.

There was a measure of spite in the other's voice as she unfolded a bundle of native clothing. 'You will know the despair of being converted to an alien faith, mem-Sahib, of being wife to one of a different race, of the resentments of his people and the contempt of your own. You will bear children who will be neither Indian nor English, and who will be rejected by both, and you will cry often in the darkness for the things that you once knew.' She paused, but not yet satisfied. 'You will not be called mem-Sahib again, nor expect to be pampered like a white lady. Your husband may have three other wives, and you will walk three paces behind him with your eyes lowered. Five times each day you will pray, with your face towards Mecca, for you are now a Moslem and the wife of a Moslem. If he says, you will have your face veiled from the sight of other men, and you will speak to none but he – and then only to answer him. You will acknowledge him as your master, your life, your all; you must know nothing but the demands of your husband, to supply his demands and to never question.'

Amelia wanted to scream, but her throat was clogged with absolute terror. A Moslem? How could she be a *Moslem*? And *married*?

'But *how*—?' The situation was too overwhelmingly macabre for her to grapple with, her sense of logic numbed by the crushing events of the past few hours. She could no longer think clearly, and she stood with glazed eyes as the woman dressed her in clean cotton pyjamas and a long-sleeved *kurta*, tight at the waist and reaching to her knees, then draped a muslin shawl over her head and shoulders. Unprotesting, she followed her companion back to the *maulvis*' tent, where Mohammed Ismail Khan waited.

The *maulvi's* gaze rose slowly from her small, slippered feet to her veiled face. 'In the Name of God, the Merciful, the Compassionate.' He opened the Koran before him. 'Repeat after me: "He is God, the one, God the everlasting. He begetteth not, nor is he begotten; and there is none equal to Him . . .'

She was back in the hut in the cavalry lines, where the woman, with bad grace, had brought her a meal of chupatties, lentils and unidentifiable, curried vegetables, then left her alone. Amelia ate with her fingers from the chipped plate, listening to the unceasing murmur of noise from outside – voices, the bark of dogs, the passing wheels of occasional carts. The light was fading and, lonely and unspeakably confused, she began to shiver from the increasing chill. Then she started as the door rattled, her nails biting into her palms, and saw the ominous silhouette of her captor against the dusking sky. He grunted, then closed the door firmly behind him. There was the flare of a lucifer, an old lamp gleamed a sickly yellow, and Amelia could smell the burning smoke of coal oil. She pressed herself backwards.

He stood over her, his shadow immense on the wall and roof, uncoiling the turban from his head and shaking his hair free. Then he unbuttoned and removed his *alkhalak* and pushed his loose pyjamas over his knees and ankles. Amelia began to cry. 'Please – oh, please—'

He was enjoying her despair. 'It is time, little golden one,' he grinned, 'for me to loosen the knot of your girdle, that no man has untied before.' She had never seen a man exposed and swollen with lust, but now she did. Dear God, did all women experience this? When she had heard whispered voices through the thin walls of the bungalow, with the *punkahs* silent, had dear, innocent Mamma seen John Cook like this?

But it was too late. His hands were already humiliating her. She fixed her gaze on the flame of the oil lamp that trickled a ribbon of black smoke roofward. Let it be finished quickly, she prayed, and then she could no longer see the flame.

19

The overladen boat rolled sluggishly in mid-river under a blistering sun, moving with infuriating slowness as men flailed with make-shift paddles of torn-up deck-planks; there were no poles or oars, and the rudder had been shot away. Mowbray

Thompson had his head lowered, vomiting, as a scarecrow Private Murphy pummelled his back. 'Better out than in, sorr,' advised Murphy. 'Them nigger bastards hev sold us, sorr, an' that's fer sartin.' The wallowing craft was a ludicrously simple target for the batteries and musketry-fire from both banks as it alternately drifted and grounded on sand-beds. The survivors from one other boat, foundering after being struck below the waterline, had scrambled aboard, and living, wounded and dead lay tangled below the flimsy gunwhale. At times the vessel was barely a hundred yards from the guns among the tall *jhow*, whose crews loaded and fired, then yoked their bullocks to follow the Europeans as they moved slowly away from Cawnpore.

By midday, however, the mutineer's artillery pieces could no longer follow along a sandy riverbank into which wheels sunk to the hubs, defying even the efforts of the whip-lashed gun-bullocks. Now only the sepoys followed, swarming like red ants at the water's edge, thrusting through the scrub and the groves of wild mango to get ahead, to load and wait until the boat came abreast of them again. And then the boat swung broadside onto a sand-bed and stuck fast.

A dozen of the fitter men jumped for the water, to stand waist deep, tugging at it. Moore's shouted encouragements died on his lips as a musket ball smashed into his chest. Another shot hit St George Ashe, and a third cut down Lieutenant Bolton, who had survived the Cawnpore siege after escaping the mutiny of the 7th Oudh Horse at Chobipur. The boat was still aground.

'It's no good,' Thompson panted. 'We'll have to lighten our load.' Carrying more than a hundred people, the boat was not to be budged by a handful of emaciated men. 'The dead must go over the side.'

It was a miserable task, not made easier by the continuous volleys of shot from the shore. The dead were dragged clear of the living and flung from the side. Women sobbed, clinging to a dead husband or child, then watched with demented eyes as the corpses floated obscenely, refusing to sink or drift clear of the boat's side. But the boat moved, inch by agonizing inch, then slid into buoyancy. The hauling men clawed for the deck, with hardly strength remaining to pull themselves aboard.

Several did not. A last, single round-shot from a six-pounder hardly within effective range scythed down Lieutenants Burney and Glanville, and a Mrs Swinton, then shattered the leg of Lieutenant Fagan so that, below the knee, it was no more than a few shreds of flesh and sinew. He lay on the deck-planks, ashen-faced, his teeth bared and eyes clenched, but saying nothing. As the lightened boat rode on the slow current, Mowbray Thompson felt small fingers plucking at his arm. It was the six-year-old son of Mrs Swinton. 'Sir – Mamma has fallen overboard.'

At that moment Thompson had little attention to spare for a diminutive orphan. Within the previous few minutes the fugitive boat had lost six of its most determined defenders – the indefatigable Moore, Ashe, Bolton, Burney, Glanville and Fagan, while Major Vibart nursed an unstrapped, fractured arm and Lieutenant Harrison a severed hand. The surviving, effective officers numbered himself, Captains Athill Turner and Frank Whiting, and Lieutenants Delafosse and Quin.

For the rest of his life Mowbray Thompson would regret his brusqueness to the small boy. His attention elsewhere, he patted a tangled head. 'Your mother will suffer no more pain, son.' Thompson was a bachelor with no more than a tolerant big-brother attitude towards small boys. He was reloading his pistol with torn fingers, peering at the brown-green jumble of *dhub*-grass and stunted trees on the eastern bank that crawled with red insects. 'Go up with the women, son, and keep your head down—'

An hour later he remembered, then crawled aft, searching, but the boy had gone, to look for his mother.

The ordeal of that afternoon was as harrowing as anything suffered during the siege of the *Lal Koorti Ka Haspital*. The mutineers, enraged that one boat should survive so long, followed doggedly along both banks, racing ahead to crowd marksmen at vantage points where the river narrowed. Seldom out of musket-range, there was no respite for the Europeans. Under a broiling sun the boat's woodwork seared the flesh; there was only warm, dirty water from the river, and none had eaten since the previous evening. Again and again the boat nudged sandbanks, hesitated, then shuddered free to drift aimlessly on as the sepoys' shots and shouted abuse followed, and as people died their bodies were slid from the side; there could be no useless weight to endanger the living.

There had been a lull in the firing of several minutes when Mowbray Thompson clambered forward to stare ahead, seeking the reason. Had their pursuers been outpaced at last, or were they waiting in ambush again? Henry Delafosse shouted a caution, but Thompson raised himself. He saw the red coat of a sepoy half hidden by a tree, saw a musket flash and a feather of smoke. The bullet struck the side of his head, gouging a furrow to the skull, and he fell backward into the boat, unconscious.

When he recovered his senses he was staring at a sky that had cooled and his head blazed and throbbed with pain. Whiting and Delafosse were over him, splashing water. 'Dammit, Mowbray,' Frank Whiting growled, 'we thought you'd shuffled off this mortal coil. Gave us a bloody fright – 'specially as you still owe me two bottles of whisky from the last smoking concert.'

Thompson groaned. 'What's happened?' he muttered.

'You've got a hole in your head as big as my thumb,' Delafosse said, 'and you're bloody lucky not to be floating in the river. Apart from that, it's about five in the afternoon, and we're aground – this time hard and fast.' He glanced around warily. 'Fortunately the blacks have stopped firing. Likely they've sent back to Cawnpore for ammunition.'

'Cawnpore?' Thompson calculated. 'How far have we got?'

Whiting was chewing on the damp, unlit stub of a cheroot. 'Only about six miles. I remember the locality, Mowbray. We came snipe-shooting here after the last rains. About another six miles down the river there's a village on the Oudh side – Nuzufghur. If the local *zemindar* is still friendly we can get provisions and help, but if he isn't' – he removed the cheroot stub from his lips to stare at it morosely – 'then God help us. We'll never get past Nuzufghur.'

Major Vibart was cradling his broken arm with his good hand, his several days' growth of beard showing white through the sweat-streaked dirt of his face. Together they eyed the nearer, Oudh shore, a hundred yards away. All was very silent. Two sarus cranes stood motionless in the shallows, and the air was thick with mosquitoes, but there was no other movement. Beneath them the boat, slightly heeled, lay in four feet of water, its keel firmly embedded in the soft sand of the bottom. 'It looks quiet enough,' Whiting added, 'but there's no knowing. That scrub could be swarming with blacks, thicker than fleas in a camel blanket, just waiting.'

'Give me six men,' Henry Delafosse offered, 'and I'll find out. We can wade ashore.'

Vibart winced, eyes narrowed. 'No. We haven't got six fit men to gamble with. I've been taking stock. We've nineteen effectives – seven officers including Chaplain-Captain Seppings and Doctor Boyes, one sergeant and eleven soldiers, then two wounded officers with one arm each. The rest – nearly fifty men – are all seriously wounded, sick or infirm. And that's not counting twenty-five women and four children.' He shook his head. 'No. If Nuzufghur is hostile, we'll need every damn man we've got to even attempt to fight our way through. But we just might get past in darkness. We'll wait until nightfall, disembark everyone that can stand on their feet, then refloat the boat. After that, well, we'll have six hours to pray that we get beyond Nuzufghur before daybreak.'

They waited as the hours passed and the sun sank westward, the sky dusked to grey and the first stars showed. The men's eyes were on the Oudh bank, but they saw nothing except a few wild pigs at the water's edge and heard only the distant bicker of monkeys and birds. It was cool now and, when the near shoreline was no more than an undefinable black shadow, forty men and women lowered themselves over the gunwhale into the river. There was a moment of shock as a dozen unsuspecting wildfowl exploded into flight, only yards away, with a noise like thunder, but immediately the lightened boat rose in the current and floated free of the clinging river's bottom. Thompson, Whiting, Turner and Delafosse, at bows and stern, hissed encouragement as the heavy, clumsy hull was inched towards mid-river and deeper water. 'That's enough!' Mowbray Thompson shouted. And then he could have bitten off his tongue.

There was a faint, answering shout from the darkness of the distant Oudh bank, a musket shot and then a second. 'That's torn a bloody hole in it!' Delafosse grunted, then yelped as a bullet sheared the heel from his boot. Moments later the gloom was pitted with gun-flashes, but the boat was gripped by the current now and was gathering momentum, rudderless and yawing crazily. Although visible to the shore as a vague black shape against the grey of the river, distance must have been deceptive, and few shots were finding their target. Thompson disentangled himself from the sodden sprawl of people on the planks. 'A couple more minutes and we'll be clear. They'll not easily follow in the dark. Blast it, Frank – they were there all the time, just waiting for us to wade ashore, the bastards.'

'It's enough to shake anyone's faith in human nature,' Delafosse gritted. 'And I've lost the heel of a boot – hand-made by Gupta Sen in Delhi.'

'I've been meaning to mention those boots,' Whiting said. 'A damn disgrace to the Ridgement. Should have been mended weeks ago. That's the trouble with you infantry *wallahs*. No *esprit de corps*.'

'The Bengal Engineers, of course,' responded Delafosse, 'would know all about mending boots. In fact, they're probably the best boot-menders in India—' The muttered exchange stopped abruptly as the men flung themselves on the boat's thatched canopy, to tear free the dry straw that had suddenly erupted into flame. The night air was filled with spitting, red stars – arrows tipped with lighted charcoal that hissed into the barn-like roofing, among the congested, helpless fugitives, or sank to extinction in the dark river. 'By Christ,' Thompson seethed. 'They were ready for this! They've been waiting for festerin' hours! Either we came ashore to be killed, or they burned us alive if we didn't!' Desperately the men clawed down the straw thatch from its bamboo frame, flinging it overboard to float astern, smouldering and smoking. When every shred of straw had been wrenched free, they lay on their faces, utterly spent and with mouths gaping.

The Ganges flowed south-eastward, hardly above sea level, between thick grass jungle, trees and green bamboo thicket. It was good hunting country, with duck and snipe, pig and sambar, tiger and panther, and they knew it well – on the north side the Purwa District of Oudh, on the other the Doab of John Company's North-western Province where, roughly parallel to the river, ran the Grand Trunk Road. They had known that, too, in more normal times. Both river and road had been arteries of vital importance, the logical route of communication across the brow of India. Camel trains and creaking bullock-carts, travelling sahibs, merchants, saffron-robed priests, beggars and marching soldiers had trodden the road. Steamboats, laden barges and fishing boats thronged the river between the burning *ghats* from which the ashes of the dead were scattered. Cattle drank, children splashed, and women washed clothes or filled water-jars in the shadow of ancient temples, tombs and shabby palaces. The smell of wood-smoke and cow-dung mingled with that of frying *pillau*, of cooking *ghee*, of rice, mutton and kid – and always of people. Duleep Ram, the village headman, ran for his best turban-cloth and *salaamed* to the Sahibs of Company *Bahadur*, and the women covered their faces. May prosperity ever attend your footsteps, Defender of the Poor. Am I not an old *jemadar* of the 21st Infantry, with four medals? Would the Sahib wish to see my medals?

What had happened? The wide river, which even at night would have floated with the firefly night-lanterns of fishing craft and ferry-boats, was black and silent. No lights showed on either shore; if there were houses, they were shuttered against the night and the lawlessness that had replaced Company *Bahadur*'s rule. What had happened? Where were the Sahibs with their lobster faces and outlandish whiskers, who puffed and hawed and strutted, but were above bribery and coercion? What had happened?

What, mused Mowbray Thompson, had happened? Were those mad-dog sepoys at the *Suttee Chowra Ghat* the same men he had officered for six years? What had so poisoned the minds of long-serving men like Subedar Badloo Ram and Havildar Jodha Ram that they should want to butcher inoffensive women and chidren, burn and pillage, forfeit their honour and pensions? Had it been Kali, the Dark One, or the promises of crazed *ghazis*? Didn't they know that there could be no going back, no forgiveness? No matter how long it took, the British would return, and they would bring bitter reprisal. There would be no corner of India in which a mutinied sepoy could hide, no desert, mountain or jungle too remote for the avenging bullet, bayonet and rope.

But the death of every native of the Bengal Army would not bring back fine men like John Moore, St George Ashe, Dempster, Jenkins and Reynolds. And the women and children? What bestiality had they suffered at the *Suttee Chowra Ghat*? There were the three daughters of Major Lindsay, and the radiant and majestic Miss Yeates, for whom Athill Turner could not conceal his devoted admiration, Charlotte Newman with the hour-glass figure, Bella Blair and Ulrica Wheeler, and petite Amelia Horne, the Dâk Agent's daughter, who had soothed his broken lips with the last of her cold cream. None of them, he knew, was in the boat; they had been left at the *ghat* to die.

Had he and Moore and their fellows abandoned the *ghat* too soon? Could twenty-five men have achieved anything by fighting on? Undoubtedly not. They would have been cut down to a man, and the several score escapees in the boat would have similarly perished. Nothing they might have done would have halted the massacre. There was no justification for his feeling of guilt.

There was no moon, and blackness was complete. Eleven times they lowered themselves over the side, stupid with fatigue, to push the boat away from sandbanks. Ample water was no substitute for food, and all were near to collapse, aching with hunger. The severely wounded Henderson and Fagan were both comatose, and Dr Boyes knew they would not regain consciousness. Lieutenants Daniell, Satchwell and Master, who had been carried from the *Lal Koorti Ka Haspital*, were weakening. Without hospital attention they, too, would probably not see the end of the day.

The sun rose ahead of them, a golden orb in heavy cloud above the untidy scrub jungle. The cloud could mean that the expected rains were imminent, and rains meant the swelling of the river, a strongly flowing current and a swifter passage, but the rains might not come quickly enough, and they needed food desperately.

The boat still drifted slowly, and weary eyes searched the nearer bank. They had not passed the village of Nuzufghur during the night, Frank Whiting said. They were still two miles short of it. The boat, in fact, had travelled only ten miles in twice as many hours. At that rate they would reach Nuzufghur at mid-morning, the worst possible time if the villagers were hostile or if pursuing mutineers waited there. To abandon the boat in favour of an overland march was unthinkable; most of the hundred escapees were totally incapable of sustained physical effort. If only they could find food they might moor the boat in some obscure inlet until darkness again hid their passage down-river. Then, if the threatening rain speeded the river-flow, and they could hire or compel the assistance of some native boatmen, there would be only a hundred miles—

In the tangle of riverside jungle there were probably mangoes, paw-paws and other wild fruit. There was probably game, too, but stalking game and firing guns so close to a village of unpredictable loyalty would be hazardous. Then, without warning, there was another problem. As the boat rounded a bend they could see a brief stretch of open sand, and at the water's edge several natives were bathing.

As the crowded boat slowly approached, the natives clambered from the water to stand in an uneasy group, watching. From the boat a dozen loaded rifles were carefully levelled. 'If any of them run for it,' Thompson ordered, 'then bring them down.' But the natives could see the guns, and they did not move.

The boat grounded gently. 'They must be Nuzufghur villagers,' Whiting said, 'and that could be nasty. Bloody nasty.'

'We've *got* to get victuals,' Mowbray Thompson breathed. '*Any* victuals, and *now*. There's five of 'em. Suppose we hold four under our guns, and send away one with a promise of money?'

The Eurasian, Blenman, waded ashore with a loaded Adams pistol. They had never been entirely confident in the smooth-mannered Blenman since he had returned to the Dragoon Hospital after claiming to have penetrated seven picquets only to be turned back by the eighth. Blenman was a small man of neat, almost foppish, appearance, with a well-trimmed black moustache and beard framing a pale brown face. He spoke immaculate English, Hindi, Pushtu and Urdu, and his superior mannerisms stung those Europeans who struggled incompetently with just one tongue other than their own. Blenman was too clever by half, and he didn't know his place. Blenman was an Eurasian, and Eurasians were, well—

If Blenman was so clever, why was he only a musician of the 56th Native Infantry?

The Europeans' wariness towards Blenman had less to do with his mixed breeding than with his apparent unapproachability. True, Eurasians were not *quite* the right people with whom to be socially acquainted, but many held positions of responsibility in John Company's service, some with British subordinates. Others were accepted because of their parentage, like the children of General Wheeler, or their standing in local commerce. It was odd, people thought, that Blenman, a Christian, well educated and with a natural aptitude for languages, should choose to be only a musician in the 56th Native Infantry, when he might have been a toll-bridge collector or a postal official. Was there something unsavoury in the man's record that he didn't want questions asked? One could never tell about that sort of person. He did not mix, his manner was distant, and his appearance too fastidious for the approval of most Englishmen, but few would have diagnosed their dislike as being based on a feeling of inferiority when talking to him.

Blenman had been born Nand Ram. He knew nothing of his father except that he had been English, and by some strange arrangement the District Officer in Jhansi paid his mother twenty rupees on the first day of every month – an assured income which placed them beyond the vicissitudes of droughts, floods, cattle sicknesses and the predacity of money-lenders. Later he had attended the English school in Jhansi, and subsequently adopted the name Blenman from that of the schoolmaster from Norwich.

But Blenman was not ashamed of that aspect of his life. It had been the leopard that first betrayed him as a cringing coward.

He had never tumbled with a father, never brawled with the *ryot* children of the village on Jhansi's outskirts. When other boys herded goats, swam, fished, or took small girls into the bamboo scrub, Blenman walked with his books to school. He shrank from physical sports. Aggressive English boys wrestled, kicked balls, climbed trees and ran races. Blenman preferred history and arithmetic, and was taunted for being a book-swot.

A man-eating leopard had been terrorizing the area around Garha for more than two years, defying every effort to trap or shoot it and growing progressively more daring in its forays in search of human prey. Several times the animal had broken open doors or torn through a wall to reach a victim. Garha, however, was fifty miles from Jhansi, and it was unlikely that the murdering *bagh* would travel that far to make a kill.

But the man-hunter did travel that far, and it came by night to the house of seventeen-years-old Blenman and his mother.

Blenman slept in the inner of two tiny rooms, his mother in the outer from which a door opened onto a sunken, narrow alley. The night had been hot, and she had risen to open the door for a few minutes of cooler air. As she did so the leopard sprang from the darkness.

Blenman awoke to his mother's screams. He scrambled from his bed and to the bead-curtained opening of the outer room, and then froze with terror. His mother lay on her back on the rammed-earth floor, flailing helplessly as the leopard gripped a leg in its jaws and dragged her towards the open door and the darkness of the alley. Her face was turned towards him, mouth gaping and eyes wide with desperate pleading.

Those fleeting, terrible seconds seemed an eternity. Within reach of his hand was a *gandesa*, a heavy, razor-sharp blade with a pole-like haft, used for cutting cattle fodder. In determined hands it could be a vicious, even lethal, weapon, but Blenman did not move. He stood, appalled, as the leopard wrenched his mother bodily through the door and vanished. Moments later there was a final screech, then silence. Blenman flung the door shut and with trembling hands dropped the bar into its sockets. He fell to his knees, sweating coldly and paralysed by fear, and did not stir until dawn.

His mother's partly devoured corpse was found a half-mile from the house. There were no relatives except for the boy, and little sympathy among the villagers. The river, they complained, was too distant for a cremation that allowed the ashes to wash down to the Ganges, so they placed a live coal in the mouth of the deceased and threw the corpse into a ravine.

The District Officer in Jhansi sucked his teeth and said that he had no instructions for this sort of contingency, and he would have to write a letter. A reply would not be received for weeks, perhaps months, and in the meantime Blenman must fend for himself. The whole thing had been a nuisance for seventeen years and he, the DO, had more pressing responsibilities than other men's wild oats. Blenman could not guess what that meant, except that he was apparently destitute. Hardly considering the consequences, he enlisted in the 56th Bengal Native Infantry.

Blenman was an unpromising sepoy, and might have been 'sent away' after his first month were it not for his linguistic ability. He failed to offer the usual bribe of sixteen rupees, shared between the drill *havildar* and the company *jemadar*, for the privilege of qualifying in drill. His red coat was tight under his arms and his shako hurt his head, while his musket, pouch-belt and knapsack were a load for a coolie. The man would never make a soldier, Major Lindsay told Colonel Williams, but someone who spoke three native languages in addition to English was always an asset, and it would be a pity to relinquish him. Blenman became, ostensibly, a musician on the regimental muster list.

The circumstances of his attempt to penetrate the mutineers' picquets surrounding the *Lal Koorti Ka Haspital* had been as terrifying as his encounter with the leopard. He had not wanted to go. Several others had tried and failed, but the officers had insisted that he was the most qualified. There had been bile in his throat as he stole past Lieutenant Dempster's battery into the dark *maidan*. A note, written on the rice-paper fly-leaf from a Bible, was sewn into his turban cloth. Make southward for Ghatampur, they had told him, then turn for Allahabad.

But Blenman had not made for Ghatampur. He had crouched, shivering, in a culvert of the Ganges Canal, only six hundred yards from the *Lal Koorti Ka Haspital*, until the first grey of dawn, and had then crept back. He had talked his way past seven picquets, he told Captain Moore, claiming he had to buy cremation clothes for a dead brother. The eighth picquet had been of Moslem cavalrymen who did not care about Hindu cremation rites, and they had beaten him, robbed him of the few rupees hidden in his *dhoti* and even unravelled his turban cloth, but without discovering the note. If they saw him again, they had warned, he would need cremation clothes as well as his pig of a brother.

A few days later Blenman had watched, from the safety of the entrenchment, the attempted escape of the three Europeans and their wives, and he saw them taken by the sepoys only forty yards from the culvert in which he had cringed for a whole night. Captain Moore had regarded him silently for a long minute before nodding slowly with a tired shrug, but saying nothing. Captain Moore knew, Blenman sensed – but Moore was dead. Blenman was still alive.

Henry Delafosse and six men formed a half-circle around Blenman and the group of natives. Delafosse could understand only snatches of the exchange in colloquial Hindi. 'A quick butt in the gut,' suggested Private Sullivan, 'moight do a lot more than talkin', bedad.'

Blenman turned. 'One of them has offered to go for flour and rice if we give him five rupees. He'll leave his *lotah* with us as security.'

Delafosse nodded. 'And the others will stay here too. Tell them that if there's any treachery they'll be shot.'

The consenting native made off into the scrub promptly, but had hardly disappeared when the remaining four began to talk urgently to Blenman, nervously eyeing the guns pointed at them. Blenman listened, asked a brief question, then waved them to silence.

'They say the man who has gone is a bad man, a servant of the *zemindar*, and he will not return with food, but will betray us to the sepoys and militia in Nuzufghur. The *zemindar* is one named Babu Ram Buksh, whose estates lie further down-river on the Oudh side, and he has sworn that no Sahibs will escape his territory alive. He already knows of our escape from Cawnpore, and has soldiers and guns in Nuzufghur and Surajpur. If we are wise, they say, we will go quickly. They wish no harm to the Sahibs, and beg that we remember them when the white soldiers of Company *Bahadur* come back to Nuzufghur.'

On the boat's deck there was a hurried council of war. 'If it's two miles to Nuzufghur, and the same back,' Mowbray Thompson offered, 'we've got at least two hours' grace. Probably more.'

'That means,' Major Vibart calculated, 'that if we leave immediately we *might* get past Nuzufghur while the *zemindar*'s cut-throats are on their way here, and then scrambling back to Nuzufghur. It's rough scrub country.'

Frank Whiting was doubtful. 'Only if the *zemindar* is a bonehead, sir. If he has an ounce of dog-fat he'll realize that we *have* to pass Nuzufghur sooner or later. He's got us nicely tied with pink ribbon. We can't go back; we must go down. He can send a corporal's guard to see if we're still here. If we're not, then he sits on his pock-marked arse until we appear off Nuzufghur.'

There was really no choice. The tentative suggestion that they might now surrender themselves because Babu Ram Buksh could hardly be as murderous as Nana Sahib was dismissed without discussion. Every scruple of trust in a brown skin had been drained from them, and while there remained the flimsiest chance of reaching Allahabad they would continue to try. Besides, who knew how far the British relieving force had come? It might well have penetrated beyond Allahabad, by now – be only fifty – thirty – miles away. There was really no choice.

They pushed off the boat. The sky was heavily clouded, the air sultry and sweatily humid. With the stub of a pencil Frank Whiting wrote a brief statement of the fugitives' position and predicament, put the scrap of paper into a bottle, and threw it into mid-stream. The bottle floated ahead of them for several minutes, and then sank from sight. 'Obviously a bloody Indian bottle,' said Delafosse.

They saw Nuzufghur from a half-mile away – a riverside tangle of mud-brick walls and thatch, a roughly-paved *ghat*, melon and millet patches, a communal goat enclosure, spider-web nets, palm mats, and the usual debris floating in the shallows. At four hundred yards they could smell Nuzufghur, the musty-sweet aroma of native cooking, human and animal excrement, scented vegetation, drying fish and hot dust. But there were no women washing clothes and gossiping on the stones, no splashing urchins, no old men sitting in the shade, and the wheel of earthenware buckets that scooped water from the river was still, abandoned by its bullock. There was no sound, and nothing moved.

'I'm offering five to four that those bloody nigger minstrels are rammed and ready, behind cover, and with us in their sights,' said Mowbray Thompson.

He had hardly spoken when the boat's keel scraped bottom and, yet again, grounded hard. Seconds later, as if by signal, the clutter of Nuzufghur vomited men – shouting sepoys with muskets, local irregulars in assorted, ragged liveries, and a few mounted troops with excited dogs yapping at the horses' feet, all deploying in disorder along the river bank. There was the sickeningly familiar chutter of musket shots that had the women and wounded cowering below the gunwhale and a dozen men, with hardly strength to stand, waist deep in the river on the boat's exposed side, straining frantically at the clogged hull. Men cursed, sobbed, clawed, and cursed again as a hornets' swarm of bullets whipped up the river's surface. Major Vibart, already shot through one arm, had the other smashed. Chaplain-Captain Seppings was hit in an arm, his wife through the thigh.

'Holy Christ,' Frank Whiting croaked, 'they're bringing down a nine-pounder. If they fire canister at this range—'

A muffled thunder-clap was followed by distant sepoy screeches, and then crimson drenched the boat-deck. Frank Whiting, dead, sank into the frothed water without a sound. Captain Athill Turner flailed ludicrously with both legs shattered. Lieutenant Harrison had disappeared, and Quin, with eyes glazed, had a forearm hanging by a shred of flesh. The Eurasian, Blenman, stared uncomprehendingly at a hole in his abdomen, as big as a fist, through which his entrails were slowly spilling.

This, then, must be the end. The crowded boat was a shambles, of congested wounded, sick and dead, of bloodied, dishevelled people shorn of all dignity and restraint. Weakened in body and spirit by weeks of hunger and exposure, crushed and dejected by the loss of loved ones, and shocked by the constant horror of the past twenty-four hours' butchery, all hope of survival had now gone. Nothing, now, could save them. A sergeant tugged a despairing Mowbray Thompson over the gunwhale with torn and swollen hands. 'Blenman's got a bad one, sir,' Grady scraped. 'He's asking for a bullet to end it.'

What did it matter? The next canister shell, seconds from now, would end it for everyone. Thompson pulled himself towards Blenman, who huddled with bent knees high, his lower clothing sodden with blood. The man's face seemed to have shrunk, with eyes wide and black in shadowed pits. He mouthed urgently at Thompson, and Thompson lowered his head. And then Blenman was dead.

'They're reloading,' Delafosse warned, 'and taking their time. They've got plenty. What did Blenman say?'

'Nothing that made sense.' Thompson's apprehensive gaze was on the river bank, where jubilant sepoys and local militia were clustering around the nine-pounder. 'Something about a *bagh* – a leopard.' It would be any moment now. He could see the movements of the gun crew clearly. One man sponged, a second thrust home a canister shell, a third rammed. Thompson closed his eyes. From behind him, rising above the sobs and curses, he heard the voice of Chaplain-Captain Seppings.

'Yea, though I walk through the valley of the shadow of death, I will fear no evil; for thou art with me . . .'

Seppings' voice was drowned by an explosive whipcrack, and a woman screamed and screamed. Thompson's belly knotted. He could hear an odd rustling noise which, in a moment, was no longer a rustle but a shrill, surging hiss that stung his eardrums. There was warm wetness on his shoulders, plastering his hair over his face, choking his nostrils. The Chaplain's voice rose again to a triumphant shout. 'Goodness and mercy shall follow me all the days of my life—'

Baffled, tentatively, Thompson raised his head, to instantly flinch. Around the boat the Ganges boiled, yellow, under teeming, lashing rain that confined visibility to no more than thirty yards. The shore, the village, the gun and gesticulating sepoys had vanished behind a curtain of almost solid water. The boat trembled like a flogged animal, but remained fast. Henry Delafosse was standing upright, dancing. 'It's raining! IT'S THE BLOODY RAINS!' No muzzle-loading artillery piece would be fired in this deluge. Delafosse lifted a bewildered little girl in his arms and kissed her. 'Rain, rain, don't go away – stay with us another day!' Men and women were raising themselves, streaming with wetness, but with sudden, uncertain hope in their faces. The yellow, churned current streamed past with slowly increasing speed, swirling with river flotsam into the rain-haze, south-eastward, towards Allahabad.

20

She heard the ungreased wheels of the bullock-drawn *tongas*, accompanied by noisy voices, and saw the flicker of movement through cracks in the door, but could not think what they meant until the woman, Jemdani, came. The passing carts, said Jemdani, were transporting the surviving mem-Sahibs from the *Suttee Chowra Ghat* to the *Savada Kothi*, the Assembly Rooms, where the Maharajah would see them. One hundred and twenty-five had been taken, including *baba-log* and a few boys, but more were expected to be brought back from one boat that had briefly escaped the killing at the *ghat*. The mem-Sahibs, Jemdani smirked, were soaked, muddy and barefoot. Many had wounds bound with handkerchiefs or filthy rag, and there were two children without clothes. The mem-Sahibs and their milk-faced whelps were not so haughty now.

She saw the despair in Amelia's face, and took pleasure in adding more. 'There was one young mem-Sahib lying in a cart,' she confided, 'with blood on her clothes. She was beautiful and well-shaped, with long dark hair thrown back. It was long' – she stretched her hands downwards – 'below the top of her legs. The sepoys were saying that she was fair like a rose, an *Apsara* of Heaven, and it was a pity to put such a creature to death. They say she was the daughter of Blair Sahib, of the Commissariat.'

Bella Blair, then, had survived the killing – and Amelia had herself seen Ulrica Wheeler. Who else? Was it possible that her mother still lived? And Jemdani had mentioned *baba-log* – infants. Did they include Florence or Herbert, Agnes, Helen or baby Edward? 'The others,' she pleaded. 'Do you know any other names?'

But Jemdani did not wish to impart all her information at one time. There would be many other days for the enjoyment of the white girl's torment and humiliation. The situation was something to be prolonged. 'Your husband,' she countered mockingly, 'is he not a fine one, and perfect in shape? Is not your bed a couch of bliss, and do you not pass each night in trembling pleasure?'

Amelia flushed, shame swelling her throat and hot tears flooding her eyes. She dreaded the coming of dusk, that deepened the gloom of the hut and quietened the noise of the narrow street outside. She listened for footsteps, breathed with relief when they passed, cringed when they halted and the door-latch rattled. Then a yellow petal of flame reared from the oil lamp, guttering, and the smell of oil smoke was sickly in her nostrils. Mohammed Ismail Khan unwound his turban cloth.

For three days she had been confined to the hut. It was for her own safety, Jemdani said, for there were many who were not convinced that she was a true convert to Islam, and only the patronage of the powerful *maulvi*, Liakut Ali, stood between her and the *Savada Kothi*, where the other mem-Sahibs awaited the Maharajah's pleasure. When the *maulvi* left Cawnpore, Mohammed Ismail Khan must follow in his protection, without which Amelia would be in danger of her life.

Amelia was never certain if Jemdani always spoke the truth or wished merely to frighten her. Mohammed Ismail Khan did not converse in the accepted sense. Involuntarily, she flushed again.

Once each day, at noon, Jemdani brought her food – a scanty meal of chupatties or rice with a few scraps of mutton, sometimes a few vegetables flavoured with curry or sesame, a mango or a sour shaddock. There was a *lotah* of water, for drinking, washing, and cleaning her teeth. Her fare, Jemdani assured her, was better than that provided for the mem-Sahibs in the *Savada Kothi*, where the proud white ladies fought and scrabbled for boiled peas thrown on the floor by hilarious sepoys.

The pain and debasement of the first time had left her crushed and disgusted, incredulous that such a loathsome thing could be any part of marital relationships. Dear Mamma could not possibly have submitted to such as this, and appeared so composed at breakfast. He had lain against her, snoring, the sweat cooling on his body as she stared, sleepless, at the thatch of the roof. The flame of the lamp had died, and she was cramped, daring not to stir for fear of his waking. But he did, and reached for her again.

In the darkness his hands shocked her. Her thighs, he said, were things of beauty, her belly vaulted like an arch, her proud breasts were hyacinths and her neck was like a gazelle's. The opening of her mouth was the opening of a ring, her lips fresh and red. Her teeth might be taken for pearls and her cheeks for roses. Her eyes were black and well-shaped, her eyebrows of ebony were as the rounded flourish of a skilful writer's pen. Her brow was like the full moon in the night.

After that first time, Amelia tried to lie stiffly inert, her eyes closed and her thoughts divorced from the defiling of her body. It was not really happening to her, but to someone else. She thought of the Commissioner's garden party, of lemonade and cold mango-fool, ladies in frothy crinolines and gentlemen in white gloves, of church pews and the droning voice of the Reverend Moncreiff, and the jingling, shining guns of Lieutenant St George Ashe—

During the day she seldom saw him and, when she did, he rarely spoke and did not look at her. Amelia, although praying for news more reliable than that offered by Jemdani, could not bring herself to question him. It was Jemdani who confided that Amelia was not the only young mem-Sahib to have been abducted by men of the 2nd Cavalry. There had been three others – one of them the daughter of Wheeler Sahib, the Station Commander. The Maharajah had been angry, and had summoned the troopers responsible, insisting that the women should be given up immediately. He was unwilling for his hostages to be scattered, out of his hands. Three of the men had reluctantly obeyed; only Mohammed Ismail Khan had sworn that his captive had thrown herself down a well, and produced witnesses to support him. The witnesses had cost money, Jemdani said, and Amelia must keep herself hidden, for she would not wish to exchange her present circumstances for those of the *Savada Kothi*. Soon the *maulvi*, Liakut Ali, who had sworn the restoration of the Mogul Empire, would march with an army to relieve Allahabad, recently captured by a British force, and Mohammed Ismail Khan would go also.

Amelia wished she could believe everything that Jemdani said. If she were to be taken towards Allahabad, towards the British—

She sat, hour by hour, listening to the steady fall of rain on the thatch above her – the rain which, if it had come only two days earlier, might have meant the escape of every boat from the *Suttee Chowra Ghat*. And she listened for the footsteps, and the rattle of the latch.

For the last hour of the afternoon the torrential rain continued, thrashing the river's surface to a tobacco-coloured froth as it raced past the stranded boat, floating with tree branches, broken foliage and unrecognizable refuse. Frustratingly, the boat still refused to move, but it must do so soon. The water level was surely rising, and it was almost dusk. Rain, river and approaching darkness were in the Europeans' favour; there was hope still.

Then that hope was thrown back in their teeth. From the drenching rain-haze astern emerged a boat similar to their own, poled by natives and yawing wildly in the river's surge. As it heeled and swung towards them they could see the sodden scarlet and crossbelts of forty or more sepoys crouched on its deck.

Surprise was mutual. There were shouts of alarm through the rain and the native boatmen thrust frantically on their poles. The newly-arrived craft, apparently worked downstream from Cawnpore, in pursuit, was in no better plight than that of the fugitives. A straining boat-pole snapped with a noise like a pistol shot and flung its handler headlong into the yellow torrent. Then the boat, only twenty yards away, buried its bows in the sand and halted.

There were several moments of indecision, with the occupants of both craft staring at each other across the narrow stretch of storm-swept water; it was Mowbray Thompson who recovered first. 'Bayonets! Bayonets! Out! Out and at 'em!' But who was left? Himself, Harry Delafosse, Sergeant Grady,

Murphy, Sullivan, and a dozen other filthy skeletons who scarcely remembered if they were Queen's soldiers or John Company's, and no longer cared. It was kill or be killed, and they had just one effort remaining.

They went for the water, sixteen of them, with bayonets fixed. With odds of only three to one there was a chance of a savage reckoning with at least a few of the Cawnpore murderers. The confused sepoys were still clawing for handholds on their tilted deck when the berserk horde of British were upon them, stabbing, slashing, and crazily blaspheming. Hardly one of the mutineers had any opportunity to resist. Closely huddled in the waist, many had laid aside their muskets, which they scrabbled to find in the down-pouring rain, disputing ownership with blows. The three remaining boatmen flung themselves overboard, to be quickly followed by a half-dozen native soldiers, but for the slower thinking there was no quarter. Thompson and Delafosse emptied their five-shot pistols at point-blank range as their snarling supporters thrust and thrust again with the desperation of madmen. Hands raised in pleading were smashed aside, faces stamped on or clubbed. Within two frenzied minutes the boat's deck was piled with dead; not a sepoy lived.

'That's the way to deal with mad jackals.' Delafosse panted, sucking torn knuckles. 'Quick an' no nonsense. We'll know, the next time we have a bloody mutiny. I'll write to the *Calcutta Chronicle* about it.'

The party had suffered no injuries worse than bruises and minor lacerations. In the sepoys' boat there was a box of greased Enfield cartridges and packs of percussion caps to which, it seemed, the Hindu soldiers no longer objected. But there was no food, the boat-poles had vanished with the boatmen, and there was little advantage to be gained in transferring several dozen sick and wounded from one grounded boat to another, even if Thompson's wrecks were capable of doing so. They hauled themselves back, now racked with cold, teeth chattering.

Despite the rain, the freshening wind, and their hazardous situation, almost all were sufficiently overcome by exhaustion to sleep. Mowbray Thompson lacked the heart to order lookouts to remain awake, and determined to perform that duty himself. On his knees, he lodged himself in the angle of deck and gunwhale, convinced that the discomfort of his position would ensure his wakefulness. It did not, and he would later curse his stupidity. He might have slept for hours, or only seconds, but there were shouts, far distant, that his drugged senses wanted to ignore. He dragged open his eyes, with every stiff, aching muscle screaming protest. It was raining still, dark and shudderingly cold. but the boat was buoyant, floating. How far had they drifted – how far from the bank, and which bank? Were they a safe distance from Nuzufghur? What, in God's name, was ahead of them in this sheeting rain and night blackness?

The upsurge of optimism that the rain had promoted could not be sustained. None of the officers who still had the sense to calculate retained any illusions about the party's chances of ultimate survival; the rain had only delayed the inevitable for a few hours. The fittest of the remaining men were seriously debilitated, capable of only brief effort. Most were completely disabled by fever, injury, starvation and exposure, and even immediate, medical attention would be unlikely to save many.

'What's it look like, Mowbray?' Henry Delafosse had crawled forward. 'Is it a go? There'll be some good duck-shooting here after the rains, mark my words.'

Delafosse and himself, Thompson realized, were the last effective officers. They had to reach a decision. 'We're floating like a bung in a barrel,' he said, 'but Christ knows where. Harry—' He turned his head so that his mouth was close to the other's ear. 'Harry, we're not going to reach Allahabad like this. We've got to think of something else – and the first thing is victuals. We must get our hands on some provisions within the next few hours, or nothing else will matter. That means we have to land an armed party on one side or the other, find a village, and get back to the boat with as much food as we can carry'. He paused. 'I wish I knew the territory better. Nuzufghur is behind us, and somewhere hereabouts is Surajpur, but that's likely to be swarming with sepoys and the *zemindar*'s irregulars. Still, we can't choose, and if we get a detachment ashore at first light, with the weather to help, we might pull it off—'

Beneath them the planks jolted. The boat staggered, its stern swinging drunkenly in a half-circle and the keel rasping on the river's bottom. Delafosse's fingers gripped his companion's arm. 'The bastard!' They were aground.

Thompson stared into the rain-whipped darkness. 'Can you see anything?' he shouted.

Sergeant Grady had joined them. 'Will I get the men over the side, sir? There's about one push left in 'em.'

'No.' Thompson shook his head. 'No. If we're taking a detachment ashore, then this place – wherever it is – is probably as good as anywhere. At least nobody's seen us arrive. Sergeant, I want a dozen men ready for dawn, including yourself, for a foraging sortie. Rifles loaded and bayonets fixed, dry ammunition. Choose the fittest; we may have to move fast, and fight – and, God willing, we have to carry provisions. And see that all your men have boots. We'll likely be in scrub jungle.'

'Twelve men. Yessir,' Grady nodded. Then, 'That ain't leaving much for the boat, sir, if the blacks reach it before we get back. Not more'n five or six men as can stand—'

'I know it, Sergeant, but none of the people here have eaten for two days, and they've been on starvation rations for nearly a month. Every hour counts, and this could be our only chance to keep some of them alive. Likewise, we'll need every man we can spare for the foraging party, to carry, and to fight if necessary. I'm gambling that the weather will have dampened a lot of the mutineers' enthusiasm, and that most of them will be under cover, particularly at first light. If we don't get provisions now, we needn't think about anything else.'

When Grady had departed, Delafosse said, 'Mowbray, I hope you're right.'

Thompson sucked in his breath. 'Christ, old son, so do I.' He grinned wryly in the darkness.

Dawn came reluctantly, the temperature miserably cold for the Europeans clad in sodden rags and weak with hunger, but long before full light the painful truth of their new situation was apparent. They were no longer in the broad, main channel of the river; the boat had been thrust into the mouth of a narrow creek, and was now lodged with bows and stern against opposing banks, clogged with floating vegetation. The muddy Ganges streamed past, a tantalizing forty yards away.

Both sides of the creek, above the mud line, were curtained by soggy scrub jungle, reed grass, thornbushes, dwarf bamboo and trees trailing with creepers. Everything dripped wetness, and tangled foliage drooped under drizzling rain. They could hear the distant 'kuk-kuk-kuk' of jungle fowl, the bicker of monkeys.

But there was something more ominous than rain-soaked jungle or any of the wildlife it might contain. On the far side of the Ganges, almost precisely opposite the mouth of the creek and clearly visible in the brightening dawnlight, was a riverside village. It was sizeable, but it was not Nuzufghur. It could only be Surajpur.

'There are times,' Henry Delafosse despaired, 'when a gentleman's justified in using a little strong language.' It was damn cruel fortune that had spared them so far, baiting them with hope – and then this.

'If we can see the village,' Thompson said, 'then, any minute, they'll see us. Perhaps they have already.' The drizzling rain had ceased falling. Everything, it seemed, had turned against them. Mowbray crawled his way aft. The air was thickening with the smell of wet vegetation, and mosquitoes were beginning to swarm. Lieutenant Satchwell had died during the night, with a Mrs Fraser and a Mrs Coombe. Several others were comatose, including Daniell and Master. Major Vibart, shrugged over two smashed arms, lifted a yellow face that was twisted with pain and fatigue. 'Ah, Thompson! As messing officer you're a damn failure, and I'll have a word with the committee. My buttered eggs and gammon were cold again this morning. That *khansamah* will have to go.' His voice was weak, and Thompson guessed that the older man was beginning to lose his grip on consciousness. He outlined his earlier plan for a foraging party. 'But we daren't risk it now, sir – not with Surajpur staring at us. My guess is that we can expect visitors any time from now, and I'd like to meet them on shore instead of waiting in the boat. I've got a dozen men, and there's Delafosse and me. If we can give the blacks a shock, and make a demonstration, they might decide we're too prickly to tackle, and leave us be.' He grinned, although he never felt less like grinning. 'I can't promise buttered eggs and gammon, sir, but with luck we might manage boiled rice and mango.'

He didn't believe it, and neither did Vibart. Whatever else happened, the boat would never be dislodged from the narrow creek, nor could the sick and maimed be conveyed overland. They were as firmly trapped as they had ever been in Cawnpore or since, and their strength to resist was draining hourly.

Vibart nodded. 'But listen, Thompson. Some of us have *got* to get through to Allahabad, and it's likely to be the fittest. Get your detachment ashore, and give the blacks a hammering if you can, but if things go badly, or if you're outflanked, then you'll abandon the boat and do your damnedest to fight your way out.' He paused, wincing, 'And that, Thompson, is an order. I'm still commanding.'

Thompson, Delafosse, Sergeant Grady and eleven surviving privates of the 32nd and 84th Regiments were hardly ashore and deployed twenty paces apart in the wet scrub when the jungle around them swarmed with the red coats of sepoys, intermingled with others raffishly-clad who might have been local irregulars or armed villagers, crashing through the shoulder-high cane and matted undergrowth from every direction. There was a fusillade of wild shots. 'There's 'undreds of 'em, sir,' Grady said. 'Bleedin' 'undreds.'

'Keep your distances!' Thompson shouted. 'Don't lose sight of your flank men!' In the sodden labyrinth of tangled brush a man could walk three paces and be lost. He could hear the distinctive *kik-rrump* of his men's Enfield rifles and Henry Delafosse's pistol from the far left. Three rounds a minute, the musketry manual said, but a desperate man could load four and to hell with tight ramming. Christ, Grady was right. There were hundreds of them, like crawling red bugs, everywhere. They could be spread over a mile of jungle, and his line of fatigued men stretched barely more than two hundred paces.

The sepoys and their hangers-on, however, advancing through the scrub in no recognizable order, had been taken by surprise by the volley of rifle fire that had suddenly tumbled a dozen of their number. Accompanying villagers were anticipating the spectacle of several score dishevelled and helpless Sahibs being herded back to Surajpur in triumph, not an ambush, and the ill-disciplined militia of Babu Ram Buksh, *zemindar* of Doondriakera, had not expected to fight. Sepoys, turning to flee, threw into confusion others crowding behind. Ignorant of the numbers that opposed them, every noise and every movement in the cluttered brush was suddenly hostile. Excited natives fired at others, at a pair of buff-coloured bustard-quails that whirred frantically away, at tree trunks and unidentifiable shouts. Where were the brave sepoys of the 53rd Regiment, who had boasted of having killed all the soldiers of Company *Bahadur*? Who, then, was shooting in the jungle? Were the Sahibs coming?

A sudden glimpse of the thinly-spread line of Europeans pushing doggedly through the green cane scrub was enough to turn momentary confusion to infectious panic. There had been no concerted plan, no liaison between a dozen leaders jealous of each other. They melted away, but Mowbray Thompson, his sweating face bloodily slashed by thorns, and panting from the exertion of the moment, was apprehensive. It must take the enemy only minutes to realize how puny was the force that had checked them. They would be swarming back, and his front was so narrow that, inevitably, he would be outflanked and surrounded. Every instinct screamed that he should fall back on the boat in the creek, to hold a shorter line. But what then? Wasn't there an alternative?

There *had* to be an alternative. 'Keep 'em moving!' he roared. 'Don't let the bastards settle!' Savagely, he thumbed cartridges into his pistol. A rabble running like terrified sheep could not be re-formed for hours; and Mowbray Thompson needed hours. He shouted to his left, hoping that Delafosse, furthest from him, could hear through the soggy tangle of vegetation. 'Harry! Watch that bloody flank! D'you hear?'

There was a distant, muffled reply, and Sergeant Grady interpreted. 'He sez 'ee's flank is a seductive golden brown, sir, an' how's your'n?'

The rain had paused, but the sky was a dirty grey blanket over the tall *jhow*, and the humidity was thickening with every minute of daylight. Underfoot the earth, for months dust-dry, was like sponge, briefly glutted with water. The men were sweating profusely now, their strength taxed to the utmost by the labour of shouldering through the sodden thicket, and leg muscles were barely capable of dragging foot after foot. Cohesion was difficult. They fired at fleeting glimpses of red coats and crossbelts, the flash of a musket, or at cane brake flattening under scrambling brown legs. A hog deer broke from cover, halted, then scurried frantically away, and a flurry of pheasants erupted skyward with wings drumming.

They reeled on, firing, ramming, spitting black powder, firing again, nostrils clogged with sulphur and lips caked with blood, sweat, charcoal and mucous. And firing again. Soddin' Christ. Not a man among them could have carried more than his rifle, bayonet and cartridge wallet. Holy Mary an' Joseph – shure, there es times when soldierin' es bloddy harrd, so ut is. Shure, they didn't tell ye this ut Inniskillin'. Cartridge. Tear with the teeth. Powder in. Ball. Ram hard. Wad. Sod the wad. Ram. Cap. Cock. The bastards. Dayfid, bach, the auld sergeant's lost the spit an' wind he had in Brecon, look you. FIRE! Piss orf, you bleedin' Welsher, or yer'll get a mouthful o' teeth. Cartridge. Ram. Holloran, me jewel, wud ye be remem-b'ring Sackville Strayt in Fifty-one? Jasus, watch thet bloody haythen on ye left, or he'll hev ye fer curry. Cartridge. Ram. Scotsmen? I shit 'em; Welshers is bleedin' worse. FIRE! Yer festerin' bastard. Pick the bones out o' that, yer sod. Mister Thompson, sir – these black bleeders is thicker than shit on a blanket, they're bleedin' thousands. Thet wuzn't Fifty-one, me darlint, it wuz Fifty-two. FIRE! Jasus, me legs is loik wather. Keep yer soddin' twenty paces, yer Irish sod, or I'll spread yer like bleedin' strawberry jam. FIRE! Piss orf. Welshmen is soddin' animals. Christalmighty. Yer Bastard. FIRE! B' Jasus, shure an' I'd wroit a book on ut, ef I cud wroit.

Mister Delafosse, yer honour. Thim black divils is creeping 'round, sorr. Gawdalmighty, we aint' goin' ter stop 'em, Mister Thompson, sir. The sods is outflankin' us. FIRE—

As Privates Sullivan and Burt were saying, the scrub-lurking, widely-spread mutineers were seeping past the Europeans' flanks – or perhaps a totally different force had approached the creek from another direction. A chutter of musket shots were coming from behind as well as ahead. Uncertain, several of the men had halted, to turn, searching about them, and Mowbray Thompson choked on an oath. The thing he had feared most had happened. The enemy were between him and the almost defenceless boat while, equally disastrous, he and his detachment were surrounded.

Had they anticipated his sortie from the creek? Had he allowed himself to be outwitted by a rabble of blacks, scrambling blindly through tangling scrub while they attacked the boat in his rear? No, he didn't credit native troops with that degree of tactical acumen. He was just ludicrously outnumbered – but any first-year Addiscombe cadet could have told him that, with only fourteen effectives, he should have shortened his line, taken open order, and waited for supports. It was all written in the drill manual—

Supports? From where?

'Back! Back!' he sobbed. 'The boat!' Vibart was in the boat with two broken arms, Captain and Mrs Seppings, both wounded, and old Doctor Boyes, Daniell, Master. And there was George Nelson, the Tent Club secretary, and the Andersons, and Mrs Allen—

Jesus soddin' Christ. He'd never festerin' forgive himself if—

They were flinging themselves back on their tracks, with the fourteen staggering men splintering into disordered groups of twos and threes, noisily panting with mouths wide, savagely desperate as they smashed their way through the clawing cane behind their bayonets. The bastards. The shit-faced bastards. 'This is it, Mr Thompson, sir,' Grady croaked, wind-broken. 'This is where the boat was!'

But the boat had gone.

21

The two small rooms of the *Savada Kothi* had become inadequate for the growing number of European captives held by Nana Sahib. They now totalled two hundred and six, with the survivors of the *Lal Koorti Ka Haspital* supplemented by forty-seven others from Fatehgarh. Almost all were women and children, but there remained five men – Magistrate Thornhill and Colonels Smith and Goldie of the Fatehgarh garrison and Edward Greenway, proprietor of the Old Cawnpore Hotel, and his teen-age son Thomas.

The new prison was a house on the north side of the Ganges Canal, between the native quarter and the river. Once the residence of a native clerk of John Company, it stood among similar shabby villas only yards from the hotel in which Nana Sahib had taken residence with his entourage. Previously justifying only a numeral on an ordnance survey map, the house would hereafter be always known as the *Bibi Guhr* – the House of Women.

It was a flat-roofed, single-floor building of traditional mud brick, with two principal rooms each of twenty by ten feet, separated by a walled courtyard fifteen yards square in which grew a dusty, barren orange tree. In addition, there were several small and windowless closets, scarcely larger than cupboards, intended for native menials. The *Bibi Guhr* was marginally better than the *Savada Kothi*, but as accommodation for two hundred and six people it was excruciatingly confined.

There were no furnishings or bedding except a few coarse bamboo mats, and artefacts were limited to earthenware dishes, old soda-water bottles and the few pitiful personal belongings that the women had been allowed to retain by their predatory gaolers. One meal a day was provided, usually a mess of lentils or corn-meal with thin chupatties, brought by low-caste *mehtars*. They ate with their fingers, ground their own corn with hand-mills, and tried hopelessly to wash the children's rags in tiny quantities of water and no soap.

Heat and exposure, malnutrition, untreated wounds, inadequate and reeking toilet facilities, the swarming, infection-bearing flies, and doubtful water all contributed towards a lengthening death-roll. There were cholera and dysentery in the *Bibi Guhr*, and during only eight days a native doctor, belatedly assigned by Nana Sahib to the prison-house, recorded the deaths of eighteen women, seven children and a Hindu *ayah*. Months later investigators would read notes such as 'Name: *eck baba* (one baby). Disease: *ap se* (of itself).' Nana Sahib, alarmed at the diminishing number of hostages, ordered that all should be driven from the fetidness of the *Bibi Guhr* once daily, to sit in the open for an hour.

There were still acts of sympathy by a few natives, usually the sometime servants of European households. Small quantities of milk and bread were smuggled past the guards, and on one occasion a sepoy of the 56th purchased eight annas' worth of sweetmeats for Mrs Williams, widow of the Colonel, and her daughter Georgiana. More often, however, an overt charitable gesture or even a solicitous enquiry would be rewarded by a blow in the face from a contemptuous gaoler.

On 28 June the city of Cawnpore had been ablaze with lights, by order of Nana Sahib, in celebration of his great victory over Wheeler Sahib Bahadur, and his own consecretion as Peshwar of the Mahrattas. 'As by the bounty of the glorious Almighty,' he proclaimed, 'and the enemy-destroying fortune of the Emperor the yellow-faced and narrow-minded people have been sent to hell, and Cawnpore has been conquered, it is necessary that all the subjects and landowners should be as obedient to the present Government as they had been to the former one . . .'

Nana Sahib was uneasy about the loyalty of the civil population, particularly the more influential landowners and merchants, for many of whom the new regime was anathema. Most of the shops in the bazaars were shuttered against the activities of predatory sepoys and prowling riff-raff. There was a lack of law enforcement, prices were high, and there were increasing references to Nana *Soor* – the pig. Thousands of people earlier employed by the Sahibs were now destitute. Money and provisions for the Army were becoming increasingly difficult to requisition; the commissariat lived from day to day, uncertain of the next, and the troops complained that their pay was no better than it had been under the Sahibs and now purchased considerably less. Behind bolted doors and drawn blinds there were very many in Cawnpore who bitterly rued the disappearance of John Company's paternal bureaucracy.

The ownership of the Ganges Canal, with its toll revenues, had been presented to Azimullah Khan. To awe the populace, Nana Sahib paraded his entire military force – six regiments of infantry, two of cavalry, artillery, and irregulars and deserters from every quarter of Bengal. Nana enjoyed the compliment of a royal twenty-one gun salute, his brothers and nephew seventeen each, and General Jwala Pershad eleven, by which time the awed populace were streaming away with tingling eardrums. Equally painful for the Nana, but necessary for morale, the native contractor Ram Dabidin was publicly awarded five thousand rupees for the loss of his fleet of river boats on the previous day.

Nana Sahib's residence was now the Old Cawnpore Hotel, its verandah flanked by a pair of six-pounder guns in the manner of General Wheeler's divisional headquarters, while bored sentries stood at the door. The two largest, lower floor rooms were reserved for public receptions, the daily confusion of subedar-brigadiers and havildar-colonels, complaining merchants, *maulvis*, self-appointed ministers and hangers-on. There was a great deal to be argued over in addition to the administration of the Cawnpore district.

Fifty miles to the north-east Lucknow had not yet been subjected to direct assault, although the surrounding province was completely in the hands of the mutineers. For several weeks strenuous efforts had been made to fortify the Residency, demolish adjacent buildings, and accumulate stocks of provisions and ammunition. The news of the massacre at

Cawnpore was shattering. Lucknow was now alone. When intelligence told of approaching mutineers only ten miles away, Sir Henry Lawrence resolved not to be trapped as Wheeler had been; he would meet trouble halfway, in the open.

The enemy force was reported to be of 500 infantry, 50 cavalry and one gun, which might have been thought suspiciously meagre for the task of investing Lucknow. Lawrence marched with 300 men of the Queen's 32nd. 170 Native Infantry, 36 Volunteer Horse, 84 Oudh Irregular Cavalry, ten guns and a howitzer drawn by an elephant. Unfortunately the Commissioner's information was widely inaccurate. He found himself faced by 5,500 infantry, 800 cavalry and 16 guns. Lawrence's own native cavalry and artillerymen deserted to the enemy, and the balance of his column cut its way back to Lucknow with the loss of half of the 32nd and many of his best officers. The mutineers followed, and the siege of Lucknow was about to begin in earnest.

The high water mark of the Sepoy Revolt had been almost reached, but in Cawnpore this was far from apparent. Everywhere the Europeans had been overwhelmed, and there seemed no limit to the possibilities offered. True, the mutineers had not yet met European troops in a set-piece battle or in anything like comparable numbers but, apart from Delhi where the besieging British were as pinned down as the besieged, the only threatening concentration was that at Allahabad, to be numbered only in hundreds, and men like Azimullah Khan, Jwala Pershad and Baba Bhut were loud in claiming that the time was ripe for these puny remnants to be swept away. And why only Allahabad? There was Calcutta, where the King of the Mahrattas could sit in the Governor-General's chair in Government House, his generals occupy the fine white houses near the Esplanade . . .

In the evenings, in the Old Cawnpore Hotel, the drifting *punkahs* dispersed the haze of hashish smoke and the smell of cooking from the kitchens as Nana Sahib entertained with music, dancing and pantomime. There were hundreds of dishes, of meats, flavoured rices and sweetmeats, with sherbet for the orthodox and French brandy for the daring. To drums and flutes the dancer Oula swayed, her arms and ankles jingling softly with silver bangles. An emerald shone from her bared navel, and there were mirrors on her slim fingers, *alacktaka* on her nails and crimson betel on her lips. As her sinuous dance quickened and her skirt whirled the cross-legged audience watched with fascination. Nana Sahib, it was whispered, paid her a thousand rupees for every night of the sensuous pleasures of the rainbow arch, the turnabout, the somersault, and the tail of the ostrich.

And in the nearby *Bibi Guhr* the women lifted their children to the latticed windows to breathe the cool breeze of sunset. They could hear the noise of revelry from the hotel, and the shouts of laughter as a native entertainer impersonated a Sahib officer, prancing and puffing with gloves and cane.

Amelia no longer knew the date nor the day of the week. She calculated that the end of June had passed, and then, in almost the same thought, decided that it did not matter. Day followed identical day until she learned to judge the passage of time by the glimmer of sunlight through the cracks in the door and window. Jemdani came at noon with monotonous food, doubtful gossip and innuendo, and Amelia listened to the rolling thunder of the gun salutes from the distant *maidan*, unaware of its meaning and afraid. Then, on one occasion, Jemdani led her from the hut for an hour's walk in the noise and glare of the *Sudder* bazaar. Amelia clung closely to her companion, unrecognizable in a hot, tent-like *burqha* worn over her head and shoulders. She was not grateful for the excursion, only relieved to be returned to the solitude and gloom of the hut in the 2nd Cavalry lines, to wait, until Mohammed Ismail Khan came.

Involuntarily, inescapably, she realized, her resolution was draining, to be replaced by a submissiveness towards her captors that she would earlier have never thought possible. She was contemptuous of herself, but even the contempt was lessening. Her predicament was no longer a dream; it was real. It was her earlier life as Amelia Horne that was becoming imaginary. The education and conventions of eighteen years were becoming progressively distant, and she was beginning to think like a native, like the subjugated wife of a Moslem.

And there was something else that sickened and yet simultaneously excited her. She had struggled to remain unresponsive during the hour of carnal animalism that was a part of her every night, but she had failed. Her own flesh was betraying her. The shiver of apprehension as his mouth sought her breast was shamefully exhilarating, and there was a strange contortion within her that she had never known. Her heart pounded and she felt vaguely faint. Dear God, she screamed silently, what is this? Her mouth filled with saliva and she throbbed with an irresistible craving. This was wrong, wrong, wrong – but her legs, treacherously, were splayed, and her nails bit into his flesh. When he entered her, she choked, thrusting against him, and he laughed, his hands under her buttocks. Dear God, dear God, Mamma, Mamma—!

When the humiliating madness was finished she lay back, spent, uncaring that he kissed her lips, her thighs, uncaring that she lay naked under his gaze. He laughed again as, servilely, she washed his lower body with water from the *lotah*. 'Ah, how lustful has God made woman,' he murmured, 'and how deeply she drinks of the cup of her husband.'

Mohammed Ismail Khan was less arrogant when he and Amelia were summoned to the tent of Liakut Ali. 'There is no God but Allah—' the trooper began, but the *maulvi* ignored him, his black eyes on Amelia. She could see fragments of rice on his beard and smell onion on his breath. She lowered her gaze.

'Do you know Allahabad, woman,' he enquired, 'as I do?' The *maulvi* had once been a school-teacher in Allahabad, but his knowledge of the city's military aspects was negligible. Such ignorance in a *maulvi*, however, could not be confessed to a female.

Amelia nodded. Her heart leapt, but she kept her eyes lowered. 'I know Allahabad well,' she affirmed. She had never been to Allahabad. She was only aware that the British were there and, if Jemdani had spoken the truth, Liakut Ali intended to lead his followers in that direction. The *maulvi* leaned forward. 'Then tell me of Allahabad,' he ordered, 'to prove that you know it well.'

Only seven or eight days earlier, in the *Lal Koorti Ka Haspital*, Lieutenant Delafosse had been talking to Amelia of Allahabad, but she had scarcely listened. Now she groped for memory. 'It is like Calcutta – which you will also know – but smaller, and greener than Cawnpore. There is a red sandstone fort at the junction of the rivers, and a bridge of boats, but elephants can swim the river with their *mahouts*.' She considered. 'There is a *maidan*, and a tree-lined Mall' – all Indian cities had a *maidan*, and there was sure to be a Mall – 'and public gardens with a bandstand. Then there's the Bengal Club, the Breakfast Club, the Allahabad District Bank, the offices of the *Indian Planters' Gazette*, the orphanage and the Europe Shop—' She might have been describing any Anglo-Indian location from Calcutta to Peshawar.

'That is exactly correct,' Liakut Ali said. 'And do you know the approaches to the fort, and the gun positions of the *topkhana*?'

'I know the roads,' Amelia nodded again. 'My great-uncle, who is an indigo-planter, lives in Allahabad.' That at least was true, but she had met him only once.

The *maulvi* was convinced. 'I am pleased. You will follow with my army, which is of thousands. It is possible that your knowledge will be of some help, for although I know everything you have described of Allahabad, and much more, I cannot do all things. In the name of God, the Compassionate, the Merciful . . .'

Two days later the three thousand followers of Liakut Ali streamed south-eastward along the Grand Trunk Road in the direction of Fatehpur and Allahabad. At the head of the column rode Liakut Ali and his subordinate *maulvi*, Mohammed Ameerun Ali, behind them twelve guns drawn by plodding bullocks. The army for the liberation of the holy city of Allahabad straggled over five miles – companies of sepoys with shakoes and trousers abandoned for turbans and *dhotis*, cavalrymen in silver grey and irregular horsemen in ragged *alkhalaks*, feudal militia, carts piled with baggage and bedding, camels and elephants, ash-smeared *sadhus* and beggars, robes of crimson, plum, bronze, amber, green and saffron, straw umbrellas, ammunition limbers, *nautch*-girls, grass-cutters and *bhisties*, children and dogs. In a bullock *tonga* with shrieking wheels was Amelia, her *zeinab* – beauty – hidden by the suffocating *burqha*, for no man but her husband could look upon her unveiled.

Alongside the cart Mohammed Ismail Khan rode a grey Arab that had once belonged to Colonel Larkins of the Bengal Artillery. He was in a sullen humour, for Liakut Ali, it seemed, valued him less than the woman, and had ignored him in her presence. Did not he, Ismail Khan, deserve to be a Rissaldar-Major? Was not the woman his? And did he not have the Colonel's horse?

Major Sydenham Renaud, Madras Fusiliers, who had marched from Allahabad on 30 June with 200 of the Queen's 84th, 200 Fusiliers, 120 Sikh horse and two guns, had advanced only forty miles, repairing the telegraph wires as he went, when the news of Cawnpore's surrender and massacre reached him. Renaud's philosophy regarding an enemy was similar to that of his commanding officer, Lieutenant-Colonel Neill. In two days he had hanged forty-two men at the roadside and burned to the ground every village on his route. Then, on hearing of Cawnpore, he shot twelve natives who had failed to prostrate themselves as his column passed. The bloody chapter of British vengeance had been opened, and would not be closed for more than two years.

If the reports of the total annihilation of the Cawnpore garrison were true, then, from Havelock's viewpoint, a measure of urgency had been removed from his relief attempt, tragic though the reason might be. True, there was still Lucknow but, so far as he yet knew, Lucknow was not under close siege and was, moreover, a stronger defensive position than Wheeler's miserable entrenchment around the Dragoon Hospital. Havelock's force in total was small enough without frittering it away by the madcap dashes of small detachments like Renaud's which, despite their ferocity, could achieve only localized successes unlikely to seriously contribute towards the ultimate pacification of Bengal. Havelock ordered Renaud to burn no more villages, to halt at Lohunga, and wait until overtaken by the main column which would march from Allahabad on the following day, 4 July.

The order to halt incensed not only Renaud but also Lieutenant-Colonel Neill, still in Allahabad and still smarting with frustration, ready to dispute any action by a man who, only weeks earlier, had not even been in India. Neill committed the unforgivable sin of telegraphing the Commander-in-Chief, Sir Patrick Grant, requesting that the order be rescinded. In Calcutta, where clerks and merchants in wideawake hats were drilling with bayonets, women were at pistol practice, and clergymen roared the Lord's vengeance from every pulpit, Grant acquiesced, compounding Neill's disloyalty by ordering Renaud's continued advance. It would be the first of several breaches between Havelock and his impetuous subordinate.

Havelock's force now mustered a thousand strong, the majority comprising the balance of the Madras Fusiliers and 84th Foot, a battalion each of the 64th and the 78th Highlanders, 130 Sikhs, 18 mounted volunteers and six guns. With too few bullocks for the baggage carts, however, the march was again delayed. It was not until the rain-swept afternoon of the 7th that the hastily-gathered force moved off, leaving only 150 men to hold the fort at Allahabad. The Highlanders had exchanged their hackled bonnets for curtained forage caps, but still wore scarlet woollen doublets with buff facings, plaid kilts, woollen half-hose, pipe-clayed gaiters and boots. The other Queen's soldiers were no less encumbered, and only the Fusiliers enjoyed the relief of white duck trousers and smock-coats.

It was a wretchedly uncomfortable march. Intervals of heavy rain soaked and chilled the men, and then they steamed under a hot sun, sweating and itching, plagued by flying insects. The *kunkur* road surface – crushed limestone – turned to ankle-deep grey slime. The column halted after three hours, having outstripped its carts despite the conditions, and most of them slept on the waterlogged earth without tents or blankets.

The second and third days were similarly difficult, with no

more than ten miles covered on each, but the men were fiercely eager, neither complaining nor needing any urging. Every mile provided evidence of the passing of the advance force under Renaud, and Havelock's face grew progressively grimmer. Corpses hung from trees, putrefying, fly-blackened and torn by scavengers. Huts and *dâk* bungalows were charred, sodden ruins, and natives fled at the Europeans' approach or fell to their knees. Livestock had been driven off, crops abandoned to the elements.

Meanwhile, Renaud had marched into trouble. He and his command were at Syranee, deep into rebel-held country and in imminent peril of being swept away by a native army of 3,500. The muddied men of the advance force were in extended order, facing the skyline to the near westward from which the enemy was expected to deluge at any moment. It was Renaud's first collision with the full weight of an organized army of mutineers, and it was promising to be his last. The enemy commander, Tantia Topee, had been watching Renaud's headstrong approach for a week, and had carefully planned a reception from which there could be no escape for the 400 Europeans. What Tantia Topee did not know was that, on Renaud's heels, were Havelock's thousand infantrymen, weary and blistered, but provoked to savage petulance by the rigours of their march from Allahabad. Native patrols had reported only a short, double line of white soldiers half hidden by tall grass, smoking their pipes and spitting, and Tantia Topee had an answer for tall grass. It was going to be very easy.

When the news of Renaud's predicament reached him, Havelock was still seventeen miles away, his column halted for the night in the shelter of mango groves. Many of his men had not experienced hard marching for many months, and their performance under the prevailing conditions was admirable. Still, there was no alternative but to drag them from their huddled, drugged sleep and form them up for a night tramp. The destruction of Renaud's force following so quickly after the Cawnpore disaster, would exalt rebel morale and further damage British reputation in the eyes of those native rulers who still held back from the conflict.

Havelock was aware that, as a result of his inherent caution, he was not a popular commander, but on this occasion there could be no cause for complaint. Numbed with fatigue, his men stumbled into the night. The enemy, Havelock calculated, would attack Renaud at dawn.

In the van were the 78th Highlanders, the Ross-shire Buffs, a battalion to which Gaelic came easier than English and of which almost all its soldiers claimed one of only seven surnames – Mackenzie, MacDonald, Tullock, Macnab, Ross, Gunn, or Mackay, and fully half boasted the first name Donald. Captain Francis Maude, Royal Artillery, had dashed from Ceylon with only 30 regular artillerymen and no guns, but had made up the deficiency from the Allahabad magazine, and reinforced his gun-crews with infantrymen from the 64th. Both the Madras Fusiliers and the Queen's 84th had earlier sent detachments to Cawnpore, to die, and they were in a mood to march their feet bloody and fight like madmen. The gentlemen volunteers – displaced officers, planters and burned-out merchants – would need to be curbed rather than exhorted. Only the Sikhs' loyalty was an unknown factor.

Mile followed lurching mile, with the humid blackness of the night vibrant with the chirruping of millions of crickets, the croaking of bullfrogs, the incessant whine of insects, and foul with the smell of wet lime trees. At two in the morning there was a distant shout, scattered cheers swelling to a roar, and then the triumphant wail of the Highlanders' bagpipes. Renaud had been overtaken, only four miles from Fatehpur – and Fatehpur was less than fifty from Cawnpore.

As if startled by the skirl of pipes, the moon suddenly appeared from behind heavy cloud, to flood the wet landscape with brilliant silver. Renaud had his men in open order on both sides of the Grand Trunk Road, in tall grass on a shallow ridge that commanded the road for a mile in both directions and the flat grassland on each flank. In the dry season it would have been excellent cavalry country, but it was now studded with great ponds of water and, off the road, little better than a swamp in which a man could sink to his knees. Somewhere ahead was Fatehpur, on which the yet unseen rebel army was centred. It needed two hours to dawn, and Havelock needed those two hours. He sent his eighteen volunteer horsemen ahead to reconnoitre the road, then ordered everyone to breakfast and rest. Every minute that Tantia Topee delayed his attack allowed Havelock's reeling, rear-marching troops to come into line, to swill water, cram their mouths with food, to remove clenching boots and rub blistered feet with beef-fat, draw and reload weapons, take a bite of black plug, spit, and make ready. When Tantia Topee's bugles sounded the advance, just after seven o'clock, it was already too late. He had missed his chance.

Further westward, beyond Fatehpur, the leading files of the army for the liberation of Allahabad slouched to a halt. From somewhere ahead, far distant, came the rumble of cannon-fire. It must be Fatehpur. Who fought at Fatehpur? Amelia could hear the gunfire, like a far-away drum, and within her the ember of hope that had almost died was suddenly rekindled. Was it the British? As near as Fatehpur?

The *maulvi* was clearly worried, frowning with narrowed eyes as he listened, but the distant rumble had faded. It might have been only thunder below the clouded horizon, bringing rain. 'We will go on,' Liakut Ali decided. 'The rest is the will of God.'

Northward, on the bank of the Ganges, Mowbray Thompson put a filthy finger to cracked and blackened lips. 'Harry – listen! For Chris' sake, isn't that artillery?'

Delafosse nodded, but uncertain. If a starving and exhausted man could see a mirage, he could probably also hear one.

'What's in that damn direction?' Thompson insisted. 'Fatehpur?'

They waited, listening impatiently, but they could hear nothing more than the murmer of the river, the hum of mosquitoes.

Havelock would later write that the whole affair was decided in ten minutes and, if true, they must have been ten of the most vital minutes in the history of India. The engagement before

Fatehpur was modest in dimension, would never be referred to as a battle, nor would the name be embroidered on the colours of the regiments participating. Even so, a defeat suffered on this occasion could have been catastrophic. Apart from the British clinging tenuously to the Ridge outside Delhi, Havelock's force represented the barrel-scrapings of both Queen's and Company available military resources; if it was overwhelmed, almost nothing would stand between the mutinous native armies and Allahabad, Benares, Patna, and even Calcutta. Lucknow must fall, and the Delhi Relief Force would be isolated. Those native princes who waited to see which way the tide turned might well be tempted to throw their weight behind the mutiny, and the Punjab, held by a thread, would be in general revolt. Nepal, Afghanistan and Persia might become involved, and there was always Russia waiting on the sideline, still angrily smarting after the Crimean War. A great deal depended on the little British force astride the Grand Trunk Road before Fatehpur.

Hundreds of men were sitting or lying among the wet grass, many with boots removed, slapping at flies on reddened necks. The sun was warm on their backs, and behind the shallow ridge the kettles of the 64th were steaming with porridge stirabout. Maude's guns, now eight in number, loaded, and with bullocks in their traces, were in battery across the road which bisected the centre of the line, screened by a hundred infantrymen with Enfield rifles. The Highlanders, standing with water over their boots, occupied the right centre, and the Madras Fusiliers the right flank. The 64th held the left centre, with the Sikhs, under Captain Jeremiah Brasyer from Allahabad, drawn up on the far left. As Havelock interrogated two natives driven in by the picquets, the eighteen gentlemen volunteers came spilling over the skyline from the direction of Fatehpur, their horses' feet splashing. Seconds later a 24-pound shot struck the road only six yards from the commander and then ploughed on among the 64th's camp kettles.

A bugle sounded, limpid on the morning air. Thirteen hundred infantrymen climbed to their feet, rifles rising to the present with bayonets glittering in the sunshine. Thirteen hundred hands unbuckled expense pouches, thrust home percussion caps. The murmured conversation of moments earlier had died to complete silence. Behind the guns the sergeants whirled their glowing fusees, and Havelock drew his watch from his cummerbund. 'A fine early start,' he approved.

The long wall of enemy cavalry came into view, a mile distant, advancing at a leisurely walk, stirrup to stirrup and in excellent order of spaced squadrons, as they had been taught by British officers in the schools of Etawah and Sultanpur. Among them could be distinguished the dark blue and scarlet of the 6th Bengal Irregular Cavalry, the French-grey of the 3rd, the pale blue of the 2nd. The sodden ground deadened the drumming of their hooves, but there was an audible, steely whisper as a thousand sabres rasped from scabbards, and the waiting British could hear the shouts of native officers, faint, but shrilly English. 'Trot! Trot out!' And then, '*Sivaji ki jai!*'

A trumpet trilled, and the trot became a canter, with the rissaldars' sabres stretched sideways at shoulder height to check the pace and dressing of the jingling lines that followed. All was precision, a drill-book cavalry movement. Would not the Colonel-Sahib have approved? How could two short ranks of infantry stand against such as this?

They had not noticed, yet, that fifteen hundred yards ahead waited rather more than two short ranks of infantry.

'Prepare to receive cavalry front!'

Hidden enemy nine-pounders were firing at extreme range, with the shot jolting into the road and spinning away dangerously. The mounted volunteers clattered into the lines, and Lieutenant-Colonel Fraser Tytler, Quartermaster-General, dismounted to make his report. Havelock nodded. 'Thank you, Colonel. We shall let them get just a little closer, I think, and then we shall see.' Another hundred yards, and the approaching cavalry would be within range of the British rifles.

In that instant the lines of cavalry splintered into confusion, with hundreds of troopers wrenching at their reins, horses rearing, screaming and tangling. Now they could see – not the flimsy detachment they had expected to ride into the ground, but *battalions* of infantry drawn across the sodden green of their front, a long paint-slash of congealing scarlet, white, blue, tartan, stippled with the glitter of bayonets like silver grass. And saddling the road – *jeldi, kubbadar!* – the black mouths of eight nine-pounder guns. At only one thousand yards—?

Havelock grunted, annoyed. He snapped at an aide. 'My compliments to Major Stirling, if you please. He will advance a hundred riflemen to that copse—' He pointed. 'And to Captain Maude. His battery will move forward in support. If they won't come to us, we'll have to go to them.' He splayed his fingers, red-blotched with prickly heat. 'Mohammed said it first.'

A hundred men of the 64th cascaded untidily down the ridge, with sergeants shouting and the impulsive volunteers following in their wake. Maude's gun lascars slashed, the bullocks threw themselves into their traces with heads low and eyes bulging, and the clogged wheels of guns and caissons scudded, crushing their way over ground as water-logged as a paddy field. Ahead, the temporarily disconcerted cavalry was breaking away to left and right, momentum lost, but revealing for the first time a mass of native infantry, several gun batteries and, to the rear, two gaudily caparisoned elephants. It was plain that the bulk of the rebel army was still unaware of the increased number of British troops, for their batteries opened fire immediately and the closely formed sepoys, intermingled with groups of gesticulating riff-raff, continued to swarm forward.

Havelock's situation was far from invulnerable. He was outnumbered by three to one, and a determined flanking movement on the part of the enemy could roll up his line. 'We can't let ourselves be bearded like that,' Havelock decided. 'Sound "General Advance".' The General's field bugler, Dick Pearson of the 78th, lifted his bugle.

Lieutenant-Colonel 'Wattie' Hamilton of the 78th, his face scarcely less scarlet than his tunic, turned his horse about. 'Highlanders! There's space for every name of ye dead in the *Inverness Courier*, and the minister'll read ye names in the kirk every second Sunday in July! Pipe-Major! Ye can stretch ye lungs wi' "Johnnie Cope".' He drew his claymore. 'Ross-shire Buffs! At the double – fooor-WARD!'

Highlanders, Fusiliers, Queen's infantry and Brasyer's Sikhs surged forward in pursuit of the 64th's skirmishers. Maude's battery had halted, fired once, then plunged left from the road, his gun-wheels hub deep in the swamp and the lascars and artillerymen heaving, feet scrabbling. The volunteers, riding wide, reined only four hundred yards from the enemy to volley, and saw three native troopers spin from their saddles. At a mere two hundred yards – point-blank range for the nine-pounders – Maude halted again, and his men flung themselves on their guns, hand-spiking them around. Behind, at deploying distance, came the European infantry.

The effect of Maude's fire was shattering, clawing down sepoys in their dozens, but there was worse to come. The Enfield rifle was sighted up to 900 yards and lethal even further. There had been no formal training with the new weapon, and most men were only vaguely familiar with the purpose of a calibrated rear-sight; many thought the figures referred to muzzle velocity, not range, and invariably selected the highest. Even so, the superiority of the rifle over the older smooth-bore was never more plainly demonstrated. The sepoys, halted in their tracks by Maude's artillery, but confident that they were beyond the reach of small arms, now reeled back, confused and unbelieving, as the distant rifle-fire scythed them down. How did the Sahibs' guns kill *before* they were fired? As one sweating Fusilier put it, the nigger minstrels were going to have the Enfield cartridges, one way or the other, cow-fat or no cow-fat.

On Havelock's extreme right the fire-eating Renaud blasphemed his Madras Fusiliers to the crest of a knoll, deployed, then poured rapid fire into the retreating mutineers who could do nothing in retaliation. The retreat, reluctant at first, quickly became beyond the control of the cane-slashing jemadars and, when the Highlanders with their bizarre kilts and bagpipes were within 150 yards, the natives broke, streaming away from the guns that had hitherto maintained a commendable rate of fire. Few had ever seen more than a few dozen European troops at one time, and none had seen Highlanders.

The engagement was going almost too well for the British, and Havelock had cause to be apprehensive. The men of his force must be reaching the limits of their physical endurance, and the terrain over which they now advanced, sheeted with water, would have exhausted the fittest. The disordered enemy was falling back on Fatehpur, surrounded by high-walled garden enclosures and embracing many houses of substantial construction – a warren of narrow streets among which the British superior rifle-power would be nullified. If the sepoys were given time to reform, Fatehpur could be a spiteful obstacle. Already another rebel battery had begun firing from beyond the clumps of mango trees that stood like islands in the marsh, and droves of native troops were congregating as an officer gesticulated from the back of an elephant. The Grand Trunk Road, where it disappeared into the outskirts of Fatehpur, was barricaded by upturned carts and piled logs.

Captain Francis Maude, Royal Artillery, had never laid and fired a nine-pounder gun at an elephant in his life. He did not recall anything being said in Woolwich or Hythe about elephants. He sighted carefully along the 'line of metal' – from the top of the barrel's base ring to the top of the muzzle – with a finger raised as a panting artilleryman inched the gun-trail in traverse with a hand-spike. 'Make ready!' He was satisfied and stepped back, groping for his glass. If the target did not move, he calculated, there was going to be one bloody surprised elephant— 'Fire!'

Even as the gun erupted and reared backward, the elephant, six hundred yards distant, turned slowly, presenting its rear. Maude swore, but the hurtling shot struck the animal under its tail, ploughed through bowels, paunch and lungs, then smashed bloodily from its chest. The shocked monster screamed, and crashed sideways into the marsh as men scattered desperately in all directions.

'They'll never believe it in the mess,' Maude lamented. 'Not a bull's-eye, but an elephant's arse.' He did not know that the man who had scrambled from the splintered *howdah* of the fallen elephant, soaked but only bruised, was Tantia Topee, the Nana's general, who had survived to fight another day, to be a greater trouble to the British than any other rebel leader.

But the destruction of the elephant had an instantly unnerving effect on the sepoy companies beginning to form up across the road and among the mango groves that curtained the first few houses of Fatehpur, and they were turning away in droves. A few scattered detachments still fired from the grey jumble of walls and the barricade, but the gun batteries had already been overrun by the Highlanders, who left them where they stood and pushed on, bayoneting the wounded and stumbling over half-submerged corpses. Maude's guns had limbered again, and then the intermingling flank men of the 64th and 78th, on the road, carried the barricade in a scrambling rush.

The Fatehpur engagement was almost over. Only a few stubborn mutineers chose to make a token resistance in the streets and compounds of the town; the vast majority streamed westward, abandoning stores, baggage and all twelve guns. By three in the afternoon Fatehpur was secure. Casualties had been light, involving a dozen men felled by heat and exhaustion who would be dead before the next dawn.

Pursuit beyond Fatehpur was unthinkable. For the previous twelve hours the British troops had been sustained by a savage determination to come to grips with the mutineers as quickly as possible. They had done so, but the action had been mildly disappointing. It had been a victory – of the importance of which they were yet unaware – but hardly the massacre they had looked for. Now, with Fatehpur taken, and the relative anti-climax of a cease-fire, they flung themselves down where they stood, to sleep, in alleys, ditches and out-houses. Many were too exhausted to even eat, and meat freshly butchered that evening would be bad by morning. A few incorrigibles reeled from house to house, seeking liquor and loot.

Only a mile from Fatehpur the army for the liberation of the holy city of Allahabad came to a confused halt. On the road ahead a rabble of sepoys, native cavalrymen, women, lurching carts, animals and terrified townspeople swarmed towards them. The Sahibs were coming, they shouted – thousands and thousands of Sahibs, some dressed like mem-Sahibs, and all the soldiers from the Crimean War, with guns that killed from six miles, or ten. The English commander was Havlook Bahadur, eldest son of the *Buna Ranee*, Vittori. He ate kippers, babies, and cow-milk cheese. *Cow-milk cheese!* See, many sepoys had cut the throats of their women to prevent them falling alive into the hands of the English. *Ayee! Ayee!* And the elephant!

Amelia's cart had jolted to a standstill with the others, their progress arrested by the stream of Tantia Topee's sepoys, stumbling in the opposite direction. She pulled herself to her knees. Beyond the hot tangling sea of turbans and muskets she could see the first few houses of Fatehpur, a clutter of flat roofs and blank-faced walls leprous with peeling whitewash, monsoon ditches overspilling with filth, a few tired trees dripping with water. Dear God, *could she hear bagpipes*? Those distant flecks of scarlet behind the chack-chacking spits of smoke—She saw a darting figure, then a second, a third—

Dear God, they wore *kilts*?

But the Moslem trooper had read her thoughts, and sidled his horse towards the cart. There was no hope. She shrank back into her *burqha*.

The *maulvi*, Liakut Ali, had no wish to collide with the British at Fatehpur; it was something he had not bargained for. Besides, hundreds of his followers were draining away with the defeated men of Tantia Topee's army. They had not come to fight thousands of Sahibs, only to inherit.

Liakut Ali turned his straggling column northward, then north-westward, parallel with the Ganges, to look for a crossing-place that would place him beyond the immediate reach of the British, who were marching for Cawnpore. Allahabad would have to wait. The army for the liberation of the Holy City was beginning to disintegrate. Some wanted to make for Delhi, others Lucknow, or Farrukhabad, or Kalpi. Trooper Mohammed Ismail Khan, who wanted to be a Rissaldar-Major, remained with the *maulvi*'s following, and with him went Amelia Horne.

22

Mowbray Thompson, Henry Delafosse, Sergeant Grady and eleven ragged and filthy soldiers stared at the empty creek. 'Is this the same place?' Thompson asked. 'It looks the same—'

Delafosse trod into the muddy water until he stood knee deep, then turned. 'It's the same place. There's a corpse in the water. I think it's Daniell.'

They were breathing hard. 'They couldn't have got off by themselves, could they?' Thompson choked. 'And if they had, they wouldn't have left us?' He would swear that the boat had been firmly aground across the stream, its refloating beyond the capabilities of the people aboard. But there was no place for it to go except the wide Ganges, forty yards away; if it had not been carried by a sudden, unlikely surge of the current it must have been taken off by the insurgents.

'If the blacks have got 'em,' Thompson decided, 'they're blasted done for, Harry, and that's for certain. They'll be poling up-river, for Cawnpore, and we'd never overtake 'em in this bloody scrub. Jesus Christ.'

'Beggin' yer pardon, Mr Thompson, sir,' Grady offered, 'if the blacks 'ave taken our people, it's more'n likely they've taken 'em across to that place, Surajpur. Them local levies, they'll want to show 'em off to their own village before turning 'em over to Nana Sahib.' He spat into the creek. 'Sir, you jes' say, and we'll go over there an' knock seven kinds o' shit o' them blacks.'

For the moment, Mowbray Thompson was unable to think clearly. He had made a blunder; he should never have gone beyond sight of the boat, never have attempted a blind, running battle against natives who probably knew every inch of the country. It was likely they hadn't been running away, only drawing him off from the boat – and he had let himself be led by the nose—

Delafosse waded from the creek. 'There's been a sizeable force here, Mowbray.' He pointed at the churned mud of the bank. 'Including horses.' Delafosse's appearance was grotesque, his face sore-covered, the remnants of his shirt revealing a hideously blistered torso, and his trousers so torn as to constitute only a misshapen, slovenly kirtle to his knees. 'Do we fight or run, Mowbray?'

Someone *had* to get through to Allahabad, Vibart had said, and of course he was right. Of the thousand or more Europeans of Cawnpore, these fourteen were the last remaining at liberty, assuming the boat to be lost. Someone had to survive, to carry the story of the Cawnpore massacre, to provide intelligence for the recovery operation which must be mounting – Christ, someone was entitled to survive, and were fourteen too many?

'Mr Thompson, sir,' Grady repeated, 'you jes' say.'

'Shure, an' that's roight, Captain sorr,' contributed Private Sullivan. 'Jasus, if it's a foight them bastards is wantin', we're jes' the bhoyos, sorr.'

'Allahabad is all of a hundred miles, Mowbray,' Delafosse cautioned, slowly, 'and, as far as we know, it's all rebel country. If we had our people with us – the sick and wounded, I mean – there wouldn't be a hope in hell for any one of us.' He fingered his black, crusted lips. 'For the fourteen of us there's not much chance either, but one or two might – just might – get through—'

Sergeant Grady spat in the creek again. 'Sir, likely it's not my place ter say—'

'That's right,' Thompson snapped, 'nor anyone, except me.' He had made one mistake, and he would not compound it by another, by losing authority. Still, he compromised. 'We'll follow the river, eastward. If we see the boat, or any of our people, we'll fight. If we don't, we'll make in the direction of Allahabad. That's how I interpret my last orders, and now they're yours. We'll move in open order, with no bunching, which'll lessen the effect of any hostile musketry—'

The gunshots began spluttering almost as soon as they moved off, from their rear and the direction of the river, with the marksmen, however, careful not to leave the cover of the bamboo scrub. As their distance from the river increased, so did the terrain change. Vegetation was becoming more sparse, giving place to almost grassless, rough ground broken with shallow ravines and littered with stones and shale that clawed painfully through the men's thin boots. The sun was high. Shrinking cover and an occasional volley kept the pursuers at a respectful distance, but they could be clearly seen now, and there were hundreds of them – the familiar rabble of sepoys and villagers, running, crouching. 'They're bloody persistent, Mowbray,' Delafosse commented hoarsely, 'and they're not taking chances. They're going to wear us down.'

They had stumbled almost three miles, and all of them, Thompson knew, were near to dropping. He could see the sun's glitter on the Ganges again, a hundred yards distant, and underfoot the earth was rutted with crude plough-furrows, long abandoned. They would have to halt, now, or the men would start going down, and that would be the beginning of the end.

'Mr Thompson, sir!' It was Sergeant Grady, pointing ahead. 'Ain't that a Sammy house?'

The reference was that commonly applied by British soldiers to the small, rustic temples or shrines that stood on the outskirts of village, near *ghats*, crossroads or halting-places, or simply anywhere, where Hindus for five thousand years had daily greeted the Giver of Life, *Gangi Mai*, the Ganges, with the *Gayatri*, the oldest prayer known to man, offering flowers, fruit, grain, a sacrificed goat, to elephant-headed Kanesha, or Kali, or Siva himself. The temples might be of white marble, more commonly sandstone, or humble mud-brick and wood, but to the British they were always Sammy houses. They might be crowned with richly carved cupolas that reared above tamarind trees and tall flagpoles, or crumbling ruins providing a gloomy sanctuary only for bats, pigeons and snakes.

Mowbray Thompson nodded, then shouted. 'The temple! Harry! Make for that temple!' The building would give cover, shade from the sun, and a period of respite. There might be water, even fragments of food offerings left by natives. In any case, there was little choice. They had to halt.

The Sammy house was a simple cubicle of local sandstone crusted with decaying plaster and surmounted by a domed roof. One of the four walls was pierced by a doorway, the others being completely blank of any opening. The whole stood on a squared, brickwork base three feet high, in turn mounted by steps below the door. The fourteen men broke into a shuffling trot, and from behind them came shouts, a fresh fusillade of shots. Sergeant Grady turned, lifting his rifle, but a musket ball smashed into his head.

The remainder flung themselves through the doorway, utterly spent, as bullets splintered the plaster on all sides. It was dark to their glare-blinded eyes, but cool, and shafts of sunlight broke through holes in the roof. The chamber was small – smaller than a bungalow drawing-room – the floor thickly covered with soft dust, dead leaves, bats' droppings and flaked plaster, the inner walls carved with contorting, foetus-like figures smeared with red. There was a stone altar, in the centre of which was a basin-shaped cavity, half-filled with stale and putrid water which they cupped with their hands and sucked down gratefully. They could find no food offerings. If there had ever been any, they had long rotted or been taken by scavengers.

There was just space for four men to fire from the doorway while, behind them, the others reloaded rifles and passed them forward. The field of fire, however, was limited to only one side of the building. The pursuing sepoys and armed villagers, angrily frustrated by a situation they had apparently not anticipated, swarmed towards the little temple in a disordered mob, and a dozen were torn down by the rapid British fire before scattering to right and left, out of sight.

For several minutes there was silence. 'Well,' Delafosse observed, 'we're here, and they're out there.' He had been sounding the walls for an alternative loophole, but there was none. The old walls were thick, and the holes in the roof beyond reach. It was stalemate. The single doorway was easily defendable while ammunition lasted, but the defenders were blind to three sides of their position, and although they fought from good cover against natives who must move in bright sunlight, the brick platform on which the temple stood allowed the enemy to crawl within a few feet of the door with impunity. 'Sooner or later we're going to have to break out,' Thompson ordered. 'Time's not on our side.' They had been calculating the number of insurgents surrounding them, deciding there must be five or six hundred, of whom roughly half were trained sepoys. 'We'll hold 'em off until nightfall, then we'll see. Our only chance is the river, and it's only a hundred yards away. When it happens, we'll all go together, clear them with a volley, and then it'll be bayonets. Anyone who's brought down will be left where he falls. Nobody will attempt to carry a wounded man – and that includes Mr Delafosse and me. At the river, it'll be every man for himself. Strike out towards midstream, then let the current take you.'

He paused. 'It's imperative that someone reaches our relief force. We know it reached Allahabad, but it could be nearer. You'll know soon enough. The local blacks won't be so bloody belligerent with a British punitive force around. Half of 'em will be hanging from trees and the other half crawling.'

But it was barely noon. It would be ten or twelve hours before darkness made a breakout possible. They sat on their haunches in the gloom, some sleeping, others talking in low voices, taking turns to watch from the door or checking the cartridges and percussion caps in their pouches. Private Murphy carefully tied a wallet filled with rupees below his right knee – his wages for drawing buckets of water from the exposed well in the *Lal Koorti Ka Haspital.* There was a smell of dust, dung and ancient blood. From outside there was almost complete silence – an occasional, distant shout or a brief, unidentifiable noise beyond the wall – but a careless movement by a man at the door incited a rattle of musket shots that gouged plaster from the brickwork. A ricochet tore the rifle from Private Ryan's grasp, breaking a thumb.

'My father,' mused Delafosse, 'always said that if you couldn't send your son to Oxford, then send him to Addiscombe. If you couldn't make him a gentleman, then at least make him an officer. He was a Bengal Artilleryman, y'know. Afghanistan with Pollock, and all that – when an officer never campaigned without his field tent, carpets, mahogany furniture, silver and glass, table linen and brandies by the crate. The old lad's field baggage needed thirty camels.' He chuckled. 'I wonder what he would have made of this situation?'

The mention of artillery caused Thompson to sit up. 'Is that why they're so damn quiet outside?' he calculated. 'Do you suppose they've sent off for a gun? This local *zemindar* – Babu Ram Buksh – he had a nine-pounder at Nuzufghur. If the blacks bring it up before dark—' Then he shook his head. 'No, they'll not get a gun over that rough in less than twenty-four hours, by which time we'll be gone, I fancy.'

The mutineers surrounding the little temple, however, had decided on tactics that did not involve artillery. The first became apparent in mid-afternoon, when the Europeans heard the sound of pickaxes against rock. It took only seconds to determine that the noise came from beyond the wall opposite the door, and the meaning was both obvious and ominous. The enemy was attempting to breach the foundations in order to plant explosives, and there was nothing the occupants could do to prevent them.

The noise of digging continued steadily for an hour, and then suddenly ceased. Inside, there was also a silence, punctuated only by the men's breathing, as they listened, their bodies crawling with fresh sweat. Was this the moment? It seemed a festerin' pity, after all this, to be buried under a mountain of sandstone, without a chance to have one more screaming sepoy at the end of a bayonet. 'Mr Thompson, sir,' appealed Private Murphy, lowering a ragged trouser leg over his wallet of rupees. 'Wud ye not think we'd be better having a run fer it?'

'Shut up!' Thompson hissed. He was listening. 'These old temples were built like fortresses, and I'll swear that one hour's not enough to drive a sap under the foundations. Anyway, Hindu sepoys are too bloody lazy, and I doubt if they'd know how to lay a mine, even if they had the material.' He sucked in his breath. 'It's a chance in three. One – they *have* laid a mine, in which case we'll be blown to Kingdom Come within the next few minutes. Two – they want us to *believe* we're mined, and are waiting to shoot us to rags when we run out like stampeding goats. Three – they *tried* to dig a sap but found that their great-grandfathers were bloody good masons, and they've thrown in the towel.' Mowbray Thompson palmed the sweat from his eyes. 'The odds are two to one in our favour, and that means we *wait*!'

A minute passed, agonizingly, then a second, a third. Nobody spoke or moved, and when a steelshod boot rasped against stonework a dozen pairs of eyes fastened accusingly on the culprit, as if the slightest noise threatened disaster. Private Sullivan swallowed apologetically. Mowbray Thompson grinned, then heaved a breath. 'I think we're all right. I reckon they've decided there are easier ways of skinning a cat. Likely they'll wait for the nine-pounder.'

'And we bloody ain't,' said Murphy.

'No. As I said, we'll move out as soon as it's dark enough. I fancy some of the local irregulars will be drifting away for the night, and some will be sleeping. There won't be much moonlight. Given ordinary luck, we should reach the river.'

'B'Jasus,' Private Sullivan recalled, 'I ain't swimmed since I wuz a boy in Dundalk.'

'I ain't never swimmed at all,' confessed Private Malpass, 'but I ain't got time for soddin' lessons.'

The besieging sepoys, however, did not intend to wait for nightfall or for the nine-pounder. A dozen of the more bold had crawled to within a few feet of the door and, remaining out of sight, were throwing armfuls of brush and chopped wood, primed with occasional broken cartridges, to form a growing mound at the top of the steps. In minutes the combustible pile had climbed to almost the height of the door, and the intention was plain. 'Damn cunning, these Orientals,' Delafosse decided. 'It's going to get warmer, any moment from now.' A burning, oil-soaked handful of rags was flung, and the brushwood sputtered, then exploded into flame.

Furnace-like heat flooded the temple chamber, tearing at lungs, and the men pressed themselves to the floor. Fortuitously, a light breeze was carrying the fire's smoke away from the steps, and the sepoys, wary of the defenders' rifles, had been unable to place the brushwood sufficiently near to completely choke the door. Even so, the fire could be replenished with impunity, and the heat was becoming intolerable. The British crouched, hands over faces, sucking air through clenched teeth, the streaming sweat that soaked their rags drying in seconds. Nearer the door opening, the dried leaves that littered the floor were curling, beginning to char, and a dragon's breath of sparks whirled towards the roof. It was impossible.

'It's got to be now!' Thompson croaked. 'Are you listening? We've got to break out *now*! Make sure you're loaded, and bayonets fixed. When I say, we'll go. And I mean *go*! – both sides of the fire, like bats out o' bloody hell. The blacks'll be waiting for us – they know we've got no choice – and it's broad daylight. Some of us will get winged, and no mistake, but I've told you before. Nobody plays hero. Those who reach the river go straight in and strike out, until the current takes you.' He paused, gulping. '*Have you heard me?* NOW!'

They leapt from the door into a red oven of heat that seared off eyebrows and lashes. The sun-glare blinded them, but they plunged on desperately, ready to kill.

Instantly, a fury of musket fire poured into them from three directions. Mowbray Thompson flung himself from the brick parapet, felt his feet jar against the ground and, his leg muscles inadequate, fell to hands and knees. The mishap probably saved him; on each side a man was scythed down, to sprawl, cursing. He scrambled upright, lurched forward, firing at sepoys who, in their scores, seemed to have materialized from nowhere and were running in all directions in chaotic disorder. Delafosse was a yard ahead of him, ludicrous in the flapping rags of his trousers, and Sullivan, Murphy, Ryan, and two or three others. Thompson's legs were like water, and the distance seemed endless. He reeled through a wall of tall cane, arms outflung, and he could see the river. A skeletal, cream-coloured cow stumbled from his path and his legs buckled under him, but he was among riverside reeds, and only a dozen paces ahead was the Ganges, wide and mud-coloured, shimmering in the sun.

Almost all the sepoys had opened fire at the first, sudden

appearance of the Europeans, and there would be a few moments of grace as they frantically reloaded. Thompson counted six of his men wading into the shallows, preparing to plunge. He threw a glance over his shoulder and realized that none followed. Six, then, had gone down already, and the rabble of sepoys was surging forward again. Some had already reached the river's edge on the far left and were jostling to take aim. The water was reaching almost to Thompson's waist, and he felt as if he were wading through stiffening glue. He turned once more to fire the last shot from his Adams pistol, flung it down, and then let the water take him.

He plunged deeply until his fingers clawed at the glutinous bottom, kicking feebly with his spent legs and aware that there was probably an insufficient depth of water to conceal him, but there was nothing else he could do. Distantly, there was a renewed chutter of musketry, and he tensed, waiting for the hammer-blow that would smash his spine or tear off the back of his head. Filthy water fouled his mouth and nostrils and, choked and despairing, he broke surface. This must be the final moment; it was impossible that the river had carried him more than a few yards, and he would be a helpless target for dozens of waiting muskets. The sun flared in his face as he gulped air.

But the Ganges current was stronger than he had supposed. He was thirty, perhaps thirty-five, yards from the nearest sepoys, and he heard Delafosse shout, 'Go it, Mowbray!' The river bank was a blur, of sepia mud and dirty green, crawling with the red and white of native soldiers, yelling, howling. Within an arm's reach of him was a floating corpse, its shirt ballooning, but he could not recognize it. He struck out with the last of his strength, and felt the tug of the river lift him.

Mowbray Thompson remembered very little of the next two or three hours during which, alternately, he swam weakly, floated, sobbed for breath, and sometimes drifted into semi-unconsciousness, only to thresh desperately as the water closed over him. He had fleeting visions of the gymnasium at Addiscombe. Class of 'Forty-nine, and crop-haired Sergeant Malster's swimming instructions: 'Fill yer lungs with *hair*, Mister

Thompson, lift yer chin, and yer can't sink. Keep it hup! Keep it hup!' It was confidently rumoured that old Malster could not swim a stroke, but merely quoted freely from *Commander Ogle's Manual of Swimming & Rowing*, and the Sergeant had said nothing about swimming in the Ganges while being shot at by two or three hundred mutineers.

'Six miles?' he heard himself saying. '*Six miles?* Christ, I couldn't swim *six miles*!'

'You just have, old son,' Delafosse's voice assured him. 'Leastways, you dived in like brave Horatius, six miles upstream, and now you're here. Welcome to the club. The membership's getting a little thin.'

The haze of misapprehension slowly cleared. Thompson's head ached, every muscle throbbed with cramp, and his lungs felt as if they were being crushed in a vice. He was sitting waist deep in warm water, a few feet from the deserted bank, and looking at him were Henry Delafosse, Murphy and Sullivan. The sun was hot on his shoulders, and he could hear the chatter of birds. 'There are two long-nosed muggers eyeing us from the sand-bank,' Delafosse went on, 'but I think they've already dined.'

Thompson stirred cautiously and winced with the pain of it. 'What happened? Where are the others?' He would stay where he was; not even two alligators would provoke him to move another inch.

'Ah, you may well ask, Mowbray.' Delafosse had lost the remnants of his trousers, and his gruesomely blistered body was completely naked. 'Seven of us reached the river, but two were shot before they could swim clear. The blacks followed, screeching and shooting, for a couple of miles. Then Ryan began to flounder, and made for the shallows. The blacks waded in and clubbed him to death.' He shook his head. 'There was nothing we could do, and if the blacks had continued to follow, I fancy we'd have come to the same sticky end. Gradually they peeled away, and the last we saw was a mounted trooper, twenty minutes ago, who decided he didn't want to tackle us alone – not that we could have put up much of a show. There's not a weapon between us, and none of us had the strength to spit. Anyway, we've not seen or heard a thing since.' He grinned at Thompson. 'And your appearance, Mowbray, is positively indecent.'

Thompson glanced down. His sole garment was a shredded flannel shirt. He had no trousers or footwear. Both Murphy and Sullivan were naked and, like Delafosse, hideously punished by the sun, their month-old beards congealing with suppurating scabs, eyes puffed and bloodshot, lips black and broken. But Thompson's senses were clearing. 'All right,' he nodded, 'there's four of us left.' Four survivors from more than a thousand, none of them with strength left to crawl from the river, starved, emaciated, weaponless, naked, and with still a hundred miles to travel over terrain that would test the capabilities of a fully equipped column. 'We can't sit here all day like virgins in the bloody bath.'

There were several moments of indecision, and then Private Sullivan said, 'Mister Thompson, sorr, it's likely we ain't going ter be arst. There's a soddin' *ridgement* coming through the jungle!'

From beyond the nearest tangle of reeds came the sound of approaching, excited voices and, instinctively, they lowered themselves back into the water, incapable of any further effort. If they were discovered now, there was nothing they could do but resign themselves to surrender and whatever followed. It was a pity, Thompson mused, a pity. They had come so far and endured so much, and all of it for nothing. Now there would be no survivors of the massacre at Cawnpore, and never an account of it from the lips of a European. It was a pity, and somehow so bloody unfair.

The voices ceased suddenly, and then there was a shout. 'Sahibs! We have found you! Sahibs! Do not swim away! We are friends!'

Mowbray Thompson raised himself with an effort. On the bank was a throng of eight or nine natives, Hindus by the look of them, none resembling a sepoy but carrying matchlock muskets and swords. They stared down at the half-submerged British, and one of them was speaking. 'We had heard that some Sahibs and mem-Sahibs had escaped from Nuzufghur, and we have been searching all day. Are there no more of you? The Rajah is waiting at Moramhow.'

'Rajah? What Rajah?'

The native seemed surprised at Thompson's ignorance. 'Dirigbijah Singh of Moramhow, Sahib, who is a good friend of Company Bahadur, and we are his people. See, this is the Salon District of Fyzabad, and you are safe.'

Safe? Could it really be true? Thompson glanced at Delafosse, who shrugged. 'It could be a bloody trick, Mowbray, but they don't have to wait for us to go ashore. They can walk in and kill us as soon as they like.' Murphy and Sullivan remained silent.

The native spokesman shook his head. 'If you do not trust us, Sahib, we will throw our guns and swords into the water. See, across the river' – he pointed – 'Havlook Sahib and the *Lal Koorti* are coming – many white soldiers and guns – from Allahabad, and Sereek Dhondhu Punth, who calls himself Nana Sahib, will be blown from the muzzle of a cannon. You are safe now, Sahib!'

Thompson wanted to cry. Safe? 'Christ,' Delafosse croaked, 'I think he's telling the bloody truth, Mowbray. I think we've done it, old son. *We've bloody done it!*'

Thompson nodded, his throat swelling uncontrollably. 'All right,' he said. They began, slowly and painfully, to crawl for the bank, and the natives came forward to meet them.

'It is *Khuda ki-mirzee*, Sahib – the will of God,' the spokesman declared. He and a companion lifted Thompson from the water. 'Our village is less than a mile away, and I am its *lumbardar*. We are a poor people, Sahib, and can offer you only *chupatties* and rice and buffalo's milk. And we have blankets. Tomorrow, after you have rested, we will take you to the Rajah at Moramhow, where you may sleep and eat all day.'

Private Sullivan sighed. 'B'Jasus – slayp and ayt all day. That's jes' what I'm goin' ter do. Slayp an' bloody ayt all day.'

23

Rumours of the advance of a British relief force had been filtering through from Allahabad, and there was an air of uneasiness in Cawnpore. There were stories of hundreds of mutineers hanging from trees along the Grand Trunk Road like rotten mangoes, of prisoners being lashed to the muzzles of field guns and blown to pieces. In Cawnpore there was a sudden increase in the number of sepoys deciding to visit relatives to the far westward, and merchants who discovered pressing business in the opposite direction. Nana Sahib issued a proclamation.

'It has come to our notice that some of the city people, having heard of the arrival of the European troops at Allahabad, are deserting their houses and going out into the districts. Be it therefore proclaimed in each lane and street of the city that regiments of cavalry and infantry, and batteries have been despatched to check the Europeans, either at Allahabad or Fatehpur; that the people should therefore remain in their houses without any apprehension and engage their minds in carrying on their work.'

The citizens of Cawnpore were not impressed, and the Nana had resorted to a different tactic. The Sultan of Turkey (may Allah perpetuate his kingdom) had received news of the passage of 35,000 troops from England to India, and had instructed the Pasha of Egypt that the infidels should not be permitted to reach Hindostan, where they intended to forcibly convert all Indians to Christianity. The Pasha, said Nana Sahib, had mustered his own army before Alexandria, and when the Europeans arrived had fired into their ships from all sides, sinking them all and killing every English soldier. His Grace the Peshwar of the Mahrattas swore it.

But the advance of the British from Allahabad was not going to be halted by proclamations, and Nana Sahib and his senior staff knew it. The drums were beating in the bazaars, reluctant sepoys driven from brothels, carts and ammunition limbers loaded. The Ordnance Office had reported an inexplicable shortage of percussion caps, and hundreds of percussion muskets had to be hurriedly converted to a doubtful matchlock action. The rains had begun, and there was a demand for waterproof greatcoats, a luxury that native troops would not have expected in normal times. And if the Sahibs campaigned with tents, why should not the sepoys, who had supplanted the Sahibs?

On 9 July the army marched – thirty-five hundred men and twelve guns – overwhelmingly adequate to deal with the four hundred British infantry approaching Fatehpur, commanded, it was reported, by a Major Renaud. It would be all very easy for General Tantia Topee, who would be accompanied, on elephants, by Jwala Pershad and Baba Bhut, the Nana's brother.

The news of the defeat before Fatehpur on the 12th, only 48 miles away, was shattering. In the Old Cawnpore Hotel, Nana Sahib paced behind lowered venetian blinds, cursing the intelligence that had never mentioned Havlook Sahib, his thousand men and eight guns. Why was he served by imbeciles? And could not his generals win battles when they outnumbered the British by three to one? And what stupid story was this about hundreds of English draped like women?

But the thought of women reminded him. He had two hundred English women in the *Bibi Guhr*. The English were fools about their women, and would do nothing that might endanger his captives. Did he not have, as the English were fond of saying, a trump card?

Nana Sahib had himself bled by his doctor to relieve his explosive petulance, then sent for Oula, the *nautch* girl who had once pleased the King of Oudh. She knew how to soothe him.

The following day every sepoy, cavalryman and local irregular in the Cawnpore district was drummed in, mustered and equipped, every serviceable field gun brought from the Magazine at Nawabgunge and gun bullocks yoked. Hindus, Moslems and Sikhs poured eastward along the Grand Trunk Road, the band of the 56th Native Infantry braying a distorted 'Royal Windsor'. Nana Sahib now had more than five thousand men in the field, all comparatively fresh, with a short line of supply and ample ammunition reserves. Havelock led possibly 1,400 men, of whom almost the entire cavalry element, Brasyer's Sikhs, was of doubtful loyalty. Under normal circumstances, the Nana knew, European troops were expected to remain in the field for two or three days and fight one battle. Any more extensive activity necessitated a slow-moving baggage train and five camp followers for every fighting man. Havelock's troops had already fought their battle and must have exhausted their resources. The concept of the 'movable column', self- sufficient and capable of rapid deployment was new and effective. Just how effective Nana Sahib was to learn very quickly.

His plan to stop the British at Fatehpur was nonsense almost before he marched from Cawnpore. On 14 July Havelock's force fired the town and moved westward to smash an enemy infantry position before the village of Aong. Rebel cavalry, following an irrelevant demonstration, withdrew hurriedly, leaving baggage and stores strewn over miles of wet countryside. The British, however, were beginning to pay with casualties, among them the fire-eating Major Renaud. Like Fatehpur, the Aong action might have developed into an irreversible rout of the loosely-disciplined rebel forces, but again Havelock's lack of reliable cavalry did not allow for a pursue-and-destroy operation which might have scattered Nana Sahib's army beyond recall. Havelock's performance was limited to the daily marching capability of European infantry and ten miles, under the prevailing conditions, with the possibility of a battle to fight at the day's end, were as much as any troops could sustain, even though sustained by an insensate lust to kill every Indian within reach.

It was therefore not unreasonable for Nana Sahib to assume that Havelock would be satisfied with the success at Aong for one day's activity, and would halt, so giving the mutineers a breathing space in which to regroup and consolidate. A defensive position was formed behind the Pandu Nadee river, six miles from Aong.

The Pandu Nadee was a formidable natural obstacle. Normally fordable, the river was now heavily swollen by the rains. It could now be crossed only by a narrow, stone bridge, of which one of the arches was mined, while also being commanded by a 24-pounder gun and a 25-pounder carronade. The possibility of the British attacking on the 14th, however, was considered remote. For them to cover the six miles from Aong in only two hours was incredible, and when a skirmishing line of blue-capped Madras Fusiliers burst from a concealed ravine, and five of Maude's guns, unexpectedly, began scattering segment-shell among the sepoys' positions, there was new consternation.

Even so, the position was almost unapproachable and, if the bridge was demolished there were no possible means of advance without boats or a pontoon. Recovering a degree of confidence, the entrenched rebel guns began to reply, and the deployed British infantry were ordered to lie down on either side of the Grand Trunk Road. One Highlander, raising himself from behind a small hillock, had his head smashed by a roundshot, only a few yards from Havelock, and the commander could not resist an opportunity to sermonize. 'It was a happy death, men,' he offered. 'He died in the service of his country.'

A shout from nearby indicated that at least one soldier was unconvinced. 'For mesel, sir, gin ye've nae objection, I wad sooner bide *alive* an' *unhappy* i' the service o' ma cuntra!' Laughter rolled among the prone Highlanders.

There was another shout, more urgent. 'There goes the bridge!' A pall of white smoke had mushroomed over the distant bridge and, seconds later, there came the heavy reverberation of an exploding mine. The laughter of seconds earlier turned to groans and oaths, and soldiers climbed to their feet, spiteful and disgusted. They had wanted to get within bayonet-thrust of the enemy, to be able to thrust and slash, kick and crush, to kill, kill—

But the bridge had not gone. When the obscuring smoke had cleared, it still stood, solidly intact. A section of the parapet had collapsed and there was a wide hole in the road, but the arches were untouched and the narrow causeway, hazed by thinning smoke, was empty of debris. Nothing could have restrained the blaspheming Madras Fusiliers who now streamed towards the naked link with the opposite bank, and behind them spilled the Scots and the grit-tough gutter-scum of the 64th and 84th. The Fusiliers reached the bridge first, and in clattering seconds were across. Native gun lascars flung down sponges and rammers, and scattered, but too late. The Fusiliers poured into the entrenchment, bayoneting every native artilleryman and sepoy who could be cornered and driving others over the scarp's edge into the river. The enemy cavalry had already flown and, when the Highlanders swarmed angrily across the bridge there were no enemy left to kill.

Havelock pushed his command forward a further mile and then halted. He had lost thirty men during the day and had outmarched his carts, but he was now only 23 miles from Cawnpore.

During the early hours of the 15th the news of Aong and Pandu Nadee reached Nana Sahib.

24

Bala Rao, nephew of Nana Sahib, had ridden from the Pandu Nadee with an English bullet in his shoulder, and he flogged his jaded horse to the Old Cawnpore Hotel, where his illustrious uncle was engaged in furious debate with a clamouring throng of subordinates, all of whom were realizing that the conduct of a military campaign was not just a matter of wearing Wheeler Sahib's best regimentals and strutting along the *Chandni Chauk* smoking cheroots. In the Indian lines, in the evenings, when the fire-sparks had whirled in the dusk and the young men boasted, it had all seemed so easy, and the Brahmins had promised. Who, they had asked, were these pot-paunched, sweating Sahibs, haw-hawing and breathing port fumes? And who were these arrogant, pink-cheeked boys who referred to veteran soldiers as *jawans*, village lads? Were they better than subedars and jemadars of forty years' service?

It had all seemed so easy, but nothing had progressed as they had anticipated. They had been unable to overcome the puny defences of the *Lal Koorti Ka Haspital* by force and had been compelled to resort to treachery. The commissariat was a shambles, pay was in arrears, the sepoys were insubordinate and the civil population was simmering with discontent. It had been publicized that Nana Sahib had sent a messenger on a camel to seek the aid of the Czar of Russia, but there was no news of the expected seventy or eighty thousand Russian troops marching into India. When Hindostan had been swept clean of the English, the victorious Bengal Army was to embark for England and would conquer that country; the holy men had promised that Hindus would suffer no harm to their caste providing they cooked no food on the voyage.

Why had things seemed so regulated and easy under Company Bahadur, and so differently complex now that Havlook Sahib was approaching? If the English soldiers reached Cawnpore – and they were already across the Pandu Nadee – they were likely to be very angry. Perhaps it would be advisable to retreat towards Bithur or Fatehgarh. And what of the two hundred hostages in the *Bibi Guhr*?

The problem of the prisoners in the House of Women was becoming increasingly worrying to Nana Sahib, and Azimullah Khan was equally uneasy. 'Excellence, what is your intention? If the British reach Cawnpore it will be impolitic to have so many people with stories to tell.' He had apparently forgotten his earlier assurances that the British were inept, paper tigers, that those who were not already running for their ships in Calcutta could be swept aside with ease. The British were getting ominously near, and there was talk of a gallows that could hang four men at a time. 'The British are coming only because we have their women, Excellence. If we no longer had the women – if they were dead – why would the British fight battles for a few corpses? We have killed hundreds of Sahibs already. Will the British forgive us it we spare these others?'

At four in the afternoon several men of the Nana's bodyguard went from the hotel to the *Bibi Guhr* and ordered the few surviving English adult males to emerge. Colonels Smith and Goldie, Edward Greenaway and his son Thomas were accompanied by a youth of fourteen, apparently grateful to be classified a man. A throng of women pressed around the door as they left, but the sentries thrust them back. All day the *Bibi Guhr* had seethed with hopeful rumours. A British relief force under General Havelock was only hours away! Who was General Havelock? When would he reach Cawnpore? Today? Tomorrow? Emaciated women searched children's hair for lice, examined their own haggard faces in fragments of mirror, or wrote final entries in grubby diaries or the fly-leaves of Bibles.

'Entered the barracks May 21st. Cavalry left June 5th. First shot fired June 6th. Aunt Lilly died June 17th. Uncle Willy died June 18th. Left barracks June 27th. George died June 27th. Alice died July 9th. Mamma died July 12th.'

The five men were herded towards the hotel. A sizeable crowd of natives had gathered, sensing some interesting development, and in the shade of a lime tree stood Nana Sahib, Azimullah Khan, Tantia Topee, Jawala Pershad and Bala Rao with a bandaged shoulder. At the gate of the hotel compound the Englishmen were halted and immediately surrounded by sepoys as if by prearrangement. No orders were necessary. A dozen musket shots hammered at the hot afternoon air, and then silence. Azimullah Khan laughed, pointing at the slumped corpses in the dust. 'There,' he said, 'is the Governor of Bengal, there the Governor of Madras, and there the Governor of Bombay.' The watching circle of natives, shocked, applauded nervously.

The growing excitement in the *Bibi Guhr* was abruptly extinguished. The five men had not been taken to parley with the Nana Sahib, to discuss a safe-conduct for the prisoners. They were dead, only thirty yards away, and that suggested only one thing. Could it be so horrifyingly possible? Mrs Henry Jacobi, who had carried the Nana Sahib's surrender terms from the *Savada Kothi* to the *Lal Koorti Ka Haspital*, was convinced that she had earned security for herself and her children. They would be spared, no matter what happened to the others. Mrs William Probett, widow of a Dâk official and the daughter of an artilleryman, had no such confidence. She called the havildar of the guard. What was to happen to the women and children? Whatever flimsy justification there had been for the massacre at the *Suttee Chowra Ghat*, what could possibly excuse the murder of imprisoned and helpless women and infants?

The havildar was evasive. 'If there were any such orders, mem-Sahib, I would have heard of them.' He shrugged, trying to disguise his own apprehension. The Nana Sahib's moods were unpredictable. He, the havildar, had enjoyed watching the discomfort and degradation of these arrogant white ladies and their milk-faced whelps, but enough was enough. The euphoria of the earlier days of the mutiny was dissipating. Vicious retribution was approaching from the direction of the Pandu Nadee, and there were going to be a lot of necks in hempen nooses. 'Do not be afraid, mem-Sahib. We shall never lift our guns against you. You will remember our kindness when the Sahib soldiers come—?'

At five o'clock, as the shadows were lengthening and the air beginning to cool, five men, each carrying a cavalry sabre, came to the door of the *Bibi Guhr*. Two were Hindu peasants – one tall and fair-skinned but with one eye milkily opaque and blind. Two more were muscular Moslem butchers from the native bazaar. The fifth was Survur Khan, an officer of the Nana Sahib's bodyguard, thick-set, with hairy hands and arms. The bystanders who had earlier witnessed the shooting of the white men now shrank back nervously. The vicinity of the *Bibi Guhr* was a place to be avoided.

The havildar did not like the simian Survur Khan, a Moslem, but he mustered his guard detail on the verandah. The native doctor and several menials waited unhappily by the door, wishing they were elsewhere. 'By order of the Peshwar,' Survur Khan said, 'the women are to be killed. You will place your men at the windows and fire through the slats. Do it quickly. Those that escape your guns we will finish with our swords.'

The havildar shivered, pouring with cold sweat. '*Ayee!*' There was a terror in his belly that he had never known. 'This is a terrible thing. Have we not done enough? What is the profit?' He wished he could be anywhere but here. Anywhere. The hot-blooded killing at the *Suttee Chowra Ghat* was one thing, but how could anyone expect men to shoot down these starved, pathetic wretches who huddled in the *Bibi Guhr*? He shook his head. 'This is a terrible thing, *Kiladar*, a terrible thing!'

'*Jeldee, kubbadar*,' Survur Khan warned. 'Eight sepoys have been shot for disloyalty since yesterday. The Peshwar is still master in Cawnpore.'

There could be no argument. The havildar mouthed an order and six of his sepoys moved along the verandah, churlishly, glancing at each other from the corners of their eyes. An hour before they had been talking together in low voices, but they did not trust each other to keep the resolution they had agreed in those muttered moments. What did a man gain by being shot today instead of a hanging tomorrow?

They pushed their muskets through the slats of the windows.

A child screamed. 'Mamma! Mamma!'

Mrs Jacobi, dishevelled, clawed at the door. 'No! Please – tell the Peshwar! I'm not one of these—! I've been promised – and my children! We're not to be killed! Havildar! Havildar! The Peshwar promised—!'

The muskets crashed in succession and window-slats splintered. The verandah was fogged by grey-black smoke, and from within came a discord of shrieks, of children's sobs and the shocked oaths of barrack-room women. But Survur Khan, incensed, flung a sepoy aside. 'Pigs! You pigs! You have shot at the roof! Reload! Reload! Pigs—!'

The havildar bridled. 'We have done as you ordered. We have fired. It is not our fault if our guns are old and useless.'

'Then fire again!' Survur Khan snarled. 'Reload and fire again!'

The havildar drew himself up, his dignity regained. 'We have no more cartridges.' He stared stonily at the sky above the other's head.

Survur Khan shivered and his large hands opened and closed around his sabre. 'What is your name, spawn of a sweeper? The Peshwar will hear of it.'

'Havildar Ram Ghulam, 56th Infantry, of forty-one years' in the service of Company Bahadur, with three medals, and two sons in the Ridgement. You may tell that to the Peshwar.'

Survur Khan spat, then strode to the door, threw back the bolt, and beckoned his followers with a twist of his head. '*Are! Chul!* Everyone,' he gritted, 'everyone will be dead before dark.' The man with a blinded eye, Souracum, laughed and wiped wet lips with the back of a hand. They filed in, and the door slammed behind them.

There were several moments of silence, overlaid by the murmur of shocked voices and weeping, of women calling for children and then, suddenly, an awful cacophony of human terror that sent the native doctor to his knees with his hands over his ears. From beyond the peeling wall and the broken window-slats the horror broke over the verandah like a scalding sea, of screams and blasphemies, of Mrs Jacobi pleading, 'There's been a mistake! Tell the Peshwar! I've been promised.' Of a shuddering *chrump-chrump* of steel against bone and flesh, sanguinary male laughter, a pathetic few voices breaking into a hymn: *All hail, the power of Jesus' name*—

Terrified, the menials ran from the verandah, the women with their *chudders* shrouding their heads, but the havildar remained motionless, his face to the sky, while yards away a sepoy stood with eyes clenched, muttering. *Om! Tat Savitur varenyam, bhargo devasya dimohi, diyonona prachodayat* . . . The laughter from within had ceased, replaced by masculine, sobbing grunts that punctuated the erratic frenzy of animal screeches, the wailing of infants abruptly silenced, choked cries of agony and shock, scuffles and the retch of torn clothing – and all the time, unceasing, the *chrump-chrump* of sabres, again, again, again. Mrs Jacobi no longer screamed for the Peshwar.

In less than a minute the door reopened and the native doctor cringed, terror-struck, as Survur Khan emerged. He was sweating and panting, and the blade of the sabre he held had broken off below the hilt. He flung it down in disgust, glared belligerently at the havildar, and hurried away towards the Old Cawnpore Hotel. In a further minute he had returned with a fresh weapon, and again the door slammed behind him.

Lamps were beginning to glimmer from the windows of the Old Cawnpore Hotel, and the strains of 'The Lincolnshire Poacher' drifted across to the *Bibi Guhr*, where the havildar and his sepoys stood woodenly and the native doctor still crouched on his knees and elbows, his face to the dust. Daylight was fading, the air cooling, and when the rosy flush of the westward sky drained below the rooftops, the havildar stirred, shivered, then whispered, '*Shanti! Shanti!* Is it finished, then?' The spine-crawling noises of death had almost ceased; there continued a few sobs, a choked groan, men's voices in jerky conversation, incomprehensible. '*Bhuk se marte!*' a sepoy breathed, 'but I shall not eat tonight, nor tomorrow. I swear it.'

It was fully dark, however, when the door of the *Bibi Guhr* opened for the last time, and Survur Khan and his party reappeared on the verandah. The Moslem bolted the door firmly behind him.

The appearance of all five was ghastly. Each man was drenched with blood from his turban to his ankles; clothing dripped blood with every movement, swords, hands and arms were totally crimson, spattered with bone fragments and tangles of clotted hair. They walked unsteadily, like men exhausted, with eyes glazed and weapons lowered limply. 'We will wash in the Canal, where the bullocks are watered,' Survur Khan said hoarsely, 'and return in the morning.' A mumble of sobs and choked groans still came from the *Bibi Guhr* to his rear. 'It is too dark to see dead from living.'

The sun rose, low and bright, over the eastward Ganges and the slate-blue dust plain of Oudh. There was mist among the *jheel*-grass and the tang of cow-dung smoke from the confusion of houses in the native quarter. Women were abroad, wending their way to well or river with bright water-pots balanced on heads, and naked infants crawled from cavernous doorways to seek the gutters. Shrivelled *pi*-dogs, corroded with mange, lifted speculating snouts and sniffed, then slunk the shadows, lured irresistibly across the Bithur road and the churchyard by the strange stench that was beginning to come from the *Bibi Guhr*, the House of Women.

It was eight o'clock before Survur Khan and his companions of the night, swollen-eyed, met at the steps of the Old Cawnpore Hotel and walked slowly to the *Bibi Guhr*. With them trailed seven or eight sweepers and *pariahs*, the outcaste disposers of filth, conscripted unwillingly from their hovels. On the road, an elephant, made nervous by the gathering dogs, halted and curled its trunk, then trumpeted. The *mahout* jabbed angrily with his goad. '*Chai ! Chai !*'

And in a few days' time an interrogated witness, cringing under the bayonets and the vicious eyes of Fusiliers and Highlanders, would give an account that was corroborated by many others.

'The bodies were dragged out, most of them by the hair of the head. Those who had clothes worth taking were stripped. Some of the women were alive. I cannot say how many, but three could speak. They prayed for the sake of God that an end might be put to their sufferings. I remarked one very stout woman – a half-caste – who was severely wounded in both arms, who entreated to be killed. She and two or three others were placed against the bank of the cut by which bullocks go down in drawing water. The dead were thrown into the well first. Yes, there was a great deal of people looking on; they were standing along the walls of the compound – mostly city people and villagers, but also sepoys.

'Three boys were alive. They were fair children. The eldest, I think, must have been six or seven, the youngest five years. They were running around the well, but there was none to save them. No, none said a word or tried to save them.'

The chosen depository for the two hundred corpses was a deep, dry well behind a clump of trees nearby, already used for the disposal of night excrement, still-births and other refuse. By nine o'clock a sizeable crowd had accumulated, none approaching too closely but all morbidly hypnotized by the grisly occasion, by the naked bodies of mem-Sahibs savagely hacked and bloody, dismembered infants, trunks without heads, limbs and heads without trunks, crawling with flies and beginning to bloat in the sun's growing heat. Mongrels bickered and snapped, were kicked away, to return panting and slavering.

The smallest of the three surviving children, crazed with fright at the spectacle of a mangled but feebly sobbing woman flung into the well's fetid depths, threw himself at the wall of spectators, but nobody moved aside. Survur Khan, his attention arrested, barked an impatient order, and Souracum, with the blinded eye, drew his knife. Seconds later all three children had joined their seniors in the tangled and stinking horror of the well.

25

Liakut Ali had abandoned the relief of the city of Allahabad, the holy *sangam* where the muddy green Ganges was joined by the blue waters of the Jumna. His dwindling, untidy force was displaying a marked reluctance to face the Sahibs who had scattered Tantia Topee's army at Fatehpur and who were now driving relentlessly in the direction of Cawnpore. The sacred relics of Allahabad could wait – the Temple of the Undying Banyan Tree and the shrines to Ganesh, God of Luck, Lakshmi, Queen of Beauty, and Mahadeo, Holy Ghost of Hinduism. Neither Allah nor the Hindu pantheon, it seemed, were hurling thunderbolts at the British for the moment.

But Delhi, at least, still resisted the British, and Delhi was a safe 300 miles from Fatehpur. Liakut Ali pointed to the north-west. The bullock-drivers shouted '*Chalo bhai!*' and the dry wheels of the carts screech-screeched. Amelia, choked with disappointment, and angry that she had not flung herself towards that fleeting glimpse of kilts and scarlet, sweated under the stifling *burqha* that shrouded all but her eyes.

There was a need for her swathings beyond the demands of Moslem *purdah*. In the long, straggling column of unkempt sepoys, carts and bullocks, women and horses, resentment against anything remotely British was intense. At every halting place, at Company toll-houses and dâk stages, all notices and signposts written in English were wrenched down, English-style garments earned the wearer a pelting with rocks and filth, and the betrayal of Amelia's nationality could have spelled her death despite the patronage of the *maulvi*, Liakut Ali – for the *maulvi*'s authority was weakening. His promises had not borne fruit; his shabby army of liberation was wearying of tramping endless miles of Grand Trunk Road in search of victories that were never achieved and riches that never materialized. Had they left Cawnpore only for this – to be homeless, soaked by rains and reduced to peasant fare? Where were the rubies as big as pigeons' eggs? Where were the sapphires and pearls, the silks, the rupees and the gazelle-eyed women? *Ayee!*

Mohammed Ismail Khan still rode the grey horse that had once belonged to Colonel Larkins, but it was no longer the glossy creature that had arched its proud neck as the jingling guns of the Bengal Artillery passed in review. Now the animal's head drooped, its flanks were muddy and matted, and the thin grazing at roadside halts was no substitute for commissariat corn. The trooper was surlily unrepentant. Did he have a *syce* to daily brush and pamper the horse, to mix bran mash with eggs? Or was the dust of the *maidan* laid by sprinkled water so that polished hooves and leathers were not spoiled?

And Mohammed Ismail Khan was becoming increasingly apprehensive about his abduction of Amelia. True, she was submissive, even responsive, but the novelty of possessing a white woman was beginning to lose its early piquancy – and she was not so white-skinned beneath her *kirta* as other mem-Sahibs, although only he could know that; her hair was as dark as any Indian woman's. He speculated. What would a golden-haired woman be like under her clothes? Would she be tufted with golden hair between her thighs, with golden coins on her breasts instead of bronze?

There were more serious considerations. The British avengers were advancing from the eastward, and there was a general, if unspoken, suspicion that they were not going to be denied. Nobody, yet, dared to say so, but there was silent evidence in the face of every tired and hungry sepoy, in the hesitancy of Liakut Ali, and the trooper saw it in the taunting, half-closed eyes of Amelia as she lay on the camel-blanket, no longer ashamed. Now he pinched out the lamp before pushing his pyjamas over his knees, and cursed himself for it. He no longer wished to shock her with his masculinity, and in that second before the lamp-glow died he knew himself identified – a pock-faced peasant boy from the village of Payagpur, illiterate, incapable of being even a Lance-*Naik* in Company Bahadur's service. Do what you wish, *ryot*, her eyes told him, for your time runs short. The English soldiers are coming in anger, and you will crawl like an animal. There will be no pity from the men of my country; you have fouled a white woman, which is the one sin that the English will never forgive or forget.

Mohammed Ismail Khan knew it. In Fatehpur, it was said, the retreating sepoys had cut the throats of their own women to avoid their being captured by the Sahibs, who would surely butcher them in revenge for the mutineers' treatment of Europeans. It was also said that Sikh cavalrymen loyal to the English had burned alive captured sepoys, and even in Bombay innocent natives had been shot dead for speaking the word 'Cawnpore'.

He knew it. To be caught by the English in possession of this white woman would be damning. Not for him a quick death by bullet or rope, but his head and beard shaved, his genitals severed, fried with pigs' intestines and excreta and thrust into his throat and rectum with a smoking red bayonet, the savage Irishmen kicking out his eyes with their steel-tipped boots, and he sprawling, dying slowly as drunken, kilted Scots stamped his face. Then they would wrap him, still breathing, in the skin of a pig, to hang for long hours, turning on a rope—

Amelia, however, possessed less confidence than her captor supposed. Every mile of the Grand Trunk Road diminished her chances of rescue, and now that Liakut Ali had turned back from Allahabad he was unlikely to be unduly concerned over her welfare. Despite the cloak of *purdah*, she did not always succeed in impersonating an Indian Moslem. At wells and riverside other women paused in their chatter to watch her curiously. Men's eyes stripped the guise from her and they spat, muttering. She avoided associating or conversing with anyone, remaining in or near to the hooded bullock cart – a behaviour that only served to deepen suspicion. Her command of Hindi was only that of a mem-Sahib who spoke occasionally to servants, and of Pushtu even less; her inadequacy betrayed her immediately. Sooner or later, she was certain, she would be denounced, and neither Liakut Ali nor Mohammed Ismail Khan would be able to save her from a mob that was growing daily more contentious.

Or, if the British net tightened, would her Moslem master cut her throat and thus relieve himself of her damaging presence?

And there was something else, almost equally shuddering. The nightly hour of obscenity to which she surrendered unchastely must have its price. She knew much now that earlier she had only guessed at; it was inevitable, she decided, that she would become pregnant. It was an inescapable conclusion to any such relationship. What did pregnancy feel like? Mamma's waist had always been embarrassingly swollen, she was unwell in the mornings, and Doctor Boyes came with his bag and the *ayah* took the children for a picnic with the dog-cart. When they returned, Mamma lay cleanly washed and weakly proud and, magically, there was another small and lobster-red member of the family.

She could detect no swelling below her waist. How would she first *know*? That the Moslem trooper's seed was within her secret body she was certain, for many times in the humid darkness she had recognized the moment for what it was, had been half intoxicated, half despairing – relishing that she had drained the man of his animal lust but sickened by her own shameless involvement.

She would have to resign herself to delivering an infant under viciously insanitary native conditions, attended by a native midwife more concerned with bizarre religious ritual than obstetric skill, not averse to coating an arm with cow-dung and plunging it into a uterus to extract the unborn child limb by limb if the birth threatened to be difficult.

And if Amelia and the child survived, what then? Already she was a *karanie*, a half-caste – tolerated by European society but not enjoying *quite* the status of ladies from Cheltenham and Guildford. For a white lady to bear a child fathered by an illiterate peasant *sowar*, however unwillingly the circumstances, was beyond the sympathy or even the comprehension of the ladies from Cheltenham and Guildford, who would have chosen death as an alternative. An Anglo-Indian woman in such circumstances would, of course, be merely reverting to type. Native blood would out. The Company maintained orphanages in Calcutta, Madras and Bombay to accommodate the offspring of such indiscretions, but made no concessions towards the female parent. The children in due course became domestics, 'baboo' clerks, or joined the ranks of the Madras Fusiliers or the Bombay Light Infantry. The woman, brown or half-brown, vanished, unregretted, among the crawling millions of India's native population.

There had been no rain for a whole day, and the sun was hot, clawing at sleeping villages, white shrines, mango groves, ragged bamboo shrub and pig jungle, until steam rose from the sodden earth and high above, wild geese flew, almost unseen. Bloated pumpkins aired on thatched rooftops, and old men sat in the sun, watching the long, tired column of Liakut Ali's army come down to the Pandu Nadee – dishevelled sepoys and their women, camels and bullock-carts, cavalrymen slumped in the saddles of neglected horses, beggars and lepers, monkeys, ash-smeared holy men, an elephant with bloody feet, more sepoys, sore-covered dogs and toddling infants with eyes blackened with flies, erratic, screaming wheels and rising dust, more sepoys, spitting betel, women crouched under incredible loads, chanting, moaning, '*Sachi, sachi* . . .'

The old men sat in the sun, watching. All day there had been a grumbling thunder from the eastward, where men said was

Fatehpur – although they had never seen Fatehpur, the biggest city in the world. And all day an unceasing stream of people had passed, and many had cried for water, for a moment of shade.

The old men sat in the sun. It was all so puzzling. Where were the Sahibs of Company Bahadur, with their pink faces and comical whiskers, who were incorruptible even if they did smell of coconut oil? Why were the sepoys pulling down the pumpkins, and shouting? Shouting about what? Where were the Sahibs?

As Amelia's cart lurched into the water of the Pandu Nadee she cautiously raised a flap of the straw-matting canopy. It was a shallow place, only inches deep and easily fordable with the river bottom made firm by rammed limestone, but progress was slow as thirsty bullocks halted to drink. Amelia's cart was stationary in mid-stream for several minutes, and she watched idly the water chuckling gently around the wheels, wishing that she could walk barefoot in its coolness, but not daring to. Then she realized, with horror, that in the water only a yard away was a pair of children's leather boots, each enclosing a severed leg. She lowered the flap hurriedly.

Beyond the river there were more desertions, but most decided that there was security in Liakut Ali's numbers, and remained. '*Dilli dur ast!*' the sweat-streaked, laden women mourned. 'Delhi is far away!' The *maulvi*'s influence was draining, but there was none other to command. He sat his horse, a straw umbrella over his shoulder, accompanied by several subordinate *maulvis* and a clutter of raw-boned, starving dogs around the horses' feet, snatching at excreted dung and fighting viciously over discarded food scraps. The long, dusty column of carts, animals and humans snaked on. '*Dilli dur ast!*' It had avoided Cawnpore and reached Araul, where Liakut Ali was met with shattering news. Delhi, it was reported, had fallen to the British. Dehli, the impregnable, the bastion of Hindostan, was lost, and the old king, Mohammed Surajoo-Deen Bahadur, was in an iron cage.

The report was false; it would be almost two months before Delhi was retaken after seven days of the most savage fighting of the Mutiny, but Liakut Ali could not know this, and the all-devouring advance of the British from Calcutta, the reverses at Benares, Allahabad and Fatehpur, all contributed towards the growing feeling that anything could happen, that the vengeful Sahibs would not be stopped. Nobody questioned the plausibility of the hysterical report from Delhi. Liakut Ali, terrified of being crushed between the hammer of Havelock and the anvil of Delhi, needed a sanctuary. It must be Rohilkhand Province, where the local Rohillas, of Afghan stock, led by Khan Bahadur Khan, had been joined by the 10th and 41st Native Infantry and the followers of the Nawab of Farukhabad. The *maulvi* pointed ahead at the endless ribbon of the Grand Trunk Road, and the weary column trudged on, for Farukhabad.

Amelia trembled with secret elation at the discomfiture caused to the mutineers by the news of Delhi's downfall. How was this possible? they lamented. Were there not sixty thousand sepoys behind the fortress walls of Dehli, with the biggest magazine in India, and less than five thousand ragged British, Sikhs and Ghurkas to contend with? There were some who recalled that Mohammed Ismail Khan harboured a mem-Sahib convert to Islam, and watched for her, to spit and hurl insults. The trooper was increasingly sullen, sensing her silent jubilation. As appeasement to his fellows' jeers he resorted to petty actions calculated to annoy her. He urinated in her presence, left her food that was cold and stale, and when the long caravan forded the Kali Nadee he made her wade on foot, clinging to his horse's tail like a low-caste coolie woman.

Araul, Makanpur, Kannauj. How burning the heat, how thirsty the land! Yesterday it had deluged with rain but today the earth was dust-dry as if it had not rained for years. Thousands of men, women and weary children had turned the road into a slow river of jostling humanity, bearing bedding, cooking-pots, *lotahs* of holy water, *hookas*, sugar cane and bags of flour or rice, smelling of sweat and the eternal hot dust. There were glazed eyes of hemp-drinkers, pitifully small infants, infested with flies and dripping with dysentery, carried by diminutive mothers of eleven or twelve years. Vultures watched from the roadside peepuls and banyans, and a cadaverous cow, its rectal area a crawling mass of maggots, lay dying in the road. The human river streamed around it, unseeing. The vultures waited patiently.

But it was Farukhabad at last, with the familiar glitter of the Ganges beyond, and the human river diffused into the sea of squalor, of ramshackle booths, tents and straw-matting shelters, the sprawling camp of Khan Bahadur Khan, who boasted that he commanded the loyalty of 30,000 men. The claim was optimistic in the extreme, but Liakut Ali had no desire to dispute it. 'God is everlasting,' he affirmed. 'God is sufficient. God is he beside whom there is no God.'

26

On 16 July the first real battle of the Indian Mutiny was fought seven miles from Cawnpore. Five thousand men and eight guns under Nana Sahib had been smashed by Havelock's force after a day of bitter fighting and sent reeling back on the city. Hundreds of defeated, frightened sepoys, increasing in number with every hour, swarmed across the race-course and the canal, past the demolished *Lal Koorti Ka Haspital*, flinging down weapons and equipment, snatching food from bazaar shops, and scattering for the Kalpi road, or the bridge to Oudh. Townspeople, too, who had curried favour by supporting the mutinous regime, frantically loaded carts, watched by the spiteful eyes of those who had waited long for this day of reckoning.

By dusk the roads westward and northward were choked by refugees, laden vehicles and baggage animals, goaded to panic by the rumble of gunfire that came nearer with every minute. Disillusioned sepoys, tearing off their incriminating regimentals, cursed the incompetence of their officers. A provost party, with a beating drum, was shouting that there was nothing to fear, that only a hundred English still lived, and whosoever brought in the head of a Sahib would be paid a hundred rupees. The sepoys laughed bitterly, recalling the savage tide of tartan and dirty scarlet that had erupted from the village of Maharajpur, with bagpipes screaming and the Sahib wolves singing 'Auld Lang Syne', the bayonets, the snarling, unshaven faces and the segment shell that had scythed down the rebel lines like dry grass.

A hundred rupees for a Sahib's head? The sepoys jeered. You'll find the Sahibs, they retorted, just south of the native lines, at the 120th milestone from Allahabad, and you may earn all the rupees you wish. Soon the provost party abandoned the drum and joined the fleeing crowd.

At nightfall Nana Sahib clattered into Cawnpore on a chestnut horse that was drenched with sweat and bleeding from savage rowelling. As he reined outside the Old Cawnpore Hotel for the last time the charcoal sky to the northward, beyond the roofs of the native quarter, suddenly flushed to a salmon pink that illuminated the smudged clouds overhead. Seconds later the ground trembled as if stamped on by a giant foot, and then there was a grumbling roar that had the lathered horse flattening its ears. It was the Magazine at Nawabgunge, which General Wheeler had failed to earlier occupy or destroy, now exploded by the Nana's retreating troops. If he had nursed any further hope of organizing a further stand against Havelock's advance, it had disappeared with the shattered Magazine.

There was no time to be lost, and the few followers with him – Bala Rao, Tantia Topee and a number of personal retainers – were impatient. Nana Sahib flung a glance at the gloomy, silent and deserted *Bibi Guhr*, wetting his lips with the tip of his tongue. 'We will go to some country,' he ordered, 'where the Sahibs are not in power.' Then, optimistically, 'And when they have been driven from India, we shall return.'

The party of horsemen spurred on anxiously, past the ghostly-grey tower of Christchurch, the mission house of the Society for the Propagation of the Gospel and the freemasonry lodge, onto the Bithur road, past the wrecked Sessions House, the Gaol and the Treasury with its broken windows and fouled courtyard beneath a long-dead clock. Five miles beyond was the Palace of Bithur, sometimes called Brahma-wat because, it was said, Brahmâ himself had once walked the *ghat* that flanked the holy river.

Nana Sahib halted only long enough to collect his immediate family – his fourteen-year-old wife, Kasi Bai, whom he had married when she was ten, and the widow of Bajoo Rao, the late Peshwar. But there was time for him to perpetrate his last act of spite against the detested British. Mrs Carter, the widow of a murdered toll-collector, who had been given sanctuary by the Bithur women six weeks before, was dragged from her room with her month-old baby and killed. His earlier sparing of her, he commented, had been worthwhile. Instead of one British life, he now took two.

Finally, as his women sobbed, he pushed into a pocket the fabulous *Nau-lakha*, the principal jewel of the Peshwars, a long necklace of pearls, diamonds and emeralds valued at one million rupees. Fresh horses were saddled and, as a yet unseen sun streaked the sky with yellow, the shrouded cavalcade boarded a barge for the Oudh bank of the Ganges.

Havelock, reluctantly, had resisted the temptation to send his troops into a night-darkened Cawnpore. His battle losses had been heavy, there was widespread heat exhaustion, and the surgeons were reporting cases of cholera. He did not anticipate organized resistance, but he knew too well the penalties of launching deprived, empty-bellied soldiers into a town where unlimited alcohol and loot could be had for the taking. 'If there is liquor remaining in Cawnpore,' he telegraphed Calcutta, 'it will require half of my force to keep it from being drunk by the other half, and I shall scarcely have a sober soldier in camp.'

Before first light, however, obsequious natives brought him the news that he most dreaded to hear. His 120-mile march had achieved nothing; the two hundred surviving women and children of the Cawnpore cantonments had been slaughtered by order of Nana Sahib.

The report was too incredible to believe immediately. There was conceivably some explanation, some glimmer of mitigation, for the killing at the *Suttee Chowra Ghat* on 27 June. The sight of eight hundred Europeans being conveyed to safety after the unsuccessful siege might have been too much for the discipline of the frustrated sepoys, who would have needed no orders to open fire. But to deliberately murder two hundred women and children who had been captives for three weeks was surely an act beyond the capability of any human being. Before dawn Havelock mustered his senior officers – Colonel Tytler, Colonel Hamilton, Majors Stephenson and Stirling, Captains Maude, Brasyer, Grant and Fraser. They drank coffee, listening to the same story again and again as the picquets brought in more natives. The *Bibi Guhr*, they told the grave-faced Sahibs. It was all true.

Patrols in strength were sent forward as soon as dawn began to show. A hundred men of the Queen's 84th, under Captain Henry Ayton, were the first to reach the long echelon of half-built barrack houses, now shot-pitted and blackened, in which the railwaymen under Jenkins, and later Mowbray Thompson, had fought. Despite the recent rains, the soil was parched and dusty, but grass was pushing through the rubble, and the patrol stumbled over hidden round-shot and broken skeletons. They could see the ruins of the *Lal Koorti Ka Haspital* and its crumbling *sangar*, the redan, and the embrasures once occupied by the batteries of Dempster and St George Ashe. A half-mile distant, to their left, were the charred lines of the 2nd Cavalry, deserted of life.

Life was apparent, however, as soon as they crossed the Canal into the cluttered native quarters. Apprehensive townspeople emerged from doors and alleyways, genuflecting over their hands, or offering milk, sweetmeats and cheroots to the tramping company of dirty, grim-visaged soldiers. '*Huzoor*, Sahibs!' There was hissing, anxious whispers. '*Jai Company ki!*' A brown hand pointed. '*The Bibi Guhr*, Sahibs!'

Ayton did not immediately identify the undistinguished building. He halted at the Old Cawnpore Hotel, which informants had said was the Nana Sahib's headquarters. The hotel, predictably, was abandoned, littered with papers, empty bottles and refuse, reeking of native cooking, hashish and perfume.

When the Captain regained the freshness of the street he found that his detachment had been overtaken by another, a mixed company of Highlanders and 64th under Lieutenant Richard M'Crea. Thirty yards away the Lieutenant had kicked open the door of a flat-roofed house of white-washed brick. Then, followed by two men, he vanished from sight.

Ten seconds later M'Crea reappeared. He staggered from the door drunkenly, his eyes bulging in a grey, distorted face that mouthed frantically like that of a lunatic, but no voice came from his throat. He saw Ayton on the steps of the Old Cawnpore Hotel, lifted a beseeching hand, and then vomited. Ayton ran. M'Crea's boots, he realized dully, were crimson.

The interior of the *Bibi Guhr* was like an abattoir, the entire floor carpeted with congealing, glutinous blood which in places was inches deep, bristling with black flies and additionally strewn with the pitiful relics of the building's last occupants. There were scraps of blood-drenched clothing, children's pinafores and babies' shoes that still contained tiny feet, bloodied straw bonnets, earthenware, broken toys, smashed daguerreotypes, hanks of hair torn from living flesh, leaves of Bibles, crumpled letters. The lower inches of the walls and the square-cut pillars were hacked and splintered by sword-cuts, where helpless children or women had crouched under a frenzy of death-blows. The higher plaster was scattered with the red prints of clawing hands.

There was evidence that at least two women had been tied to pillars while their throats were cut, and that a child had been impaled by its chin on a meat-hook. The handles of several inner doors were tangled with strips of dresses, as if in a vain attempt to secure them against the horror outside. The open courtyard was similarly littered, with infant trousers, combs and frills, a locket of hair in a folded cardboard marked, 'Ned's hair, with love,' and a Bible flyleaf written, 'Mamma, from her affectionate daughter, Isabella Blair.' Straw matting oozed spongily with blood, and the orange tree, hitherto barren, was spattered with grey-white brain matter. The stench of corruption was thick and nauseating, the air swarming with black, bloated flies.

The men with Ayton and M'Crea were no strangers to blood and mutilation, no stomach-weak recruits new from England. In nine days they had marched 126 miles in the hottest season of India, fought four battles and a dozen skirmishes. Gutter-bred, they were pitiless, callous men, with emotions blunted by years of hard knocks and privation, the daily blasphemy and brutalizing discipline of the Army, alcohol, and the constant threat of death by bullet, cholera, sunstroke or typhoid. A man was not a soldier until he had received fifty lashes over a gun-wheel, nor if he could not walk unaided away from it with a contemptuous curse. Dysentery, malaria and pneumonia were matters of insignificance, and a man who winced when a clumsy scalpel probed for a .75 calibre slug in his flesh was a milk-sop. In 1857 the Army in India was the toughest profession in the world.

The *Bibi Guhr*, however, was too much for even these men's stolid senses. Their curiosity provoked, they jostled to enter, remained for shocked moments, then stumbled to escape, retching, sobbing, cursing obscenely, and glaring malevolently about them with red-shot eyes until the timidly-gathering natives backed away, their ingratiating *huzoors* fading. Only a few of the bolder stepped forward. The *Bibi Guhr* was not all. Would the Sahibs like to see the well?

The well was less than twenty yards away, behind a cluster of small trees on a weed-choked area of waste land. Its mouth was uncovered, and from its depths issued a ghoulish, sonorous humming – of millions of flies. The dark shaft, sixty feet deep, was choked to within an arm's reach of its brim with dislimbed torsos, severed heads with blood-caked hair, arms, legs, hands and lacerated feet, hacked babies, a hopelessly tangled mass of human fragments, unidentifiable and stinking with putrescence.

27

Amelia recalled her occasional glimpses of the native quarter of Cawnpore, before the sepoys' revolt – when Harry Delafosse had escorted her through the squalid maze of the *Sudder* bazaar. She had worn crisp white lace then, carried a dainty parasol, and the natives had moved from their path, respectfully bowing over their hands.

Farukhabad was one huge *Sudder* bazaar – the same narrow streets, stiflingly humid, with filthy, clogged gutters, people, dogs, bullocks, wailing music from dark doorways, skeletal beggars, brown faces, brown bodies, brown legs, and the stench, the pervading stench—

But there were differences. Harry Delafosse, of course, was dead, with all the other young officers of the 53rd and 56th Regiments, with their smiling gallantries, immaculate dress regimentals, brimming with confidence and authority. And Amelia no longer wore a daring new bonnet from Dent's Emporium in Calcutta, or a padded binder under lavender-scented, frilled petticoats, or tiny shoes. She had not enjoyed a change of clothing since the woman Jemdani had impatiently thrust her into native pyjamas and pulled a Moslem *burqha* over her face. Her slippers had worn to shreds, and she walked bare-foot, although in Farukhabad she did not walk far.

The fine white houses and bungalows in the European quarter had been quickly occupied by natives, each building accommodating a score of families with often several to a single room, and within days becoming unrecognizable as the once fastidiously maintained residences of magistrates and civil servants. Furnishings and doors had been chopped up to feed cooking fires, carpets fouled and ceilings blackened with smoke. Compounds swarmed with women, children, goats and chickens, treasured lawns were grazed by bullocks and shrubs trampled. A ramshackle shanty-town of grass-mat shelters and ragged tents spread along the wider thoroughfares, and it was in the Moslem precinct of this teeming, human ant-heap that Mohammed Ismail Khan brought his bullock cart, his horse, and Amelia.

Mohammed Ismail Khan condescended to speak to her only rarely, and then usually in monosyllables, his general apprehension reflected in his contemptuous tone, his desire to humiliate, to relegate her to the level of a menial in the eyes of others. Amelia spent endless hours in the shelter, veiled and sweating, listening to the confused clamour of the street outside. Itinerant vendors offered foodstuffs, but only her Moslem master bargained with them, and his absences were brief.

A few days earlier, Amelia had heard, the Nawab of Farukhabad had massacred twenty-one Europeans. His soldiers had saved until last a fair-skinned English girl, whom they sported with by firing blank cartridges at her from close range, blackening her face and singeing her hair. Sobbing, she wiped her eyes with a rag of a handkerchief, whereupon they fired at her feet, howling with glee as she danced frantically. When she fell to her knees, exhausted, the men loaded their muskets with small shot, which tore her face to a sightless horror of blood and soot. Finally, tiring, they cut her throat from ear to ear.

And that, Mohammed Ismail Khan warned her, would be her fate if she were denounced as a mem-Sahib. Amelia needed no such assurance; she was determined, for the present, to behave in all respects as a Moslem.

Her role was difficult. She could not remain permanently hidden in the crowded native community. There were personal ablutions to perform, however discreet, prayers to say, and no man kept a woman who did not fetch water several times daily. At the well the veiled women expected to gossip as they waited with their jars balanced on their expert heads. The periodical chore at well or river-bank was the Moslem woman's only relief from a hot, airless tent or windowless room, the brief few moments when she walked in the sunlight, albeit shrouded, met other women's eyes over her *burqha*, and talked as she was unable to talk to her husband.

And a strange woman who stood apart, who did not share

the shallow, chattering gossip, who carried a water jar clumsily in her pale arms, was an object of still more gossip, of suspicion.

They came for her during the first hour of evening, when a blue haze of smoke lay over the dark trees that screened the Ganges – the smoke from the pyres of the day's Hindu dead. The tempo of movement had slowed; the cooking fires were reduced to glowing ashes, children's bicker was muted, and from the hidden distance came the first faint drum-beats of a *nautch*. They were Moslems who came, eighteen or twenty men, a few women pointing silently. Terrified, Amelia shook her head. 'Your women are wrong! I am a True Believer, and have submitted to God and His Divine Will! Does not the voice of *mullah* call me from my bed? The *maulvis* will tell you. Do I not pray five times each day, say the Hundred Beautiful Names of God? See, here is my prayer mat, which waits for sunset!' There was no sympathy in their faces, and she turned appealingly to Mohammed Ismail Khan, who stood unmoving. He shrugged. 'It will be as God pleases,' he muttered.

Drawn by the commotion, people were gathering quickly in the fading light. Another mem-Sahib? Would her throat be cut, like those of the others? It would have to be done tonight, for tomorrow was Friday, the day for prayer, for tolerance, and kindness towards the weak.

She was no True Believer, a man accused. She was an infidel mem-Sahib, and worse, she had profaned the Name of God, the Merciful, the Compassionate. Thus was the deceitfulness of women. She would be killed, if it please God, but not by the knife. The lascars of the Artillery had loaded a cannon, and she would be blown from its mouth. A hundred cavalrymen and a hundred infantry would parade for the occasion. Then, if it please God, they would decide what to do with the man who pretended to be her husband—

'It is not the will of God!' An angry voice came from the fringe of the crowd. 'It is the talk of evil men who have not heard the Prophet, the salutation and mercy of God be with him!' Liakut Ali, the *maulvi*, pushed his tall figure through the throng. Men drew back, and women, stooped, ran for their tents. 'Do you not know, my brethren, that only a *maulvi* can judge the True Faith?' He pointed a derisory finger at the crowd's spokesman. 'And are you a *maulvi*, the voice of God? There cannot be two of us. Come, let us meet, we and our disciples, and examine each other. We will discuss that which has come from God the Almighty! We will see who is the true *maulvi*!'

The object of his attention drew back among his fellows and Liakut Ali nodded grimly. 'Such are men whose eyes remain closed to the light, and who are deprived of the assistance of God, the Lord of all Being.' Amelia shrank to her knees. Death, she knew, was very near. She listened numbly to the voice of the *maulvi* above her as he harangued the crowd that now numbered several hundred. She could not know that Liakut Ali, with his eyes white in the dusk and spittle on his beard, was scarcely more confident than she. For weeks he had experienced the weakening of his authority. He cared very little whether Amelia lived or died, but she had been his convert, and any condemnation of her inferred serious doubts with regard to his own judgement and integrity. He must reassert his authority by defending her; if he did not, he could be irretrievably compromised.

Did they not know the teaching of the Holy Koran? he shouted. Did they not know that infidelity could be judged only by a *maulvi*? It was written. Tomorrow, if it please God, they would examine this woman, and if she must die, we shall so decree. *And we pray to God, who directs everything for the best – and there is no other God than He – to lend us his help, and lead us in good ways; for there is no power nor joy but in the high and mighty God . . .'*

It was not easily done. There were many who had come anticipating a killing; Europeans for killing were becoming progressively fewer, and soon there would be none. Amelia's claimed acceptance of Islam was irrelevant. She was a mem-Sahib, and that was enough. Nobody, however, dared to openly challenge the *maulvi*'s reasoning. Liakut Ali had the Koran on his side. There were sullen mutterings, shuffled feet, a spit in the dust, but their initial, angry determination had gone. They began to drift away, sulkily assuring each other that they would return for an answer tomorrow.

But Liakut Ali had no intention of examining Amelia in the presence of fellow *maulvis*. She might well fail the test, in which case he would have gained nothing. Three hours after midnight, the wheels of the cart were gritting on the road southward, seeking a place to be poled across the river to the Mullaon District of Khyrabad. Mohammed Ismail Khan rode ahead. Take her away from Farukhabad, the *maulvi* had ordered. Take her anywhere. Take her to Lucknow.

Amelia, however, was not alone under the straw-mat canopy. Confined with her was another woman, an ample, dark-skinned Moplah widow ready to follow anyone in exchange for subsistence. It was a hundred miles to Lucknow, and they would be halted a dozen times by armed bands seeking fugitive Europeans. At each such challenge Mohammed Ismail Khan gave the same answer: 'The cart carries my women, who are in *purdah* and will not speak or be spoken to by strangers.' In corroboration, a flap of the canopy was lifted and a plump, black hand extended for a few seconds, then modestly withdrew. The cart screeched on, to Lucknow.

On 20 July the little steamer *Brahmaputra* had reached Cawnpore with reinforcements, arriving almost simultaneously with a column afoot under James Neill, now a Brigadier, who had hitherto remained in Allahabad, simmering with anger at being deposed by Havelock. Relationships between the two men were now openly hostile, each disputing the other's actions merely for the sake of it. Neill would soon glean satisfaction from the news that Havelock, also, was to relinquish overall command to Major-General Sir James Outram, even if the appointment did divorce him, Neill, still further from leadership.

For the moment, however, Neill's ill-humour was exacerbated by finding himself left in Cawnpore with three hundred men while Havelock launched his first bid to relieve Lucknow, 49 miles away. It was just another illustration, in Neill's view, of his senior's determination to steal all the glory for himself.

Savagely, Neill turned his attention to the disciplining of Cawnpore – a task for which he had no equal.

Rebel prisoners were being driven in daily, voluntarily surrendering or being hunted and betrayed by the same baying mobs of natives who, a week or two earlier, had dragged Europeans from hiding and jeered them to their deaths. Times had changed, and the Sahibs were masters again. *Huzoor*, Sahib, Defender of the Poor! May prosperity ever attend your footsteps! See, Sahib, this is a dog who killed mem-Sahibs at the *ghat*, and there is another! *Jai Company ki!*

No captured sepoy could expect mercy. There was a parody of a trial, a nod from the presiding officer, and an immediate hanging. For prisoners of rank and high-caste Brahmins, Neill devised an additional ordeal. They were taken into the *Bibi Guhr*, forced to their knees and compelled to clean a section of the blood-caked floor with their tongues. Any reluctance was dispelled by a lash in the hands of a muscular provost sergeant. 'To touch blood is most abhorrent to the high-caste natives,' Neill wrote. 'They think, by doing so, they doom their souls to perdition. Let them think so. My object is to inflict a fearful punishment for a revolting, cowardly, barbarous deed, and to strike terror into these rebels.'

There were no graves, no burning-*ghats*, no ritual, for dead sepoys. Their corpses were flung contemptuously into ditches, to be devoured by pariah dogs, jackals, or the ghoulish vultures with their soulless eyes and snake-like necks. Whitened bones, tangled with rotting, scarlet rags, littered the roads for miles. Vengeance was no longer the Lord's. It was Neill's.

28

Amelia was acquainted with Lucknow, but not the tangle of native hovels on the low ground flanking the Gomati river – a replica of the native quarter in Farukhabad, crawling with deprived, starving humanity, rank with vermin, and a malodorous breeding-place for disease. Mohammed Ismail Khan, for a few pice, had rented a tiny, dilapidated hut from a Hindu dyer. Cows fed on mango leaves, with no other form of feed or even water to drink, passed urine, known as *peuri*, which was highly valued for dyeing processes. The hut, large enough to accommodate only a broken string bed, was stifling, hot, and reeked sickeningly of cows' urine. Locked in, Amelia panted and sweated away the daylight hours. With dusk the trooper allowed her to emerge, to breathe cool air and to satisfy sexual demands which were becoming increasingly more calculated to debase and humiliate. Amelia submitted or starved. She was not of proud mem-Sahib material; there was no fate worse than death. She was young and wanted to live. Dear Mamma could not have remotely envisaged her daughter's experiences, which were totally beyond the imagination of an English lady, but it did not matter. Each passing day was another day survived.

She could hear artillery fire and musket shots continuously, shouts, the moans of wounded, and knew that the British still clung to an entrenched position based on the Residency, but the river and the rebel lines separated her from the siege position. If there remained sufficient light in the evenings she could see, beyond the Gomati and the debris of shelled houses, the Water Gate, the coloured rag that flew from the roof of the Residency, the Church and the Hospital, all locations that she had once known well. It was bitterly tantalizing to know that a British garrison was less than a mile away, English voices shouted, and even English women and children. She pushed rice into her hungry mouth with her fingers, but now she did not weep, and when the trooper occasionally did not return from his day's duties she went famished until the following evening. Then the trooper spitefully placed the food beyond her reach until she had served his lust. Her confinement and her servile compliance had, she knew, reduced her to an animal level, but it did not matter. She was still alive.

She overheard snatches of gossip. The local rebel leader was Ahmed Ullah, *Maulvi* of Fyzabad, reputed to have murdered all the British in that town in addition to fourteen women, children and native Christians in Lucknow, dragged from the cellars of a large European residence, *Tara Kothi* – the Observatory. Ahmed Ullah was infinitely more influential than Liakut Ali and fanatically served by his followers, who revered him as a prophet immune to English bullets, although this was a claim made by many *ghazis*, who flung themselves on the English guns, and died, riddled with shot, as easily as anyone else, and bled just as much.

The continued resistance of the British under Lorrens Sahib – Sir Henry Lawrence – against the holy powers of Ahmed Ullah was a matter for great surprise, but of course it could not be for much longer. The Sahibs would all be killed, like those in Cawnpore. When Lucknow fell, all the remaining English in India would jump in their ships, but the *Maulvi* and his army would go to England. The *Maulvi* would put Quini Vittori into his *harem*, or he might give her to the Czar of Russia if she could not cook good, dry *pulau*. And the sepoys would parade on the *maidan* at London, and drink tea in the *Gunter's Kothi*.

Mind, there was a worrying rumour that Cawnpore, fifty miles away, had been retaken by an English force under Havlook Sahib, and that hundreds of large English mem-Sahibs with bayonets and bagpipes were marching up the Cawnpore road towards Lucknow – but, of course, these were Sahibs' filthy lies.

As in Farukhabad, however, the trooper's attempted concealment of Amelia, and occasional glimpses of the pale-skinned captive, were generating suspicion among the congested community in the vicinity of the dyer's hut. Several times, from beyond the flimsy door, she heard raised voices, angry accusations and references to a mem-Sahib pig of an infidel, followed by Mohammed Ismail Khan's sullen retorts. There were moments of terror when, during the trooper's absence, the door rattled and insults were shouted. Then, in the quiet of night, the trooper ordered her to cover herself well, for he had found another place, and they must leave before their neighbours' threats turned to violence.

He led her over a narrow, iron bridge to the south bank of

the river, over a canal, through weed-choked gardens, ruins, and streets of darkened houses. Occasionally they detoured to avoid the glowing brazier of a gun battery or a picquet post, where she could hear the low murmur of voices, a man's cough, or the familiar spit of betel juice. Several locations she recognized – the turreted walls of the Alambagh, the Cawnpore road where she thought she heard English voices in the darkness and the trooper tugged her on. It was a long tramp of several miles, and Mohammed Ismail Khan was impatient with her slowness. At dawn, with the first clatter of water jars and the smell of cow-dung smoke, she saw the 32nd Regiment's officers' mess-house and then the Observatory, which the natives called *Tara Kothi*, or the Star Mansion.

The main rooms were occupied by sepoys who came and went noisily at all hours and who seemed, for the moment, to give little attention to the shrouded woman brought by the trooper. Amelia's new prison was the kitchen, windowless and still confined, but luxurious by comparison with the stinking dyer's hut. There were nostalgic relics of European occupancy, rejected by looters – candlesticks, a coffee mill, aspic dishes, a jar of rancid Cold Meat Sauce, and a tin of sardines but no means of opening it. Amelia pulled her *burqha* over her face and sat in a corner, unwilling to attract notice. The guns and the noise of fighting were much closer. She was in constant dread of the native soldiers who stamped the rooms and obscenely cursed the Sahibs, but, for the present, they shot only unseeing glances at her as she crouched with veiled head lowered. And she still lived.

Would there ever be an end to her ordeal? Would she ever be returned to English society and the life she had once known? As days became weeks her hopes fought a losing battle with resignation. She had become native in her habits. The food she ate gladly with dirty, broken-nailed fingers was, she knew, the scraps left by the sepoys, and the water she drank had been carelessly drawn from a river that floated with sewage and the ashes of the dead. Her girlish plumpness had gone, her skin had coarsened and her hair was lank and dull; she had the odour of a native woman, and her crude ablutions would have revolted her in Cawnpore. Now, it was becoming increasingly unimportant. She was seeing through the eyes of an Indian, to even think in Hindi.

Amelia's native identity, however, was less convincing to others. The siege, from the rebels' viewpoint, was not prospering. Although the circumstances of Lucknow's defenders were dismal, the position was better fortified and provisioned than the *Lal Koorti Ka Haspital* and, moreover, the lesson of Cawnpore – the massacre following a negotiated surrender – had been learned. There was no possibility of Lucknow surrendering; the garrison would fight to the last man, and the sepoys were beginning to realize it. They were not all holy men, immune to English bullets, and a lot of them were going to die before the Residency was overrun. After each day of heat and frustration they clattered into the *Tara Kothi*, throwing down their muskets and haversacks, arguing and accusing, even exchanging blows. Later they would sit on their haunches, smoking hemp through their cupped hands, hawking and spitting, debating the day's fighting and seeking a scapegoat, a target for their ill humour. Increasingly, inevitably, their curiosity was aroused by the woman in the kitchen, with European features and skin still paler than an Indian's.

Did someone say she was really a mem-Sahib? A mem-Sahib in *purdah*? It was just the sort of thing to expect from a pig of a Moslem trooper. The Hindus were doing the fighting while the Moslems sported with captive mem-Sahibs. The woman was probably a spy, passing messages by some secret means to the Sahibs in Lucknow, who then knew exactly where to expect attacks and could dispose their forces accordingly.

Mohammed Ismail Khan showed little inclination towards disputing the sepoys' allegations, and his absences from the house became deliberately more prolonged, on one occasion being away for three days, during which time Amelia had only a few dry betel leaves to chew. She dared not ask for food or water, but sat on the floor with her back pressed into a corner, her knees to her chin. She was a *kaffir soor*, the sepoys taunted, and her throat should be cut like a sheep's.

When the trooper returned, his face betrayed his surprise at finding her still alive. Amelia was no longer ashamed of her own relief at seeing him, and brazenly spoke. 'I beg that you take me from here to a safer place. If you leave me here again the sepoys will kill me.'

He glanced away. 'It will be as God wills,' he said. He had returned too soon, or perhaps he should not have returned at all. The sepoys would have solved the problem for him.

'Have you not converted me to Islam, and made me your wife?' she pleaded. 'Does not the Koran teach that women should be honoured?'

He was unmoved. 'It will be as God pleases,' he repeated. If he were free of her, he decided, he would return to Payagpur, his village. It was an insignificant place that the Sahibs would not trouble themselves with, and the *maliks* would not betray him.

'Is it right that Hindus should insult a Moslem woman?' – she insisted – 'a woman who carries your child in her belly?'

She was ignorant of such matters; there had been no change in her that might suggest pregnancy, but the claim was one to which he could hardly be indifferent. His dark eyes fastened on her, startled, calculating. 'How can you tell?'

Amelia raised shoulders under her *burqha*. 'How does any woman tell? There are signs.' She hoped he was as ignorant as she.

The trooper grasped her with one hand and pushed the other under her clothing, flattening it against her abdomen. 'There,' she said. 'Do you not feel it?'

His eyes were doubtful but, to voice his doubt would infer a lack of confidence in his own procreative abilities. He nodded. 'Praise belongs to God, the Merciful, the Compassionate.' She was probably lying, but he could not be certain. If it was truth, it changed everything. To acquiesce in the murder of a woman who carried his child would damn him for an eternity. The eventual fate of Amelia was irrelevant; he had derived pleasure from breaking a mem-Sahib's spirit, from seeing her humiliation; but if she carried his son—

'I will take you to Haji Ahmed Ullah, the *Maulvi* of Fyzabad,' he told her. 'He will decide.'

* * *

Westward from the Residency and close to the river was a suburb of fine houses and gardens belonging to the princes and state officials of Oudh. One of these was the palace of Ali Naqi Khan, sometime chief minister, which was now occupied by Haji Ahmed Ullah, *Maulvi* of Fyzabad, adviser to the Begum and the acknowledged leader of insurrection in Oudh. He had the dark skin of Madras, aquiline features with deeply sunken eyes that bored into Amelia's like gimlets. He wore a turban of dusty green, indicating that he had kissed the Ka'aba in Holy Mecca, and his short, trimmed beard was slashed with grey. Expressionless, he listened to Mohammed Ismail Khan's stumbling story, then nodded. 'In the name of God: God is great. Leave us. I would speak to the woman alone.'

When the trooper had gone, Ahmed Ullah turned to Amelia. His eyes were suddenly less frightening and his English was impeccable. 'I have been to England,' he confided, 'to London – Cable Street. Do you know Cable Street?' Amelia did not, She had never been out of India. 'Upper Chapman Street,' the *Maulvi* asked hopefully, 'or Dock Street?' She shook her head. 'No, *Hajji*. I have never been to England.'

He was sympathetic. 'Ah, a pity. London is a very fine place, and bigger than Bombay. Do you know that Bombay belonged to my forefathers? Rightfully I am the Peshwar of Bombay, which the British know, for the Lieutenant-Governor offered me the hand of his daughter in marriage.' It was highly improbable, but Amelia refrained from comment.

The Koran, the *Maulvi* went on, predicted that he would suffer minor reverses in the war against the British, but he would achieve a complete success in six years. 'It has been said that I shall make Queen Victoria my wife, but this is not true, She will be forty-four years of age, which is too old to marry. But I will make her a servant in the kitchen of my house. If I take wives, they will be younger women.' His hand was on her knee, lightly, and she kept very still.

He continued in the same vein, apparently grateful for an opportunity to expound on matters of high policy. He was not boasting, Amelia realized, but naïvely sincere in his preposterous plans for the future. No power would compel him to sheathe his sword in this holy war, and there was no doubt that the Czar of Russia would help him to exterminate their common enemy, the British.

The small room in which they sat, cross-legged on the floor, was becoming warm, and Amelia's eyelids were becoming heavy. Facing her, inches away, the *Maulvi* talked on. They were intimately close, their knees almost touching, and she watched his lips as they moved, compelling herself to remain attentive. Complacency could be fatal; this man had savagely murdered women and children and had officer prisoners decapitated. He could order her death as easily as snap his fingers. There was sweat in the creases of his face and she noted idly, he had a front tooth raggedly broken. She could feel the warmth of his breath, tainted with garlic and cinnamon. There had been a similar moment, she recalled, before Liakut Ali in the tent in Cawnpore, a lifetime ago.

She jerked her attention back to his words. 'And you have come to me, my daughter, for my protection? So it shall be.' He took a sticky sweetmeat from a dish, broke it in his fingers, and gave her half. It was the sacrament she had experienced before, and she ate dutifully. 'And now,' he said, 'you may remove your *burqha* in my presence, for no things shall be hidden.' Amelia slipped the shawl from her head and flushed. She had become so accustomed to the veil that she felt naked without it, exposed before his eyes. He nodded, and his hand was on her knee.

'It is not easy for a Christian to follow the path of the True Faith, but you will be my *mureed*, my disciple, obeying me in all things and following wheresoever I tread.' His hand moved from her knee to her thigh, gently, and she steeled herself against flinching. 'You will observe all the holy festivals of Islam, keep every fast, and pray with your face to Mecca five times each day. In the Name of God, the Merciful, the Compassionate . . .'

She had a room to herself, light, cool, and with the luxury of a window that overlooked a sun-drenched courtyard. Twice each day a meal was brought to her – meat and fish, flavoured rice and vegetables, chupatties stuffed with onions and honey, eggs and milk. There was ample fresh water, clean napkins, and new clothing – pale blue velvet pyjamas, embroidered slippers, a jacket of silk brocade and a delicate Kashmir shawl for her head – and myrrh-water for her toilet. A serving woman bowed respectfully over joined hands.

After her weeks of deprivation, her situation was deliciously comfortable. There was a price, to which Amelia had resigned herself when the *Maulvi*'s black fingers had stroked her thigh. She was no longer the innocent young Miss Horne who had blushed at the merest thought of flesh against flesh, and she was prepared to pay with the only currency she possessed. What did it matter?

He came to her after the prayer at midnight, and often again before dawn, to join with her in devotions, he explained. He was not an animal in his lusting like Mohammed Ismail Kahn, and was easily satisfied. She lay obediently, more discomfited by his unpleasant breath than his inept thrusting. There were moments when, almost pitying, she encouraged his flagging exertions, and when, drained, he gratefully scrabbled at her body, her pity became contempt. Was this abject old man the awesome Hajji Ahmed Ullah, *Maulvi* of Fyzabad, before whom she had trembled in terror? This lean-shanked grey-beard who whined like an excited puppy when she took the damp rag between his thighs in her increasingly expert hands – was this the great Moslem leader of a holy war against the British?

Amelia was no longer the humiliated; she was the possessor. Once, a man had made her crawl. Now the *Maulvi* crawled to her.

29

For five days the rain had lashed into the courtyard under Amelia's window. She could see a leaden sky overhead, while below only an occasional menial ran for shelter with head covered and bowed. Ahmed Ullah had been absent for almost a week.

At least she was unmolested. Her only exchanges were with the native woman who still brought her food twice daily – of distinctly poorer quality but more than adequate. The woman, of low intelligence, was at first reticent, setting down the dishes and withdrawing with seldom a word, but as the days passed her reserve disappeared, and she would sit on her heels, watching Amelia as she ate. Her knowledge of events beyond the walls of the palace was sketchy, usually incomprehensible to her and so of little relevance. She lit fires, brought water, cooked food, washed clothes; nothing else concerned her, or could be changed by her. The world belonged to men. Even so, to achieve the favour of the concubine of the *Maulvi* of Fyzabad might be rewarding.

The Sahibs were approaching, she told Amelia and the *Maulvi* had gone to fight them. Amelia was unable to feel excited. The Sahibs had been coming for weeks, months, but they never arrived. It was a threat with which to frighten naughty children – *Jeldee, kubbadar!* The Sahibs are coming! Where were the Sahibs? And how many? The woman did not know, but their leader was Hafloo, or Haplook, or something like that, and almost all the sepoys and the big guns on wheels had gone eastward, to the Alambagh and the Charbagh districts. Only a few picquets patrolled between the palace and the Residency. It might be possible, by night, if the lady wished to try—?

Amelia considered the possibility, but only briefly. The palace was a full two miles from the Residency, and the woman's information could be totally false, even if unintentionally. Her doubts were reinforced when the woman confided that the building in the courtyard, seen from the window, had been a stateroom of the Begum of Oudh. Beneath it was a cellar in which, covered by only rubble and an old verandah blind, were jewellery and money to the value of three crores – thirty million – rupees. Such a fortune was impossible, a figment of native imagination. All the rest was probably imagination also.

She would believe. Amelia decided, only when she heard English shouts, or saw soldiers with white faces. Here in the palace, even if a prisoner, she was well fed, clothed and quartered. Her skin had regained its sleek smoothness, her arms were plump and dimpled, and her hair was like black silk. True, the *Maulvi* might return, and come to her with his wet lips, breathing garlic, but she had acquired the ability to blanket her squeamishness, to lift her thoughts beyond the carnal sordidness of it. It was not Miss Amelia Horne who lay here with this panting old native, but someone else – some woman 'of a certain type', as her dear stepfather, John Cook, occasionally mentioned, and Mamma lowered her eyes to her sewing. Poor, dear Mamma.

Was there a different future for her? She had lost her entire family – parents, brothers, sisters – and, so far as she knew, everyone who had ever known her was now dead, with the exception of her mother's uncle in Allahabad, whom she had met only once. In one respect this was an advantage. If she were ever delivered from her present circumstances there would be nobody sufficiently privileged to ask intimate questions, or expect a detailed account of her months of captivity. She would survive an initial period during which strangers would be politely inquisitive, and there would be gossip, knowing whispers and innuendo, but as soon as possible she could disappear into a limbo of anonymity, change her name, perhaps marry. Marry? Would she dare? How would she react if she met St George Ashe, or Harry Delafosse, or Mowbray Thompson?

But of course she would never meet any of them. They had died at the *Suttee Chowra Ghat*, and their bodies had been eaten by turtles and vultures.

If she stood on a rush-topped stool she could just see over the outer compound wall, which was eastward, the Gomati river and, she knew, the further bank and the dyer's hut in which she had spent so many miserable days. But she could see only the tops of a few roofs and trees, hazed by rain. She could hear the same leisurely rumble of gunfire that she had heard for weeks – the rebels shelling the Residency. Lorrens Sahib, the native woman said, was dead, but the British relief force had reached the Alambagh, the Garden of the World, only four miles south of Lucknow.

On the following day Amelia believed. The broken rumble of gunfire had become a continuous thunder, and the courtyard below the window surged with sodden people. There were muddy, aimless peasants with children and bundles, scurrying sepoys anxious to dispose of regimentals and muskets, peering into rooms for remnants of substitute clothing. There were wounded and blinded, with rag-swathed heads and limbs, red-soaked, reeling from wall to wall or, abandoned by comrades, slumped in corners and doorways, their choked appeals ignored until, resigned, they appealed no more. The rain fell without pause, and the sky was only an arm's reach above the flat roof of the palace, pressing downward like a wet, charcoal-coloured blanket. The serving woman had come and gone hurriedly. The Sahibs were coming. The Sahibs were coming.

Even if there were still any guards at the compound gate, Amelia calculated, they would be unlikely to concern themselves with one Moslem woman who carried nothing of value, and if she could get clear before the *Maulvi* returned, then crouch somewhere until she saw British soldiers—

There was no warning, except for footsteps that clattered on the stone stairs, and she turned quickly, raising her *burqha* tightly under her eyes. At the door stood Mohammed Ismail Khan, wet, filthy and ragged. She stared, cringed, wanting to scream.

He towered over her. His *alkhalak* was torn, his beard had not been trimmed for weeks, and his turban cloth trailed untidily. The knuckles of the hand that gripped her shoulder were crusted with dried blood. She tried to twist away. 'The *Maulvi*—!'

'With whom be the mercy and salvation of God,' the trooper nodded grimly.' The Sahibs have crossed the Charbagh bridge, and the *Maulvi* is on the Sitapur road, riding for his life, without a thought for his little *mureed*. But you must not be afraid. Your husband is a good Moslem, and will keep you safe from the white soldiers. If they find you, they will make you sing hymns and eat pork, and walk with your face naked before men. Come. There is no time to be wasted.'

Amelia pulled away, but he was too strong for her. A hand

was under her armpit, vice-like. He half lifted, half dragged her to the stairs as she struggled hopelessly. Below, his horse was tied – not Colonel Larkins' grey but a lean, rope-galled troop-horse that sidled away with white eyes as the trooper reached for its bridle. Amelia made another frantic effort to tug free, then screamed as her foot was chopped to the bone by an iron-shod hoof. Unmoved, the trooper raised her like a bag of flour to the saddle and swung up behind her. The horse flung up its head with nostrils flared and cantered away. Amelia, with her foot shrieking with pain, wet hair tangling with the veil over her face, struggled frenziedly, tearing with her nails, but then her head crashed against the low arch that spanned the gate and her senses hazed. The horse plunged on.

A half-mile westward Mohammed Ismail Khan drew rein, glanced over his shoulder and laughed. 'There they are – the white monkeys. See?' Brutally he wrenched her throbbing head around. Distant, yet so near, she could see trotting groups of kilted soldiers among the white walls, and already surrounding the palace of Ali Naqi Khan, from which she had just been taken. 'Ah, they have the cunning of monkeys, these Sahibs,' the trooper jeered, 'and their habits. Do they not sniff their food before they eat it, and pick for vermin in their hair?' He laughed again, then kicked his horse forward.

Day followed day, week followed week in pitiless sequence, uncounted. The rains had ceased and the roads returned to dust, always stretching endlessly ahead. Numbed, Amelia was aware only of a meaningless mosaic of movement, sounds and unrelated events, of pad-footed camels, bullocks with fly-rimmed eyes, lizards in crannies, crumbling villages with cactus hedges, native women with naked infants astraddle hips, betel trees, ak plant and patches of millet, deep-fringed bananas, cow-dung smoke – and always the hot, red dust that penetrated everywhere.

Her dainty, embroidered slippers had long disintegrated, and her feet were bare and lacerated from cutting stones – one still only half-healed from Lucknow – but she dragged herself in the wake of the plodding, jaded horse, which the trooper rode. Occasionally, when she sweated with fever and her limbs ached with ague, he reluctantly conceded the saddle, resenting that a woman should ride while a man walked.

Every road was thronged with fugitives from British pursuit. The Sahibs were coming, shooting, bayoneting, hanging, torturing and burning, blasting sepoys from cannon. For the next century, the Sahibs swore, Indian natives would crawl on their knees when within a hundred yards of a European. If a native so much as raised his eyes in the presence of a mem-Sahib he would be flogged bloody. Cawnpore and Lucknow had been retaken and – *Ayee!* – Delhi, the mighty bastion of Hindostan, had fallen to a British assault. The old king, Bahadur Shah, had been captured and his sons shot like rabid dogs. *Ayee!* The holy *Maulvi* of Fyzabad, sometime leader of 30,000 men, had withdrawn into Rohilkhand with a handful of adherents and the British on his heels. *Ayee!* Where were the *lakhs* and *lakhs* of rupees that every village *ryot* was to have? And the big houses and servants?

Amelia had lost all count of time, distance and direction, except that she recognized that a journey of normally four days now needed twenty because of the British or the rumours of British. Mohammed Ismail Khan seemed to have no clear intention other than to avoid capture, like hundreds of other mutineers who roamed Oudh and Rohilkhand like hungry *pariahs*, stealing from local people, waylaying travellers or demanding protection payment from merchants, but all the time wary of the approaching threat from the eastward. The Moslem trooper made towards Delhi, then sheered away when he heard the news of the city's capture. Two weeks later a shuffling, hollow-eyed Amelia saw a broken East India Company toll-house notice that told her she was in the Sultanpur District, and the number of a gutted bungalow of the North-West Dâk Company allowed her to roughly calculate, from her memory of John Cook's wall map, that she was near Bareilly, only fifty or sixty miles from Cawnpore, where it had all begun.

She realized, with a jolt, that she had spelled out the words on the toll-house notice slowly, like a child. How long had it been since she had read English lettering? Eight months? Nine?

Mohammed Ismail Khan was becoming increasingly apprehensive. Except for religious fanatics, and criminals who still saw advantages in a state of anarchy, disillusionment with the mutineers' cause was almost complete among Bengal's civil population and, with the British net drawing slowly closer, there was a growing anxiety to disassociate from mutinous activities. When the Sahibs returned – it was now *when*, not *if* – there were going to be a lot of questions to find answers for, and there would be witnesses and informers eager to point a righteous finger in exchange for favours.

Amelia had become a liability. The native ill will towards Europeans had not suddenly changed to affection – there were still occasional British being dragged from months of hiding, and murdered – and the presence of a mem-Sahib still provoked resentment. Mohammed Ismail Khan could see it in the uneasiness of village *lumbardars*, in the narrowed eyes of other mutineers as they fastened speculatively on Amelia. Kill her, someone whispered to him. Kill her and leave her body to the jackals in some lonely *nullah*. A man could travel faster without a woman. Besides, the Sahibs could not kill the entire Bengal Army. Sooner or later there would have to be an amnesty. But not for a Moslem trooper who had abducted and forcibly married a mem-Sahib. The Sahibs would follow him to the ends of the earth.

Better to be rid of her now, while there was still time. Soon, it might be too late.

But it *was* too late, the Moslem realized bitterly. There were too many who knew that Trooper Mohammed Ismail Khan of the 2nd Bengal Cavalry had taken a mem-Sahib to wife after converting her to Islam. It was known in Cawnpore, Farukhabad, Lucknow, and a dozen other places; there would be whining grovellers enough to take the story to the Sahibs. And then the hunt would be on.

No. If it pleases God, there must be an alternative.

It was at dawn, in the village of Goothree, burned to charred ruins by Renaud's Fusiliers ten months earlier, and only a few miles from Allahabad, that he hesitatingly broached the subject.

'It is being spoken by men,' he said slowly, frowning at the smoke of the fire, 'that the Sahibs have made a proclamation.'

Amelia, sitting on her heels, lifted her head. She was damp and cold, her limbs ached with rheumatism, and a diet of rice and lentils had turned her bowels to water. She had not seen her face in a mirror for many weeks, but did not wish to, fearing that she would see the face of an old woman. Her hair was falling out, and there were lice in her rags. Utter weariness slowed her every movement.

'It is said,' the trooper went on, 'that the Sahibs will grant a free pardon to all who deliver up prisoners unharmed.' He did not look at her.

Amelia's heart pounded, and her throat was suddenly choking. What was he saying?

The trooper was embarrassed. His role of supplicant was one to which he was unaccustomed, requiring a major effort. 'Can the Sahibs be trusted?' He shrugged, but his air of unconcern was forced. 'Is it just talk – a trick? Or can it be believed?' At last, his eyes flickered towards her.

Amelia did not recognize her own voice. 'If the Sahibs have said so,' she assured him, 'then it is truth.' Her head swam, and there was a yawning in her belly that told her that her bowels were about to disgrace her. Her eyes were misted with tears. 'The Sahibs' word can be trusted.'

It was what he wanted to hear, and he had obviously given the matter earlier thought. 'If that is so,' he nodded, nonchalantly, 'then you may go back to the Sahibs and be a Christian. But first I must have a paper, which you will sign with your name. It will be written that I have saved you from death, and fed and protected you, also that, if I am taken by the English, you will speak for me saying that I took no part in the killing at Cawnpore, or Lucknow.'

Amelia, in that moment, would have promised her captor anything, surrendered her body eagerly, abased herself in complying with his most obscene demands. The sun was suddenly shining, and birds sang. She was alive, and life was so wonderfully sweet. Would it be today? Tomorrow? Dear God, she promised, whatever he asks, I will do. Anything, anything.

Mohammed Ismail Khan, however, was not to be hurried. Illiterate, he did not trust the letter of safe-conduct to Amelia's writing. He found an English-speaking *munshi*, a native teacher, who wrote to his dictation, and then he eyed the document doubtfully for a long time, turning it one way and another. Finally satisfied, he folded it carefully.

'It is well,' he agreed. He waved a conciliatory hand eastward. 'You may go. Praise God, the Compassionate, the Merciful, for your deliverance.' He paused 'Do you think you will ever find a Sahib who will please you as much as I have?'

She found a police post at Synee, with a listless Union Jack hanging from a pole, some tethered horses and, in the shade of a tree, several officers in soiled whites leaning over a map spread on a camp table, but a tall Sikh Duffadar looked down at her enquiringly. 'I wish to be taken to the officer Sahibs,' she said.

He was surprised that a ragged native woman should address him so boldly, and in English better than his own. 'If there is anything you wish to say to the Sahibs,' he countered, 'you must tell me first. I will decide.'

She drew herself up. 'You are impertinent. I am an English lady, and you will take me to your officer immediately. *Jeldee!* At once!'

The Sikh was taken aback. 'Delafosse Sahib will be angry—'

Her heart sang. 'I assure you,' she smiled, 'he will not.'

POSTSCRIPT

Of the five survivors of the Cawnpore massacre, Private Sullivan died of cholera within a few weeks of reaching safety. Five years later, however, Private Murphy, on his discharge, returned to Cawnpore to become the custodian of the memorial garden located on the site of the well in which so many had been buried.

Both Thompson and Delafosse served with distinction during the remainder of the Mutiny; both survived the century, Delafosse retiring as Major-General.

Amelia married a railway engineer, William Bennett. She was still alive in 1913, in Howrah, near Calcutta, where Colonel Neill had entrained his Madras Fusiliers. Aged 73, she wrote an account of the siege and her subsequent experiences in captivity.

The ultimate fate of Nana Sahib is one of the mysteries of the period. Pursued and harassed by the vengeful British, he and his melting band of followers fled into Nepal. There were numerous reports of his death, none of which could be fully substantiated, and the Nepalese authorities were not helpful, but it is more than probable that he died in the bleak Himalayas in 1858. There subsequently emerged several impostors to his title, one as late as 1874, who was sentenced to four years' imprisonment which he did not survive. In 1895 an aged beggar, arrested for creating a disturbance, said he was Nana Sahib, and claimed the protection of Sir Jang Bahadur, the Nepalese prime minister of the Mutiny period, who had died years before. The old man at first excited only ridicule, but he insisted that he should be Peshwar, and an examination revealed physical marks similar to those of Nana Sahib. The Indian Government was consulted, but Calcutta, wisely, ordered that the man should be set free.

If there was any truth in the old man's claim, there is hardly a more desolate picture in history than that of Nana Sahib, senile, discredited, half-witted, wandering the icy roads of Nepal, his identity contemptuously ignored and the laughing-stock of every passer-by.

The five mass-murderers of the *Bibi Guhr*, the House of Women, are more difficult to trace. It was known that one of them, a Hindu named Souracum, had an eye milkily white and blind. Early in 1858 two natives in the Cawnpore district were arraigned and sentenced to death for the murder of a Eurasian. One had an opaquely defective eye. On being sentenced and being led to the gallows, both were violently abusive, protesting against being hanged for so trivial a crime as the murder of one miserable half-caste when they had shared in the slaughter of scores of mem-Sahibs and children in the *Bibi Guhr*, by the order of Nana Sahib. If they must be hanged, could it not be for the greater crime?

There survived only two European eye-witness accounts of the siege of the *Lal Koorti Ka Haspital*. One of these, as mentioned, was that of Amelia Bennett, née Horne, fifty-six years later. As a teen-age girl her knowledge of military technicalities must have been slight and, with her memory dimmed, there is little doubt that she refreshed that memory by referring to the other record, written by Mowbray Thompson. Even so, Amelia's story is invaluable for its description of her own experiences and emotions, particularly following her abduction.

Mowbray Thompson's account was perhaps written too soon after the event – within two years. It lacks the benefit of information, statistics and native viewpoints which were not available for some time. Not surprisingly, there are inconsistencies in names, dates and times between all accounts, sometimes on neighbouring pages of the same book, but they are minor, and most can be logically recalculated.

There were, of course, no survivors of the massacre in Cawnpore's *Bibi Guhr*, and the subsequent statements of natives questioned by unsympathetic British officials must be viewed with caution. These natives said what they thought their questioners wanted to hear; their necks depended upon it, and native necks were cheap. There is no doubt that much anti-Indian evidence was fabricated, but genuine circumstantial evidence is so sickeningly overwhelming that an objective picture of the circumstances can be recreated without difficulty.

Of the regiments mentioned, the 32nd Foot were later retitled 1st Duke of Cornwall's Light Infantry. The 64th became 1st North Staffordshire Regiment, the 78th the 2nd Seaforth Highlanders, and the 84th became 2nd Yorks and Lancaster Regiment. After being transferred to the Crown in 1859, the Bengal Artillery was absorbed into the Royal Artillery. The Madras Fusiliers became the 102nd Foot, and was retitled Royal Dublin Fusiliers in 1881. It was one of six Irish regiments disbanded in 1922 following the establishment of the Irish Free State.

BIBLIOGRAPHY

Adye, Sir John: *The Defence of Cawnpore*, Longman, 1858.

Banerji, B. N.: *Tha Last Days of Nana Sahib*, Historical Records Commission Proceedings, Vol. 12, 1932.

Barnes, R. M.: *Military Uniforms of Britain and the Empire*, Seeley Service, 1968.

Bartram, Mrs Katherine: *A Widow's Reminiscences of the Siege of Lucknow*, James Nisbet, 1858.

Bellasis, M.: *Honourable Company*, Hollis & Carter, 1952.

Bennett, Mrs Amelia: 'Ten Months' Captivity after the Massacre at Cawnpore,' *The Nineteenth Century*, June/July, 1913.

Benson, A. C. and Esher, Viscount: *Letters of Queen Victoria*, John Murray, 1908.

Berrey, R. P.: *The Right o' Line*, James Nisbet, 1904.

Bhargava, K. D.: *Two Unpublished Proclamations of Nana Sahib*, Indian Historical Records Commission Proceedings, Vol. 25, 1948.

Blackham, Col. Robert: *Scalpel, Sword & Stretcher*, Sampson Low, Marston, 1926.

Blackwood, R. M.: *The Battles of the British Army*, Simpkin, Marshal, 1909.

Bonham, John: *Oudh in 1857 – Some Memories of the Indian Mutiny*, Williams & Norgate, 1928.

Brock, Rev. William: *A Biographical Sketch of Sir Henry Havelock*, James Nisbet, 1858.

Chattopadhyaya, H. B.: 'The Sepoy Army, Its Strength, Composition and Recruitment', *The Calcutta Review*, May/ July/ September, 1956.

Collier, Richard: *The Indian Mutiny*, Fontana, 1966.

Corbett, J.: *The Man-eating Leopard of Rudraprayag*, Oxford, 1954.

Cornet: *The Broken Link*, Geoffrey Bles, 1951.

Dunbar, Janet: *Golden Interlude*, John Murray, 1955.

Edwardes, Michael: *Battles of the Indian Mutiny*, Batsford, 1963.
Edwardes, Michael: *Bound to Exile – The Victorians in India*, Sedgwick & Jackson, 1969.
Evans, R. J.: *The Victorian Age*, Edward Arnold, 1950.
Farwell, Byron: *Queen Victoria's Little Wars*, Allen Lane, 1973.
Forbes, Archibald: *Havelock*, Macmillan, 1891.
Forrest, G. W.: *Selections from the Letters, Despatches and Other State Papers preserved in the Military Department of the Govt. of India, 1857–58*, Calcutta, 1902.
Gibbon, Frederick: *The Lawrences of the Punjab*, Dent, 1908.
Gubbins, Martin: *An Account of the Mutinies in Oudh and of the Siege of the Lucknow Residency*, Richard Bentley, 1858.
Gupta, P. C.: 'Nana Sahib at Bithur', *Bengal Past & Present*, Vol. 77, 1958.
Hutchinson, Maj.-Gen. George: *Narrative of the Mutiny in Oudh*, Smith, Elder, 1859.
Jerrold, W.: *Lord Roberts of Kandahar*, Partridge, 1900.
Judd, Denis: *The Victorian Empire*, Weidenfeld & Nicolson, 1970.
Landon, Perceval: *Under the Sun*, George Bell, 1906.
Lord, John: *The Maharajahs*, Hutchinson, 1972.
Mackenzie, Mrs Colin: 'English Women in the Rebellion', *The Calcutta Review*, September, 1858.
Macmunn, Lt.-Gen. Sir George: *Always into Battle*, Gale & Polden, 1952.
Macmunn, Lt.-Gen. Sir George: 'Devi Din, Mutineer', *Blackwood's Magazine*, April, 1928.
Masson-Oursel, P. and Morin, Louise: *Mythology of India*, Batchworth Press, 1959.
Mayo, Katherine: *Mother India*, Jonathan Cape, 1927.
Moki Singh: *Mysterious India*, Stanley Paul, 1938.
Norgate, T. and Phillpott, D. C.: *From Sepoy to Subadar*, Baptist Mission Press, 1911.
Norman, C. B.: *Battle Honours of the British Army*, David & Charles, 1971.
Pandit, V. P.: *Trial of an Impostor of Nana Sahib, Peshwa*, Indian Historical Records Commission Proceedings, Vol. 30.

Rogers, H. C. B.: *Weapons of the British Soldier*, Seeley Service, 1960.
Rogers, H. C. B.: *Artillery through the Ages*, Seeley Service, 1971.
Russell, William Howard: *My Indian Mutiny Diary*, Cassell, 1957.
Sherer, J. W.: *Havelock's March on Cawnpore*, Nelson, 1898.
Thompson, Capt. Mowbray: *The Story of Cawnpore*, Richard Bentley, 1859.
Trevelyan, Rt Hon. Sir George: *Cawnpore*, Macmillan, 1865.
Vibart, H. C.: *Addiscombe, Its Heroes and Men of Note*, Archibald Constable, 1894.
Wylly, H. C.: *Neill's Blue Caps*, Gale & Polden, 1925.
Yeats-Brown, F.: *Bengal Lancer*, Victor Gollancz, 1930.